DAYS OF RAGE

Also by Brad Taylor

One Rough Man
All Necessary Force
Enemy of Mine
The Widow's Strike
The Polaris Protocol

DAYS OF RAGE

Brad Taylor

A Pike Logan Thriller

DUTTON
— est. 1852 —

DUTTON
—• est. 1852 •—

Published by the Penguin Group
Penguin Group (USA) LLC
375 Hudson Street
New York, New York 10014

USA | Canada | UK | Ireland | Australia | New Zealand | India | South Africa | China
penguin.com
A Penguin Random House Company

LIBRARY OF CONGRESS CATALOGING-IN-PUBLICATION DATA
has been applied for.

ISBN 978-0-525-95398-2

Printed in the United States of America
1   3   5   7   9   10   8   6   4   2

Set in Sabon Ct Std.
Designed by Leonard Telesca

This book is a work of fiction. Names, characters, places, and incidents either are the product of the
author's imagination or are used fictitiously, and any resemblance to actual persons, living or dead,
business establishments, events, or locales is entirely coincidental.

To my wife Elaine, my own personal Jennifer

In 1946, Robert Oppenheimer, the father of the Manhattan Project, was asked in a closed Senate hearing room "whether three or four men couldn't smuggle units of an [atomic] bomb into New York and blow up the whole city." Oppenheimer responded, "Of course it could be done, and people could destroy New York." When a startled senator then followed by asking, "What instrument would you use to detect an atomic bomb hidden somewhere in a city?" Oppenheimer quipped, "A screwdriver [to open each and every crate or suitcase]." There was no defense against nuclear terrorism—and he felt there never would be.

Rolf Mowatt-Larssen, *The Armageddon Test*, Belfer Center
Discussion Paper, Harvard Kennedy School, 2009

"Send forth the boys."

Prime minister of Israel Golda Meir initiating
Operation Wrath of God

1

Summer Olympic Games, Munich, Germany
September 5, 1972

Yakov Freidman felt the skids to the Bell helicopter touch down, and knew they had reached the first leg of their destination. Next stop: Cairo. Seeing only darkness behind the blindfold cinched to his head, he rubbed the leg of the Israeli athlete next to him, using the rope around his wrists to make contact. A small effort at solidarity. A reassurance that everything was going to turn out okay. That they would all be released alive from the maniacal Palestinian terrorists that had captured them.

He didn't believe it. And neither did the man he rubbed. The Palestinians had already killed enough people to prove that wouldn't happen.

The engine whine began to decrease, the shuddering of the frame growing still. He heard the terrorist in the hold with them shout at the German pilots, screaming in English to keep their hands in sight. He only assumed the pilots had, because the shouting stopped.

He sat in silence for an eternity, waiting, straining his ears to hear something. Anything to indicate what was transpiring. He hunched his shoulders and rubbed the knot of the blindfold on his back, causing it to shift a millimeter. Enough to let in a sliver of light and a small piece of vision.

He saw two of the terrorists walking to an unlit Boeing 727, parked off to the edge of whatever airfield they had landed within. They went up the stairs, took one look inside, then began running back down.

He felt a cold fist settle around his heart, his body tensing at the sight. The athlete to his left shifted, understanding something had occurred, but not knowing what. Yakov wished he were still in blessed ignorance. He knew they were dead. All that remained was the action.

The two terrorists made it halfway back to the helicopters before the first round cracked through the air, sounding like a pop from a child's firecracker. It was followed by another, then another, until at least four rifles were firing from the roof below the airport control tower.

The terrorists began screaming and firing back in a wild display. Yakov saw two crumple to the ground, flopping grotesquely in the harsh mercury lighting. The remaining killers hid underneath and behind the helicopter he was in, firing back toward the roof.

Pushing through the noise of the gunfire was the low groan of a diesel engine. Yakov saw two armored personnel carriers splice through the darkness, rolling toward the helicopters and the terrorist hidden underneath. He knew the armor would force an endgame.

He yelled to the bound men in the helicopter and began to frantically chew through the rope bindings on his wrists. He saw a terrorist rise up on the other side of the Huey, his face a mask of rage. The terrorist raked the inside of the cabin with an AK-47, puncturing the Israelis inside. Yakov ripped off his blindfold, shouting at the man to stop. He was hit twice in the leg, snapping him upright in pain.

The terrorist tossed something inside, then began running across the tarmac, firing at the men spilling out of the armored carriers. Yakov focused on the device the terrorist had thrown, his vision coalescing on a spinning round metal egg. A hand grenade.

Yakov screamed, and the grenade exploded, sending fire and shrapnel throughout the cabin, igniting the Huey's fuel and turning the helicopter into an inferno. Incinerating all inside.

The world received the news in horror and shock but managed to recover soon enough, not even stopping the Olympic games from continuing. For Israel, it was much, much worse. The 1972 Olympics already had them on edge, as it was the first time Germany had hosted the games since the fateful ones in 1936, when Hitler was the chancellor. For the fledgling state, returning to the land of the Holocaust held special significance, and now it was met with special horror.

The earth continued turning, and, like all tragic stories that have no concrete linkage with the person listening, after a couple of weeks the images of death faded from public consciousness. But that hand grenade had special significance to some. A terrible line had been crossed, and, as often happens in the toil of human events, the Israeli reaction was a precursor of things to come.

It would be three decades until 9/11. But the grenade's pin lit more than just the fuse. It ignited the original Global War on Terror.

2

Beirut, Lebanon
January 22, 1979

"I have a birthday party to go to, then off to Damascus. I don't have time to sit here blathering on about the revolution with you. Was there something in particular you wanted?"

Vladimir Malikov leaned back from the steering wheel, wondering if the Palestinian in the passenger seat had grown soft. Possibly fatally so. Vlad glanced out the window, seeing the Land Rover full of hired guns. Men with bandoliers and mirrored sunglasses, but little skill. Ali Salameh's protection. Aka the Red Prince. Aka Abu Hassan. The Palestinian went by many names, but none worked as a cloak to protect him. He was the most wanted man on the planet, and had been since September 5, 1972.

Vlad said, "You really should take your protection a little more seriously. The Zionists have long memories."

Salameh scoffed and said, "Not since Lillehammer. Not since they killed an innocent man. The world hates them more than me. Besides, I have protection from my new friends. Friends who seem to care more about our cause and less about just causing trouble. They would tell me if the Jew dogs were planning something."

Vlad felt a slow boil. He knew exactly whom Salameh was talking about. Knew Salameh was now playing him.

"Don't fuck with me," he said. "I'm the man who made you who you are. I'm the one who gave you Munich. I got you the passkeys to the Israeli dorm. I'm the one who provided the layout, provided the clear path, reduced the police presence. You're the one who screwed it up. You sit here now, convinced you're a celebrity, but it's on the sweat of my country, and you'd do well to remember that. Black September would not exist without the USSR."

Salameh studied him for a moment, clearly feeling secure with the Land Rover full of muscle in front of them. He said, "Perhaps I should let the Zionists know that. Maybe such information would help my future. At least get them hunting someone else, since you seem to fear them so much."

The words raised a warning in Vlad's mind. A sense that he was losing control of his most valued asset. He'd been working the backwater of the Middle East for more than a decade, and had achieved many, many successes, but few were higher than Salameh. He was the heir apparent to the Palestinian Liberation Organization, and Yasser Arafat's number two. Because of it, Vlad considered him the crown jewel, but only as long as he was worth it. Talking with enemy intelligence agencies or threatening to reveal secrets was a step on the road to destruction.

Maybe he'll have to be dealt with.

Vlad shook his head, the weariness creeping out of his voice, "Salameh, believe me when I say this: We help you because you help us, but the people I work for are just as vicious as the Zionists. Why do you insist on antagonizing us? Why are you talking to the CIA?"

Salameh laughed and clapped Vlad's knee. "I'm just teasing. You Russians are so serious. I understand how much you have helped my people. Arafat understands. But the CIA can help us as well, and that is all I care about. Don't be jealous. Be more helpful."

"What have you told them?"

"About you? Nothing."

Vlad sensed a niche. An angle that could prove helpful in the future. "How long have you been talking to them? I know it's been years, so don't pretend."

"It *has* been years, but they've done nothing to help me, unlike your people. Don't worry. I use them for information only. You don't have an inroad into the Zionist state, and they do."

"Do they know about Munich?"

"Of course. Everyone knows about Munich. It's why I have to live with such security."

"No, no. I mean, did they know about Munich before it happened? Were you talking to them then? Did they know and do nothing?"

Salameh remained quiet, understanding the answer was critical, but not understanding why. He chose to ignore it. He opened the door to the beat-up Datsun and said, "I'm late for my niece's birthday. We can talk again next week."

Vlad clamped his hand on Salameh's arm and said, "Did they *know*?"

Salameh said, "Yes. They did. And they did nothing to stop it."

Vlad let him exit the vehicle, spinning the ramifications in his mind. Wondering how he could use the information for the USSR. He glanced once more at Salameh, watching him talk to his security, then enter the drab station wagon, sandwiched between two bodyguards and followed by the Land Rover full of meat. Israel wouldn't be getting him today, but it was good for Vlad to study his security. In case Israel would need to be blamed for something in the future.

He put his car in gear and jumped ahead of them, not wanting to be bogged down with the circus that always surrounded Salameh. In his rearview mirror he saw the two-car protective detail pull in behind.

He drove down Rue Verdun, barely conscious of the ebb and flow of life in Beirut. Even with the nascent civil war, this area maintained an image of calm. An island of protection in a land splitting apart at the seams, this section had yet to feel the effects of the fighting.

He passed an apartment, glancing at a woman on the balcony, painting the setting sun with a bevy of cats walking to and fro. Erika Chambers. A British eccentric that the KGB had long ago dismissed as a reclusive nut. All she did was paint on her terrace and feed her pride of felines. Day after day.

The sun caught her hair and he saw her drop her paintbrush, opening her mouth as if she was screaming. Confused, he focused intently. When she brought both hands to her ears, he knew exactly what she was doing. Opening her mouth to equalize the pressure.

A bomb is going off.

He saw Salameh's convoy draw abreast of a parked Volkswagen Golf, and he floored the engine, his little Datsun jumping forward with a complaining whine.

He saw the light of the explosion before he felt the heat, a brilliant flash that caused him to swerve to the right and lie down on the seat, opening his own mouth like the little old lady on the balcony.

The shock wave shattered his rear window, coating him in sparkling glass and causing his ears to pop, then ring from the noise. He sat up in a daze, shaking his head to clear it.

To his rear he saw twisted metal and flame, the explosives in the Volkswagen crushing both the station wagon and the Land Rover following. He saw a body in the street, lying inert, then another staggering about on fire. Running and screaming, his face a mass of melted tissue, he no longer resembled a human visage.

He put the Datsun in gear, not even considering checking on Salameh. He knew the man was dead, and he knew it was Israel who had done it.

Their dedication was astounding. Munich had happened more than seven years ago, and yet they hunted still. If they found out about his help to Salameh, he knew they would come after him. They held nothing sacrosanct. Being from the USSR meant zilch.

Driving away, he reflected that it was a good thing the Zionists preferred to kill instead of capture. Had they interrogated Salameh, he would be next on the target deck. He regretted losing his finest asset, but maybe it wasn't such a bad thing that Salameh was dead.

The trail of Munich would end with him.

3

Plovdiv, Bulgaria
Present day

Confused by all of the Cyrillic street signs, Aaron Bergmann folded his map and sighed. Why was it that a town predicated on attracting tourists did nothing to help them navigate? The damn place was a maze. And he thought Jerusalem was bad. This town was worse.

He grinned, knowing that wasn't really true.

He continued in the same direction, following the crowds walking down the large promenade. He hoped to see something that would trigger in his mind from the research he'd conducted before he left Tel Aviv. An historic house, church, mosque, or other landmark he would recognize. He saw a circular hole in the ground, about a hundred feet across, and walked toward it. Getting closer, he sighed with relief, recognizing the remains of an old Roman stadium. Only a small piece had been excavated, with the rest running a hundred meters under the pavement of the modern streets, but it was a landmark he could anchor against.

He got his bearings and took a left on Saborna Street, entering the cloistered cobblestone of the old city. He picked up his pace, seeing he'd burned his entire time cushion wandering around trying to find his location. He passed other tourists out sightseeing, but didn't ask for any help. Very few spoke English, and none spoke Hebrew, but he was fairly sure he could find the remains of the old fortress on the tip of the hill. From there, he'd locate the beer garden with the man he was paying to meet.

They'd had some success penetrating Hezbollah and the Syrian opposition forces, but no stone would be left unturned. The Mossad looked everywhere and anywhere for intelligence, and when an oligarch from Russia had made contact, claiming he not only had information on Russian geopolitical history and future goals, but on the Syrian government's intentions with WMD, he'd been launched to investigate. The oligarch—code-named Boris—had picked the place and Israel had brought the money. There was little risk if he ended up being a bust, but the potential for payoff was great.

Aaron wound his way through the cobblestones, knowing as long as he was headed uphill, he was going in the right direction. He passed a youth hostel, seeing a tent and a clothesline in the courtyard behind an open door, wondering how they washed their clothes before hanging them up. Did they have automated washers, or do it by hand? For that matter, did they have a shower in the compound, or did they simply pay for the security of a lock on the gate?

He would have liked to experience the world as they did, freely tramping about, no worries and no greater ambition than to explore, but that had been taken from him in the first Intifada when a suicide blast on a Tel Aviv bus had shredded his parents.

He had been fourteen, and his childhood had disappeared. He had worked to contain his hatred at the same time he had worked to find an outlet. He'd shown a fierce drive and an uncommon intelligence during his mandatory military service, striving for and being accepted to an elite Special Forces unit known as Sayeret Shimshon—or Samson—tasked with clandestine penetration of the Gaza Strip, the hardest counterterrorist missions in the IDF.

He'd learned to blend in as a Palestinian Arab. Learned to harness his fear while walking in the belly of the beast, to succeed against all odds, locating and eliminating terrorists in their own backyard. He'd lived through many missions that he would have considered suicidal before, and had had the art of the impossible hammered into him.

In 1994, right about the time he'd begun to grow comfortable with the mission, the Gaza Strip had been given back to the Palestinians, and because of it, his unit had been disbanded. For about a day.

Before Aaron could even wonder what he would do next, the Mossad had called, wanting Samson's skills and promising future missions.

Now the commander of the unit, he'd made a deal with the devil and found his team doing more Mossad tasks than manhunting. A necessary evil to keep the support. He, as the Samson commander, was not immune, which was why he was in Bulgaria attempting to glean intelligence on Syrian intentions.

Aaron turned a narrow corner and saw the cobblestone run up to the ruins at the top of the hill. To the right was a smattering of picnic tables perched on an overlook two hundred meters above the town.

Must be the place.

He went down the steps, purchased a bottle of Kamenitza beer, then casually surveyed the deck. Full of students and backpackers, he focused on singletons and found his contact fairly quickly. A large, overweight man of about sixty-five or seventy, he was sitting at the very edge of the overlook, next to a small trail leading precipitously down. He had a porkpie hat on the table to his front, and a tourist map laid out. The map was the identifying bona fide, and the hat was the safe signal. Had he been wearing it, Aaron would have taken his beer elsewhere and simply reported back, letting his higher command in Mossad reinitiate contact and determine what had gone wrong.

Aaron took one more look around the deck, checking for anything out of the ordinary, once again searching for singletons who didn't fit in. He found none, but that didn't mean there was no threat. Just that if there *was* a threat, it was well trained.

He approached the man known as Boris and said, "Sure is pretty up here."

The man said, "It is, but I prefer Moscow. Have you been there?"

Aaron sat down opposite of him and said, "No, but I've always wanted to go."

The correct words exchanged, with both men satisfied they were talking to the correct person, Boris wasted no more time.

"Did you bring the money?"

"Yes. Well, I brought a card and a PIN. You can draw the money from any ATM or bank, but the card won't be activated until I get what I came for."

"How do I know you aren't tricking me?"

Aaron smiled and said, "How do I know you have any information that's worth a shit?"

Boris said, "The Americans thought it was good. They have paid me handsomely."

"You've already sold this to the CIA?"

"Yes. Perhaps you'd like to wait on them to pass it to you." Boris smiled again.

"What am I buying?"

"Have you heard about Edward Snowden?"

"The American traitor? The one who gave all the secrets to you people? Is that what this is about?"

"No, no, I just mean are you aware of the large cache of documents he stole from the American National Security Agency? I am like him. I have a treasure trove of documents, from the KGB's help of terrorists against your state in the 1970s to what they're planning to do today. Russia is worse now than it was under the USSR, and the KGB is alive and well in the FSB."

Aaron knew that Boris was prior KGB himself, and understood that he—like many, many KGB agents—had made a fortune plying his skills for less-than-savory individuals before returning to the new federal security apparatus—the FSB. He was no saint. No white knight out to expose Russian corruption. No, he'd been turned out into the cold for some transgression, and now he was looking for a final golden parachute. An augmentation of his retirement fund to be earned by selling the souls of the people he'd worked with for decades. It made the Israeli sick to his stomach.

Aaron said, "Let's just get this done. How do I get the information? You'll earn no money until that happens."

Boris said. "I figured as much, but a man can hope. I didn't bring the information here with me. Bulgaria is easy to get to, but very, very dangerous for me to operate within."

He smiled, his teeth cracked and yellow from a lifetime of tobacco. "If you'd walked up with an umbrella, I would have jumped off the cliff. The KGB may be gone, but they can still kill pretty ingeniously."

Aaron knew he was talking about the death of a Bulgarian dissident named Georgi Markov, assassinated by the Bulgarian secret police in London in 1978. While waiting on a bus, a man had approached and injected a ricin tablet into Markov's leg using a spring-loaded umbrella. Markov had died three days later.

Aaron said, "I have no weapons. I have a card I'm willing to activate if you have information."

Boris nodded and said, "Taped underneath my chair is a key. It opens a lockbox held by a man at an Internet café in the main bus station in Istanbul. He's waiting for you. You give him the key, and he'll call me. You'll give me the PIN to the card, and I'll have him pass you the thumb drive. I get the PIN and I'll give you the password to the encryption. Fair enough?"

Aaron started to reply when Boris slapped his chest with both hands, his eyes squeezed shut in pain before popping open wide in shock. He swayed a minute, then fell out of his chair. Aaron raced around the table and grabbed his shoulders. "Hey, what's wrong?"

Boris said, "Heart. Heart. Pacemaker. Stop . . ."

Aaron propped him up with one hand while sweeping his other under the chair, retrieving the key. He cloaked the movement by shouting, "Is there a doctor here? Anyone have medical training?"

A crowd had gathered, but nobody moved forward. Aaron looked into Boris's face and saw his eyes go flat. Something he'd seen many, many times.

Boris was dead.

4

Yuri Gorshenko watched from the rear of the crowd, gawking like the rest of the people at the dead Russian. Finally, two men pushed through the throng, ostensibly some sort of medical team. He saw the Israeli stand up and fade to the back. Yuri waited until he had disappeared from view before leaving himself.

Figuring the Israeli would take the shortest route out of the old town, Yuri kept to the high ground, circling the ancient cobblestoned streets until he was standing next to a Roman theater from eons ago, now equipped with modern sound and advertising contemporary shows. He found a small table in the sun and sat down, giving the Israeli time to clear the area. Killing time, he fiddled with an electronic device, checking the readout for a sniff of a vulnerability, but it came up empty.

No pacemakers around here.

Looking like a scientific calculator with an antennae, he marveled at how quickly it had worked. He'd practiced with it endlessly, but had never used it live.

Worth the risk going to San Francisco.

The device was nothing but a bunch of plastic and silicon, harnessed together like any other modern gadget, from a Nintendo portable game player to a digital cell phone. The difference was its purpose. There would be no joy working this device, unless one liked watching people die. Using a wireless connection, it injected malware into implanted medical devices. In plain language, it caused pacemakers to flame out with eight hundred volts.

The vulnerability had been perfected by the FSB over two years ago, and had been used quite successfully until the back door had been discovered by an American hacker named Barnaby Jack. Last year, he was all set to reveal what he'd found at a hacking conference called Black Hat when the FSB had intervened. They'd spent too much time and effort refining their technique to allow their back door to be exposed, and so they'd decided the risk of operating in the United States was worth it. Barnaby Jack died under "mysterious" circumstances in San Francisco, causing a mountain of conspiracy theories, but none as outlandish as the truth.

Yuri checked his watch, seeing thirty minutes had passed. He had about forty-five minutes before he had to report to his Control, something he didn't want to be late for. He stood up and walked around the outskirts of the theater, then followed the cobblestones downhill until he intersected Knyaz Aleksandar Street. He blended into the crowds out shopping, and wandered south, past the ugly Communist-era post office, the building blanketed with graffiti.

The supposed benefits of capitalism.

Yuri passed behind the post office and turned right, walking toward another squat, ugly four-story building at the edge of a large wooded park. The location of his Control, it was a Communist-era military club, still used by the old Bulgarian military men. A sort of veteran's affairs association from the USSR of the past.

He entered, seeing a geriatric man guarding the front door, the room inside paneled in old wood, dark and dank. In Bulgarian, he said, "I'm Jarilo. Someone is here to meet me."

The man showed nothing but boredom, having seen and heard many odd things in his eight decades of life. He nodded and said, "Upstairs. Last room."

Yuri turned without a word and walked across the open ballroom, his feet clacking on the marble floor. He entered the stairwell and climbed to the top, his steps now causing echoes that bounced back and forth in the narrow confines.

The clatter stopped in the hallway, his footfalls smothered by the threadbare carpeting, something he was sure was left over from the Bulgarian revolution.

From the thirteenth century.

He found the last door and paused, checking his clothing to ensure he projected a professional appearance. He had nothing but disdain for Control, as the man had never entered the arena—never risked his life in the great game—but he *did* outrank Yuri and was someone who could affect his career.

Yuri knocked, heard a muffled "Come in," and opened the door. What he saw on the other side rendered him speechless.

5

Before the man in the room even turned from the window, Yuri knew it wasn't his Control. When he did face about, Yuri thought he was surely mistaken. Seeing the wart on the man's temple, right next to his left eye, he was sure.

Vlad the Impaler? Here? Why?

Vladimir Malikov said, "Don't look so shocked. I do get out into the field occasionally. I'm not decrepit yet."

Yuri snapped to attention and said, "Sir, no, sir."

Vlad walked to a wall covered in books, seemingly studying them. He said, "Stand at ease, Jarilo. I'm not going to bite."

Yuri tried to relax, but it was impossible. The leader of the new and improved FSB—the successor of the KGB—Vladimir Malikov was a legend who'd earned the nickname Vlad the Impaler from some of his operations in the Middle East. Yuri waited for Vlad to say something more, but the man remained silent, his labored breathing the only thing disturbing the peace in the room. A rattle that sounded like an Arab smoking a water pipe, it ended in a string of coughs, then a hacking spit into a trash can.

Vlad lit a cigarette, drew deeply, coughed again and said, "These things will fucking kill you."

Yuri nodded, remaining silent.

"Jarilo. Slavic god of war. Did you pick that code name?"

"No, sir. Just lucky, I suppose."

"But you believe in it. Like it."

"Yes. I guess."

Vlad turned from the books. "How did the operation go?"

Yuri pulled the electronic Bluetooth device from his pocket. "It went absolutely perfect. The traitor is dead, and I have now identified the Israeli. He is exposed and doesn't even know it."

"Did you get the cache of information?"

"No, sir, but neither did the Israeli."

"How do you know?"

"Because I watched the entire affair. The traitor passed nothing, and his death put the Israeli in a dilemma. He could not explain to the authorities what he was doing with a Russian national without giving up that he was an Israeli spy. Nothing he said would fit his cover. He fled at the earliest opportunity, leaving the body for others to clean up."

"Good. And the information?"

"We'll have to do some investigation. The traitor hid it somewhere."

Vlad moved back to the window, saying, "Okay. Not your issue, though, is it?"

Yuri was unsure how to respond, as his taskings ultimately came from the man in front of him.

Vlad said, "You have served with distinction on many fronts. One of the few who remained after the fall. Tell me, did you do this out of duty, or out of fear of a brave new world?"

"Duty, sir. I have no fear of any new world. I saw how others made their fortunes, and I could have done the same. I could have eclipsed them all."

Vlad considered, finally saying, "Yes. Yes, I believe you might have. You ran the Berlin group, did you not?"

"Yes, sir."

"And the Chechens learned to fear you."

Where is this going? Vlad was reciting things that were old news.

Missions that had been hashed out over two years ago. Yes, he'd run an assassination cell out of Berlin, and had killed Chechen terrorists everywhere from London to Istanbul, including the former Chechen president—in Qatar, no less. It was what the Vympel were trained for. Blending into a foreign culture and sowing the seeds of destruction.

He said, "Yes, sir. I did as I was ordered."

"Did you believe in the mission?"

"Belief has nothing to do with it."

"No. You're wrong. I've learned over time that belief has *every-thing* to do with it. You can order a man to attack, but you'll only succeed in the assault if he *believes*. A man who believes is worth ten who simply follow orders."

He faced Yuri, standing a full head shorter, but his lack of physical stature in no way interfered with his ability to instill obedience. "Tell me, what do you think of the United States? Do you wish Russia to emulate them?"

"If that is what you think is best."

Vlad waved his hand. "Give me an answer that isn't just supplication."

Yuri said, "Okay . . . no, sir. I don't think we should emulate the US. I despise them and their arrogant worldview. I hate the humiliation they have heaped upon our country."

"You mean you despise the fact that we went from a superpower to a has-been. From an equal player to a shell that lives for pinpricks on the UN Security Council."

Yuri said nothing, unsure how to respond.

Vlad said, "Can I trust you? Trust what you say?"

"Yes, sir. Of course you can."

Yuri considered for a moment, then said, "There is a terrorist here in Plovdiv. A Nigerian from the group Boko Haram. He's a wild-eyed, radical, suicidal monkey. The worst I've ever seen. But he's also a tool. Something I intend to use to equal the playing field with the United States. Remember what caused our undoing?"

"The United States spreading the lies of capitalism to our federation, causing our satellites to run blindly toward a dream that didn't exist."

"Really, now, I expected more from you. That was an outcome. States choosing a different path because the one they were on was failing. Why was it failing?"

Yuri thought for a moment, then said, "Afghanistan. Getting involved in Afghanistan. It bankrupted both our moral fiber and our bank account."

Vlad smiled, pleased. "Precisely. And I believe the United States is ripe for that very thing."

"I don't understand."

"You will in due time. I've taken over as your Control. I have a special mission for you. But first, I need to meet this Boko Haram savage. I was going to introduce him to a Syrian Shabeeha leader. A man from Syrian Air Force intelligence who is working external operations. Someone who would help us attain our goals, but I'm afraid the savage has been compromised. I believe the United States is tracking him, and I need that to stop. I need you to confirm his status."

Yuri nodded. "I can do that. My team is here right now."

Vlad's face grew stern. "It's more than that. If he's being tracked by the Americans, I need you to dissuade them from continuing. Buy me enough time to set up and execute a meeting."

"How? Have them arrested? Get them involved with whores? That's really not my skill, sir. Others in the FSB can do that much better than my team."

Vlad's face split into a macabre smile, disconcerting even to a man like Yuri. He began to understand where the nickname Impaler came from. "No, no, Yuri. I precisely want your skills."

He pulled a folder off of the table and handed it to Yuri.

"I want you to kill them."

6

Yuri watched the parking lot with a pair of binoculars, waiting on the Boko Haram man to leave. Praying he could follow simple directions. He put the binos down on the seat and a chilling thought entered his head.

What if he can't drive a car?

He'd taken the folder provided by Vlad—a dossier of the Boko Haram facilitator, to include local habits and lodging—and had spent five days studying the man. It took two just to make contact without contaminating his team, then another three to determine that he was, in fact, under surveillance. It was loose surveillance, to be sure, but it was there nonetheless.

Knowing what he did about such operations, he decided that the surveillance wasn't designed to capture the facilitator, but was intended to lead to further information. They were trying to see who he met or talked to, what actions he was taking. They were building a pattern of life.

Given that, he had to assume that every electronic device the facilitator used was already owned by the Americans, making his job much, much harder. On the plus side, since the Americans weren't looking at the facilitator as an imminent threat, they'd back off if he hit the team. If he killed one or two members, he was sure that the Americans would focus on the death and not the mission. To that end, he'd set up a pretty good trap, but now, not having the luxury of phys-ically meeting the Nigerian facilitator, he wasn't sure the man could actually accomplish what he'd planned.

He looked at his team member in the passenger seat and said, "Dmi-tri, you think this savage can operate a vehicle? I mean, you think he would have said he couldn't after we transmitted the plan to him?"

Picking the binos off the seat, Dmitri said, "Honestly, I don't know. We never got a chance to vet him. But surely he couldn't travel here for a meeting with a Syrian colonel without having some rudimentary skills."

"I'm not so sure. Did you read the dossier? The guy is a lunatic. A fanatic. I hope Control knows what he's doing."

Looking through the glass, Dmitri said, "He's just exited the build-ing. Moving to the car. I guess he found the keys we placed in the dead drop. That's a good sign."

Yuri tensed, knowing the building was boxed in by American sur-veillance. Planning on using that to trap them. First, he'd peel them off, then he'd peel one car for real. He said, "See any correlation?"

One of the first ways to spot surveillance was to correlate activity around the target. Did someone get on a cell phone right as you left a building? Did a car sitting stagnant for four hours pull into traffic at the same time you did? Probably not a coincidence.

Little things like that didn't *prove* surveillance, but were an indica-tor. Yuri was past the indicator stage, though. He'd already deter-mined that the target was being chased. Now he just wanted to confirm that the chase was happening today.

Dmitri said, "Yeah. Northeast corner. Vehicle just pulled out. It's way outside of effective control, but also out of view of the target. Someone triggered by radio. If they're good, that's the surveillance."

They're good all right.

"Let him go and keep looking. We know where the target's headed. See if the box collapses."

From their vantage point on the side of a hill, they could see the entire surroundings of the parking lot, to include the three different exits. Like clockwork, each exit had a vehicle break away and start to chase the target. When Yuri was sure they were all on the move, he put the car in gear.

"Now we get to see if this savage can follow instructions."

The target entered Highway 86 heading south, toward the town of Asenovgrad, the follow now forced to trail behind. Yuri picked up the rear, happy that the target—so far—was driving as instructed.

They passed the road to the Plovdiv airport and the target pulled into a petrol station. Just as planned.

Yuri watched the follow cars spread out and slow, taking lefts and rights in order to wait until the target moved again. Yuri blasted past them all, as the whole point of the stop was to get him in the lead. Get him in a position to execute his plan.

He pointed at a small duffel bag in the footwell and said, "You sure that thing is going to work?"

Dmitri said, "Yes. It's really simple. The hard part will be you driving close enough to use the Bluetooth connection."

"How sure? These men are no amateurs. If it isn't swift, they will realize they're being hunted, and the entire mission will be in jeopardy."

"Then why don't we just shoot them?"

"Control wants it to look like an accident. He wants a Vympel hit."

"Fuck Control. That bastard doesn't even know what he's asking for."

This Control does. Yuri hadn't told the team of his meeting, unsure if he was allowed to. As far as they knew, they were working for their original chain of command.

"We have our orders. These aren't a couple of Mafia men. We can't do anything that looks like an offensive attack. The repercussions will be profound if we can't execute clandestinely. Will it work?"

"Yes. Believe it or not, the United States Department of Defense paid for the research, then published a paper showing how it's done. All I did was establish the connection wirelessly. You get him on the fortress road, and I'll cut the brakes, flood the accelerator, then jerk the wheel. It'll work, I promise."

Yuri nodded, passing through the town of Asenovgrad. He reached the Cheplare River and veered off the main highway, clawing up a side road that plied steeply uphill.

Climbing higher and higher, he could see the little ribbon of Highway 86 far below, the cliff itself a jagged shelf with an almost-vertical drop-off.

Perfect.

He studied every switchback, determining which would be the best for attack. Everything was focused on the tactics. The killing itself never entered his mind.

Yuri had grown up at the end of the cold war, joining the KGB in time to watch the USSR implode. He'd been insulated to the upheavals for longer than most, training for years to attain the honor of serving in the Vympel of the KGB's First Directorate—back when the mission was targeting the west.

Designed to blend into the population of foreign countries, its mission was to conduct sabotage operations in the event of all-out war. He'd spent three years learning four foreign languages, a host of foreign customs and mores, along with some decidedly lethal skills. Because of this, he had been hammered on the righteousness of the motherland and the evils of the capitalists more than most other soldiers of the USSR. He was tasked with penetrating deep into the societies of his chosen target, and the politburo had to make sure he wouldn't decide to simply remain in his assumed role and abandon his mission. His preparation was very, very specific.

The training stuck, leaving Yuri a fierce defender of Mother Russia— even after the fall of the USSR and the disgusting way his comrades raped and pillaged whatever they could, creating oligarchs that became

rich off the skin of the people. Exactly what Communism was designed to prevent. In his mind, it proved the failure of capitalism, and
was the primary reason he never left the service.

His team was composed of men who had been recruited after the
fall, when Vympel joined the FSB after the KGB was disbanded. They
didn't have the skill in cross-border operations that he had, but were
still pretty damn effective. With Vympel no longer tasked with penetrating foreign societies in preparation for World War III, they'd spent
the majority of their time fighting the Chechens, either head-on in
Grozny or outside Russia in a stealth war.

Yuri had worked hard to instill his sense of patriotism into the
team, and would not tolerate anything short of absolute devotion and
perfection. Mistakes would be tolerated. Once. After that, he'd punish
a team member just as easily as an enemy. Kill him if it became necessary. It was how he was trained in the old days, with the old ways, and
he'd expect nothing less from Vlad the Impaler. And knew he wouldn't
be disappointed.

7

They reached another hairpin turn, and Asen's Fortress appeared on an outcropping of rock. An ancient citadel built to protect the valley down below, it hung out into space in an impossible display of construction from a thousand years ago.

How on earth did they build that thing way up here? Without modern tools?

They circled around the hairpin to a small parking lot. Yuri pulled in beside a panel truck and killed the engine.

Dmitri said, "How long will I have in the vehicle?"

"At least ten minutes. The rabbit will go all the way across the road, then walk the footpath on the outcropping to the old church. He'll enter and take a seat. The surveillance won't want to burn themselves, so they'll stake outside until he leaves. My only concern is the follow-on team. If another car comes up here, they might stay right here in this parking lot. It'll make things a little tricky breaking into the empty vehicle."

"What will we do then?"

"Nothing. Come up with another plan. But I'm betting they won't stop. If it were me, I'd continue on so as not to create a signature, parking out of sight up the mountain and waiting on a radio call. These guys will do the same."

Fifteen minutes later the Nigerian turned around the hairpin driving a beat-up Lada two-door sedan. He parked as instructed, waited for about a minute, then exited the vehicle. Yuri strained to see the follow-on surveillance, not too concerned about being remembered by the opposition because he didn't intend for this car to report back to anyone.

Thirty seconds later, a Ford Escape rounded the turn and parked. Yuri recognized one of the men inside as part of the surveillance effort. He waited until the men had exited the vehicle and crossed over a hillock in the middle of the hairpin, circling around picnic tables and a small children's play area. When they'd disappeared from view, Yuri scrambled along the same path, taking a seat at a table that allowed him to view both the road up and the crosswalk that led to the entrance of the ancient fortress across the road.

Seeing a single car headed toward him, he spoke into an earpiece. "Stand by. Vehicle approaching."

The car made the hairpin, slowed in the parking lot, then continued on up the small ribbon of road, heading deeper into the mountains. Yuri couldn't confirm if it was part of the surveillance team, but he assumed it was. He triggered the operation.

He saw Dmitri exit the vehicle, sidle between the cars, then slim-jim the door of the Ford. He opened a bag, flopped onto his back, and began working a small device into the onboard diagnostic port, allowing him access to the controller area network that facilitated the various electronic control units of the Ford Escape.

Ordinarily used by mechanics to determine faults with the car, the onboard diagnostic port also allowed a pass-through for the entire brain of the vehicle. A brain that would now be controlled by the follow-on car.

Dmitri finished, and Yuri settled in to wait for the Nigerian to leave. It took longer than he expected, but a little over twenty minutes later he saw him approaching the crosswalk. He knew that the surveillance wouldn't be too far behind.

Yuri scrambled down the hill and entered his car, asking a question without saying a word.

"It plugged in fine," said Dmitri. "Shouldn't be an issue."

"We need to do more than just pull the brakes. They have to go over the cliff. I can't trust them to lose control."

"You won't have to. The Ford Escape has parking assistance. It'll parallel park the vehicle for you. Which means the computer controls the steering. I'll have that control. You just need to be close enough."

They watched the target leave, driving back down the hill, and waited, feeling the heat build in the car from the sunshine. Within seconds, the vehicle that Yuri had seen travel up the road earlier came flying back down, now taking the lead on surveillance and allowing the team that had penetrated the fortress a gap in time to protect them from exposure.

Yuri no longer cared about the active surveillance or the rabbit. He waited on his target. Eventually, they fired up the Ford and began driving back down the mountain. Like a snake tracking his prey, he slid in behind the car.

Driving directly behind the target, he said, "Two turns. You've got two turns."

Dmitri said, "Working it."

Yuri glanced his way and saw him stroking the keys to a laptop, a USB cable stretched out on the dash with an iPhone 5s attached to it. They passed the first turn.

"You've got a little over a mile. Status."

"I have contact, but I can't manipulate."

"What the fuck does that mean?"

Fingers flying over the keyboard, Dmitri said, "I can talk to my device, but it's not talking to the car."

Yuri closed his eyes for a second, then applied the brakes. Dmitri said, "What are you doing? I have to maintain our connection."

"I'm not going to burn us for this circus."

"It'll work! Give me a chance. Back off after the kill-zone if it's still not working."

Yuri grimaced, and increased acceleration. Dmitri rattled off a string of numbers designed to instill confidence, but they meant nothing to Yuri. Dmitri continued to manipulate the keys. He called a signal strength that might as well have been describing the fluid dynamics of a rocket launch as far as Yuri was concerned.

Dmitri said one more mix of computer language and Yuri snapped, "Shut the fuck up. Is it working or not?"

Dmitri smiled. "Yes. Yes, it is. Tell me when."

Yuri surveyed the road ahead, knowing the hairpin was about a half mile away. He said, "Cut the brakes in ten seconds. Hit the gas in twenty."

Dmitri nodded. Ten seconds later he stroked the keys. Initially, there was no reaction from the car in front of them. Four or five seconds later, the car swerved left, then right, then continued straight. At the twenty-second mark, Dmitri typed something new, and the car jumped forward, racing straight into the hairpin turn.

Yuri could only imagine what the driver was doing, frantically slamming the brakes into the floor, jamming the gearshift into low, and scared to death because the accelerator was pouring gas into the engine as if a ghost were in the machine.

He saw the passenger's arms waving in the air, scrambling for something in the backseat. He had no idea what it could be.

The turn approached much faster than anticipated, as they were now flying down the mountain at a good fifty miles an hour. Fast enough for him to lose control of his own vehicle, but he had to maintain his proximity or lose the Bluetooth connection.

His knuckles grew white on the steering wheel as they approached the turn, realizing too late that his plan might be the death of both of them. He saw the car enter the hairpin and screamed, "Now!"

Oblivious of his own impending fate, Dmitri continued to tap the keyboard and Yuri watched the car snap to the right, crash through the minuscule guardrail, and sail into space, as if it were trying to leap across the chasm.

Yuri had no time to appreciate the view, as his own vehicle hit the curve at over fifty-five miles an hour. He slammed on the brakes and torqued the steering wheel, fighting to keep from following the car over the cliff. He bounced against the guardrail, eliciting a shout from Dmitri, then slid to a halt, the passenger side grinding along the metal rail for close to forty meters.

Yuri sagged against the wheel for a second, panting, then looked behind him, seeing a cloud of smoke rising from the valley below.

Dead. The Vympel way.

He'd executed exactly what Vlad the Impaler wanted, believing he'd set his country on the path of redemption. Using the best-trained men the Russian Federation had to offer, he'd accomplished what few on earth could do: a targeted killing with no evidence of foul play. He smiled to himself, failing to realize that the men he'd just killed would awaken a combat skill that was more than his equal.

Failing to realize he'd declared war.

8

The beer commercial on the bar television was a counterpoint to the somber mood of the crowd around me. I watched the impossibly beautiful people prance about on the wide screen, each drinking a bottle of nectar guaranteed to get them laid, and realized I'd lost a segment of my life somewhere along the way.

I was older than the people in the commercial.

When did that happen?

It seemed like just yesterday I was younger than them, looking at their beauty and waiting until I was their age to savor the goodness of the life they portrayed. Then, in the blink of an eye, I was older, somehow having skipped that beer-commercial generational gap, and never experiencing the Promised Land shown.

It made me a little melancholy. Made me wonder if I had missed out on what others had experienced because of my chosen career. Had I wasted my life chasing terrorists in the burning sands and fetid jungle while others danced at NFL parties, hooking up with impossibly gorgeous women just by drinking a beer?

I wondered if Turbo or Radcliffe had experienced the golden life portrayed in the commercial before they had died. I hoped so. We hadn't exactly seen eye-to-eye in our unit, but that didn't prevent us from having a deep connection because of our shared sacrifice. They had been inside a brotherhood that few on earth had experienced.

The official burial at Arlington Cemetery wouldn't happen for a month, and the bodies hadn't even been escorted home from Bulgaria, but we always did this little private wake as soon as possible, spreading the word and starting the grieving process early. It was a chance for a very select group of people to not only mourn, but to learn the specifics of the deaths, something that was hard to do in our compartmented little world, where everything was "need to know." We always held them at the same bar, and always at the same time. We'd done way too many of them since the unit had been created.

I felt someone bump my elbow, bringing me out of my trance. I turned and saw Jennifer, my partner in crime, and the only female in the entire group. Her eyes were red, but even with that she brought a smile to my face, a light that always managed to penetrate the darkness. The melancholy evaporated.

I said, "You doing okay?"

"Yeah," she said. "It's just such a waste. I feel for their families. They shouldn't be going through this." She wiped her eyes and smiled ruefully. "I wonder if they gave their wives as hard a time as they did me. Turbo and Radcliffe were tough to please."

That's putting it mildly. Along with me, Turbo and Radcliffe were members of a counterterrorist unit full of meat-eating he-man womanhaters. I'd recruited Jennifer to join, and they, like most of the unit, about lost their minds. We had women intel analysts, a smattering of case officers, and a few other female support types, but none had ever crossed into an operational role the way Jennifer had. They'd tried hard to keep her out, but had failed. Jennifer's sole experience with them had been as antagonists, but she was above all of that, and truly mourned their passing.

She said, "You guys live this life and you expect the worst to come from an enemy bullet or bomb. It doesn't seem real that two Taskforce operators would die in a car accident."

The unit we were in was so top secret it didn't have a name. Just some code words that would never see the light of day. We had to call it something, and the Taskforce had seemed to stick. Jennifer was right, though—it was a tragedy to lose two operators for something as stupid as a car wreck. She waved a hand around the bar, full of men all wearing a coat and tie.

"You're supposed to be indestructible. This reminds me that you're not, and the rules that apply to everyone else also apply to you."

Which was exactly how I felt. Apparently, Radcliffe was driving and had gone straight over a cliff, killing them both. I knew the inglorious nature of their deaths was weighing on everyone in the room.

All of the males in the bar were operators pulled from various special-operations units within the Department of Defense and the paramilitary arm of the CIA, now working for a unit that doesn't exist and living a lie in their everyday lives. In truth, there was a danger in all of us coming together like this, because we were working under different covers, but the commander of the Taskforce, Colonel Kurt Hale, believed the grieving process was more important. And he was right. Anyway, nobody was going to question us because the suits did nothing to dampen the raw aggression in the room. People instinctively knew to leave us alone.

There were no support folks here or representatives of any of the various cover organizations that we used to infiltrate an operational area. No pilots, oilmen, cellular technicians, or anyone else from the myriad different clandestine activities at the Taskforce's disposal. It wasn't that they weren't respected, but this wake was reserved for operators only. Well, except for Jennifer and me.

I said, "I can't figure it out either. Both those guys trained to drive just about anything from snowmobiles to rally cars in Dakar. It doesn't make any sense."

A man came up with a beer in his hand, long wavy black hair and a neck choker, like some sort of 1970s commune dweller. Aggravatingly enough, outside of the hippie hair, he was as handsome as the men in the beer commercial. He said, "Who let you in here? Turbo hated your ass."

I smiled and said, "I'm not the one who beat the shit out of him for punching Jennifer." I snatched the beer out of his hand. "Thanks for the suds."

Jennifer said, "Knuckles, did you get any skinny on what happened over there? Nobody will talk to me."

He winked at me and said, "That's because this is for active counterterrorist commandos only. America's finest. I guess you two don't rate."

Matching his sarcasm, I said, "Maybe it's because I still hang out with you."

While Knuckles had been a teammate of mine, I'd actually left the Taskforce a couple of years ago, and Jennifer had never served a day in the defense or intelligence communities. Together, we were business partners who owned Grolier Recovery Services, one of the Taskforce's cover organizations. On the surface, it was designed to facilitate archaeological work around the world, but in reality it enabled the Taskforce to penetrate denied areas and capture or disrupt terrorists out to harm the United States.

Basically, if a diabolical plot was hatched in a country that had some old shit in it, we could use our corporation to infiltrate a team of killers without the state or the terrorists knowing we were coming. Which, given that ninety-nine-point-nine percent of the countries around the world had some type of archaeological site, meant we could penetrate anywhere we wanted. With Jennifer's anthropology degree and my military experience traveling the globe, we looked legit. Hell, we *were* legit, having found an ancient Mayan temple in Guatemala on our own a couple of years ago.

So why were Jennifer and I allowed into the sacred wake? Some of the greener operators, having come on since I left, gave us a sideways glance, but the old-timers knew better. Before I'd left the Taskforce, I was the leader of the team that had successfully prevented more terrorist activities than the next three teams combined. I was also a plank owner of the Taskforce, one of the first men recruited, and I'd helped build it from the ground up. I'd put most of the men in the room through Assessment and Selection to join the unit, so as far as the tribe went, I was alpha male. And Jennifer was, well, Jennifer.

Probably half of the men in the room despised her presence for no other reason than irrational fear and caveman feelings, but she'd also been through Assessment and Selection, with Turbo and Radcliffe running it, so there was no excuse that anything had been given to her. On top of that, she had proven herself on a number of missions.

Our company was unique in the Taskforce stable: a cover organization that was run by operators, and could do much, much more than simply provide an infiltration platform.

My old team—now ostensibly employees of Grolier Services—were the only ones who had operated with Jennifer. They'd seen her skill, and they were now believers. Their tolerance, coupled with my reputation, was enough firepower to shut up the he-man woman-haters. That, and the fact that she was a hammer to look at.

Knuckles smiled again and said, "Maybe you're right. Me being seen with you is tarnishing my reputation. Maybe I should see what I can do about getting you two out of here."

He looked over my shoulder at someone behind me and said, "Maybe I should tell the commander about the fraternization going on in your little company. That ought to do it."

His words punched a sore spot, friend or not. "Maybe you should keep your mouth shut."

Jennifer heard my tone and touched my arm, saying, "He's just kidding, Pike."

I said, "That's not something to joke about. Kurt might really take it seriously."

Over my shoulder, I heard, "Take what seriously?"

9

I glared at Knuckles, seeing him grin at the foot I'd placed in my mouth. I turned around and shook Kurt's hand, saying, "Nothing. Knuckles was just talking about Taskforce members getting administrative leave for same-sex marriages, since Virginia doesn't support them."

Knuckles's mouth fell open, and it was my turn to smile. Kurt said, "Is that so?"

"No . . . no. That's not what we were talking about," said Knuckles.

Kurt went back and forth between us before giving up and saying, "I'm sure whatever it was, I don't want to know about it."

We spent the next twenty minutes talking about Turbo and Radcliffe, laughing at some of their antics and somberly reciting their sacrifices. The usual thing that happened at any military memorial. Eventually, Kurt got around to asking about our company and our current schedule. My antennae went up immediately, because I'd known him for over fifteen years and could read him like a book. He wasn't making small talk.

I said, "Company's fine. We're still in the black and getting requests from real clients."

He laughed and said, "You mean like that last client looking for pirate treasure?"

"No, real clients," I said. I punched Knuckles in the shoulder. "Unlike the ones this shitbag comes up with."

Kurt cut to the chase. "You able to travel? No notice?"

That completely took me aback. "What?"

"Hey, I know I promised you guys two months' warning before operations, but I could use you right now."

"Doing what?"

"Turbo's team was getting a pattern of life on a Boko Haram leader. The guy is still out there, and I'd like to make their deaths mean something. It grates on me to let it go. He's probably not worth the effort, but I don't want to quit."

I got Jennifer's eye. She shrugged, telling me, *I'm game. Why not?*

I said, "Why us? Why not just slot Turbo's team a new leader? I know it would be rough, but they've got the better handle on the target. Why start over?" As soon as the words were out of my mouth I wanted to take them back.

Kurt looked at me for a moment without answering, then said, "You really asking that? Turbo's team is pulled. If it were a crisis or imminent threat, of course I'd keep them in the hunt, but it's not. They're on downtime until I can sort out the chain of command."

Our missions weren't like combat in Fallujah or *Saving Private Ryan*, a hellish cyclone of violence where a leader dropped and someone automatically took his place. We worked in the netherworld of covert operations, with the Taskforce itself operating outside of the bounds of US law. As such, the greatest pressure on an operator wasn't a gunfight but blowing our cover in a hostile country and exposing the Taskforce for all to see. It was a narrow beam we walked, as we all understood how quickly the organization could go bad.

Being a Taskforce operator meant having a moral compass that could withstand just about anything. It took a clear head and nerves of steel, with the judgment to bring violence only when violence was necessary. Not a place for anyone who wasn't one hundred percent, like Turbo's team. They were probably looking for a fight.

Most civilians thought us supersecret commandos had some type of on/off switch, where we could shunt our emotions to the side, and to a certain extent they were right. But we were still human, and the worst thing about a unit like ours was the very selective nature of it. We worked together for years, with teams literally coalescing because of shared attitudes and personalities. You became closer than family. Much, much closer than any other unit I had served within, and when someone on the team died, it was just as harsh as losing a brother or wife. It was devastating.

I said, "Yeah, sorry. Forget I said that. But why us? You've got four teams in here right now. Why not them? Jennifer and I are just the infiltration platform."

"The target is in Plovdiv, Bulgaria. Believe it or not, it's the oldest continually habited city in Europe, which means it's ripe for your cover. I have a Taskforce cover contract set up with UNESCO to look at some Roman ruins that are being destroyed by automobile exhaust and vandalism. You fit the bill perfectly."

I caught Jennifer's eye and saw, like me, she didn't believe it. "So it's the cover only? Who's developing the pattern of life? What team am I infiltrating?"

Kurt said, "No. It's not just the cover. I want *you* to develop the pattern of life as well, Pike. I need success on this. Set that guy up for an Omega operation. The Oversight Council is getting skittish because of Turbo's and Radcliffe's deaths. The team's cover is holding up just fine, but there's talk about closing down for a while. I need a success to calm them."

The Oversight Council was our own unique body of authority. Since we operated outside the bounds of the US Constitution, we didn't fall under traditional DOD or Intelligence Community oversight. Because of this, Kurt, along with the president of the United States, had built their own oversight, realizing that every organization like ours had eventually morphed like a cancerous growth into something evil. Composed of thirteen trusted individuals from the private sector and the government leadership, the Oversight Council was designed to prevent that, as they had approval over all Taskforce activities.

I was surprised he wanted *me* to execute the mission, but my ego sort of enjoyed the attention. Kurt and I had worked together for years, even before the Taskforce was created, and I appreciated the vote of confidence in my abilities. But I still had a few questions.

I said, "So the Council approved of this deployment? On such short notice?"

Usually, Taskforce approvals took months before we could execute, with a slow buildup until everyone was satisfied with the endgame. Then, if we were lucky, we'd be granted Omega authority for a take-down.

He smiled. "Not so much. You're deploying under Turbo's authority. Honestly, we've never had a situation like this, where a team is pulled because of death from nonhostile activities. The Council already sanctioned the mission. You're just executing."

I nodded, letting that soak in. I caught Jennifer's eye one more time, seeing she was okay with it. I said, "I need more than just Jennifer and me. I'm going to need the team."

Knuckles said, "Hey, wait a minute. We're off cycle. We've got a deployment in two months and need to finish the train-up package. I don't have time for this."

Kurt ignored him, saying, "You got it. Whoever you want."

Knuckles said, "What the fuck? I'm the damn team leader here, and I'm telling you we can't go."

I ignored him as well, saying, "I need four in addition to Jennifer. Buckshot's wife is pregnant, right?"

Kurt said, "Yes."

"I'll take Knuckles, Retro, Blood, and Decoy."

Knuckles began huffing and puffing, incredulous that we were talking about his team as if he weren't there. I let him, enjoying the show.

He said, "Sir, Pike's no longer active. If I go, it's my mission. He's just the facilitator."

I heard the words and realized it was no longer fun and games. I was overstepping my bounds. Knuckles *was* the team leader, and I was about to cause a fracture in our chain of command. I was nothing but a cover company, no longer an operator in the Taskforce. I hadn't expected Knuckles to fight it, primarily because of my ego and the fact that I used to be his team leader, but I wouldn't usurp his command if it caused an issue. I'd made my choice to leave the Taskforce, and he'd stuck by me on a number of missions after that. I had no right to take his team.

I put my beer on the counter and said, "He's correct, sir. It's his show, not mine."

I saw the gratitude on Knuckles's face at my words.

Kurt said, "Jesus. You people are like a bunch of high-school drama queens. I don't have time for this bullshit. You need to fly today."

I waited for what Knuckles would say. He looked at me, then Jennifer, and finally Kurt.

He shook his head and said, "Aww, screw it. It's your company." He pointed at Jennifer and said, "Besides, you and spider monkey here wouldn't listen to me anyway."

10

Yuri checked in with the four other Vympel team members inside the park, each situated at an ingress route to the meeting site. None had seen the target.

The park was fairly crowded and very large, making Yuri concerned that Vlad's Nigerian had somehow slipped through, but he knew that was just nerves. It was highly unlikely his men would miss a six-foot-tall African in a Bulgarian park. Even so, he wanted to ensure there was no screwup. For the first time since the USSR had fallen, Yuri felt he had a purpose. A chance to make a difference.

He had been adrift for over ten years, striving to do what was right only to see his efforts wasted, watching the abuse from the leeches that fled the security services when the USSR fragmented, only caring about themselves and what they could gain from the carcass of the country he loved. He had thought he might be the last person who cared, until he met Vlad. A man who had a vision for the country. A man who understood the purpose of power, and was willing to do what was necessary to attain it. To do what he must to reestablish Russia in its rightful pantheon among the other global leaders.

After the successful ambush of the Americans, he'd reported back to Vlad, letting him know the surveillance effort was in disarray and the men he'd attacked were dead. Yuri had remained on the fortress road just long enough to confirm that the Ford had plunged straight down, exploding in a violent fuel-air ball of fire, incinerating the men inside.

They'd kept a loose countersurveillance eye on the remaining men of the American team, only pulling off when it was clear the horrific crash had overcome any attempt to remain in contact with the Nigerian. From afar, he'd watched the team frantically scale the hills attempting to get to the wreckage, clearly seeing the pain on their faces through the binoculars. He felt no remorse.

Back inside the military club, he'd expected some praise from Vlad, but the man had simply nodded and said, "On to the next step."

Chagrined, he'd waited for his next orders. Vlad had said, "Have a seat."

He did so, still not saying a word.

Vlad said, "The Boko Haram savage is named Usman Akinbo. The group is fighting the government of Nigeria, but with my prodding, Akinbo has decided to make the fight global. We wish to help them on this path."

"Why? Don't we have enough problems with Chechen terrorists? Why are we helping an Islamic radical?"

"We are not helping him. We're helping ourselves. He has no idea who's behind him. As far as that savage knows, he's being assisted by any number of different terrorist groups."

"But we *are* assisting him. He'll be blowing up Russian interests soon enough."

Vlad poured two shots of vodka, handed one to Yuri, then held his glass out for a toast. Yuri tapped the glass and waited.

Vlad said, "You need to think larger. More strategically. Akinbo will only strike once, and his attack will be the catalyst that ensnares the United States into one more quagmire war. The final one that will cause its bankruptcy."

"I don't understand. America has been burned from both Iraq and Afghanistan. There's no way they'll get involved in another war. Look at Syria. Ten years ago, the United States would have done whatever it took to cause the downfall of Assad. Now they watch from the sidelines while our own president manipulates them like a puppet."

"Yes. You're right. But Syria is all part of the plan. The Americans have refused—in their words—to put 'boots on the ground,' but they haven't been properly incentivized. All it takes is an attack that will trigger a response. I told you there was a Syrian Shabeeha coming. He's bringing a package of Sarin nerve gas."

Vlad saw Yuri's eyes squint and said, "Contrary to what the press reports, Syria isn't giving up its chemical weapons."

Yuri grimaced and said, "That's great. Wonderful. Another country we'll back until it bankrupts us. So how will this help?"

Vlad glared at the words, causing Yuri to backpedal. "Sir, I didn't mean—"

The Impaler waved a hand impatiently. "Let me finish, child, before you give me your keen grasp of world events."

He took a sip of vodka, then said, "Akinbo will release the weapon in the west. He thinks he's on his jihad—which I guess he is—but the true response will be from America. The threat from Boko Haram will go from regional to global, and America—just like they did in Afghanistan— will be forced to invade Nigeria to remove the global menace. On top of that, the Americans will trace the tags from the chemical munitions. When it tracks back to Syria, they'll invade that cauldron of violence as well, flailing about trying to stem further WMD leaks.

"We, on the other side, will ensure the fight continues for years, bleeding dry the American economy. The US will flood both countries with its army and state department, and all it will cost us is weapons. They will reach a tipping point. Just like we did in Afghanistan in 1989."

Sitting on the park bench, Vlad's final words still made Yuri smile twenty-four hours later. The chance to be instrumental in the great game was a breathtaking gift, something he had only dreamed about. No longer would he or his team hunt Chechens in a tit-for-tat pinprick war.

His earpiece chirped, bringing him out of his reverie. "Akinbo in sight. Headed in from the fountain. Five minutes out."

Yuri left his position and moved closer to Vlad's location. Seated on a plastic chair surrounded by old men playing chess and backgammon, Vlad blended in perfectly. With his worn clothes, he looked like any other geriatric killing time in the park.

Yuri settled onto a park bench ten feet away, but outside the concrete circle of board-game players. When Vlad looked his way, he twitched his head in a slight nod. Vlad gave no indication he even saw the signal, turning back to the chess game he was watching.

Akinbo entered the small circle of tables and moved to Vlad. He took a seat, and Yuri saw Vlad press a button on his lapel, turning on the microphone that allowed Yuri to hear the discussion, and in so doing, giving him early warning to protect his Control should the Nigerian do something stupid.

The radio was tinny in his ear, with scratchy static that spiked occasionally, causing him to flinch, but the words were clear enough.

Vlad: "I'm glad you could come here."

Akinbo: "I'm not sure why I did. My leader sent me, but I'm not
sure you are worth the effort. You are just as bad as the *kafirs*
we fight in Nigeria."

Vlad: "Your leader is wise. Take the help you can, regardless of
who gives it. It's how you win."

Akinbo: "What help are you offering?"

Vlad: "You have been fighting for an Islamic state in Nigeria for
years. Why have you failed? If your group is so strong?"

Akinbo: "The rapists of my country. You."

Yuri heard what he thought was laughter, then Vlad continued.

Vlad: "Me? My country has done nothing but help the revolution.
You mean my enemy the United States?"

Akinbo: "Yes. The United States. They keep the corrupt government in power. They prevent us from winning."

Vlad: "Do you see how the United States operates? If you bloody their nose, they quit. Look at Lebanon, Somalia, Iraq, or Afghanistan. They don't have the heart to fight. You hit them hard enough, and they'll leave Nigeria to you. Can you win if that occurs?"

Akinbo: "Yes. Yes, we can. We have many, many supporters. But how will I bloody their nose? What can I do?"

Vlad: "I have a man I want you to meet in Istanbul. A person that has a very potent weapon. If you release this weapon in the west, it will cause them to react like a child touching a candle flame. They'll leave the country to you."

Yuri heard nothing for a long moment, enough to make him think his radio had failed. He moved his hand to the small control unit, then heard Akinbo say, "I would welcome such an opportunity, as long as you are telling the truth."

Vlad: "I am. But there's one thing you must know. You will become a martyr by using the weapon. It isn't discriminatory. When you release it, you will die."

Akinbo: "I am prepared for that. It was understood when I came here."

Vlad: "You need to create a statement of some sort. Something to let them know it was Boko Haram that caused the attack. Otherwise, it will be a waste."

Yuri was amazed at the duplicity Vlad was espousing. He was actually using Akinbo's own vanity to accomplish exactly what he intended.

Akinbo said, "Of course. It would be my high honor to let the world know who caused the pain. I will make a videotape that my cell will release when I'm gone."

Yuri saw Vlad hand over a package, then heard, "This is a new cellular phone. Throw yours away. It is undoubtedly being tracked. Along with that there are four different SIM cards. Make no more than five calls before switching SIMs. If you need to call family or friends, do so from a public phone."

Akinbo took the package, but seemed reluctant. "I don't want your electronic help. I can do this on my own. You give me the weapon, and I'll perform the jihad."

Vladimir said, "You *will* take the electronics, because without them you will be dead. I'm willing to help you, but I won't do so just to see you fail. You work well in Nigeria, but you are in the real world now. And you've already had men hunting you. Why did you think you were ordered to the fortress in the mountains?"

Akinbo's eyes grew wide and Vlad leaned into him. "You will do what I say. Do you understand?"

Akinbo nodded. Vlad slid across a passport, saying, "This has visas for Turkey, the United States, and Bulgaria. It is what you will use from here on out. The Bulgarian visa will also get you into any EU country."

Akinbo nodded again, remaining mute.

Vlad tapped his hands on the table, then said, "I see you thinking, and that's good, but know I've already saved your life once. Go now. I'll call with instructions tonight."

Yuri watched Akinbo collect his passport and phone, then waited until he was out of view before approaching Vlad.

He said, "That seemed to go fairly well."

Vlad shook his head and said, "You can never tell with an asset. You want them to execute what you ask, but they have a mind of their own. Either way, we need to get him moving out of here before another American team comes."

"You think they will send another?"

"Yes. I'm sure of it."

"What do you want me to do if they arrive before we evacuate Akinbo?"

"Do what you do best."

11

R etro gunned the drill, causing bits of sawdust and insulation to float down onto my face. I looked to the ground, but that was all I could do to escape the rain of dust, since I was bracing the table/chair pyramid we'd made so he could reach the ceiling.

He said, "I don't know why we don't just put in a Wi-Fi transmitter. This guy isn't some super-spy. He's not going to pick up a signal coming out of his room. He'll just think it's part of the hotel's Wi-Fi network."

"I'm not worried about the target," I said. "I'm worried about the hotel. This *is* Bulgaria, after all. Past heart of the Communist empire, now the heart of the Mafia kingdom. I'm not taking any chances."

He continued drilling and said, "Come on, Pike, hardwiring a microphone is a hell of a lot of work, especially one of these shielded ones. We're not in the Kremlin."

The microphone he was installing was made for serious covert usage, with all components protected from emitting any electromagnetic energy. I'll admit that it was a little overboard, but we had no middle ground. It was the only wired device we'd brought. Everything else transmitted a signal. Much easier to emplace, but also easier to find. At least I knew this one would remain undetected.

We'd flown in early this morning, landing at the airport in the capital of Sofia and renting cars to come south to Plovdiv. It would have been much more convenient to land at the Plovdiv airport, but we were flying a Gulfstream IV, and I didn't want to spike anyone's interest this close to the target. We jokingly called the aircraft the rock-star bird because, well, that's what rock stars use. It was a specially constructed piece of Taskforce equipment that could hold a large array of equipment hidden within its walls, and it was how we got the technical kit into Bulgaria that we were now installing. The aircraft was "leased" to Grolier Recovery Services, and was a pretty convenient way to travel, but sometimes it wasn't prudent to brag about that luxury. Landing at Plovdiv's small airport would probably get tongues wagging.

We'd checked into the same hotel as our target, and, through some manipulation of their computer system from hackers at homestation, managed to get a room directly above his. After scanning his room and ensuring it was empty, I'd placed Decoy and Blood in the lobby as early warning, and left Knuckles in the room above us, ready to help with the install.

Retro pushed the drill hard, causing the pyramid to sway. I braced my feet and stabilized it, while he slammed his arms into the hanging light to stop himself from falling. He said, "Are you holding this damn thing?"

I grinned and said, "Maybe we should have Jennifer do this."

From the corner of the room, where she was preparing various beacons for operation, she snapped her eyes up with an unspoken question.

I shook my head at her, hearing Retro say, "Jennifer won't do any better than me with your lack of help. I'm telling you, this is a waste of time. This hotel room looks like the set of *Three's Company*. They won't have any technical capability."

I said, "Well, then you'll fit right in," bringing a smile to Jennifer's face. Retro got his call sign because he refused to buy new clothes simply because the old ones were out of style. Thus, if a garment was still capable of performing its intended function, he kept wearing it. He looked like an advertisement from a 1980s Sears catalog. He did have a point about the hotel, though.

The Trimontium Princess was pretty utilitarian. Despite being one of the finest guesthouses in Plovdiv, the rooms were still fairly outdated. The TV was an old twenty-four-inch tube, the thermostat apparently a decoration, and the bathroom fixtures antiques. But they did have Wi-Fi, so that was a plus.

Truthfully, that description was a little harsh, as the hotel was very clean and the staff did everything it could to please us. It was just a little tired and on the wrong side of the old Iron Curtain, but it still had a lot of life left. Jennifer, of course, loved every inch of it. Primarily because she loved anything at all that was older than her.

She'd wanted to start building our cover immediately, which meant going out and looking at UNESCO heritage sites, but I wanted to get a handle on our target first. She was correct in her intentions, but in this case, we knew the guy was gone and we needed to seed his room.

I'd read the dossier of the target on the flight over, including the pattern of life developed by Turbo's team. Usman Akinbo was a leader in the terrorist group named *Jama'a ahl al-sunnah li-da'wa wa al-jihad*, but known to the world as Boko Haram, an indigenous Nigerian organization that was determined to create an Islamic government ruled by Sharia law. A familiar refrain heard in quite a few different Muslim countries, especially with the Muslim Brotherhood leading the charge of the Arab Spring. The difference here was that the conflict didn't pit Islamic fascists against moderate Muslims, but against Christians. The northern part of Nigeria was Muslim, while the southern part—including the seat of government—was Christian. A volatile combination, and a microcosm of the global clash of civilizations, playing out here in a single state.

Given that, Boko Haram was different in another way. It was one of the most puritanical terrorist groups I'd ever seen. The name itself said it all: Directly translated, it means "Western education is sinful." The members themselves believed anything coming from the West was an affront to God, and did whatever it took to counter that encroachment. Forget about "normal" whacko Islamic screeds. For them, saying the earth was round or studying the theory of evolution was outright heresy. Needless to say, their human rights record, including the treatment of the fairer sex, wasn't that high on the scale. It hovered somewhere below Idi Amin.

Originally, the group was focused solely on creating an Islamic state and spent all its energy fighting the Nigerian government. It had no global aspirations, but, like just about every Islamic terrorist group in existence, it was now branching out.

The Taskforce had intercepted intelligence indicating that members of Boko Haram had coordinated with al-Qaeda in the Islamic Maghreb, and were being recruited for attacks against Western interests outside of Nigeria. Because their nationality and ethnicity had much less of a chance of getting profiled for terrorism, the Nigerians were being wooed by the broader global terrorist networks.

Usman—whom Turbo's team had given the code name Chiclet due to the size and whiteness of his teeth—was one of the Boko Haram men who had spiked interest. We didn't know for sure if he was planning or coordinating an attack outside of Nigeria, which is why we had him under surveillance. Our mission was the same as Turbo's: confirm or deny that Chiclet was a threat.

I heard the drill stop and looked up. Retro pulled out the bit and peered at his tiny hole. He keyed his radio and said, "Knuckles, see if you can feed it through."

Ten seconds later a thin wire with a little bump on the end appeared, snaking out next to the plate that held the 1940s wiring for the hanging light. Retro extended the microphone wire just enough to go inside the plate, then seated the microphone with a bit of glue. He slid the base of the light back over the plate and screwed it down, then admired his handiwork for a minute.

I helped him down and he said, "I'm going for a sound check. When I call, go to each corner and count to five."

I told him fine, then checked on Jennifer. She'd embedded two beacons, one into the Nigerian's suitcase and the other in the heel of a pair of shoes, but was stymied with the third one.

She said, "I've got this last DragonTooth, but I can't find anything to put it in."

The DragonTooth was a beacon about the size of two quarters stacked together. It worked off a combination of the cellular GSM network and any available Wi-Fi node to determine its position, and would relay a location on a preprogrammed time. It wasn't as accurate as a GPS, in that it wouldn't give us a grid to within three meters, but on the other hand, it didn't need to see the sky in order to access satellites like a GPS required. I could live with the greater circle of probable error; knowing the building Chiclet was in should be good enough.

The beacon was also disposable, and had its own self-destruct mechanism. When the battery reached a certain level and was about to be exhausted, it would use its remaining juice to fry the circuit board inside. Thus, if it was recovered later, nothing of its history would remain. With continuous use, the battery life was only six hours, and I needed to stretch that out. I'd programmed them to signal twice a day, which should give us about two weeks.

I said, "Don't worry about it. Two should be good enough."

She began packing our kit while I picked up a wand that registered the emanation of electromagnetic radiation from electronic devices. I climbed our rickety ladder and turned it on, seeing the needle jump. I said, "Turn off the light."

She did, and the needle dropped to zero. I smiled. *Not going to find that bug without digging.*

I began climbing back down and saw the needle jump again, a small spike that shouldn't have registered among the wood and fabric of the table and chairs. I stopped and did a slow sweep with the wand. The needle spiked over the center of the chair, an old relic with faded, dusty upholstery. I looked below, seeing only the cloth covering and four wooden legs. I pulled the cushion up, finding nothing unusual. I bent down and looked closer at the fabric underneath. It too was faded, but there was something out of place. A little incongruity that had triggered in my subconscious. It took a second before it registered.

The staples holding the fabric to the chair were new.

12

I removed the chair from the table and set it on its side. I held the wand over the center of the fabric. It buried into the red zone.

Jennifer said, "What's up?"

I pulled my knife and knelt down, saying, "Get the table back where it was. Make sure the legs go back into the indents in the carpet."

She did so, not saying another word. I slid the tip of my blade underneath the corner staple and slowly worked it free. Slicing the fabric would have been a hell of a lot quicker, but it would also leave no doubt that we'd been in the room if someone had to retrieve what I thought was underneath.

I popped the staple, set it aside, then worked on another one. When the corner and the two staples left and right were out, I shined my light in and saw a modern electronic device. A digital recorder. And it was running.

Next to it was a small microphone-looking thing that was long and thin, covered in foam. On the other side was a battery pack, lead wires running to the recorder.

The implications were profound.

Someone else is tracking our guy.

We'd scanned our rooms as soon as we checked in, and they'd all come up clean, which meant this device was placed for the person in this specific room. *Chiclet. My target.* When the wand first triggered,

I thought maybe it was something innocuous or a piece of kit left over from the Cold War, when this hotel was probably wired for sound better than the Met. Now it could mean only one thing.

My earpiece chirped and I heard Retro say, "Ready for sound check."

I said, "You owe me a case of beer. This hotel does have some technology."

"What are you talking about?"

I pulled up my smartphone's camera and said, "Standby." I took a picture and sent it to him, asking, "What do you think?"

Retro was our team's resident computer geek, and if I was imagining things, confusing a digital voice recorder for some type of pesticide ultrasound, he'd let me know.

He came back on. "It's a digital recording device. The thing to the left is a combination boom mike and initiation switch. It only records when there's sound to save battery life. You make a noise and it turns on."

Great. High-tech. So much for the Cold War. "What's the battery life?"

Knowing that would give me a good idea of how long ago it had been emplaced. Maybe it was for the guy who had Chiclet's room earlier. Before he could answer, Decoy cut in. "Break, break, break. Chiclet entered the lobby. I say again Chiclet entered the lobby."

Shit.

I said, "I need someone to stall him. I have to erase the last ten minutes of this digital memory or we're burned."

Blood said, "You need to exfil."

I hissed at Jennifer, "Hold this light. I can't see the buttons."

Blood said, "You copy?"

"Blood, we have to neutralize this device. Figure out some way to stall him."

"What do you want me to do, go up to him and ask what a brother's doing in Bulgaria? He's already at the elevator."

Blood was African American, and that was his idea of a joke. He came back on and said, "Decoy, let the elevator start to close, then holler at him to hold it. We'll both get in. You push the first floor, I'll push the second."

Chiclet's room was on the third floor—which was actually the fourth in American terms—so that was all the delay I was going to get. I snaked my hand into the small hole and stopped the recording. "Retro, Pike. How do I delete just my stuff? Can you tell me how to do that from looking at the picture?"

I heard Decoy shouting, "Hold that door, please."

Retro said, "Yeah. I Googled the owner's manual when you sent it. See the circular dial? Click the 'menu' button below it, then click on 'graph.' The entire recording will come up in a graphical line. Use the left arrow on the dial to walk it back however far you want, then hit 'delete.'"

I heard Blood say, "Second floor, please," and knew I was running out of time. I followed Retro's instructions, looking at my watch and making an educated guess as to how far back to go. Before hitting delete I said, "Jennifer, once I'm done here, no more talking. Help me get the fabric back on, then we're out of here."

She nodded, and I pressed the button, then reset the microphone back to its dormant status.

Over my Bluetooth I heard, "Pike, this is Decoy. I'm out."

I gave a double-click, acknowledging his words, then pulled the fabric tight against the frame, nodding at Jennifer. She picked up the staples and worked the first back into its original hole, lightly tapping it in with the back of my knife. It might have triggered the microphone, but I didn't really care, as the noise wasn't confirmation of anything. It could have been Chiclet knocking on a wall.

She started on the second and I heard, "Pike, Blood. I'm out. He's on the way. I hope you're clear of the room."

Knuckles came on. "I accessed the stairs to his floor. I'm headed down the hall from the east end. No Chiclet yet, but once he's committed to this hallway, you guys are trapped."

Jennifer locked eyes with me and I nodded to the chair. She placed the last staple and tapped it home. I flipped the chair upright and set it exactly where it had been before. Jennifer moved to the door and I picked up the garbage bag we'd laid on the floor to catch the shavings and sawdust from Retro's drill, folding it up and shoving it into my pocket.

We were just about to crack the sill when Knuckles said, "Too late. He's in the hall. He's going to see you exit. Come up with a story. Send Jennifer out first, and start bullshitting."

Damn it. No story we could create would alleviate all the suspicion with this guy. He was used to being hunted, and was naturally paranoid. On top of that, both Jennifer and I would be permanently burned for further surveillance work.

Looks like it'll be Knuckles's mission after all.

The room had two very large windows that went from the ceiling to about two feet above the floor. They opened like a miniature sliding door, and had no screens. Jennifer sprinted to one, dragged the heavy drapes aside, and threw it open, exposing a faux balcony with a cast-iron railing. She looked back at me, then dove out.

What the hell is she doing?

I raced over to the window in time to see her stand up on the railing and point above her head. I leaned out and saw that the fourth floor—our floor—had a small ledge all the way around the building. But there was no way we could both climb simultaneously, and there wasn't enough time to do it one after the other.

Jennifer had realized the problem before she'd even exited. A former Cirque du Soleil performer, there was very little she couldn't climb. She had no fear of heights and was as comfortable climbing the side of a building as a squirrel running up a pine tree. Standing on the iron railing, she shucked her shoes, letting them fall to the earth four stories below. She pointed at herself, then the other window balcony over ten feet away. Before I could do anything, she launched herself in the air, leaping with her arms stretched out in front.

I leaned out as far as I could, my heart in my throat. I watched her snag the lower rail with a single arm. She swung under, then back, wrapping her other hand onto the rail. She pulled herself up, and I wanted to scream at her for the stupid risk. Instead, I clambered out onto the balcony railing, then slid the window closed. There was nothing I could do about the drapes. Hopefully he'd think the maid had moved them.

I got on the radio and said, "Retro, need some assist out of your window."

He said, "What? You're coming up the wall?"

"Yeah. Koko committed me."

I saw Jennifer scowl at her call sign, then leap up and snag the ledge below our room. She pulled herself up until she could grab the railing of our own faux balcony, then began to haul herself to the window.

She made it seem easy, but it was a long, long way to the ground below, and my subconscious mind was revolting against a leap of faith to the ledge. It was only about a foot higher than my outstretched arms, but that was the longest twelve inches I had ever seen.

Jennifer climbed up the railing until she could pull her feet onto the ledge, then glanced back to me, a question on her face. Through the glass I caught a glimpse of Chiclet's door opening and committed, leaping up and clamping my hands on the ledge in a death grip. I executed a chin-up, the fear of the long drop flying through my body. I slapped my right hand onto the lower railing, then the left, grateful to have the iron to hold on to instead of the rock ledge.

Using brute strength, I shimmied up the railing as fast as possible so I could get my feet on the ledge. No style points whatsoever; all I wanted was to get my weight onto the stone. Away from the drop of death. After I felt I'd gone far enough, I swung my feet, kicking the wall and feeling for the ledge.

When my left foot hit it, I slapped my right in the same location, then relaxed, letting the adrenaline subside. I looked over at Jennifer, seeing she had pulled herself all the way up and was sitting on the railing. She smiled at me, then began putting her hands together in a silent golf clap.

I said, "You have lost your fucking mind. Next time, how about you ask if your idea is worth it first instead of just jumping out the window."

She said, "What's the big deal? It wasn't that hard, was it? And now we're not burned."

Chagrined, I said, "No, it wasn't hard, but it *was* a little risky."

She gave a look of mock surprise. "Really? Because I was going to ask you to do that to get to my room tonight. After the guys go to bed."

Retro opened the window next to her, cutting off the conversation. She winked at me, then crawled inside. When he got to my window, he said, "Not sure what you did, but she's giggling about something."

I shook my head and said, "She's trying to drive me into an early grave."

13

Aaron Bergmann leaned back from his computer, annoyed and exhilarated at the same time. Annoyed that Mossad said it was going to take days to crack the encryption of the trove of documents promised by Boris, but exhilarated that Boris's proof of value had delivered much, much more than Aaron would have thought. Clearly, Boris had wanted his PIN to the bank card, because the unencrypted documents had exposed a current, valid threat, and had shown that Boris did indeed have excellent placement and access to cutting-edge Russian secrets.

A proof of value was simply a taste of what a source could provide. Boris knew that Aaron wouldn't transfer the PIN simply by getting a thumb drive full of encrypted documents. For all he knew, Boris had encrypted the morning paper and said it was top secret. Thus, he'd included several documents that were not protected to show the quality Aaron was buying, and it was high quality indeed. Aaron had sent the documents to Mossad headquarters, and they'd come back with an answer: a Syrian intelligence officer posing as a Shabeeha was attempting to bring a weaponized container of Sarin nerve gas to Istanbul. Aaron couldn't think of a single piece of intelligence that would spark Israel's interest more.

The Shabeeha were the death squads roaming around Syria slaughtering anyone who opposed the regime. Ostensibly just local yokels who'd spontaneously begun running amok, killing anyone who disagreed with President Assad, their actions were perversely held up by the regime as proof of Assad's grassroots popularity. In reality, they were exactly what they appeared to be: thugs paid to kill to advance the dictator's agenda. They were controlled and rewarded by the Syrian security establishment. In this case, a Syrian Air Force intelligence officer, posing as a Shabeeha commander, had evacuated an artillery round filled with Sarin GB, the deadliest nerve agent on earth.

The documents didn't disclose what the Syrian officer intended to do with it, but it was a forgone conclusion that it wouldn't be good. So much so that Mossad had decided to err on the side of caution. Instead of attempting to penetrate and determine intentions, linkages, and further exploitation, the Mossad had designated him a Samson target.

Aaron's target.

He reread the Hebrew on his screen to be sure he wasn't mistaken, but the words didn't change. His Samson team was inbound to Istanbul with a mission: Eliminate the Syrian, and do it in such a manner that would send a message.

The Mossad is finally understanding our worth.

Aaron and Samson had worked for the Mossad for twenty years, but some still considered him an IDF castoff. Not worth the trouble.

After Israel gave the Gaza Strip back to the Palestinians, Aaron's unit became superfluous. The high command still maintained Sayeret Duvdevan, the sister counterterrorist unit tasked with the penetration of the West Bank occupied territories, and thus had no use for the Gaza unit, but they hesitated to throw away something that had been very difficult to create.

The Mossad had stepped in.

In 1979, the Wrath of God operations had ended with the killing of Ali Salameh, the archetype of terror. After that hit, the Kidon—or bayonet—teams had been reassigned back to general Mossad operations. In 1987, Hamas had formed, and the blood began to flow on Israeli soil. By 1994, some in Mossad were beginning to think disbanding the Wrath of God teams had been a mistake, and were looking to rekindle the Kidon mission, but convincing the command was another story. Too much training. Too much overhead. Too much everything for too little gain. Then Samson fell into its lap. Almost a Kidon element in its own right. All it needed was a little sharpening of a few global edges.

The Mossad went to work, and the results began immediately, with the 1995 killing in Malta of Fathi Shaqaqi, the creator of the Palestinian Islamic Jihad. There were a few missteps after that first success, the worst being two operatives captured in Jordan in 1997. They'd injected the Hamas political bureau chairman, Khaled Mashaal, with poison, but were swiftly captured by Jordanian police, leading to enormous political repercussions. The mission ended with Israel flying in an antidote to the poison, forced to admit its hand in the operation.

The teams learned quickly from those mistakes, and had some notable successes, including the 2008 killing of Imad Mughniyah—a master Hezbollah terrorist—in Damascus, Syria, and the 2010 killing of Mahmoud al-Mabhouh—the founder of Hamas's militant wing—in Dubai, UAE.

Even with these successes, without a burning desire to keep the mission—without a Munich—people in the upper echelon of Mossad still questioned the expense and waste of teams dedicated to targeted killing. After all, they did nothing for years at a time. Couldn't Mossad simply put a team together when necessary? Did Israel really need dedicated assets for the mission?

With the target on his computer, it appeared Samson had finally turned the corner, and their worth was being proved.

Aaron reflected on the profile for a moment, running through various options in his mind. Of course, the target himself had a vote, and would dictate to a certain extent what was possible, but sending a message required a specific signature. Mossad wanted Syria to know it was *them* who had taken the life, but needed to ensure the prime minister of Israel could say *No comment* with a straight face. In other words, everyone would know with a wink and a nod, but nobody could prove anything.

He pulled up the location of the meeting on Google Earth, and thought about the atmospherics. *Yes. It would work.*

The initial Shabeeha meeting with other unknown personnel was just outside the Istanbul Grand Bazaar, in a rat warren of small streets and side alleys too small for a car. But not too small for a moped, which is what zipped around that area like little demons. A perfect mode of assault. Wearing helmets, a Samson element could blast up on a small motorcycle and assault the meeting site, surgically killing the Syrian without harming anyone else in attendance. *Exactly like the scientists.*

Over the past several years, five Iranian nuclear scientists and the commander of Iran's cyber warfare unit had been assassinated, all by attackers on motorcycles. Some were killed when a limpet-shaped charge was magnetically attached to their car door, others were simply gunned down in a drive-by, but all were the work of the Mossad, and the world knew it. True, the missions were executed by surrogates and not an actual Samson team, but everyone understood who the puppet master was. Using the same signature here would ensure the Syrian regime instantly recognized this hit for what it was.

Aaron smiled to himself. It looked like conducting "ordinary" Mossad case officer work in between Samson missions was paying off, even if Boris had died before he could provide the encryption key.

He'd left the Russian lying on the ground, heart quivering like a spastic colon and brain slowly dying. He dearly wanted to search the man, but there was no time. He had no way to explain their relationship to any authorities that responded to the medical emergency. No way to plausibly describe why the two were sitting together.

He'd had a lot of strange things happen during his time in the Mossad, to the point where he never discounted the impossible from interfering with his mission, but this topped them all. His source having a heart attack at the most vulnerable time—with the case officer next to him.

He'd settled for the information he already had, along with Boris's physical key, and immediately headed for Istanbul, Turkey. Boris had provided one anchor—an Internet café in the Istanbul bus station—and Aaron was determined to find it.

Five minutes on the Internet revealed that Istanbul had a glut of bus stations, but only one that could be considered *the* Istanbul bus station. The Esenler Otogar. It was the third-largest bus station in the world, with more than three hundred different platforms utilized by buses leaving for destinations all over Europe and Asia. If Boris had left the documents at a bus station, this one was the first on the list for Aaron to check.

He'd taken a taxi to the station and found himself swallowed by a never-ending stream of people running about like ants. The place was a huge horseshoe, with bus platforms ringing a central building and metro station. After exploring some of the terminals, he shifted focus. Somewhere there had to be a central shopping district for all of these people. While chaotic and large, at the end of the day, it wasn't unlike a modern airport, with gates servicing transportation just like an air terminal.

He exited a platform and observed his surroundings, focusing on the central building in the center of the horseshoe. He dodged through the traffic, passed by stairs to the underground metro station, and entered the building.

Full of shops selling everything from running shoes to vegetables, he wondered how they stayed in business. Did travelers really want a bushel of beans or a new stereo before getting on a bus?

He saw a sign proclaiming Internet access with an arrow pointing up a flight of stairs. Before mounting them, he assessed his status.

Could he penetrate here and not be remembered? Did the atmospherics facilitate a play for the documents?

He had the key, but nothing else, and the only way to succeed was to portray himself as knowing exactly what he was doing. But he had no real idea of what actions he was supposed to take, because he hadn't been able to confirm the bona fides for the café. Thus, he was forced to fish, and he studied the area to determine if he could do so without anyone wandering inside the station remembering him.

He'd decided he was good. The place was a beehive of activity, with everyone within an hour of being on a bus to a different country. He mounted the stairs.

Reaching the top, he'd found three different Internet cafés and one phone center. He studied them for a moment, watching the people coming and going, along with the men behind the central desks. He focused on one with a younger Turk, seeing him conduct several transactions that had nothing to do with the Internet. Transactions that were probably less than savory, given the furtive nature of the customers. He approached.

The young man looked at him expectantly, and he removed the key, eyeing the people on the computers, relieved to see they all were engrossed in their web experience.

The clerk said something in Turkish, mistaking Aaron's Mediterranean appearance as a local. He answered in English, and the man said, "You want computer?"

Aaron held out his key and said, "No. I want the box to this."

The man looked at him in confusion, and Aaron knew he'd made a mistake. He said, "Sorry. I'm in the wrong place."

He exited, kicking himself, but he knew there was nothing else he could have done. Getting out swiftly was the best chance of not being remembered. He surveyed the other two cafés and began thinking like Boris. Thinking like a spy. Who would he trust? Not a kid. Someone else. Someone who'd probably done espionage for Boris in the past.

He studied the clerks from the other two Internet shops and focused on the smaller café, with only three computers that were years out of date. How did that guy stay in business with the other cafés next to him using more modern systems?

He approached and repeated his request. The man saw the key and became wary, saying, "Where did you get that?"

"From a friend."

The clerk took the key and bent down, removing a metal lockbox. He used the key to open the lid, then pulled out a sheet of torn paper, reading the words. Inside, Aaron saw a thumb drive.

The man picked up a cell phone and dialed a number from the paper, a number that Aaron knew wouldn't be answered. He waited patiently until the man put the phone down. He said, "I'm sorry. My instructions were to call and confirm. I cannot help you until the man answers. Perhaps try again tomorrow."

The clerk was visibly shaking, worried about his answer. Aaron smiled, disarming him. "Of course. I would expect nothing less. I'll come back tomorrow."

The man smiled in return, nodding.

Aaron left, took a seat outside, and waited.

14

Aaron had grown bored from the stagnant sitting, hating the slow pace and tedious reality of intelligence work. Used to planning missions, then executing with a definitive result, he had little patience for the endless pools of potential outcomes that was the life of a case officer. He dealt in concrete operations, with a clear-cut end state, but the world of Mossad was not like that. It was a universe of possibilities, with the case officer trying to decide if this or that dedication of effort would pay off, but never knowing for sure if he wasn't missing an opportunity elsewhere.

Eventually, as the night grew long, the clerk left his shop. Sitting in a chipped plastic chair next to a barbershop, his head nodding, Aaron caught the movement and perked up. He concentrated on the security in play at the café. To his relief, there was none. The clerk turned on no alarms nor set any other electronic trip wires. He simply locked the glass door to the little cubicle he'd rented in the bus station. Which, given the location, made sense. It would be very hard to break into his shop inside a bus station that operated twenty-four/seven, especially since the café to the left—the one with the kid—never closed.

Aaron focused on where the clerk put his keys, then faded back, letting the man take the stairs. He followed discreetly behind.

The clerk went directly to the metro station, descending into the darkness. Due to the time of night, there wasn't a lot of traffic accessing the train, and Aaron realized he was in trouble. If he entered, the clerk would recognize him from his previous encounter, precluding any further operations. He hung outside for a moment, debating, then heard a crowd approaching. He looked behind him and saw a large crew of men and women, all wearing waiter and waitress uniforms. Something had just closed for the night, and the employees were giving him some cover.

The group walked down the stairs and he tagged along in the back, reaching the station platform five steps behind them. Dodging in the flow of people, he located his target, now standing at the edge and waiting for the train.

The platform was fairly new and clean. He would have appreciated something a little more archaic, with faded lighting, strange odors, and shadowed crannies like other countries he'd operated within, but this one was modern, well lit, and had digital cameras on the fore and aft of the platform.

A tougher nut to crack, but not impossible. He'd be on camera, but if he did it right, he wouldn't spike. The man wouldn't even know he had been there.

He needed five seconds. An accomplished pickpocket would only take a second or two, but he would have to get the key, press it into clay, then return it to the rightful owner without him knowing it had gone missing. Of course, it all depended on the situation and the target, but having done this multiple times, he knew the average was five seconds.

He worked his way through the crowd, getting right behind the target, wishing he had a Samson teammate here. Using three people for the operation would guarantee success. But wishing didn't make it so.

He positioned behind the man and considered his options. Like a street magician, he needed the target to focus on something else while he picked the pocket.

The crowd was thick just to the left of the target, and the workers from the restaurant were rowdy. Two girls were bouncing up and down and singing, while the men cheered them on. One girl was dancing closer and closer to the edge of the platform, imitating the twerking she'd seen in US music videos. Everyone was looking at her, including the target, ogling the antics with lecherous grins.

Aaron shifted his position and waited. He saw the headlights for the metro train in the distance and paused until the light bathed the platform itself. When he was sure of the timing, he backed into one of the waiters cheering on the dancers and gave him a hip check. Caught off guard on the edge of the platform, the man windmilled his arms to regain his balance, which he managed to do. But not before bumping into the girl.

She fell onto the tracks.

The crowd went wild, screaming and yelling, dashing in to help her back onto the platform. The target joined the fray, and Aaron glided in behind. The old clerk leaned over, offering his arm, and Aaron slipped his hand into the man's coat, retrieving the key ring.

He turned away, pulled out a container the size of a small soap dish, and imprinted the three keys on the ring in a block of clay. Jamming the lid closed, he whirled back around and helped pull the woman to safety, slipping the keys into the pocket of the target to his left.

Getting her off of the tracks, the target recognized Aaron, his eyes puzzled, but he said nothing, focusing on the hysterical girl's near-death experience. Back on the platform, everyone began a relieved discussion, talking and shouting at how close disaster had been as the train pulled into the station.

In the confusion, Aaron slipped away.

Two days later he returned to the bus terminal, armed with three keys. He repeated his static OP at the barber shop, watching the clerk leave the station. Waiting an additional hour, he approached the Internet café as if he belonged. He worked through the keys until he found the one that matched the lock. Glancing to his left, he saw the kid at the adjacent café looking at him curiously. He ignored him and entered, moving straight to the location of the lockbox.

He pulled it out and opened the lid, seeing the thumb drive inside. He'd just put his hand on the drive when he heard, "What are you doing in here?"

Aaron snapped his head up, his body now fired with adrenaline, only one thought in his mind: *Eliminate the threat.*

He said, "I was supposed to get this. The clerk gave me the key."

He held them up while cursing himself for not learning the clerk's name. For not preparing a suitable cover.

The kid said, "Mustafa never lets anyone in here after he closes. Why didn't you get it when he was here?"

Aaron said, "Close the door. We need to talk."

The glass of the café was mirrored with privacy film, leaving the open door the only access to witnesses. Of which there were many wandering about outside. Stupidly, believing his story, the kid did as he asked, sliding the glass door until it clicked.

He said, "So what are you doing?"

Aaron said, "Nothing. Like I said, I'm just getting something Mustafa owed me. Come here. I'll show you. I'm not stealing anything."

He held up the thumb drive and said, "This is what I came for."

The kid approached for a closer look, and Aaron struck.

Having spent over twenty years studying Krav Maga, Aaron's biggest threat was killing the kid outright. The art itself had no subtlety, and was designed simply to destroy an opponent. There were no subduing or compliance holds in Aaron's repertoire.

Aaron whipped his elbow around and caught the teenager directly across the nose. He heard it shatter with a gristly pop, followed by an explosion of blood as the kid began to collapse, arms flailing about, eyes squeezed shut in pain.

Aaron caught him, then lowered him to the ground. He dragged the body just outside of the door to the café, then hollered into the adjacent shop, where the kid worked, looking for a manager. When people gathered, leaving their computers to help, he professed innocence, acting confused and scared by the blood. As the crowd grew, he had faded back, leaving the scene. He knew the entire scenario would make the highlight reel on local television, but Turkey wasn't Israel. It would be investigated and dropped within hours due to a lack of leads.

The kid would do what he could, but with the thousands of people passing through the bus station, the investigation would reach a dead end that the police would have no heart pursuing. Logically, the old man in the café wouldn't lift a finger to help the investigation, even when he saw the thumb drive missing. He knew he was doing wrong, and wouldn't want to get on the bad side of Turkish authorities. He'd proclaim no knowledge, and the kid with the broken nose would end up living with the mystery for the rest of his life.

He'd worried that the sloppiness of the action would cause his Mossad masters to question his judgment and perhaps even his leadership of Samson. Now, staring at his computer screen and seeing the threat Boris had exposed, he knew his activities had been worth it. It wasn't clean by any stretch, but Mossad actions were rarely clean. Risk was an inevitable part of the game, and the Israeli Special Forces lived to push the envelope. He'd made a choice, and his decision had been right. Because of it, one of the most efficient killing machines on earth was coming his way.

His men.

15

Keeping my distance, I sat down on a little park bench while surreptitiously watching Chiclet. Jennifer followed suit, pretending to enjoy the sight of the children playing in a fountain to our front, but I knew her real focus: trying to determine if there was someone else conducting surveillance on our target.

After our little climb yesterday, we'd made it inside the hotel without getting compromised—the closest being when Jennifer went to retrieve her shoes and had to explain to the bellboy why she was walking around the premises digging in the bushes—and had begun to monitor Chiclet's hotel room.

The first thing we had done—before installing the microphone yesterday—was to initiate a cell phone IMSI grabber while we knew the room was still empty. A device about the size of a laptop with a small cellular antenna poking out of the side, it duplicated the actions of a cell tower and tricked any cell phone within a hundred meters into registering with it. It would suck them in, record the mobile subscriber number—the IMSI—then reject it back into the cell network. What we wanted was a footprint when Chiclet wasn't around so that when he returned, we could repeat the process and identify his phone.

After getting recovered into Retro's room from our monkey climb, we'd fired up the IMSI grabber, knowing Chiclet had a cell phone that was sniffing for a tower. Siphoning out all the previous phones from the earlier grab, we ended up with four new ones. Four was a little too much to hand to the NSA for content. They'd call it a fishing expedition, and with all the troubles they'd had recently, they would be in no mood to play ball, sending enquiries we at the Taskforce didn't want to answer.

It was hard enough getting our requests into the greater system without questions, and an enormous Taskforce infrastructure had been built to do just that. The employees of the CIA, NSA, NGA, and every other three-letter agency screamed at anyone who would listen that they were following the law, and that was true, but they didn't know about the Taskforce. We were an element working outside their scope, doing exactly what they claimed they weren't.

It was a dangerous place to be in today's world, but it was necessary. We'd prevented some potentially catastrophic attacks in the last few years, but we couldn't do it on our own. We weren't omnipotent. We still had to leverage the leviathan known as the US Intelligence Community. We just had to do it in a manner that remained beneath the radar—a radar that had become particularly sensitive in the last eighteen months. Because of it, feeding four numbers to the NSA was too many. It was something we'd have to refine ourselves.

We'd waited, listening on our installed microphone until we heard him begin to dial his phone, then waited a beat more until we heard him talking, ensuring that his cell was connected and passing data. We fired up the IMSI grabber, sucking in his phone, disconnecting it from the tower, and identifying his specific number. It was interference I didn't like, as it was a direct manipulation. Although benign—after all, cell phones dropped signal all the damn time—it was something a paranoid person could run with, seeing spies in the woodwork.

And everyone we tracked was paranoid.

It turned out that we didn't have to worry about Chiclet's paranoia. We had to worry about our own. The NSA ran the number through its giant metadata repository, and the phone had a link to a US num-

ber. So they wouldn't track it. Wouldn't listen to it. Wouldn't do anything *at all* with it.

The very database that was supposed to help find terrorists was
now being used to identify numbers that they would in no way, never,
ever look at. Since this phone had talked to a US cell sometime in the
past, it was now off-limits until we could prove its terrorist heritage
or get a warrant through the FISA court. Never mind that the phone
we wanted was clearly a foreign target—and well within the legal
framework of the NSA—because of public reaction to fantastical news
stories they had become reactionary, refusing to investigate anything
that had a US person's taint without first covering their asses with
paperwork. Since we in the Taskforce couldn't prove anything at all
without exposing ourselves—much less go to court for a warrant—
Chiclet's phone was done. A delicious irony, to say the least.

In the end, crying about it was a waste of time. I just had to get the
NSA what they wanted: a phone that wasn't tainted.

Chiclet had made that single call during the night. Because of the
NSA proscriptions, we couldn't get the transcripts from both parties,
but at least we had what he said through our microphone implant
earlier. He was going out to meet someone, and that someone would
give him further instructions. Which meant we were swinging into
action.

We wanted to do two things: one, identify the person he met for
further exploration and intelligence, and two, drive him to a different
cell phone so we could track his conversations.

The first objective would require a full-court press with the entire
team, but the surveillance would have to be very, very loose. Someone
else was potentially tracking him, and we didn't want to get snagged
in their surveillance effort. We had no idea who it was, but clearly they
weren't working with him, as the digital recorder had been emplaced
without his knowledge. We'd just have to be very careful on the follow, checking to see if he had anyone on him.

As for the second objective, that was easy. Jennifer and I staged in the lobby of the Princess hotel the following morning, drinking coffee. Chiclet had repeated the meeting time, so we knew that. We just didn't know the location. We set up way early to catch him in case he had some other plan in mind. Which he did, coming out of the hotel a full hour and a half before the meeting.

Jennifer saw him exit the elevator and hissed, giving me barely enough time to pull up our Stiletto. An electromagnetic pulse device, it looked like a compact telephoto lens mounted on a rail with a pistol grip. When triggered, it sent out an EMP that had the ability to render any small electronic device unusable. Basically, it fried the circuit boards of modern electronics like a mini–nuclear blast.

On the surface, it sounded cool, but the gun wasn't a panacea since it had issues with backsplash that could cause the person using it to lose everything from his digital watch to a complete communications suite, depending on how shielded the electronics were.

Jennifer scooted her chair to the left, blocking my actions, letting me bring the gun to bear. She held up a menu, and I fired from the hip, seeing the small LCD graph at the back of the gun begin to trip like a seismograph registering an earthquake. I held it in place, tracking Chiclet's movement until he was out of the building. Frying his phone and anything else electronic he had on him.

From there the team picked up surveillance, following Chiclet all over the place. He remained on foot and our follow was very, very loose, but he didn't meet anyone. Eventually, Jennifer and I rotated back into the mix as we switched out surveillance operatives, and we had him for the last few minutes.

The team followed him for close to two hours, and saw nothing to indicate he was under another team's surveillance, so maybe whoever was on him was just bugging his room. Maybe it was the Bulgarians, keeping tabs on someone they thought was potentially bad. Maybe it was nothing.

I watched Chiclet go across the promenade to a small convenience store, buying a bottle of water. From there, he came back across, walking right by us as if he had a destination in mind. He stopped outside a McDonald's, the ubiquitous symbol of democracy, and checked his watch. I'd seen earlier that it had hands, but if it had a battery, it wasn't going to help him any.

It didn't. I saw him shake it up and down, then grab the shirt of a man to his left, asking a question. When the man replied, Akinbo hurried away, running to a storefront next door and entering.

I raised my eyes to the signage above the door and saw he'd entered a casino. An intrusion point that would demand a response, as I was pretty sure he wasn't looking to increase his bankroll. Watching the children play in the fountain, I urgently wanted to get someone inside. Preferably me, but that would be stupid, since Jennifer and I had been on Chiclet long enough to raise our heat state. It was time to switch the eye, but not before I determined if someone else was on him.

I waited a few more seconds, until I was sure anyone that would have been following him would have committed, running through my head the heat state of everyone on the team. I keyed my mike. "Decoy, Decoy, what's your status?"

"At your six. I have you in sight."

"Roger. You see the casino to my three o'clock? Efbet Casino?"

"Yeah."

"Chiclet's inside. Need you to conduct an intrusion."

He said, "Roger," then I heard Knuckles come on. "You sure, Pike? He'll be on candid camera from a thousand different angles."

"I know, but this is the endgame. Chiclet panicked a minute ago before he entered. He's meeting someone in there, and we need to confirm. If it burns Decoy, it burns him."

I keyed off in time to see Decoy enter the front door.

16

From inside the surveillance room of the casino Yuri kept an eye on the entry chamber, but nobody cracked the door. Nobody had entered the entire time he'd been there. All he saw was the initial security man and the bag-check girl, both chatting with each other. On a Sunday afternoon, the floor was a little sleepy, with a couple of Bulgarians playing slots and several very attractive female dealers looking bored around the blackjack table.

He wondered how much they would cost, and whether he'd get a discount as a member of the Russian security services. One in particular caught his eye. A blonde with a slight overbite and a big rack, highlighted by the way she was leaning over her table, dealing cards to no one. The flicking of her wrists caused jiggles in other, more interesting places.

"Status?"

The speaker transmitting Vlad's voice snapped him out of his fantasy. He whipped his head to the camera feed from the little room on the second floor, finding Vlad staring at him uncannily. As if he could actually see Yuri in the darkness. Yuri punched the microphone button and said, "Nothing yet. Still no entry."

He watched Vlad grunt, no sound coming through the speaker, then heard, "Where is that dumbass? You positive the only phone call he got yesterday was ours?"

"Yes, sir. Absolutely positive. When he began his surveillance detection route, we penetrated the room. The only thing besides TV noise on the recorder is him talking to you. He's called no one."

"What about Internet?"

"We'd still hear Skype, and he has no laptop anyway. I suppose he could have used the business center, but I thought you'd vetted this guy. Do you think he's playing us?"

Vlad shook his head. "No. No, I don't. He's just an unreliable African. No different than an Arab. I should have expected as much. He doesn't show in another thirty minutes, and I'm going to have to pay for this room a second time."

Yuri was unsure how to respond. In truth, he was uncomfortable with the entire setup. After the fall of the USSR, and the subsequent turmoil in the KGB, many men had left the service and taken their skills to the highest bidder, working for criminal groups bent on succeeding in the brave new world of capitalism. But this type of capitalism bore little resemblance to any other industrialized country in Europe. It was a jungle, where the KGB skills came in quite handy. Espionage and covert action were executed more than the servicing of supply and demand, with the stakes as real as anything between governments. Actually, more real, as the end result wasn't a wink and a nod, with a prisoner exchange. It was a meat hook after a healthy amount of pain.

The Bulgarians had marched to the top of the pyramid, building criminal networks that rivaled anything the Sicilian Mafia could brag about. Now in a majority of countries in Europe, extending all the way to the United States, the relationship between the Russian FSB and the Bulgarian criminal groups had become symbiotic and intertwined. The state security apparatchik, in an effort to exert control of the capitalist experiment, had been co-opted to an extent that it was hard to see who was using whom.

For Yuri, a man who'd never tasted the nectar of freelance work, it was confusing. And a little disgusting. Vlad walked between the two worlds with ease, and Yuri was sure he commanded respect in both.

He saw a flash of light from the outside door opening, and watched as a dark male entered the casino. He waited until the man approached the bag-check station, turning over a butt pack. The man looked into the camera, and Yuri recognized Akinbo.

"Sir, Akinbo just entered. He's at bag check."

Vlad nodded on camera, then said, "You know what you're looking for."

"Yes, sir."

Akinbo entered the casino, escorted by the security guard manning the door. He looked hesitant and lost, following blindly behind the guard and clearly not there to gamble. He disappeared from the camera in the anteroom, then reappeared inside the casino. Yuri tracked him all the way to the second floor and the little room labeled MAN-AGEMENT ONLY.

He returned to the camera focused on the front door, seeing the security guard reenter, and hearing Vlad talking to Akinbo.

"You're late."

"I'm sorry. I became lost following the directions you gave."

"You should have called. I've been sitting here for over thirty minutes."

"My cell phone no longer works."

"What? You mean the battery's dead?"

"No. I mean it's broken. It fails to do anything. When I left the room it was fully charged."

"The phone I gave you? That's the one not working?"

"Yes."

Yuri heard the conversation and glanced away from the front door video feed, the words causing a heightened awareness. He saw Vlad pass across another cell phone, saying, "Take this. As before, do not call anyone but me on it. Understand?"

Yuri saw him pass across a sheet of paper and a netbook computer. "This laptop is clean. Never used. The e-mail address on that paper is what we'll use to communicate. Use *only* that e-mail for operational matters. It is protected from the United States."

Vlad continued by passing across a wad of euros. "Go to the bus station and get a ticket to Istanbul. There is a bus leaving in thirty minutes. You still have the passport with the visa, correct?"

"Yes, but I can't get back to my hotel room and pack in thirty minutes. Why didn't you say something yesterday? I would have made arrangements."

"I didn't plan on you leaving so abruptly, but that was before your cell phone quit working. I don't believe in coincidence. I want a clean break. Buy what you need with the money I gave you."

"I'm going back to the hotel room. I have time if I leave right now."

On the monitor, Yuri saw the front door open and a man enter. Blond-headed and about six feet tall, he looked fit. He handed across his passport, as everyone had to do if they wanted to gamble, and Yuri saw he was American. A spike, but not much of one. The man had appeared much slower than a person conducting surveillance would have.

He entered the casino and wandered around, playing a couple of slot machines, then taking a few hands from the chesty blonde. Yuri watched his demeanor closely, seeing the man's eyes rarely made it to the dealer's face. He smiled inwardly.

No threat.

He continued studying the man for a few more hands, hearing Vlad arguing with Akinbo in the background. After three deals Yuri perked back up. In between bets the man was casing the establishment. Searching for something. It was by no means obvious, and he would have missed it had he not been looking for this very thing, but it was there, nonetheless.

He leaned over and keyed the microphone, giving Vlad a code word. Without shifting a beat, he heard Vlad say, "Never mind. You won't be making that bus. There's another one leaving at four."

Yuri saw Akinbo scrunch his eyes in confusion, but Vlad ignored it, giving new instructions. "Remember the trip we had you make the other day to the fortress? You're going to repeat it."

17

President Peyton Warren thanked the assembled crew and stood up, signaling the meeting was over. One more presidential daily brief completed, and, as usual, the world was on the brink of disaster from forty-seven different directions. Also par for the course, every analyst had an opinion on how it should be handled. But none had the mantle of responsibility.

Syria, Iran, North Korea, Brazil, you name it. They were all one giant cluster fuck. The only good news today had been when Bruce Tupper, the director of national intelligence, had described the treasure trove of information purchased from a former KGB man, now an oligarch selling information to the highest bidder. Russia's own version of Edward Snowden, he'd apparently raided the new FSB for everything it had.

Most of the information had been historical, and the DNI was still going through the repository—a mountain of documents, all in Russian—to see what else could be gleaned. Warren hoped it would be something they could leverage in their quest to negotiate with the egotistical whack-job running the Russian Federation.

President Warren checked his calendar on an iPad, seeing his next meeting was with the principals of the Taskforce Oversight Council and the Taskforce commander, Colonel Kurt Hale.

Shouldn't be too contentious.

Apparently, Kurt had deployed another team in place of the one that had lost its team leader a few days ago. The sticking point was he'd done it without proper oversight. At least that's what was going to be discussed. Well, that and the fact that the team he'd deployed was Pike Logan's. Someone who gave the Council fits because Pike routinely ignored the word *oversight* in its title. Pike listened when he wanted, and pretended not to hear when he didn't. But at the end of the day, he'd earned the right to get more rope than other teams since he had a nearly flawless track record. It was just a question of whether he'd ever hang himself with the slack. So far, he'd proven adept at dancing through the raindrops.

President Warren sat down and saw that the DNI, Tupper, was still in the room. Which was going to cause an issue with the Taskforce meeting.

Outside of the president, the director of national intelligence was the highest position within the Intelligence Community. The one person who was read on to *everything*, be it CIA covert action, NSA signal intercepts, or simply mundane Army intelligence about the intentions of the Taliban. The one person whose "need to know" automatically applied to every bit of intelligence collected in the name of the United States.

And yet Bruce Tupper wasn't read on to the Taskforce. He had no idea that an illegal intelligence organization was operating under his nose. In fact, if he were aware, he would immediately demand its closure. He would never have authorized the Taskforce to purchase a single pistol, much less rampantly conduct illegal operations throughout the world.

Unfortunately for him, he'd been appointed DNI after the Taskforce and Oversight Council had been created, and President Warren had decided to keep him in the dark. It wasn't an insult, as only thirteen persons sat on the Oversight Council, a mix of civilian and government personnel all handpicked for their temperament and expertise. Hell, President Warren had even kept his vice president in the dark for close to two years, only allowing the VP to be read on when he—as the president—had become bedridden with the flu, necessitating the action in case the worst occurred.

At any rate, the Taskforce was a temporary thing. Something created after 9/11 because the traditional Cold War intelligence and military establishments weren't up to the task of combatting twenty-first-century terrorist threats. It had come about for the same reasons as the creation of Tupper's position of director of national intelligence in 2004.

Recently, there had been some discussion among the Oversight Council about disbanding the unit, given that the heady days of 9/11 were long gone and the US population had begun to think government counterterrorism efforts were worse than terrorism itself, but every time that bubbled up the Taskforce had managed to avert a catastrophe and validate its worth.

No, in President Warren's mind, there was no reason to mess with success. The Taskforce was clicking just fine. In fact, he wanted to expand its mandate. Broaden its portfolio beyond terrorism. The intelligence and military bureaucracy had grown unwieldy, with it practically a foregone conclusion that any mission conducted would not remain secret. Not so with the Taskforce. They were very small and very nimble. Maybe his successor would see it differently, but in his mind, living with the risk of exposure was worth the protection.

He routinely conducted backroom deals on everything from sugar subsidies to EPA legislation, burying his principles in a cesspool of human frailty in order to keep the leviathan of the US government working, but there was one thing he would never compromise. One thing he knew would keep him awake long after he'd left the presidency if he did: the deaths of US citizens that he could have prevented. He knew that protecting the life and limb of American citizens was his clearest, most fundamental task, and he'd do whatever it took to guarantee it, regardless of the less-than-legal nature of the work. Something the DNI would definitely take issue with.

While a good man, Bruce wasn't exactly the bend-the-rules super-spy of movies and novels. Far from being James Bond, he had been selected for two very mundane skills: one, he had proven very good at collating and integrating disparate organizations with different agendas, something the DNI needed in spades, and two, he was a fervent by-the-book bureaucrat.

While the job of DNI sounded sexy, in reality, it was so far removed from actual intelligence work that the position had turned off potential applicants who lived for the field. Men who would—and did—bend the rules where necessary. Men who could—and had—caused embarrassment because of a myopic vision of what was necessary for the United States.

President Warren didn't want anyone like that at the helm of the US intelligence community. He had enough of a vulnerability with the Taskforce's very existence. What was needed to rein in such men was a manager like Bruce. A man who took the rules seriously, and would drop the hammer to maintain compliance. If it wasn't codified into law, then it wouldn't be executed by any agency under his control.

Bruce had grown up in the Central Intelligence Agency at a very difficult time, thrown into the maelstrom of the Middle East during the seventies and eighties. He'd been tangentially involved with Iran-Contra, an effort to free US hostages in Lebanon through less than legal means, and had thought the entire effort was an abortion. A huge, dancing polar bear of a circus designed to avoid US law.

The mess had spawned a plethora of second-guessing on other intelligence operations where none was required, but he understood why. If you did secret things, you needed to ensure you walked the line. The minute you didn't, people assumed you had strayed long before with much broader implications than the ones they were looking at. Like what was occurring now with the Snowden revelations.

President Warren knew that Bruce had his hands full dealing with the constant barrage of leaks, trying to stem the sea of distrust springing forth from Internet conspiracies. He didn't envy the man, but that's why he had been hired. He wondered what had caused Bruce to remain behind, knowing it wouldn't be good.

He said, "Can I help you, Bruce? Was there something else you wanted to say?"

The DNI shuffled forward, his thinning hair and wire-rimmed glasses making him seem much older than he was. Making him look like a librarian instead of a spymaster. President Warren knew those looks were deceiving.

"Yes, sir. You remember the Boris file we were discussing? About Russian intentions with Syria and Iran?"

"Yeah? What about it?"

"There's more than just Russian intentions in those documents. There are Russian reports of American activities, and some of those activities are volatile."

President Warren waited a beat, then said, "And?"

"And they could have a significant impact on the current trust in government if they were exposed right now."

Warren leaned back into his chair and studied his DNI. It was the first time the man had ever suggested hiding something for reasons other than to prevent the loss of sources or methods. The first time he'd ever broached the subject of burying something simply to protect reputations and the facade of trust.

He said, "So don't let it out. What's the big deal?"

Bruce shifted on one foot, then the next, clearly uncomfortable. He said, "Boris, our source, apparently sold the same package to the Israelis, with some cutting-edge intelligence we weren't privy to."

"So it's the new stuff we need to worry about? Something we didn't get?"

"No. Sorry. I'm confusing the issue. From our sources, the Mossad got an encrypted drive that held all the historical information we received. That's what's volatile."

President Warren said, "What do you mean? How could something from the past affect us now?"

Bruce took a breath and said, "Remember the seventy-two Olympics? The massacre of the Israeli athletes? The documents prove that Russia—or the USSR—provided crucial assistance to the Palestinians. Assistance that allowed the attack to occur."

"Okay. I'd think that would help us. Give us some leverage with that asshole running the country."

"It's more than that. It also talks about US involvement. We knew about the attack before it was going to occur, and we did nothing to stop it."

President Warren took that in, incredulous. He leaned back in his chair and said, "Are you telling me the CIA knew the Palestinians were going to murder Israeli athletes, and we did nothing? Seriously?"

"Yes. Well, no. I mean, we didn't *know* they were going to do it. We only had indications, and the head of Black September—Ali Salameh—was helping us deal with the Middle East. We were using him to further American interests. The reporting was just like a hell of a lot of other stories being spewed at the time. There was constant chatter about attacking Israel. We didn't know it would actually happen. We didn't *know* . . ."

President Warren heard Bruce's voice break, and understood something more was going on. "Okay, Bruce, okay. What's that mean to us right now?"

"Boris passed an encrypted drive, then died of a heart attack before he could give the password. Israel will crack the encryption given enough time. Boris was very thorough about protecting his return on investment. If it's like our pass, the drive will simply give the location to another thumb drive. We need to prevent that from falling into Israeli hands."

"Because they'll find out about our supposed complicity in the attack? It's old news. Nobody will care about that now."

"Because it will expose the fact that we could have prevented the slaughter of innocents. The Munich massacre was horrific for Israel, and if it comes out that we could have stopped it, it will be the straw that breaks the camel's back. After Snowden, this will cause the American people to forever lose trust in our intelligence community. It can't come to light. It *can't* come to light."

"Calm down. It won't be that bad. We can firewall it. Blame it on some guy that left the service decades ago. Trust me, political games are easy. We just need to manage the release. Defang it before the Israelis get the documents."

"You can't do that here. You can't fake it. The documents name *names*. It can't be hidden."

"So we find the man who got the intel and prep him for a fall. How bad could it be? The guy's got to be retired. The only way it could hurt us now is if it was someone still active in the intelligence community. You're worried about nothing, trust me. I've lived in this world of political BS for much longer than you. Shit, the only way it would be a problem is if your name came up."

Bruce winced, and President Warren felt his skin grow cold. He said, "Don't tell me that. I don't want to hear that."

Bruce nodded. "I was Ali Salameh's case officer. I'm the name on the disk."

18

Waiting on a SITREP from Decoy, I watched Jennifer walk across the square to a convenience store that looked like it had been built into a closet. *Walk* was probably the wrong word. More like *glide*. She had an economy of motion and understated strength that reminded me of a jaguar I'd seen at the Singapore zoo.

Strength she needs, carrying that leather duffel bag around.

She called it a purse, but the thing was larger than some carry-ons I'd used. I'd made her stow the Stiletto EMP gun because of it, but I had no idea what else she had buried inside. Makeup? Ninja kit? It was another female mystery.

She bought a bottle of water, then turned and held it up. I shook my head with a smile. She'd asked if I wanted water before she'd crossed the plaza, but she still wanted to make sure.

Always wanting to help out the other guy.

Even when we'd first been thrown together, at a time when I was just as likely to punch someone as talk to them, she had shown her altruism. In fact, it was quite possibly the reason I was still alive. And I mean *literally* alive, not some metaphorical thing. If we hadn't collided—which is probably the best way to describe that first encounter—I would more than likely be dead.

She sat back down on our bench and took a pull of water, surveying the crowd. She felt my eyes on her and said, "What? You want a sip?"

Embarrassed, I realized I'd been staring. "No, no. I'm good."

She caught my eye again and raised an eyebrow in a theatrical way, making me laugh. She smiled back and it was hard to remember we were on a mission. Sitting in the warmth of the summer sun, kids playing with the fountain to my front, I felt like a teenager, wanting to take her out for ice cream.

Dangerous thoughts.

We *were* on a mission, and this type of bullshit was *exactly* what Knuckles had warned me about. A distraction that could cause me to screw the pooch on a decision. I needed to get my head back in the game and forget about our relationship. Somehow, I needed to figure out a way to switch between team leader and partner, and do it in such a way that I wasn't making decisions precisely *because* I was making a switch.

Something must have flitted across my face, because Jennifer said, "What?"

I said, "Nothing," then changed the subject. "What else do you have in that duffel bag besides the Stiletto? A bicycle?"

She leaned over and held it open, and underneath the EMP gun I saw a mini folding grappling hook attached to a spool of 8mm kernmantle cord, causing my face to break into a grin.

It *was* ninja gear.

I said, "What the hell are you toting that around for?"

"You guys are always telling me to climb stuff without any warning. After yesterday I decided to start bringing some help along."

I said, "Hey, that was your damn decision. I was going out the front door. Anyway, I'll give you an A for effort, but an F for cover. Someone sees that there's no way to explain it. You should know better."

She rolled her eyes. "Like I can explain this EMP gun anyway."

Touché.

Before she could continue, Decoy came on. "I'm in. Place is about empty. I had to show my passport, which they ran through some type of scanner, and I'm sure they've taken about forty photos of me. Moving to a table."

Jennifer closed the purse and I said, "Roger. No sign of Chiclet?"

"Not yet, but this place is a little dark. Let me get inside. A lot of focus on me, I'll tell you that."

I waited a few seconds, then heard, "I'm claiming this gambling money."

I said, "Fine, but if you win, it goes to the government."

I heard a low whistle, then, "Man alive. Sorry I bitched about coming in. The blackjack dealer is a hammer. And she's driving with her headlights on."

I grinned and Jennifer mouthed, *What does that mean?* Probably thinking it was some arcane Taskforce surveillance code.

Decoy said, "Boy, oh boy, does she have some *big* headlights."

I saw the realization dawn on Jennifer's face, her confusion replaced by a scowl. I became all professional. Instead of saying, *Send me a picture*, like I wanted, I said, "Get me a lock-on for Chiclet."

He said, "I don't see him, but I can't wander around in here asking everyone if they've talked to a black man. Give me a minute."

I heard him playing a few hands and talking to the dealer, plying his man-whore ways, and wondered if he was really trying that hard to locate Chiclet. Fifteen minutes later, he said, "Got him. He's coming down from the second floor. He's a singleton, so no make on who he was talking to. He's headed straight out the door. Want me to pick him back up?"

"No. We got him. Keep your cover. I'm sure that won't be too hard. Just don't get blinded by the high beams."

"Roger all. Pike, everyone in here is Bulgarian and white. He sticks out like charcoal in the snow. Whatever he's doing, it isn't with other members of Boko Haram."

I saw Chiclet exit, thinking about what Decoy had said. Trying to piece together the connections by reviewing all of the intelligence summaries I had read. And coming up empty.

I got a status on Knuckles, Retro, and Blood, then began working the surveillance again, following Chiclet to the parking lot adjacent to the Princess. When I was sure he'd committed to his car, I folded them in, and we began a mounted surveillance effort. Something that was both easier and harder. Easier because the guy we were following was now in a large, distinct hunk of metal that was locked onto paved roads—unable to dart into a store or crowd, for instance—but harder because we were also locked onto the road, and would by necessity end up chasing him in another large, distinct hunk of metal that was easier to identify over time and distance. Easier to unveil the surveillance effort.

I let Knuckles take the lead, driving by himself in a Hyundai sedan. For backup he was followed by Retro in a Ford and Blood and Decoy in a Bongo truck. Including Jennifer and me, that gave us four vehicles—two with the ability to launch dismounts if that became necessary. We took trail, driving a Volvo C30. Since I was the team leader, I'd made damn sure we didn't get the Bongo truck. The Volvo was a strange little two-door hatchback, with the hatch made completely of glass, but it was comfortable. I probably could have made it fly if I could figure out all the electronics inside.

I gave Knuckles, as the eye, a chance to clear the area, then left the parking lot myself, saying, "Lock on, Knuckles. Still south?"

"Yeah, he's two cars up and headed straight down Highway 86. I've got Retro to my rear ready to pass."

"Roger all. We're to your six, dragging anchor. Let me know when to commit."

We went maybe ten kilometers without a change, hearing Knuckles's monotonous recital of the same thing every few seconds: "Chiclet still southbound on 86."

Thirty seconds later we heard, "Intending left, intending left. Chiclet headed toward Plovdiv airport. I'm off."

Like clockwork, Retro said, "I got him. I got him. This is Retro, I have the eye."

Still out of sight of the action, I wondered what he was doing. He couldn't be getting on a flight. He'd never gone back to the hotel room for his luggage.

Retro said, "He's pulled into a gas station. I have the eastbound road to the airport. Knuckles, can you take the southbound Highway 86?"

I heard, "Got it," then keyed the mike. "I've got northbound and the trigger. I can see the gas station."

Retro said, "Good to go."

The entire exchange had taken seconds, but like a well-oiled machine my team had just laid a blanket over Chiclet, with every man plugging a hole he could use. It gave me a great amount of satisfaction. We were clicking. I came back on. "Knuckles, when I trigger, I'll pick up the eye. I don't want to commit you again."

He gave me a "Roger," and after a five-minute wait, Chiclet exited the store and reentered the highway, heading south. I pulled in behind him, and Jennifer said, "This is the same profile he used with Turbo. The same actions."

Staying behind him, I realized she was right. I keyed my radio. "Decoy, Blood, pull off and check that station. This is the same thing he did when Turbo's team was following. I'm betting it's a dead drop or a load signal for a dead drop. See what you can find."

I got an acknowledgment, passing Knuckles on the side of the road. He pulled in behind us and Chiclet left the highway for a slim ribbon of asphalt heading into the mountains. I saw a sign reading ASEN'S FORTRESS and felt déjà vu.

Jennifer said, "This is the same road he took when Turbo was on him. This is the road where Turbo and Radcliffe died."

19

Waiting on Kurt Hale and the principals of the oversight committee to arrive, President Warren reflected on what Bruce Tupper had divulged. It was volatile, no doubt, but Warren wondered how much of Bruce's motivation was protection of the United States and how much was simply protection of himself.

In the end, he supposed it didn't matter. It wasn't a zero-sum game, and Bruce had accurately predicted the fallout. Trust in the US government was at an all-time low, and hovering at the bottom of the bowl, right around the IRS and Congress, was the Intelligence Community. The last time there had been such a groundswell of skepticism and outright hate had been 1974. That year had culminated in the Church Committee, which eviscerated the CIA for various misdeeds that they had been involved in throughout the previous decade. Had the revelation come out then that the CIA could have prevented Munich two years before, there would no longer be a CIA.

If it came out today, no matter what the extenuating circumstances at the time, it might do the same thing. Especially when it was revealed that the man the president of the United States had personally chosen to act as the overarching leader of all intelligence was the one who could have prevented the massacre. They'd all look like collaborating liars. There would be no way to spin it. No way to overcome the hysteria in the press. On top of that, Congress, smelling something that would take the heat off of them, would pile on as "champions" of the American people.

He saw his national security advisor, Alexander Palmer, glance at his phone, then stand up. He said, "Kurt's at West Wing security. Apparently he's not on the list."

President Warren said, "Go get him."

After he'd left the room, the president surveyed the three remaining men. While it took all thirteen members of the Oversight Council to make any binding decisions regarding the Taskforce, these men were usually the driving force due to their expertise and experience. Over the past few years they'd been unofficially dubbed the "principals," and the president had taken to consulting them on situations that were a little in the gray area.

President Warren said, "So, what's the take? Is this going to be contentious? You guys want to pull Pike's team?"

Jonathan Billings, the secretary of state, said, "Colonel Hale really should have asked permission before launching another team. This sets a bad precedent. It dilutes the authority and leadership of the Council, delegating it to the commander, which is *exactly* what the Oversight Council was set up to prevent in the first place."

Mark Oglethorpe, the secretary of defense, snorted and said, "I don't think it's that big of a deal. We gave permission for a Taskforce team to deploy to Bulgaria and develop the situation. We gave Kurt Hale Alpha authority, but *he* picks the team. We wouldn't even be talking about this if that accident hadn't occurred. He could have rotated people left and right."

Billings said, "That's precisely the point. When the environment changes so drastically, we need to reassess the mission. Reassess the risks of exposure."

The SECDEF just shook his head, telling President Warren he

thought it was a bunch of chicken-shit excuses. Warren tended to agree. He nodded at the last man, the director of the CIA. "And you, Kerry? Where do you stand?"

"All these decisions should be judged in light of the mission. You can't just look at the action in a vacuum, and in this case there was no real urgency to deploy. We don't have anything at all on Akinbo other than his affiliation and some random chatter, so the potential risk wasn't worth the deployment without prior analysis. Kurt acted out of emotion, and he knows it."

"So you think we should bring them home?"

"That's up to you, sir. At this stage, we don't know the potential downside because we haven't analyzed the impact of Turbo and Radcliffe's deaths. Was there an investigation by the police? Is their cover solid, or are Americans under greater scrutiny? Will pulling the team cause even more interest since they just got there? Answers we won't have without analysis."

The SECDEF said, "Well, hell, why don't we spin ourselves into the ground with potential what-ifs? Maybe they'll get hit by a meteorite if we don't pull them now."

Billings started to protest, and President Warren held up a hand. A thought had flashed in his head. A compromise that might kill two birds with one stone. He said, "What about a change of mission? Order the team to do something else? Let Kurt know we're pissed about him sending the team, but since he did we have a real mission for him."

Billings said, "Like what?"

President Warren laid out what the DNI, Bruce, had disclosed, finishing with the idea of Pike's team recovering the thumb drive. Kerry Bostwick, as the director of the CIA, understood the threat the information posed and warmed up to the idea immediately. Billings, the secretary of state, wasn't as confident. "I'm not so sure we want to redirect Pike's team. Remember, he was chosen because of Grolier Recovery Services's cover ability in Bulgaria, but I'm not comfortable leaving a civilian in charge. He's not even in the government anymore. Maybe we should think about replacing him completely since his cover is no longer necessary."

The SECDEF said, "You sure you're not just skittish about Pike?"

"Well, yeah, that's part of it. He always ends up in the center of the cyclone, but I think I have a valid point. Anyone here feel the same way?"

Kerry said, "Once again, measure the action with the mission. Boris had the heart attack in Bulgaria. Pike's already there. It makes less sense rotating the team out."

President Warren nodded and said, "So it's settled. When Kurt gets here, we'll redirect the team to the Boris thread. Get them off Boko Haram."

He saw the shadow of a smirk on the D/CIA's face. He said, "What?"

"It's just ironic. We're going to use an illegal organization to steal intelligence from an ally so that we can prevent the loss of trust and confidence in our intelligence community. In effect, we're doing exactly what the public is afraid of in order to prevent them from thinking we're doing what they're afraid of."

Kurt Hale, entering just in time to hear the statement, said, "Should I be worried about something?"

20

Jennifer said again, "This is the road where Turbo crashed. Chiclet was up here last week. This isn't a coincidence."

Has to be a dead drop. He's getting a message up here.

My adrenaline fired at the thought of getting evidence of Chiclet conducting an operational act. Of proving this asshole was up to no good, and hopefully making Turbo's accident mean something.

On the radio, I said, "All elements, I think he's servicing a dead drop. I'm betting he stops at Asen's Fortress, just like he did with Turbo. If he does, Jennifer and I will conduct the intrusion. Knuckles, you continue north. Decoy, Brett, finish with the gas station, then you guys block the exit back to Highway 86."

I got acknowledgment, and it unfolded exactly like I thought. We wound around a mountain road, doing one switchback after another, rising higher and higher. At one turn we passed a segment of yellow tape, strips strung out between the metal guardrail like a Halloween exhibit.

Jennifer said, "Jesus, Pike, that's . . ."

She didn't need to finish the statement. It was where Turbo had died. A man who had served twenty-two years in the defense of our nation, fighting in overt combat in Iraq and Afghanistan, followed by clandestine missions in every shit hole on earth, protecting US lives with little fanfare and absolutely no thanks. The only thing heralding his contributions to the nation was a strip of yellow caution tape spread between the torn guardrails. It was sad. And probably all I would get myself someday.

We kept winding around the mountain, and eventually Chiclet parked, exactly like I thought he would. He exited his vehicle in a small lot around the bend, just to the west of the fortress, then wandered across a knoll of picnic tables and a kids' playground. He crossed the road and took the path into the fortress. Jennifer and I gave him a minute, then followed.

As we walked through the gate, I felt like I was passing into another dimension. The fortress was flat-out amazing, carved through brute strength into the side of a cliff. I could only imagine the feet that had trod the same path I was on. Jennifer, of course, began giving me the background on the place before I even asked, clearly enjoying the surroundings. She had the ability to make any tourist trap the most exotic thing in the world, bringing to life what would have been nothing but moldy passages or broken rock.

We went down a narrow walkway that would have made the safety freaks in the United States pass out, literally a rock passage with a cliff to the right that fell unimpeded for five hundred feet. No railing. I guess the Bulgarians figured if you were stupid enough to hang over the ledge, you were stupid enough to suffer the punishment.

We could learn something from them.

Of course, our lesson would be that we needed to administer a written test before entry to prevent idiots from falling, complete with a new government agency to oversee the testing.

We circled around the walkway until we reached the ancient Orthodox church, constructed when life was still a competition for survival. Carved out of stone on the side of a cliff, I could only imagine the congregation that had attended it. Something from *Game of Thrones*.

From the outside I could see Chiclet sitting in a pew, a reconstructed piece of lumber made to look like something from the hardscrabble life of the people who had created this church.

He was doing nothing overt. Simply staring to his front. Remaining still.

The sanctuary was only about thirty feet long, and had little to see other than stone and a few dripping candles, but Chiclet seemed enamored. We waited outside, pretending to take in the incredible views of the knife-edge mountains dropping to the valley below.

I debated sending in Jennifer. I decided not to. If it was a drop, he'd already retrieved it. Wouldn't do any good to put her in close proximity. I decided to wait until he left, which he did after another seven minutes.

Jennifer penetrated, then came back to my location, telling me she'd found nothing. The place was clean. No residue from tape, no chalk markings, no nothing. Retro called to say he was on Chiclet in his vehicle, and we left at a slow pace, letting them continue the follow.

I fired up the Volvo and Jennifer said, "Too much coincidence here. He's doing something, and it isn't a drop. This place is horrible for that anyway. It's a damn tourist attraction. Who'd put a drop in here? With all the people coming and going? Especially from a fanatical Islamic sect? Inside an historical Christian church? Not happening."

I started working the hairpin turns and said, "What else could it be? He was up here with Turbo a week ago."

She said, "I don't know. We keep on him and it'll become clear."

I had no idea how soon that would occur.

We were rounding the second hairpin, on the steepest part of the road, when my brakes failed. I jammed the pedal into the floor to no avail. We picked up speed rapidly, the force of gravity more powerful than the gas pedal I was no longer using. I pumped the brake again, working the steering wheel to stay on the road.

We began flying down the road and Jennifer's hand slapped the roof of the vehicle. She pumped her foot on an imaginary brake pedal and exclaimed, "Pike!"

I said, "Hold on. This is going to be tight."

We screamed through the next hairpin turn and I saw a straight-away dropping down before me, a rock wall on the left and a cliff on the right falling free for several hundred meters to the river below.

I worked the wheel, allowing the gears of the car to keep us in check, then felt a subtle shift in the vehicle. We started to pick up velocity over and above what gravity was providing. My gas pedal was working on its own. My car was trying to kill me.

In an effort to slow our progress, I jerked the wheel, hammering the wall of stone to my left, causing the car to grind against the rock. It worked for a split second, the engine still screaming as if I had floored the accelerator, then the car skipped off the wall and hurtled straight down.

I knew we were going too fast to make the hairpin. The velocity was much too great to navigate the turn, and the only way to stop it would be to kill the engine. I jammed the "stop" button and jerked the wheel in one more futile attempt.

Jennifer screamed my name again and I attempted to ram the gear-shift into park, getting no response. We picked up speed until we were doing over sixty miles an hour. Jennifer slapped her hands on the dash, and time actually slowed. I could see the yellow tape marking Turbo's death in front of me, lazily flapping in the breeze.

I shouted, "Stiletto! Kill this fucking thing!"

Jennifer whirled around and grabbed her purse, yanking out the EMP weapon and saying, "Where do I shoot? What do I hit?"

We got within fifty meters of the turn and I screamed, "Anywhere! Kill it before we go over!"

She pulled the trigger, I heard a small whine, then the entire car went dead. Radio shut down, lights quit, clock on the dash blinking out. Our velocity slowed immediately, but we continued to roll forward, the weight of the vehicle struggling to overcome the lack of power. Straight to the yellow tape as if it had a suicide pact.

I manhandled the wheel, the action much harder with the power steering dead, like dragging a chain through the mud. The front wheels split the tape, and we went over, landing on a slope and picking up speed again. It was a false cliff, but the real one was right in front. I tried to open my door, but the dead electronics had left it locked. I ripped the handle back and forth in frustration, then tried jamming the brakes again. I couldn't stop the slide over the edge. Out of the corner of my eye I saw Jennifer jerking her door handle with the same result before diving into the rear of the vehicle.

I saw the edge of the cliff grow like a cancer in my vision and knew I was done. Following in Turbo's footsteps. In a land of violence, another embarrassing death.

Jennifer rolled onto her back and mule kicked the glass hatchback with all of her might. I heard her shout something unintelligible, and in the rearview mirror saw the hatch fling sideways, held on by one hinge. She kicked again, and it fell free, exploding in a shower of glass as soon as it touched the ground. I abandoned the steering wheel and followed her into the back, clawing my way past the driver's seat like a drunk on a bus.

She had her grapple in a fist and flung it out, the rope snaking through her hand. She tossed me the end of the line and I felt the car lever over, exactly like a child's seesaw. With us inside. I wrapped my hands into the nylon of the running end, watching the hook scrape and bounce across the ground. The car crossed the point of no return and I felt the sickening drop of gravity in my stomach. We went into free fall.

I closed my eyes, and the hook bit, cinching the rope into my hands hard enough to draw blood and jerking us both out of the vehicle. Jennifer, holding on to the rope four feet above me, slammed her legs into my head just before my body smashed into the rock of the cliff face.

I held on for dear life, seeing the car bounce down the precipice before shattering on the rocks below. It ticked for a minute before a low *wump* split the air, and a fireball burst far beneath me.

Jennifer's feet left my shoulders and began scraping against the rock, seeking purchase. I did the same. When I found some footing, some stability to prevent me from falling after the car and becoming a sacrifice for the inferno below, I took stock.

I said, "You okay?"

"Yeah. I'm okay. I think."

She started to climb back up the rock face, toward the yellow tape and the road. I held what I had, letting her get out first. I took a deep breath, willing myself to relax, and everything that had just happened clicked in my head. A crystal truth that sliced through my tumultuous thoughts like a razor carving out gangrenous flesh.

Not an accident.

I said, "Jenn, quit climbing. Hold up."

She said, "Why?"

My mind was still working through the event, and hanging on the side of the cliff wasn't helping my decision making, but one thing penetrated the fog.

Turbo was murdered.

I said, "This wasn't an accident. Someone's probably on the road watching to confirm we're dead. They won't hang around long, but I don't want them to see you."

The more I tossed the idea about, the more certain I became. Someone had set a trap. Someone had purposely killed Turbo and Radcliffe. *Someone just tried to murder Jennifer and me.*

As the realization began to take root, an impotent rage bubbled up. The murderers, whoever they were, had perfected a kill zone, and I had blindly walked right into it. A unique targeted killing that looked like a simple accident. They were very, very good, but they weren't immune to mistakes. They'd made the biggest one on the side of this mountain.

They'd left me alive.

21

Yuri saw Vlad raise his glass of water, signaling one of the Efbet Casino waitresses, and Yuri pointed to his own while listening to his cell phone.

He caught Vlad's eye and nodded, saying, "Understood. Return to base."

He hung up and said, "Mission complete. Second team interdicted. Dmitri confirms the car went over, and that nobody could have survived the fall."

Vlad said, "Good. Akinbo should be on a bus by now, headed to Istanbul. I want you to take your team and do the same."

Yuri hesitated, then said, "Sir, taking my team to Istanbul is a risk. Turkey is still looking for the people that hit Musayev in 2011. My previous Control wouldn't allow it for that reason."

"Your previous Control was a dilettante playing at espionage. They're looking for Alexander Zharkov, correct? Isn't that what your passport said?"

"Yes, sir."

"And does your passport say that now?"

"No, sir, but I might have given them biometric data when I entered under that name, and they'll definitely be scanning for our electronic footprint. The FSB cover we used there, the e-mails, the encryption protocols, all of that is compromised, but I don't have anything new to replace it."

He saw Vlad's face grow dark and hastily added, "I'm sure Control was going to give it to me soon. I didn't mean it was the service's fault."

Although that was precisely the truth.

Vlad said, "Don't worry about it. For one, you'll be driving, and the border crossing isn't as sophisticated as the airport. You won't go through an iris scan or give up a fingerprint. For another, I don't want you to do anything active. I just want you available should I need it. Get there, get a hotel in the Russian area, and lie low."

Vlad slid across a slip of paper and said, "Use this address to communicate with me."

"Is it encrypted? I'm telling you, sir; they're looking for our encryption scheme. They might not know what's being said, but they'll definitely know Russians are talking. That's what I was trying to tell my last Control. We don't need to be found standing over a body to get compromised. All we need to do is use the same old methods."

Yuri opened the paper as he talked. When he read the address he said, "What is this?"

Vlad said, "Secure comms without a signature. Download Pretty Good Privacy encryption and use it for every e-mail you send from that address."

"Sir, the US national security agency can break PGP."

"Yes, they can, but the Turks can't. And the NSA won't be looking at that e-mail address. Read it."

"AP dot org?"

"We have an asset inside the South American bureau of the Associated Press. That's a real e-mail address, and coupled with the encryption protocol PGP, it'll be just as secure as our own encryption because the NSA won't look past the address. We know the range of their reach now. Make no mistake, it's changing on a daily basis, but one thing they won't touch right now is the press. Calypso's revelations confirm it."

Yuri recognized the code name. "You've met him? You actually talked to him?"

Vlad gave him a sour look, and Yuri backpedaled. "Of course you have. Sorry. I just thought . . ."

Vlad said, "Yes, I've met him. I was one of the first, and he's not impressive. He's a child playing a man's game, and yet the US let him go with his treasure. Let him walk away. Makes me wonder how we lost the Cold War. If we'd have done the same with Litvinenko we would have been eviscerated on the world stage."

Yuri wondered if Vlad had mentioned the name as a warning. Alexander Litvinenko was a traitor just like Calypso/Snowden. He'd fled the Russian state and began spouting all he knew about Russian transgressions. Right up until he'd been killed in London by radiation poisoning in 2006. Assassinated by the man across the table.

Yuri said nothing, waiting on his next command.

Vlad took a sip of water and said, "I have indications that the Mossad agent did in fact get some information from Boris. I'm hearing about a thumb drive."

Yuri now knew the Litvinenko story was for his benefit, as was the thumb drive threat. Nothing had happened at the meeting with the Mossad agent, other than the Russian traitor having a heart attack. Vlad was simply keeping him on his toes.

"Sir, I watched the meeting. Nothing was passed before I killed Boris. Whoever is telling you otherwise is wrong."

Vlad said, "I agree. Nothing was *physically* passed. The thumb drive is apparently in Istanbul, waiting on the Mossad man to claim it. He doesn't know where it is, but he's working to find out."

The answer confirmed that Vlad was using the story as a means of instilling fear in Yuri that he had somehow failed. There was no way

Vlad or the FSB had penetrated Mossad, no matter how good they pretended to be, so there wasn't a way for Vlad to learn about any mystical thumb drives.

Yuri said, "What do you want me to do?"

"Get your team to Istanbul via the border crossing. Don't take any weapons with you, and ditch any cell phones you have now before you cross. I'll provide replacements when you arrive. Once you're in place, send me a message using that address. The priority is Akinbo."

"Yes, sir. You're confident that he'll follow your instructions?"

"No. But all the equipment I gave him has tracers embedded in it. I was pretty adamant with him, and he has another Associated Press e-mail account. As long as he doesn't call anyone already tainted with the new phone I gave him, he should be pretty secure. I'm more concerned about the Americans. You're confident they didn't follow him to the bus station?"

"No way. One of our men is still on him, and they would have called if they'd seen the Americans. Trust me, they're focusing on something else right now."

22

I was debating having Jennifer climb when my earpiece chirped. "Retro, this is Knuckles. Give me a lock-on. You have Chiclet?"

I cut in, "All stations, all stations, ignore Chiclet. Knuckles, you come down south, around the turn. Tell me if there's a car on the road. He'll be pulled over looking at where Turbo went down. Break—break, Decoy, you still staged?"

"Yes. Got you, lima charlie. What's up?"

"Knuckles is going to get you a description of a car. He'll be coming down the hill shortly, after Knuckles flushes him. You still at the base, on the intersection with 86?"

"Roger."

"Pick him up and start to follow. We'll be right behind you."

Knuckles came on, "Pike, I have a Renault two-door pulled over. Passenger is on the phone. Driver just tapped his brakes and is now moving downhill. That the target?"

"Yes. Get a picture and send it to Decoy. Decoy, you copy?"

"Roger all."

Knuckles said, "Where the hell are you?"

"Vehicle out of sight?"

"Yeah, what's that got to do with it?"

"Look to your right. Where Turbo went over." I pointed at Jennifer, and she nodded, starting her ascent. Small rocks rained down on my head and shoulders as she crested the ledge.

I heard, "Holy shit! Is that Koko coming up?"

"Yeah. I'm right behind her."

"What the fuck is going on? Where's your car?"

I started climbing and said, "You used the Grolier card to pay for these rentals, right?"

"Yeah . . . why's that matter?"

"You see the smoke coming up?"

"Uhh . . . you've got to be kidding."

I reached the top and found Jennifer leaning forward, one hand on a tree root, another held out. I grasped it, seeing the knuckles were skinned and bleeding. But she was alive. She leaned back, using her weight, and I crested the top, the two of us falling in a heap. We both lay on the ground for a second, enjoying the ability to feel the sun on our faces.

She said, "Man, you were right. Carrying that grapple hook was stupid."

I started to chuckle and heard Decoy saying, "I got a lock-on. Heading back toward Plovdiv on Highway 86."

I stood up, pulling Jennifer to her feet. "Don't lose that asshole. He just tried to kill Jennifer and me. And he succeeded with Turbo."

Jogging to Knuckles's little rental, I heard Decoy's voice go a little grim. "Roger that."

Jennifer got in the back, leaving the shotgun seat free for me. Knuckles started to drive, asking, "What happened?"

"I honestly don't know. Somehow, someone managed to take control of my car. It was like being on a roller coaster on rails. All we could do was hang on as it went where it wanted."

"And you think this car I just fingered is the one?"

"Yeah. No doubt. Was it a gray two-door Renault? Looked like a college kid's car?"

"Yep."

"That fucker was right behind me when the brakes failed."

Jennifer said, "Maybe it was coincidence. Maybe it just happened to be behind us and stopped when we went over. It's a natural reaction."

"And then hauled ass at the first sign of another vehicle? Is that what you would do?"

She said nothing more, and we hit 86, following behind Decoy, the target making a beeline for Plovdiv. Over the radio I said, "All elements, prepare for vehicle interdiction. This guy stops, and it's suitable, we're taking him out."

Behind the wheel, Knuckles snapped his head to me, then returned to the road. He waited a bit, then said, "Pike, we have no Omega authority here. We've got nothing like that. We can't do a V-I. We're here on Alpha."

The Taskforce called each phase of an operation a different Greek letter. Alpha meant an introduction of forces to develop the situation. To see if there was a reason to continue. Omega—the last letter—meant we'd determined the bad guy was out to harm the United States and the threat was so great we'd be allowed to take him down.

Here, in Bulgaria, we were nowhere near Omega. We were barely legal for Alpha, as the Boko Haram guy had done nothing sinister, and I was now chasing someone that wasn't part of his team. But he'd done one thing for sure: He'd killed Taskforce members.

I said, "We always have the right of self-defense. That's never taken away. We're within our mission parameters and ROE."

"Pike, that's bullshit and you know it. We're under no threat. The ROE is for a clear and present danger."

I started to say a rejoinder when he cut me off. "You and Jennifer are good to go for working outside the wire. My team is not. We're still in the government. I'm the one who'll be called to task. I'm the one who's the team leader of record. You talk a good game, but my guys will pay the price. Shit, Blood's CIA. The rest of us will be shielded somewhat because we're military, but he'll be crucified when this gets out—just to prove a point."

What he said was technically true. I *was* a civilian, but Kurt had put me in charge. Hard to say how that would work out legally, but the legal stuff was already outside our boundaries, since our very existence was illegal.

When we'd built the unit, we'd had to construct a method of punishing people inside our organization without burning it to the ground from the outside. In effect, create a disciplinary system we could use that wouldn't compromise the unit. We knew we weren't perfect, and eventually someone would do something wrong.

We ended up developing a way of filtering transgressions, then using the military's Uniformed Code of Military Justice or the CIA's civilian infrastructure for the punishment. Basically, you'd get charged with something comparable on the open-source side, then suffer the consequences. No description of the real-world action would be documented, but your record would reflect the punishment of the fake crime.

So far, we'd never had to use the system for any catastrophic mission actions. Only for minor things. Knuckles was now worried about being the first example of a mission mistake.

I said, "Are you serious? I understand where you're coming from, but these fucks just tried to kill Jennifer and me. They *did* kill Turbo and Radcliffe. Murdered them in cold blood."

I saw Jennifer in the backseat, torn by my words. On the one hand, she was dripping blood from her knuckles, a stark reminder of what had just happened. On the other, she'd caught a glimpse of the darkness in me, and I could tell she was worried about my reaction. Worried because she'd seen me do some pretty horrible things to people who'd harmed what I held dear.

Decoy came on after my last transmission, but he wasn't talking to me, even if he pretended to be. "I copy prepare for a V-I. Who'll trigger? Pike or Knuckles?"

He wasn't asking *who*. He was asking *if* we would trigger.

He'd gone through the same mental calculations as Knuckles and was now questioning whether we were pushing things outside the bounds of my authority. Outside the bounds of a civilian on Alpha, now demanding Omega.

I didn't give a shit, since this question had been brewing for a while. *Time to figure it out.*

Initially, at the inception of the Taskforce, we'd had to work through utilizing an organization that didn't officially exist, always within the confines of legacy military or intelligence architecture, like an old analog clock. It was now time to figure out how to utilize it in the digital age, with folks like me who weren't in a legacy organization like one of DOD's special mission units or the CIA's Special Activities Division. Kurt had put me in charge as a civilian, and that was a good call as far as I was concerned. It was time to push that decision. I was sick of pretending to be an infiltration platform only to get tagged running missions "off the books" because we hadn't thought through how it would work.

I waited on Knuckles's response.

Decoy came back on. "Pike, Knuckles, I say again, who will trigger?"

Knuckles looked me in the eye for a long pause, then keyed the mike. "Pike will trigger. I say again, Pike will trigger."

He'd just given me command, and all on the net knew it. He pulled the Bluetooth transmitter from his ear, ensuring his next words stayed in our car.

"I did that for the current mission, but you and I need to talk. We can't keep executing this half-assed command authority."

I nodded and said, "I agree completely."

Jennifer said, "Pike, maybe it'd be better for Knuckles to run this one. I'm not sure you're in the right frame of mind for this."

Knuckles said, "What? You don't trust Pike anymore?"

I ignored them, hearing Decoy on the radio. "Entering Plovdiv. Need a change-out."

Retro came on. "I got the eye. Pull off and reposition."

On the radio I said, "Everyone get ready for assault. That car's going to stop here in Plovdiv, and if we can interdict successfully, we do so. No killing. I want one of them alive. Keep an eye out for another vehicle. These guys probably aren't operating alone."

I turned off the mike and said, "You two stop it. I'm not going to slaughter someone just because I can."

Jennifer leaned forward, her words truculent, surprising both Knuckles and me. She said, "You sure about that? I saw the killing machine you became the last time something like this happened."

Remaining calm, I said, "Yes, you did. And so will these guys if they push the issue. I didn't bring this fight, but I'm going to finish it."

23

Once inside the city, the car became harder to track in the dense traffic. I told Knuckles to stay back, afraid of the target recognizing Jennifer or me. We passed by the Trimontium Princess Hotel on Obedinitel Boulevard, then went through the tunnel under the old town. Eventually Retro called that the target was staged for a U-turn.

I assumed that he was attempting to spot surveillance, but it wasn't the best place to do a rolling reverse because the thoroughfare we were on had a concrete median down the middle for miles. Everyone had to do a U-turn if they intended to visit anything on the left side of the boulevard, so someone following wasn't a strong indicator that he or she was surveillance. Even still, Retro pulled off of the eye and continued straight, leaving Decoy and Blood as the sole follow.

We stopped adjacent to them but three lanes over, keeping vehicles between us to block the view. The light went green, and we continued north, crossing the Maritsa River. Decoy followed the U-turn four cars back, barely making the light, and called that the vehicle had penetrated the narrow alleyways of Kapana, an ancient neighborhood from Ottoman times.

Retro pulled into a parking garage on Septemvri Boulevard, then turned around and headed south again, rushing to get back into the follow. Once across the river I had Knuckles execute our own U-turn, then pull over to the side of the road, letting the situation develop before committing. The Kapana area was very tight, so they had to be going there for a reason. It wasn't a shortcut. I hoped it also wasn't for the name of the neighborhood, which meant "the trap."

Decoy said the vehicle had stopped, and I saw my chance slipping away. I didn't want to execute with a parity of forces, and Retro wasn't in play yet.

Damn it. No way can we conduct a V-I two-on-two. I wanted at least double their forces before I committed.

I said, "Retro, status?"

"I'm fifty seconds out."

Decoy, reading my mind, said, "Not here, Pike. Not going to work. They're dismounting. Both out and walking."

Shit. Gotta get them today. If I didn't, I'd have to go back to Kurt, asking for permission and going through the entire Oversight Council. Claiming self-defense now was pushing it, but doing it tomorrow would be ridiculous.

"Okay, okay. All call signs dismount. Track where they're going."

Four minutes later I was told that they were strolling south on Daskalov Street, a brick-lined shopping promenade. I traced the road on my map, trying to anticipate their intentions, and recognized the small park with the fountain that I'd been at earlier in the day. The one in front of the Efbet Casino.

That's where they're going.

I relayed my suspicions, then got a call saying they'd split. The driver was headed uphill, over the tunnel and into Old Town, and the passenger was continuing on Aleksandar Street, closing in on the casino.

I looked at Knuckles, then Jennifer, hoping a decision would magically appear. Of course, it didn't. I studied the map, then pointed to a street on the east side of Old Town, away from the Kapana neighborhood. "Knuckles, get here."

As he put the car in drive I began giving instructions, "Decoy, Blood, track the passenger to the casino. If he gets inside like I think he will, don't penetrate. Hold fast and just keep eyes on. Retro, you stick with the driver. We're going to come in from the east side. You vector us in and we'll meet in the middle."

Retro said, "Roger that. Then what?"

"Not sure, but be looking for exfil locations that'll support extraction with a body."

We raced around the ring of hills that was Old Town, finally getting to a street called Lavrenov that went steeply uphill from east to west, into the maze of the ancient settlement. Knuckles took it, and we began to bounce along the cobblestones, the Hyundai's frame getting tortured. I was pretty sure no traffic was supposed to be in this area, but I kept seeing an occasional parked car and figured we could pretend we lived in one of the houses that lined the street, only an arm's length away. As we passed one I saw it was a museum of some type.

So much for acting like we live around here.

We reached the top in time to hear Retro say the target had entered a beer garden that overlooked the exit of the tunnel on Obedinitel Boulevard.

So he's just waiting on the passenger. Killing time. A flunky.

I directed Knuckles to pull off the road through a stone gate, into what appeared to be a car park area for an art museum. Up the street I could see an ancient church surrounded on all sides by stone or wood houses. It looked exactly like a set from *Robin Hood.* If the sheriff of Nottingham had appeared to give us a parking ticket, it wouldn't have surprised me.

Knuckles killed the engine, and I said, "Come on. Let's recce a kill zone. He comes up this way, we need to take him quickly and get him back to the vehicle."

He looked at me for a moment, then glanced around at the cobblestone streets and museum houses. He exhaled and said, "You planning on taking him out of Bulgaria? Or just interrogating and getting his electronic signature for the Taskforce, catch-and-release style?"

"What do you think? I'm for taking him, but he's not some raghead terrorist. I'm pretty sure he's working for the Bulgarian state. Might cause a few issues with the Council."

I saw him come to a decision. "Screw the Council. If these guys killed Turbo, we need to deal with them. We can go straight to Sofia, board the rock-star bird, and fly out with him. Leave Decoy and Blood to police up our luggage and check out, then they fly out commercial from Sofia."

I nodded, liking the thought. Glad that he was on board with the capture, because it was certainly going to raise a stink back home.

Jennifer finally spoke up. "Are you two serious? You want to take down an unknown target in broad daylight with no other plan than driving him to the capital for escape? The city that's the heart of his intelligence and security apparatus? No support team? No execute authority?"

I looked at Knuckles, and he nodded. I broke into a grin and said, "Yes. You're the one driving."

Her mouth opened and closed like a fish on the dock, no words coming out. I said, "Come on. Follow us so you know the plan."

She said, "Pike . . ."

I ignored her. We continued on foot about seventy-five meters up-hill, the cobblestone street intersecting the main thoroughfare of Old Town—*main* being a relative term. The immediate issue was that our road had a couple of large stone barricades set into it right at the intersection. Someone had wanted to make sure a car couldn't get onto the main avenue, leaving it safe for pedestrians. Which meant Jennifer would have to pull up here and do a forty-two-point turn to face back the other way. And we'd have to coerce our captive to follow us across the road to the vehicle, without any weapons for leverage.

We hadn't planned on an Omega operation, so we hadn't brought a full assault package. In fact, we hadn't brought anything offensive at all because the odds of it being found and causing an issue were way higher than the odds of us needing it. No way could I have pre-dicted some Bulgarian trying to assassinate us, especially since we were following a guy from Nigeria. Nothing we could do about it now, although our weapons inventory was pretty damn weak.

Knuckles had this cool ninja watchband that released a strip of nylon, allowing him to use it for a carotid artery choke, and which he'd been dying to employ since I'd known him. I had a couple of carbon-fiber two-finger loops—a modern-day brass knuckle that fit onto the first two fingers of each hand—but that was it.

We surveyed the street, seeing most of the houses were either sou-venir shops or historical venues of some kind. To the left I saw an archway of stone leading off the street, the inside strewn with bits of trash, unlike the other houses. I investigated and found it led into an abandoned home, falling apart past the portico. Amazing, since the house itself was probably seven hundred years old.

I went down the walkway, seeing a broken stone stairwell leading to an upper deck of grass overlooking the valley of the town. Appar-ently, the house had been built into the side of the hill. On the right side of the stairwell were the eves to the roof, like the ribs of a skeleton.

Further inspection showed the ravages of a fire, the walls between the rooms crumbling with ash and soot, the beams within charred.

So it wasn't abandoned.

I said, "Here's where we'll take him. We're about two hundred meters from the beer garden. He comes up here, and you push him past the portico. I'll jerk him inside, tap his ass a couple of times, then feed him back to you, tag team. You use your super ninja watch, and we take him down."

Knuckles nodded, grinning. I wondered if using the watchband had now superseded the mission. I'd always made fun of that thing, but I'd be buying some beer if it worked as advertised.

Jennifer looked around the burned-out house and punched me in the arm. "Pike, you have lost your mind. This is at least fifty meters from the connecting road. We need to back off."

I said, "Go to the car. When Retro triggers, get it in position."

Her voice turned cold and she braced me, her back to Knuckles. "Pike, you're going to kill this guy. You're not fooling me. You know you can't get him out of here to my car."

That comment took me aback. "What the hell are you talking about? I can't get any information from a dead man. Why would you say that?"

"Egypt. What you did in Egypt because of what happened to Knuckles."

Knuckles, previously looking away to let me sort out this mess, snapped his head back. "What's she talking about?"

"Nothing, damn it. When you almost died I had a little breakdown."

"What's that mean?"

"Jennifer, go get in position. I'm not going to lose control."

"Pike, I saw your face on the cliff. You were losing control right *then*. You're not so good at the control thing. You know it."

She turned to Knuckles and said, "He was questioning a guy that was involved in the VBIED that hit you, and he went batshit. He killed the man."

I held up my hands, saying, "Wait, wait, wait, it wasn't like that. . . ."

Our radios chirped, "Pike, Knuckles, target is out of the garden and headed deeper into the tourist section."

24

Looking at Jennifer, I keyed the mike. "Not headed back to the casino?"

"Nope. Apparently, he's got some time to kill."

And he's going to check out the museums on this street.

I clicked off my transmitter and said, "Go get the car ready. I'm not going to kill anyone."

She looked hard at me for a second, and I repeated, "I'm *not*."

She stood on tiptoe and kissed me on the forehead, then whispered in my ear, "It's not worth your sanity. Don't do it."

She leaned back and looked into my eyes. "I mean it, Pike. You do and I'm gone."

I'm never going to live that mistake down. She still thinks I did it on purpose.

I saw Knuckles roll his eyes at the attention and felt like I was a ten-year-old getting scolded by a teacher.

I said, "Get your ass outside."

After she'd gone, Knuckles said, "I see this whole team-leader-screwing-teammate thing is working out."

Knuckles had been the first to figure out that Jennifer and I had grown a little closer than simply business partners, and he didn't like the idea at all. He couldn't care less what happened in the civilian world, but he was sure the extra baggage of a physical relationship would destroy the chemistry of our team. So far, he'd been proven wrong, so I ignored him and keyed my Bluetooth.

I said, "Retro, give us a description."

He said, "I don't think you're going to miss him. He's literally about six feet five inches tall, and his arms and legs look like tree trunks. He's a fucking gorilla."

Uh-oh. I said, "Are you serious?"

"Yep."

"Why didn't you say something before?"

"Would it have mattered?"

"Yes! Given our half-assed plan, it would have."

"What is the half-assed plan?"

Knuckles got in position as I relayed what we intended to Retro. Knowing he'd be too far back to effectively engage in the fight, he laughed and said, "Good luck with that."

I said, "You see Knuckles in play, you'd better close the distance as fast as you can."

I got a roger, then got an up from Jennifer. I asked if Knuckles was set, and he stated he was, but he didn't sound as confident of his watch now. I slipped on the two-knuckle rings, not feeling so confident myself.

A minute and a half later, it was showtime.

Knuckles said, "Street's clear and I see the yeti. Thirty seconds."

Just inside the stone entrance, hidden by fallen timber, I tensed up. I heard, "Ten seconds, get ready."

I heard a scuffle and raised my fists expecting to see the man flung through the door. Instead I heard some smacking on the street, like someone repeatedly slapping their thigh. I heard something slam into the stone outside, then heard a gargling noise. I started to run to the entrance when I saw Knuckles jerking the guy inside by a come-along joint lock. He whirled around, using the centrifugal force to roll the beast of a man out of the lock and straight at me.

In stop-motion from the sunlight dancing between the beams of the roof, I saw him coming, a great big bear of a man, his lips already split, his arms swinging out like the limbs of an oak. Knuckles released, squinting at me with one good eye, his left one enlarged and swelling shut. I forgot about the stun plan and went for the knockout.

I met his forward motion with a fist, tagging him once, twice, three times, the carbon fiber snapping his head back. The fourth blow was a haymaker that had enough force behind it to drop a bull. It staggered him back into Knuckles, but incredibly, he was still on his feet.

Knuckles whipped out the cord from his watch and used it as leverage between his hands, cinching down on the man's carotid arteries, bending him backward with the pressure. I saw the strain on Knuckles's face as he used all of his strength to sink the cord down into the muscle of the monster's neck.

The man snarled, snapping his head back and catching Knuckles right in the nose. He followed the blow with two elbows into Knuckles's short ribs, rendering the watchband-terminator thing useless, the giant gaining enough breathing room to break out. I rolled forward on the balls of my feet and fired two more jabs into his bleeding face, the carbon fiber increasing the damage exponentially. He absorbed the punishment like it was a fly landing on him and returned the punches with one of his own, landing a sloppy right cross on my shoulder that was bone-rattling.

I slammed into the wall from the force, doing my best to raise my hands to protect myself, and he followed with a left into my lower body, punching the wind out of me. I saw another right coming and rolled under it, jabbing him twice in the gut, then snapping an uppercut unopposed into his face. His head popped back and I jammed a knee forward, spearing his groin and throwing him into the stone.

He slapped both hands down and away, grabbing my shoulder and tossing me to the ground like I was a child. My skull hit rock and I saw stars, wondering where the hell Knuckles was. I shook my head and saw him moving forward, hands held high, bobbing and weaving. I pulled myself up, doing the same. I saw a shadow, and realized that Retro had finally entered. Even with that, I wasn't sure it was enough.

The bear said something in a language I didn't understand, then spit on the ground. He raised his hands into a fighting stance, and I glanced at Knuckles with an unspoken question.

Let him go?

Knuckles blew snot-filled blood out of his nose and shook his head. We advanced forward slowly, backing the guy up.

Man, he is fucking huge.

He was taller than six five, and not like a basketball player. He looked like a normal-sized athlete that had been magnified times three, with a rustic face and ham-hock fists.

He glanced back quickly, then scooped his hand onto the ground. He picked up a broken brick and hurled it at Knuckles. When Knuckles ducked the giant took off running, hitting the cracked stone steps at the back of the room. He scrambled up them, reaching the little outdoor ledge. I followed suit, but knew I'd lost him. He'd be over the wall and away before I could stop him. He turned to kick at my head and I saw a flash of brown streak toward him.

I ducked backward from the kick as a dog the size of a German shepherd sank his teeth into the man's hamstring. He screamed and I went back into attack mode, launching up the steps and trying to grab his legs to bring him to the ground.

The dog started worrying the meat, snatching his head left and right like a shark, and the giant screamed again. He turned and kicked with his good leg, striking the beast right between the eyes and breaking the hold. The dog yelped, falling back, and the man seized the initiative, scrambling up the old stone wall of the garden.

I managed to grab his ankle just as the canine got back into the fight, chomping for more leg meat but getting only his pants. The asshole mule-kicked my head, and I let go. The dog didn't. His pants ripped straight down the middle as he escaped over the wall, now running with one leg clothed and the other naked from the beltline down.

The dog went to his lair in the corner of the ledge and began ripping his prize to shreds, flinging his head side to side in a frenzy.

I leaned against a wall and let out a breath. I gingerly touched my face, checking for damage. It didn't feel like anything had been broken, but with adrenaline, you never knew.

I saw Knuckles doing the same thing and said, "Man, that ninja watchband is the damn heat. I can't wait to get one of my own."

He stopped probing his jaw and said, "That was your idea of punching? We'd have been better off throwing Twinkies at him."

I keyed my Bluetooth and said, "Koko, don't worry about exfil."

She came back with a strident voice. "You killed him? You killed the target?"

Knuckles started laughing, then keyed his mike. "No, Koko. Calm down. If anyone was close to death, it was your fearless commando team."

The dog kept ripping up the pant leg, swinging his head back and forth and causing something to fly out from a pocket, the object falling down from the wolf lair to our level. I went over to it and found a small wallet, like travelers use for business cards. I pulled one out, seeing Cyrillic lettering on one side. I turned it over, finding English.

Knuckles said, "What is it? Who's he working for?"

I held up the card for him to see. "He's Russian. He's a diplomat for the Russian embassy here."

25

Yuri saw Dmitri's expression cloud over and understood the phone call wasn't going to be good news. Watching him hang up, his face drained of color, Yuri knew he was afraid to state what had occurred.

Initially, Dmitri had been giddy with his accomplishment of the car-hack mission. After executing the previous hacking operation, Yuri had opted to remain with Vlad, leaving Dmitri in charge. After all, the mission profile was the same, down to the location. In effect, the first one had been a rehearsal for Dmitri, and Yuri knew the greater threat was the head of the FSB misreading something that had occurred. Being near him was more critical.

Yuri had relayed the success from the initial phone call, and Vlad had demanded an in-person debriefing, wanting more information on the team of Americans.

When Dmitri had entered the small office of the casino, he'd gone through the same gamut of emotions that Yuri had upon recognizing Vlad. Obsequious, he'd begun the debrief in a halting, jerky manner, clearly intimidated. Yuri had made one attempt at helping his man, interrupting a response with his own feedback.

Turning his black eyes on him, Vlad had said, "I'm sorry, were you on the road watching the car, or were you sitting in here with me?"

"Here, sir."

"Then what makes you think I wish to hear what you *believe* has happened?"

Yuri sat back after that, not saying a word, watching Dmitri stumble through the reporting as Vlad dissected the operation.

"How do you know they are dead?"

"Sir, the car went over the cliff. It fell five hundred feet then exploded on impact. There's no way anyone inside could have survived the fall."

Vlad leaned back, his face catching the light, and Yuri saw the lethal impatience etched into his visage.

Vlad said, "I understand the physics of the mission. Yes, someone would have died had they been in the car. But *were* they inside? How do you know if you didn't check the wreckage?"

Yuri had leaned in, struggling to come up with some way to deflect the interrogation, when Dmitri's phone had vibrated. He'd exhaled, sagging in his chair, glad for the reprieve, then watched Dmitri's face. Yuri knew whatever was being said, it wasn't going to impress Vlad.

Dmitri hung up and fixated on Yuri as if he wanted to talk to him in private, but knew he couldn't say that out loud. He wanted to brief his commander, and have his commander brief Control. As was supposed to happen. Especially now that Control had turned out to be the head of the FSB, and a man who'd earned the name Impaler the hard way.

Yuri said, "What is it?"

"That was Mishka. He was just attacked."

Confused, knowing Mishka's size, Yuri had trouble understanding who on earth would attempt to rob the giant. He said, "Attacked by a gang?"

Vlad interrupted, much quicker on the uptake. "Attacked by the Americans."

It was a statement, not a question, but Dmitri nodded nonetheless as if he was answering. He relayed what Mishka had told him, with the damning information that one of the attackers was the man they'd driven off the cliff.

"So, not only is your target alive, but he had the presence of mind after the near death in the car wreck to understand he'd been attacked, then institute a comprehensive surveillance mission, complete with an ambush. Figuring all of this out while hanging from the side of a cliff."

Yuri said, "It might be luck. He may not—"

Vlad waved a hand, cutting him off. "Don't be stupid." He pointed at Dmitri. "Call the desk and see if anyone has come in since you arrived."

While Dmitri was on the house phone, Vlad said, "They followed him here. Watched him split up, then set up an ambush for the other man. This isn't some counterintelligence team from America like I had thought. They're hunters. Something different from the usual American floundering."

He thought a moment in silence. Yuri said not a word. He pulled open a laptop and went to a Russian webpage showing a moving map with Cyrillic lettering. Satisfied, he closed it at the same time Dmitri hung up.

"Nobody has entered the casino since I arrived."

"That means they're either outside waiting on you to leave—along with whomever they can associate with you—or they focused solely on Mishka after you entered here. Go downstairs and check the outdoor video feed. See what you can find."

After he'd left, Vlad said, "Akinbo is on the road to Haskovo, so he made the bus. At least we got our clean break. You need to get your men out of here immediately. Get to Istanbul. Unfortunately, you'll be doing some work there now."

"Sir, Turkish MIT are—"

"I don't give a shit about their intelligence agency. We have a critical meeting in two days and I cannot have this American team on the loose. They need to be dealt with."

"Sir, you gave Akinbo clean equipment. They have no way of knowing where he went. Right?"

"Yes, they don't have Akinbo now, but the Americans found him some way. He's clean today, but every minute that idiot is out on his own is another chance to give away his location. He'll do something stupid. I promise."

Dmitri came back with three grainy black-and-white images, one showing a Caucasian male sitting next to a black man, the other two photos showing individual head shots of each. "Sir, these are the only persons of interest. Everyone else in range of the front door has children or did not remain in view longer than thirty seconds. According to security, these two have been out front since about the time I arrived."

Vlad said, "Still there?"

"No. They left while I was downstairs watching."

Not wanting to believe how horribly wrong the events had gone, Yuri grasped at false implications. "So they can't be waiting on Dmitri. They can't be surveillance."

Vlad said, "Or they got a phone call saying the ambush had failed and we were now alerted to their presence." He turned and faced Yuri head-on. "Tell me, outside of Akinbo, how many black men have you seen in Bulgaria?"

Yuri struggled for an answer, then gave the correct one. "None."

Vlad tapped his hand with the photo for a few seconds, then said, "He's American. They both are."

Yuri shut down, reverting back to what he knew: blind obedience. "What are my orders?"

"Just as I said. Get out of here immediately. Contact me when you're in Istanbul. I'll outfit you there with clean equipment."

"What do you intend to do?"

"Give them what they want. Show them Akinbo. Only you'll be waiting instead of him."

26

U sman Akinbo felt the bus jerk over a curb and opened his eyes. They were pulling into a station somewhere south of Plovdiv, one of the many stops on the way to Istanbul. The cabin attendant rattled off a few sentences in either Bulgarian or Turkish—Akinbo couldn't tell, but it didn't matter either way—and the doors opened. He waited his turn, then exited, walking to the bathroom and ignoring the stares from the locals. He was used to it by now.

He paid a toll at the narrow stairwell leading down to the toilets, then tentatively stepped through the standing water until he reached a stall, the archaic, dripping restroom a stark contrast to the modernity of the bus he was on. After he'd finished, he climbed back up the stairs, bumping into more travelers attempting to pass by him in the tight corridor. They glared with a superior air, but they could in no way match the contempt he held for every one of them.

Born to a wealthy merchant family, he'd spent his first thirteen years in relative splendor, with private schools and personal servants. One of the few in Nigeria who could reap the benefits of the oil boom. When not traveling the world, he lived in a gated community in Lagos, on the beach of the Atlantic Ocean. A paradise that anyone of any nationality would revel within.

That changed in 2004. He'd accompanied his father on a trip to the north of the country, a little jaunt that should have been nothing more than a tour of a factory. For reasons he never fully understood, a throng had formed outside of his father's motorcade, a hostile, smelly group of men chanting and waving sticks and other implements, their clothes barely better than rags.

The crowd had grown hostile, the veneer of human compassion ripped away by groupthink and replaced by the ugly hatred of mob rule. His father's men had initially fired shots in the air to disperse the mass, then began firing into the people themselves. It did no good. In a frenzy, they attacked.

When it was over, his father's men had been beaten to death. His father had not been afforded that mercy. Forgoing a quick end, he'd been dragged behind one of his luxury Land Rovers until he was no longer recognizable as human.

Reflecting on his life, Usman Akinbo knew that he had been truly born that day.

Taken from the crowd, he'd been handed to a spiritual leader in *Jama'a ahl al-sunnah li-da'wa wa al-jihad*, known in the local language as Boko Haram.

For ten years he'd been steeped in the evil nature of all things Western and the purity of the Islamic faith. He could no longer recall what his life had been like before or stomach the degradation of wealth and corruption he had been saved from. Now twenty-three, he relished the opportunity to be the sword of Allah. The first to travel outside of Nigeria for the greater jihad.

There was a reason Allah had him born in the Christian south to a corrupt stealer of wealth. Because of it, he had a passport and some experience traveling abroad. Not a great deal, but at least he'd actually been on an airplane before, unlike the majority of Boko Haram. He had also partaken in the forbidden and deceitful Western education long enough to have learned English, something that was a necessity to travel among the Western infidels.

His life had been hard, but it had all been for a reason, one that was coming home now.

He reentered the bus, taking his seat next to the window. In truth, he could have had any seat in this row, window or aisle. The vehicle was fairly full, but the person who'd purchased the seat to his right had decided he preferred riding somewhere else.

Akinbo should have been insulted, but he didn't even notice the slight, happy for the extra privacy. He thought about making contact with his spiritual advisor. The pale Russian had been adamant that he did not, stating that the phone he'd been given would leave a trail of anything it touched, and he believed it. He'd heard the stories of how the Americans killed with their drones.

Even so, he needed to give his spiritual advisor an update, to let him know things were progressing as planned. The bus began to move, and he saw the passenger across the aisle put in his earphones and manipulate the screen embedded in the headrest to his front, while the man in the opposite window seat opened a laptop and began manipulating the keys.

Seeing the action reminded Akinbo that he had other options besides the cell phone. The bus was equipped with television, music, and a movie database, much like an international flight. More important, · it also had Wi-Fi. Akinbo decided to send an e-mail. The Russian had said to use the address only for operational planning, but also that it was shielded from the Americans. And this *was* operational planning.

He worked for Allah, not some old white-haired, wrinkled Russian.

He booted up the computer, then accessed the Wi-Fi hot spot the bus provided. Getting on the webpage provided by the Russian, he typed in an e-mail address and sent a brief message.

27

I thought I'd misheard the words coming out of Kurt Hale's mouth, mainly because the encryption for the VPN made his voice sound like he'd been inhaling helium, but the white noise generator behind me wasn't helping. Even though the room had come up clean for technical listening devices, we were taking no chances.

He saw my face through the laptop camera and said, "You heard right. Change of mission."

"Sir, did you just ignore my entire report? Turbo was murdered. Someone is hunting us, and they're tied in to Chiclet. On top of that they're Russian. I know we haven't proven Chiclet is preparing an operational act, but there's enough here to continue. We need to locate him."

After fighting the Russian grizzly bear, I'd called Brett and Decoy, pulling them off of the casino. I was torn with telling them to remain, but after the failed assault against the bear, I feared they'd be set up. I had no idea how many men we were up against, and clearly, they'd had surveillance on us while we were watching Chiclet. The fact that we hadn't seen them told me they were either very good, or it was only these two operating. I couldn't risk my men on the bet that it was just two people against us.

I'd decided to focus on Chiclet with our technical devices and back off aggressive surveillance for a day or two, repositioning to a different hotel.

The beacons we'd emplaced earlier still showed they were in Chiclet's room, so I'd left Retro behind to monitor the microphone we'd emplaced. After eight hours of nothing, I'd had him conduct a B&E of the room, fearing we'd find it cleaned out with our beacons on the floor. Instead, everything he'd owned was still there, beacons still hidden—which meant they were doing us no good. I was fairly sure that he'd flown the coop, leaving his luggage behind, which was one more indication that he was doing something nefarious.

Kurt said, "I hear you, Pike, but I've got a change of mission from the Oversight Council. I'll take your report back to them for resolution. In the meantime, get to Istanbul for the thumb drive."

I started to lose my temper. "This is fucking ridiculous. You want me to take the team and go chase a thumb drive against some Israeli we have no information on whatsoever. Meanwhile, we're going to let some seriously competent killers go free. Russians, no less."

"Pike, Russians aren't in our target deck. State systems aren't our charter."

The Taskforce had a very narrow operational profile that was predicated strictly on substate terrorist threats. If the target wasn't on the State Department's Foreign Terrorist Organization list, we weren't allowed to touch it. Instead, it would be a CIA or DOD problem set. Which begged the question about this damn thumb drive.

I said, "And beating an Israeli to a thumb drive he bought from another Russian qualifies as charter worthy? This trumps a targeting of our own men? I didn't realize we'd placed Israel on the FTO."

Kurt scowled, knowing I'd just backed him into a corner and not liking it. I could see him about to explode, like I'd seen numerous times before. I'd just pushed some buttons the wrong way. Which was tough shit. What he really didn't like was the fact that I was right about the whole damn discussion.

Even the encryption from the VPN feed couldn't hide the quiver of anger in his voice. He said, "Do not question my commitment to my men. I cannot believe you would insinuate that I'm good with the death of Turbo and Radcliffe. You aren't the only one in the fight, and we aren't in the revenge business. We work to protect and defend a nation, not execute your personal vendettas."

His words hit me slapped me, which is exactly what he wanted. My righteous indignation faded away like a snow cone dropped on a summer sidewalk. He paused a second, getting his blood pressure under control. Unlike me, he always managed to maintain a command presence, and wasn't about to start screaming at my slur like he would have liked. I felt a little ashamed about what I'd said.

He continued. "I'm going to take your report back to the Council. It may not end up in a Taskforce Omega operation, but it will end up on someone's target deck. As for the thumb drive, it's got the ability to exponentially harm US intelligence operations much greater than the loss of Turbo or Radcliffe. It's also exactly what you wanted when we created this adventure. The president is willing to bend the charter to accomplish the mission. He no longer trusts the established intelligence architecture. It leaks like a sieve. He's chosen *us* for the mission. No more terrorism only."

He was right about me wanting an expanded mission, but it would have been better if it wasn't an either/or choice of finding Turbo's killers. I said, "Okay, sir. I got you. I didn't mean to poke you in the eye."

He laughed and said, "Bullshit. Yes, you did."

"Well, okay, I did, but you have to admit we've got nothing on the Israeli. You want us to hot-rod to Istanbul, and we have no thread. What am I supposed to do?"

He paused for a moment, and I knew the other shoe was about to drop. I could see it in his face. He said, "The profile is simple. CIA has some sort of feed into Mossad. They think they'll get a location for the thumb drive through their assets, and at that point it becomes a race. I'll send you what I got from the DNI. You'll see it's pretty bad. But it's not a question of what *you* will do."

"What's that mean?"

"The Council isn't comfortable with a civilian making decisions on behalf of the Taskforce, especially one that's the CEO of a profitable business. Knuckles is taking over as the team leader."

I took that in, understanding the motivations, but knowing their excuse was fabricated. What they were afraid of was someone in charge who didn't give a shit about their hand-wringing. Someone they couldn't affect with threats through the government system or control with their rewards and punishment.

Before I could say anything, he continued. "They think it'll eventually be a conflict of interest. That you'll make a decision based on your company instead of the mission."

I said, "What do you think?"

"I think they have a point. Your decisions today had nothing to do with your company, but you sure as shit executed a potential Omega without any sanction. You hung the team out to dry because you could get away with it. And I mean you *and* Jennifer."

He read the tea leaves accurately, and it hurt.

"So I'm cut out now? Is that where we're going? You told me you wanted me to execute this mission because you wanted results. Now you're telling me I'm too volatile. Not responsive to the chain of command."

"You've always been volatile, but before I had some control. Now I'm not so sure. Mexico worked out okay, but it could have gone the other way. You made some calls down there that were tight. It gets people worried."

The comment really aggravated me because I'd actually backed off on that mission, executing only after the Oversight Council had demanded it against my better judgment, but I knew he had a point. I'd gotten comfortable bucking the system because I'd always been proven right, but today, we'd failed, and I couldn't predict the repercussions of that failure. Maybe I'd become a little too cozy thumbing my nose at the Oversight Council while using their very assets to execute missions. Assets that were entrusted to my judgment.

I said, "Why'd you say you wanted me in charge for this? I mean, if you didn't trust me."

He said, "I *do* trust you. Don't turn this into a witch-hunt. Look, let this go for a little bit. Let Knuckles take the helm. We need to work out how your company fits in. I want it to exceed other cover companies, but it's new terrain. We need to figure out how the chain of command will work. It's a different world, especially with an expanded mission set. You wanted it, and I want you in it. Get that little thumb drive and we'll go from there."

I heard the door open behind me and saw a shadow in the reflection of the glass. I heard Knuckles say, "Still no movement in the room. You want to pull Retro, or keep him in place?"

I suppose I should have been pissed at seeing him, wanting to keep my little fiefdom and protect my interests, but I didn't. I couldn't. I had no issue with giving him command. He was about as good an operator as existed, and I'd follow him under fire easily. Combat wasn't the issue. The decisions outside of combat, the ones necessary to *prevent* combat, were what worried me. I might be scary to the Oversight Council, but the very thing in me that caused their fear had also prevented several travesties. Risk early had prevented death later.

Not my worry now.

I said, "Bring him home, but before you do that, take a seat."

I turned back to the screen. "Sir, I have Knuckles here. Still nothing from the hotel. He's gone. Before we get into the meat, has anything come from Chiclet's connections?"

Knuckles took a chair and said, "What's up?"

On the screen I saw Kurt grimace, not wanting to talk to Knuckles in my presence. A painful thing that I wasn't going to make more comfortable. He said, "Are we done?"

I said, "Yeah. I got it. I'm good. Just give me anything on Chiclet. I won't chase him without your blessing."

Kurt said, "We have nothing. There's one contact to a Boko Haram spiritual leader via e-mail, but we have no idea if it's him."

I perked up. E-mail was always a good thing, both in content and geolocation. "Why? What did the e-mail say? You should be able to figure out his fingerprints fairly easily."

"All we have is metadata. The e-mail came from a protected source, and we're not getting content."

I was getting very sick of the Snowden snowball. We had a lot of capability inside the Taskforce, but it was all tactically focused on geolocation for specific counterterrorist applications. We didn't have the capability to gather any content from the massive amount of various digital and analog communications around the world. That's what the NSA was for, and there was no reason to duplicate them—and no way would we even want to, until Snowden had caused the NSA to become skittish on just about everything.

"What the hell does that mean? Boko Haram barely uses electricity, and they've sent a disciple out into the world. If he got an e-mail, it's from Chiclet."

On the screen, knowing he'd already given me enough lumps to the head, Kurt held up his hands and said, "Pike, I don't know why it was firewalled. Something about the nature of the e-mail. We've got an inquiry in through our systems to readdress, but right now, it's metadata only."

Meaning the e-mail header. But that would be good enough. It would have the ISP the e-mail went through, and with that, I could get a general location of where he had gone.

"Can you pass that to the hacking cell? Let them dig a little?"

He nodded. "Yeah. I can do that. But no execution on anything without me talking to you. You understand?"

I said, "Yeah. I got it. I'm not in charge anyway. I'll go through Knuckles."

Knuckles looked at me in confusion, saying, "What's that mean?"

28

Akinbo hung up the phone and studied the instructions the Russian had given him. He ran his fingers down a tourist map, tracing the road from his hotel and seeing it was close to a mile away. A long way to walk, but finding a taxi from here would be difficult, something he'd learned yesterday.

After eight hours traveling the Bulgarian and Turkish countryside, he'd arrived in Istanbul near midnight, only to find it might take him longer than that to go the short distance to his hotel, with not a soul speaking English once the bus stopped. He'd exited through the metro platform and been assaulted by the general chaos, a throbbing mass of people competing with bleating vehicle horns for attention even at that late hour.

He'd eventually found a taxi driver that at least pretended to speak English and presented an address to a hotel in the Kadirga district. They'd set out and Akinbo had prayed that he wasn't getting primed for a robbery. After thirty minutes, he'd complained, demanding to know their location, and the driver reassured him, pointing vaguely through the windshield, saying, "Two minutes. Two minutes."

Traveling down a narrow street with barely enough room for a single car, he was dropped off in front of a tired, crumbling brick building on the European side of the Bosphorus Strait. As they pulled up to the hotel, his mind shifted from nefarious actions of the cabdriver to the general dilapidation of the surrounding area. He was clearly in a district with little wealth, and he worried about his mission. He wondered why his spiritual advisor had recommended this place. He was on the verge of telling the cabbie to continue moving when he saw two men exit, both of African descent.

He'd decided to stay. At the front desk he'd learned that the area was filled with African illegals looking to springboard into Europe. It was the perfect place to disappear, but not the easiest to find a taxi on the spur of the moment. He'd be forced to walk to his meeting, but that was fine by him. He wanted to get out and explore.

He would have worried about leaving his belongings in the room, as it was spartan to say the least, with a simple knob lock on a flimsy door, but he had nothing to steal. He'd left all of that in Bulgaria, fleeing like a rat from a supposed boogeyman out to get him. The thought still aggravated him.

The meeting spot was adjacent to a large section on the map labeled GRAND BAZAAR, and he assumed it was a shopping area. He left the hotel much earlier than necessary, intent on spending the Russian's money on some new clothes.

Going north on the narrow street, the walk was steadily uphill, the buildings of three and four stories on either side adorned with clothes hanging to dry and satellite television dishes. They crowded right up to the street, forcing him to hop into doorways to allow traffic to pass. In short order he was winded, the hill stretching inexorably in front of him, never ending, the road winding to and fro, branching off into alleys like the roots of a tree.

He continued north until he broke out of the cloistered neighborhood into a shopping district. He crossed a four-lane road with a tram rail in the middle, the boulevard lined with modern retail stores and restaurants. He passed a metro stop and saw a string of buses near what appeared to be a cluster of awnings. He vectored toward them and found himself outside a stone portal leading to the Grand Bazaar, which, true to its name, appeared to sell everything from jewelry to clothes.

He entered and spent thirty minutes wandering the maze, looking to replenish his wardrobe but not wanting to purchase a belly-dancing costume. He passed a grill, the smell of the Turkish kabobs making his stomach grumble and reminding him of how long it had been since his last meal. He checked his phone to see if he had time and was startled to see how long he'd been roaming inside. His shopping would have to wait. He'd been late once and didn't want to repeat the displeasure he'd experienced at the hands of the old Russian.

Using a cheap tourist map, he pressed through the bazaar, trying to find the northern gate numbered sixteen. Just outside of it, on a street called Tigcilar, was a café where he was to meet his Russian contact, but he was beginning to realize that locating the gate wasn't as easy as he thought it would be. In his village in Nigeria, the directions the Russian had given him would have been easy to follow, but now he understood he'd made a mistake. This place was a nightmare of confusing alleys and streets.

He bumped into what he thought was the northern side and found a gate. The number on the stone was nineteen. He looked at his tourist map, seeing he'd marched all the way across to the eastern side, covering the entire bazaar and missing his gate to the north. He spun the map around, disoriented, sure he was wrong.

He glanced around for something to identify, and saw the same view stretched out before him, like two mirrors had been placed across from each other, showing an endless row of merchants selling goods. He felt the first tendrils of anxiety. Every alley looked like the alley before it, every stall looked like the stall next to it. There was nothing to anchor against to find his way.

He raced in a direction he thought was north, eventually hitting another wall and seeing the exit number fourteen. Across a shopping lane of leather goods was a stairwell leading up and what looked like a minbar—the pulpit of a mosque—attached to the wall.

The sight gave him pause. *An anchor*. He went toward it, then up the stairs, his speed increasing with each step. He found a shoe shelf at the top. It *was* a mosque.

He removed his shoes and entered. He stopped the first person he could find, the man looking alarmed at Akinbo's black skin and nervous manner. Akinbo gave a traditional Arabic greeting, and the man relaxed. Akinbo said something in English, his Arabic exhausted, and the man shook his head. Akinbo showed him his map and pointed to the location of gate sixteen. The man smiled and motioned for him to follow.

29

The Turk walked through the maze of the bazaar at a good clip, dodging pedestrians and slipping between booths to access the hidden lanes behind. Akinbo kept up, recognizing the stalls he had passed earlier in his wandering for the mythical gate sixteen. In seconds, they were in front of a stone portal, sunshine spilling through and competing with the artificial lighting of the bazaar. Outside was nothing more than a narrow brick lane leading away, congested with pallets, buckets, and sidewalk vendors on each side. The man pointed above them and Akinbo saw Turkish words next to the numeral for sixteen.

He thanked the Turk profusely, then took off at a trot, looking for the small outdoor café. He passed some food stalls, but nothing he would call a café. He hit an intersection and stopped, debating. Alleys led off left and right, both only wide enough for a motorcycle, the walls lined with boxes and stinking of garbage left too long in the sun. He considered asking someone else for help when his phone rang.

He answered and heard a voice he didn't recognize, but the accent was unmistakable. *Russian.*

"Where are you?"

"I'm outside the bazaar. Outside gate sixteen, just like instructed. Trying to find the café, but it's not on this street."

"Did you pass a mosque?"

Too late, Akinbo remembered the detail he'd overlooked. "Not yet."

"Then keep moving down the street."

Akinbo heard the contempt come through louder than the instructions. In thirty seconds he passed the mosque on his right. He saw tables ahead, and picked up his pace. He reached a restaurant with an interior the size of a large closet, holding only three tables, the rest of the room overtaken by cooking appliances. In the corner a man carved lamb off of a rotating spit.

He swiveled about and noticed that the majority of seating was outside, in an area fenced off by rough lumber that had been painted to look like ancient wood. The section stretched thirty feet left and right of the door, with three tables on either side.

A Caucasian man sat at the table farthest away, staring at him. There was an open newspaper on the table and a jacket draped over the back of his chair. *The meeting signal.* But he didn't recognize the man. It wasn't the old Russian. This person was much younger and fit. The man picked up a cell phone and dialed, still looking at him. Akinbo felt his phone vibrate. He answered, keeping his eyes on the Caucasian.

"What are you waiting on? Come here."

He did so. When he reached the table he said, "I was looking for the older man."

"You were told to look for a signal, not a man. If the man you'd met before had been here there would have been no need for a signal. Not only are you late, but you can't seem to follow simple instructions."

Akinbo bristled and said, "Who are you, and where is the old man? I don't like being tricked."

"You may call me Jarilo. I'm the one who will facilitate the meeting. The 'old man,' as you call him, is not able to meet without drawing the attention of others. I'll be his go-between. As for being tricked, you'll meet here again, using the same signals. That man will also be someone you don't know. That's why we sent you here today. Practice. And it looks like it was necessary."

"Why won't you be here?"

"I have my reasons, but that's irrelevant. The man will give you further instructions on where to get the weapon, what precautions are necessary, and how it can be detonated. We believe it's an artillery shell, but we're not sure. After he has passed his information, call me. I will meet you and we will discuss what he said."

"What about my target? Where am I going with the weapon?"

"That depends on a lot of factors. We'll discuss after you talk to the man. Remember, tomorrow's meeting is after dark. Will that cause you problems? Can you still find this place?"

"Yes. Of course I can. I'm not stupid."

Akinbo received a patronizing smile for the comment. "Okay. Do not be late tomorrow. The man you are meeting will not have your phone number, and will not be as accommodating as I have been. He'll leave."

Akinbo nodded.

"One other thing. Tomorrow morning, at ten, I want you to call your group."

He passed across a folded sheet of paper. "Tell them what's written here verbatim. Do not, under any circumstance, tell them anything but what is on that paper."

Akinbo read it and saw it was for another meeting, the day after tomorrow, at a different place and time.

"Why? What's this about? I was told I couldn't use this phone to contact them. The old man told me that specifically because of the Americans."

"He's changed his mind, but it *is* because of the Americans."

Akinbo started to say something else when Yuri cut him off, passing across another cell phone. "Make that call and keep the phone on you. This cell is now the new operational phone. You understand what that means? 'Operational phone'?"

"Yes. No calling friends."

Yuri nodded at him and said, "That's right. Only call us on that phone. Go. You have your instructions. Don't worry about why. Let us do the worrying."

Akinbo rose without another word.

Yuri watched Akinbo's back until he turned the corner, then dialed Vladimir.

"It didn't go as well as we'd hoped. Akinbo is not trained nor prepared for operational work. He showed up late, then ignored the bona fides. Are you sure you don't want me here for the meeting?"

"No, for the same reasons I'm only leaving the consulate for coffee. The Turks know my position in the FSB, so anyone I meet in public will be connected to me as a person of interest. I have no idea how competent the Syrian is, but he's also an intelligence operative. He might be known to MIT as well. If so, I don't want them linking to you. Akinbo is a risk we have to take. If he gets picked up, so be it."

Yuri said, "Okay, sir. But I'd recommend letting my team cover the site. Just to watch. Provide countersurveillance."

Yuri heard nothing but the hoarse rattle of Vlad's breath, the strangled wheeze making him involuntarily want to cough. Finally, Vlad said, "Okay. That makes sense. But loosely. Just observe for our protection, not theirs. Did you tell him about the call?"

"Yes, sir. He'll do it, I'm sure. My only worry is that he won't stick to the script, and instead tell other savages what's really going on."

"Doesn't matter. If he talks about the real meeting there's no way the Americans can react in time. They're still in Bulgaria, floundering for a lead. They'll take the bait and be at the second meeting. They can't help it. It's their nature. And true to your nature, you will kill them."

30

The hose jetted water, splashing the sidewalk in a tepid spray, but Bekir Kemal wondered if what was coming out was any cleaner than the splattered mess he was attempting to clean. The leftovers of a dead bird, or maybe the vomit of a drunk passerby, it needed to be removed before the nighttime rush came in for a meal.

As he had every day for the past two years, he'd come to the small café grateful to have work. Three years out of the university, he, like many young people around the world, couldn't find a job equal to the degree he held. He didn't mind, with the exception of wearing the ridiculous Turkish costume. Being near the tourist magnet of the Grand Bazaar had its hazards. Even so, others who had graduated with him were literally wondering where their next meal would come from.

He doused the pavement with the fetid water, then scrubbed the offending stain with a push broom. It did no good. He quit, aggravated, knowing he'd have to use a wire brush on his hands and knees. Disgusted at the thought.

The head cook—which is to say the only cook—shouted at him from inside, amused at the dilemma. Bekir leaned through the door and aimed the hose, as if he was about to unleash the foul water on the interior tables. The cook held up his hands, blubbering something to get him to stop.

He lowered the hose, and they both laughed. A small bit of camaraderie on a tiny street at a café that had struggled to survive every minute it had been open. One more night in an endless parade of them, each as mundane as the one before. The sun began to set, and the shadows grew longer.

Bekir had had ideas of grandeur while in school. Thoughts of changing the world, of being the next Kemal Atatürk. Those dreams had buoyed him through college, as it had for all of his university friends. Now, as a busboy with a college degree, he understood it was nothing more than an expensive myth. His place in life was limited, as was that of everyone else he knew. He would do no grand thing. He believed he was just an ant on a cog of the giant machine called earth, one of the thousands of little people who had no capacity to alter the course of human events.

He was wrong.

As he and the cook prepared for the rush of nighttime patrons, a mind-numbing task they had both done for years, they had no way of knowing that their little café was about to become ground zero for actions that had the potential to alter the balance of power among nation-states on a global scale.

Opening a caustic bottle of liquid soap that wouldn't be allowed to see the light of day in the west, Bekir splashed the stain. He knew the film he created was dangerous to leave unattended, as he'd slipped more than once using it, but it would also save him some elbow grease. He told the cook he was going to let it soak for a bit, but that he would have it up before the nighttime crowds.

He dribbled a thin line out, then decided more was better, dumping half of the container onto the street, coating the offending blemish. He watched the tendrils of soap seek lower ground, crossing the road to the shop across the way. He feared the storekeep would complain, forcing him to clean it up before it had done its job.

The merchant would not, and Bekir would have patrons much earlier than was customary, preventing him from fulfilling the promise he'd told the cook. It wouldn't be until later, after the smell of cordite had disappeared and the bodies had been removed, that Bekir would remember the soap he'd spilled on the street.

My earpiece chirped early, startling me. I maintained my stone face for anyone who might be watching, listening as Jennifer relayed that she had eyes on Chiclet. Hearing the words, I worked hard to keep the grin off of my face. I believed that we'd eventually find him, but I was in the minority. Knuckles and Kurt both thought chasing Chiclet was a waste of time, but I didn't see it that way. As long as we were sitting around waiting on the trigger of the thumb drive mission, I was willing to give it a go. Turbo and Radcliffe demanded it.

There was a risk that whoever was protecting Chiclet would recognize Jennifer, but I didn't think that would happen. As far as they knew, she was dead, having fallen off a cliff and exploded in a ball of fire.

Even so, she'd dyed her hair brunette and wore contacts that changed her gray eyes to a mundane brown. To add to the mix, I'd paired her up with Decoy instead of myself, the teammate Knuckles had given me. The two together projected a different signature, but truthfully, my greatest fear at this point was Decoy himself.

He was a notorious man-whore, and I wasn't sure he could conduct a mission profile with Jennifer on his arm without becoming focused on her other "assets." He was solid in a gunfight, about as good as I'd ever seen, but he'd been partial to Jennifer since I'd known him. Always making lewd comments and coming on to her. Which, I'm sure, was why Knuckles had given him to me. A way to get a little payback after the last videoconference with Kurt.

I'd acquiesced to the new chain of command, and things had been awkward for about thirty minutes, but I'd finally convinced Knuckles that I was good with it, let him have the helm, and begun working the hacking cell like Kurt had said I could.

Using the ISP in the e-mail header, we found out that the e-mail from Chiclet had been sent from an Internet provider for the Turkish Metro bus line, so I knew my instincts had been correct. He had fled.

While they worked for more information, Knuckles alerted our pilots and we drove back to Sofia, intent on flying to Istanbul for the stupid thumb drive mission. Kurt had also sent over the intelligence that was so controversial, but in my mind it was just a bunch of shit from the dustbin of history. Who really cared today about Black September in 1972? So the Russians had facilitated the murder of Israelis and we'd known in advance. That was worth all the hubbub? It was like reading the conspiracy theories about the grassy knoll: interesting to a select few, but old news to everyone else. Well, in my mind, anyway.

By the time we got to the plane, the hacking cell had necked down the MAC address of the Wi-Fi Chiclet had used. It was a mobile router on an actual bus. Something that worked on the cell towers but translated as a Wi-Fi hot spot to the passengers. I gave them orders to locate which vehicle, hoping that buried in the web architecture of the bus company was some sort of inventory that the hacking cell could find. Basically, neck down that mobile router X was located in bus Y. From there, I could find out where bus Y was headed.

We'd taken off for Istanbul, and by the time we'd landed, they had an answer. Well, they had a bus number. It took me about thirty minutes of calling the Metro bus line before I finally reached a person that spoke English. I gave her the information, along with a bogus story about trying to find a lost niece who'd run away, and asked where that bus was going. She told me the answer, even with the puzzlement in her voice over how I knew so much about her company. When she asked a pointed question about my knowledge, I hung up and gave Knuckles the good news: Chiclet was on a bus to Istanbul, and we'd actually beaten him to the city.

He was aggravated to say the least, but I was elated. I called Kurt, telling him what I had and demanding to put Chiclet's selectors back on the target deck. While the Taskforce was pretty damn powerful, we still had to prioritize assets, and with multiple operations ongoing around the world, Kurt had put Chiclet on the back burner. Now that we were both in the same city, I asked to have anything associated with him turned back on. He agreed, and this morning, it pinged.

A Chiclet associate—a bigwig in Boko Haram—had received a phone call from a number located in Istanbul. It was an unknown handset, but the connection was too coincidental, especially since the phone had a Russian country code. I'd begged Kurt for permission to investigate and asked him to dedicate assets to geolocate the new cell. He'd reluctantly agreed, with the caveat that if anything broke on the thumb drive, we were to redirect immediately. I promised, and then had asked Knuckles for some manpower.

With a grin, he'd given me Decoy, claiming that Brett would draw too much attention as an African American. I understood the real reason: Knuckles knew Decoy would come on to Jennifer, and he would enjoy the fireworks.

As we left he'd said, "You find Chiclet and I'll buy you a case of beer."

With Jennifer's call, I was debating whether to charge him a case of microbrew or live with the Pabst Blue Ribbon he'd buy on his own.

I keyed my radio. "I'm outside of gate seven. Can I enter?"

Not wanting to be anywhere near Chiclet due to potential compromise, I'd settled for acting as surveillance chief, although with only one element in the field, the position wasn't really necessary. Jennifer and Decoy could do fine on their own.

Decoy said, "He's exiting out the north right now, so yeah, you can enter. No threat. Give him some time before you penetrate to the far side."

I gave him a roger and entered the Grand Bazaar, immediately getting accosted by the stall owners to my left and right. According to Jennifer's little history blurb, this thing was the largest and oldest covered bazaar on earth, and had been continuously running for centuries. It was the perfect place to lose surveillance, and it hadn't surprised me at all when the handset geolocation had entered inside. Chiclet probably thought he was giving some unknown surveillance fits by roaming the bazaar, but he couldn't beat technology. He could run around inside this maze all damn day and we'd sit back waiting. Unless he ditched his traitorous phone, we could always find him again.

But we couldn't determine what he was doing.

And that, in a nutshell, was the dilemma I was facing. I could follow the phone trace all day long on a computer, but that didn't really tell me it was *him*. It could be Chiclet, or it might be someone else. On top of that, I wanted to know what he was up to, see if he met some potential Russians, which required physical eyes on. All the phone did was tell me a location, not give me a description of what had occurred at that location, but you couldn't beat the technology as a fail-safe. No more lost contact drills. All we had to do was pull back and get a lock, then reengage.

I stopped outside a stall selling leather handbags and, strangely, John Cena wrestling T-shirts, and called Jennifer on the cell, off of the group chat. Yeah, it was weak of me, but I wanted to talk to Jennifer without Decoy hearing.

31

Jennifer felt Decoy's hand slip into hers, a pathetic attempt at pretending he was solidifying their cover. Before she had time to react, her phone vibrated, giving her a reason to pull away.

"Hello? Why are you calling directly instead of group chat?"

"Just checking up. What's man-whore doing?"

She toyed with telling Pike about the hand-holding just to drive him nuts, but ultimately decided against it, instead focusing on the mission.

"He's doing fine. *We're* doing fine. Chiclet is at a café and he's seated with another man of Middle Eastern descent. I'll get you a photo in a minute. We're up the street about fifty meters away at another food vendor. We should have brought a parabolic on this. I'd love to hear what they're saying."

Pike said, "Yeah, well, I'm just amazed we found him. Get as much as you can on visual and we'll make a case to Kurt for continued operations."

She acknowledged, about to hang up, then heard, "Hey, he isn't doing anything he shouldn't, is he?"

She grinned and caught Decoy's eye, saying, "Who? Chiclet?"

"No. Man-whore."

"He's a perfect gentleman."

"Bullshit. Nobody in the Taskforce has the time of day for split tails. Let me know if he steps over the line. I'll bust his head open."

·Jennifer hung up without telling Pike how insulting the "split tail" comment was. He wouldn't get it. Pike worked in a world dominated by males, only fighting for her after he'd seen what she brought to the mission. He believed in her capabilities now, more so than anyone else. *Truly* believed, which was what endeared her to him, but he still had to be convinced initially.

Unlike Decoy.

Raised with four sisters by a mother that had left an abusive father, Decoy was an anomaly. A Taskforce operator that honestly didn't feel threatened by Jennifer. Pike was right about him bedding anything he came across, but wrong in the reason. Unlike just about anyone else in the Taskforce, he did it because he *understood* women. Jennifer knew saying that truth would just aggravate Pike, so she kept that particular insight to herself.

Even after Pike had made it clear that he wouldn't tolerate any insults to Jennifer, Decoy had spent every minute trying to get her out of her pants, but he did so without any prejudice. Operationally, he couldn't care less what her gender was. He was one of the first to recognize her talents in the covert world, and one of the first to welcome them on the Taskforce stage, treating her just like any other operator.

But he still wanted to get laid.

At the end of the day, she wondered if Decoy, given all of his man-whore proclivities, wasn't actually more open than all of the other men in the Taskforce.

Decoy said, "What was that about?"

"Nothing. Pike just checking in."

She felt his hand slink in again, trapping her wrist and bringing a grin. She knew he was doing it just to get a rise out of her. He'd figured out her relationship with Pike long before anyone else and knew he stood no chance. He squeezed her hand and winked. In the *middle* of an operation. She couldn't believe it.

Man-whore is right.

* * *

Pretending to browse a selection of silver jewelry at an outdoor stall, Yuri could just make out the elbow of the Syrian intelligence officer seventy meters away. With the canalization of the narrow street, he'd brought a minimal force to survey the meeting. Since Akinbo knew what Yuri looked like, he'd stayed on the bazaar side, near the mosque outside of gate sixteen. He'd put Dmitri inside the restaurant and had the giant of a man Mishka on the far side. Far enough away to give early warning, but not draw attention to the meeting. The man had his uses, but blending in wasn't one of them.

With the sun rapidly falling below the horizon, the heat from the day began to drop as well, and the crowds started to pick up, a mix of foreigners and locals. Yuri had the men focus on the Turks, ignoring all the tourists. If anyone was going to show interest in the meeting, it would be someone working for the Turkish MIT, but so far, the only highlight was a young waiter who was serving both the Syrian's table as well as Dmitri's.

He waited until the meeting was well under way, then called his men. He received a negative report from Mishka and a joke about the waiter's outfit from Dmitri. He grinned and checked his watch. Five more minutes and the meeting would be over. Successfully.

Five minutes.

He began thinking about the follow-on meeting with Akinbo, where they'd plan the next steps of the mission, when a flash of light caught his eye. He saw a minibike approaching, the headlight bouncing erratically over the ancient cobblestones as it wove between pedestrians, both the driver and passenger wearing full-face helmets. The driver swerved to the left of the narrow lane, and the passenger pulled something out of his jacket.

As the bike entered the pool of light spilling out from the café, Yuri recognized a mini–Uzi machine pistol. His mouth opened in disbelief.

The driver pulled up next to Akinbo on the other side of the wood rail and the passenger flipped out a small metal-skeleton stock, seating it into his shoulder pocket. Before Yuri even thought to shout the passenger squeezed the trigger, the weapon sounding like a canvas tarp ripping apart.

The Syrian held his hands up as if they could stop the death, then began twitching from the rounds shredding his body. He slumped over the wood railing next to the table, dripping dark fluid on the street, mixing in with the remains of a spilled bottle of Coca-Cola.

The pedestrians began to react as the minibike surged forward, gaining distance from the targeted killing. The driver cranked the handlebars hard to the right to get the bike turned around and aimed back up the lane, away from the dead end of the bazaar. He gunned the engine and the tires hit something wet on the street, a patch of liquid as slick as black ice. Instead of gaining traction, both tires flew out from underneath the bike, the engine slamming onto the cobblestone and spraying sparks. The passenger spilled onto the concrete and the bike ground on top of the driver, causing a scream as the exhaust branded his leg.

He pulled himself from underneath and got it back upright, but the crowds of pedestrians now blocked his way out, pointing and shouting at the killing. Running and leaping on the back of the motorcycle, the passenger yelled, jabbing his finger in Yuri's direction, and the bike jumped forward, heading right toward him.

He jumped out of the way, watching it race right through gate sixteen into the Grand Bazaar.

Incredulous, he called Dmitri. "Status. What's the status?"

Out of breath, Dmitri said, "The Syrian's dead, and I swear to God I'm looking at that female I drove over a cliff. She's got brown hair now, but it's her."

The Americans. How in the hell did they get here so quickly? How did they know about the Syrian?

The anger boiled up and he spit out, "Kill her and anyone with her."

32

Jennifer stood up so fast she knocked her chair over. On the group channel she said, "Pike, Pike, this is Koko. A motorcycle hit team just took out the Arabic man talking to Chiclet. Their egress route was blocked by civilians. They're coming right at you."

"At me? I'm in the bazaar."

Decoy, on the edge of their café, standing on a chair to see over the crowd, said, "Roger that, Pike; he's driving the motorcycle straight into it."

He jumped down, saying, "He's coming. We'll stay outside for containment."

Jennifer felt a shadow and turned around to see a giant of a man towering over her, holding a pistol in his fist, the bulbous suppressor aimed at Decoy's head.

She shouted a warning and he pulled the trigger. The weapon spit noise like a muffled clap, the sound in no way reflecting the violence it wrought. The bullet entered Decoy's head just above his nose. It channeled through his brain, mushrooming out at the resistance, then exited the back of his head, bringing with it a good section of his skull and splattering the wall behind him. Decoy dropped straight down, the life fleeing his body instantly, his arms ending up unnaturally beneath him, his eyes dimly open.

The earth stood still for a moment, Jennifer looking but not seeing

the corpse of her teammate, her brain failing to register the catastrophic damage to Decoy's visage.

She saw the weapon swinging around, the eyes of the killer lining
up the sights on her own face. The image was crystal, the details
hyperreal. She stared straight through the black hole of the barrel,
seeing the hair on the sausage knuckle of the trigger finger, like the
bristles of a hog. She saw the hairs shift, and knew the finger was
moving backward.

She exploded into action, slapping both hands over the weapon
and trapping the man's hand against the frame of the pistol. She rotated up, snapping his finger in the trigger guard and locking his wrist
joint, the weapon discharging harmlessly into the air.

He screamed, a high-pitched, feminine noise from such a large man,
and she rotated the joint, bringing him to his knees. He swung his
other hand, the fist hammering her shoulder like a mace from medie-
val times. She flew against the wall, her back sliding through Decoy's
brain matter. But she held on to the pistol.

The giant cursed at her and began to advance. She pulled the trigger, the first bullet striking the center of his chest. He staggered, but
kept coming. She continued to fire, both hands on the weapon. The
beast seemed to absorb each round and shrug it off. Frothy blood
began to escape his lips. Two more steps and he was above her again.
He reached out with both hands. She jabbed the suppressor to his
forehead and squeezed. His head snapped back in a spray and he finally dropped, landing on top of Decoy's body.

A bullet impacted the wall next to her head, alerting her to another
threat. She saw a man holding a pistol outside Chiclet's café, batting
people aside and advancing. She raised her own weapon, seeing the
slide had locked open on an empty magazine. The man began to run
toward her, darting through the chaos of the crowd.

He cleared them and held up, drawing a bead on her head, his eyes
squinting down the barrel of his weapon no more than ten feet away.

She threw her pistol at him, causing him to flinch and pull the shot. She took off, away from the café, her long legs churning the pavement, darting among the crowd to avoid a bullet to the back.

No sooner did Decoy shout the ridiculous warning about a motorcycle carrying a couple of assassins than I heard people screaming, then saw them jumping out of the way.

The motorcycle—a moped, really—came scooting by me one row over, the driver steering through the crowd and the passenger alternating between a death grip on the driver's jacket and waving his arms to get people to move. I took off after it, knowing whoever was on the back was the same person who had killed Turbo and tried to kill me.

The bazaar was shaped roughly like a square, which meant after penetrating gate sixteen on the northeast corner, they were running south, parallel to a series of exits. If they took one, they'd be on the streets and alleys leading to high-speed escape routes. They'd be gone.

I jogged parallel to them one row over, hearing the driver tooting his little horn. They were slowly pulling away from me because I couldn't get through the crowd quickly enough. While people were diving out of the motorcycle's way, they weren't doing shit for me. I saw an exit from the bazaar and took it to the narrow street outside, now able to run as fast as I could away from the chaos, but unable to see the motorcycle's movement.

I sprinted down the road in an effort to get ahead of the assassins, leaping over buckets, pallets, and other refuse. I saw another gate ahead and increased my speed, intent on cutting them off. Just before I reached it, the motorcycle popped out of the stone portal, literally three feet away. The driver turned right and goosed the engine, oblivious to my presence.

I reached out and snagged the collar of the passenger, jerking him straight off the back. He was a small man, and I slammed him to the deck with great force, seeing an Uzi machine pistol fly out. The motor-cycle spun around thirty feet away with the driver jabbing his left hand into his jacket. I raised the Uzi and squeezed the trigger, getting no recoil. It was empty. Nothing but dead weight, with apparently all of the bullets inside the Arabic man at the café.

The driver didn't know it, though. I cinched the little skeletal stock into my shoulder pocket and leaned into a fighting stance as if I was about to unleash holy hell. He dropped his attempt at getting to his weapon, thinking better of taking me on. He gunned the throttle and was gone, escaping down the road to the four-lane avenue known as Ordu Caddesi.

Before I could focus on what I'd caught, the assassin below me lashed out with a foot, catching the inside of my thigh, dropping my body to a knee, and infuriating me. I grabbed his head and bashed it into the pavement hard enough to crack his helmet down the middle, stunning him.

I rolled him onto his stomach and cinched the chinstrap of the helmet into his throat. He slapped his hands behind him, coughing and gagging. I kept working the strap, eventually seating it into his carotid arteries. He struggled a brief moment more, then relaxed, unconscious.

I dragged him into an alley, then removed his helmet. The first thing I noticed was the hair. A mess of it that had been placed in a ponytail. It confused me for a moment, then I realized why he was so slight and small.

The killer was a woman.

33

Jennifer heard the feet slapping behind her and darted into the first alley she came to. She ran flat-out, on the edge of losing control, the small lane black as pitch. Her toe caught an outcropping of brick and she went down headfirst, slamming her elbow into the ground and skidding into a wall.

She shook her head, attempting to clear it, gritting her teeth over the pain in her arm, knowing she was losing precious time. She started to rise and heard the pursuers round the corner to the alley. She tucked into a ball, pressed next to a stairwell leading down, getting as small as possible to rectify the mistake of coming into the alley. She needed to get into the light. Into the tourist crowds.

But that didn't stop them from killing Decoy. His shattered face exploded into her consciousness and she shunted it aside.

They came jogging forward, slower and more careful than her, but still moving too fast to identify where she was crouching. She willed herself to look like a pallet or garbage can, and they went by. When they were thirty feet past her, she stood and began sprinting back the way she had come.

She heard a shout just as she reached the intersection of a larger road that had actual vehicle traffic on it. She saw a puff of dust in the bricks to her left and heard the whine of a ricochet. She turned the corner without looking back. She ran down the thoroughfare, seeing the Sultan Ahmed Mosque in the distance, a thing of beauty silhouetted by spotlights, the blue tile shimmering and the six minarets spearing into the sky. It would give her a refuge, if she could make it. One of the last of the great mosques, and the most famous landmark in all of Turkey, she knew it would be well protected. A place a Russian would never dare attack.

The Russians knew it as well, and did what they could to prevent her from reaching it. She broke out into a park, seeing a crowd gathered near a large fountain. She slowed to a jog, then heard a flurry of rounds snap by her head.

She realized they were willing to harm anyone to get her. They would kill whomever it took. She was like a person pulling a trailer carrying plague, dragging the death with her wherever she went.

She couldn't be responsible for that. *Need the authorities. Someone with guns. Away from the crowds.*

She saw the Hagia Sophia museum to her left. Having once been an Orthodox church at the time the Bible was cemented, then a grand mosque of the Ottoman Empire, it was now a museum. Which meant it was closed at this hour. But surely guarded inside.

She stopped next to a kiosk that was locked, pretended to go around it, then ducked low to find her predators. She saw them less than fifty meters away and running flat out, scaring the hell out of her and short-circuiting any logical battle plan. Like a cat flushed from hiding, she sprinted across the open terrain, straight at the outside wall of the Hagia Sofia. In the dim illumination from the lights of the fountain, she saw the suppressed pistol rounds impacting the wall in front of her, searing her core. She knew if *she* were shooting, she'd miss at most twice. Pike, only once.

She jerked to the right for a split second, then went into a roll before leaping up against the stone wall. She put her left foot against it and pushed off, literally running up the wall and grabbing the top. She heard the impact of the bullets below and hoisted herself over, dropping into a courtyard of the museum.

She looked left and right, trying to see a camera or a guard post, but coming up empty. The area was well lit, but there was no overt security. The worst of both worlds.

Jesus Christ. The damn wall is the security?

She'd just dropped into a kill zone.

She heard a scraping above her and saw a silhouette. He fired once at sound alone, missing wide, but enough to keep her off-balance. To keep her from creating a plan. She ran past the entrance metal detectors and ticket gates, all turned off and silent. She kept going to the front of the church, looking for a camera. Somewhere, someone was watching this place.

She found nothing.

Even given the danger, the discovery was mildly insulting to her, aggravating her protectionist sense of history. She glanced around, looking for a hiding spot. She found several, but all were dead ends. They would protect her, but would do nothing if she was discovered. She needed something with an escape route. She entered the cathedral proper and saw an enormous cavern, dimly lit with emergency lighting.

The place was huge, but had no real area to conceal her. It was just a wide-open space, the walls ornately gilded and clearly ancient, but providing no protection. The only unique feature was a section of scaffolding stretching all the way to the roof ninety feet above her, going past a balcony that ringed the cathedral. Something erected to make repairs to the ancient building, but more than that, something she could use. A set of monkey bars that beckoned.

Like a squirrel that raced up a tree at the sight of a dog, she looked to the heights for safety. It was an equalizer for both strength and skill. A place where she knew she could rule.

She waited until she was sure they had entered, her heart thumping so loud she was positive they would hear. She heard them whisper in Russian, then split up. Not what she wanted. She needed both chasing her when she looped back around to the scaffolding on the second floor, leaving them behind.

Her hand forced, she sprinted behind them toward the stairwell leading to the upper balcony, letting them see her. She heard the snap of a single round, the bullet splitting the air by her head louder than the cycling of the suppressed pistol. She instinctively ducked, knowing it was like reacting to thunder after the lightning struck.

Someone shouted and she looked behind her, seeing only one man coming.

Shit.

She entered the stairwell and saw it wasn't stairs at all, but a hallway that went to the upper floor like an ancient handicapped ramp, switching back every fifteen meters and paved with stones that were gleaming smooth from centuries of use. A configuration that gave the man behind her the chance to shoot and kill her, since she had to run uphill fifty feet before each turn. As the balcony was sixty or seventy feet in the air, there were a lot of turns.

She sprinted as fast as she could, now depending on her athletic ability to beat the man behind her. And it proved enough. He was able to get only one shot at her before she broke onto the hall with the balcony, seeing the scaffolding before her. But it would do no good now. Getting on it would only leave her vulnerable to the man below. Like shooting fish in a barrel.

Unless I can get them to ignore the weapons. Get them to think they've won. Get them to want to interrogate me.

It was a huge, huge risk, but she saw no other alternative. She had the athletic ability to beat them, but she couldn't outrun a bullet. She needed to reduce that threat. Beat them with intelligence.

She took a deep breath and let it out, hearing the man break out onto her level. She moved into the light, hands high, and said, "Don't shoot! Don't shoot!"

He shouted something in Russian to the man below, holding the pistol on her. After hearing an answer, the man before her said, "Get on your knees. Put your hands behind your head."

She sank down in relief, interlacing her fingers on top of her head, thinking about her next move. Looking at the scaffolding four feet away.

She said, "Don't kill me. Please." She cowered down, projecting weakness.

And he believed it.

34

I searched the girl's body for weapons and found a small folding knife. Tossing it aside, I raised her into a sitting position, checking her pulse and breathing. She appeared okay, leaving me wondering about my next move. Like a dog that chases a car, I had no idea what to do with what I'd caught.

I could hear the people gathering on the street outside the alley, spilling out from the bazaar, all trying to connect why a motorcycle had raced through the place. Getting bits and pieces, they were beginning to draw a story. Some were wildly wrong, others dangerously close. I heard the peculiar sound of a European siren closing in on the action and knew I had to get away.

I called Decoy and Jennifer, getting nothing. It didn't cause concern, though, since the standard operating procedure was to put all cell phones into original equipment mode when confronted with possible compromise. In other words, turn them into standard cell phones instead of the top secret communications devices they were. Jennifer and Decoy were now at ground zero for a murder, and for all I knew were sitting in the backseat of a Turkish police car.

I considered my options. One, I could let her go. Leave her here to wake up. We weren't involved with the target, so it would be clean. But the bitch had something to do with the deaths of Taskforce members, so that option was out of the question. Regardless of the risk to my cover.

Two, I could take her with me. Drag her somewhere and get her inside a secure area. But that was just about impossible. What the hell could I do? Carry her along as my drunk date?

Three, I could kill her. I knew she'd killed Turbo and Radcliffe. Well, I knew she was on the team who'd done the mission. And she'd tried to kill Jennifer and me.

At the end of the day, this was probably the best option, because I still had the damn thumb drive mission to contend with, and that operation had no room for prisoners.

Simple.

She'd do the same if the roles were reversed.

I used one hand to hold her head still and placed the folded knuckles of my other hand against the back of her neck. Syncing where I would strike. I cocked my elbow, concentrating on the spot, not wanting to cause her unnecessary pain.

I saw her hand twitch. I felt her breath.

I couldn't do it.

The blackness that Jennifer was so afraid of didn't appear. The rage that had consumed me in the past, that had turned me into an executioner, remained at bay. What once ruled my life had decided to hide when I needed it most. Instead, something inside was telling me that killing her like this was an abomination.

I sagged against the wall, a little disgusted with myself. I let out a breath.

Shit. Looks like the drunk-date option.

She started to awaken, her eyes fluttering back and forth. It would be seconds before she snapped them open. I leaned in and rolled my knuckles into her arteries again, cutting off the blood flow to her brain. She slumped back.

I threw her over my shoulders and started moving down the alley, wondering if I had lost my killer instinct by getting entangled with Jennifer. Not regretting the decision, but wondering if I'd lost a bit of an edge, especially considering the woman on my shoulder would do it to me without question.

I thought about my past, when I was on active duty in the Taskforce. I might have killed her then, but it wasn't a given. Well, not a given before my family was taken from me. After that had happened, the question would have been whether I would have done it slowly.

But you were crazy then.

After I'd lost my family, I'd killed to release the pain, not for the mission. I'd inflicted the agony inside me onto others, conveniently using the mantle of my job to justify it. I wondered if that's what she did as well. I hoped not. That time had been horrific, and I was lucky to have made it out of the blackness in one piece. If the woman on my shoulder was a reflection of that, the world would have been better off if I'd left her in the alley with a broken neck.

I went through two intersections, sticking to festering alleys and avoiding other pedestrians, searching for a suitable place to hide. I found it down a twisting side street, a youth hostel with a flickering neon sign advertising individual rooms. A piece-of-shit place that I would never have entered if I had more than twenty dollars to spend, but a building that would now give me cover without anyone asking questions. Somewhere to sort out my next steps.

I walked in with the girl over my shoulder, causing a stir from two Australians sitting on a worn couch watching a community TV. Well, they looked like Australians. Thick beards and a quart of beer on the chipped table to their front.

I said, "Too much partying. This place have room for us?"

They gave me a knowing nod, then hollered for the manager, confirming my suspicions with their accents. He came down from a narrow stairwell, a wizened old Turkish guy. He smirked at me, then checked us in, which consisted of me handing him cash and him handing me a key. No paperwork of any kind. He smirked again and pointed up the stairwell.

Getting to the threadbare room, I tied her to the sink, then did a thorough search of her person, finding nothing but a passport from Australia.

Sure. Another Australian backpacker.

I splashed water in her face, snapping her awake. She jerked about for a moment, then looked at me.

Setting the tone, I said, "I don't want to kill you, but I will."

She said nothing. Looking at me as if I were the devil.

I said, "I know you're not Australian. But don't worry, I'm not going to raise a stink about it. What I want to know is why you've killed my friends."

I let that sink in, then grabbed the hair above her forehead, jerking her upright.

"So you know, that's the reason I'm going to make your life fucking miserable. But I have to sell this some way, so what's up with Boko Haram? Why do you kill everyone around him? Why do you protect him?"

Her eyes flicked left and right, clearly trying to determine how she could escape her fate. I yanked her head again, going so far as to hammer it against the pipe under the sink.

"Don't even think it. I'll fucking kill you right here. Trust me, that little shit downstairs won't call the police."

She looked into my eyes, and I saw Jennifer. I *saw* my weakness. I saw what was keeping the blackness under the scar tissue. And hating it. The assassin in front of me was responsible for the murder of my friends, and I couldn't generate the emotion to do what was necessary because she was female.

I released her hair in disgust and stood up, moving to the worn-out twin bed against the wall.

35

On her knees, Jennifer watched her killer advance through the shadows of the museum lighting. Convinced of his superiority, he walked right up to her and placed his left hand on the back of her head, grasping her fingers and intertwining them in her hair. He cinched down her head, forcing her to look at the ground. Reducing her ability to fight.

He shoved his weapon into a belt and shouted down in Russian to the man below. He heard a response, then said, "You will stand up slowly. If you move in any hostile manner, I will throw you over the rail. Do you understand?"

She nodded, the thought that she'd made a mistake seeping into her. Searching for the split second that would give her an edge, she said, "I'll do whatever you want. I'm not the person in charge. I'm not supposed to be here."

The man shouted in Russian again, then pulled her hair, forcing her to rise. When she was upright she rolled to the balls of her feet, getting ready. She whined, asking him to release her head, and he snorted, jerking her by the roots and turning her to face him. Giving her a target.

She speared out a knee, driving it forward with all of her weight and catching him directly in the stomach, penetrating deep. He grunted, released her hair, and staggered back, holding his midsection. She whirled and dove over the edge, going into free fall like a jungle animal, absolutely confident she'd find something to halt her descent. She dropped five feet before her hand snagged a single piece of scaffolding.

The weight of her body snapped through her shoulder, threatening to break her grip. She swung around the metal and clamped her other hand onto a steel support rod. She started to work her way down.

The man on the balcony screamed to his partner, and, as she expected, the other killer below appeared. He shouted up at her, pointing a pistol.

When she stopped climbing, he said, "Do not do anything stupid. You cannot escape, and there is nobody coming to help. I don't want to hurt you. I just want to know what you know. That's all."

She hung where she was, waiting, knowing how this game of monkey in the middle would go. Counting on it. She said, "I don't know anything. I'm not moving. I'll stay up here until they open tomorrow."

He said, "I'll kill you. Right here. They'll find your body tomorrow, wondering what has happened. All I want to know is how the Americans knew about the meeting with the Syrian. Why did you kill him?"

Truthfully, she said, "I have no idea what you're talking about. I know nothing about a Syrian, and that killing was as big a surprise to me as it was to you."

He aimed the pistol and said, "So be it."

Jennifer closed her eyes, praying that his wish to garner information would trump his anger.

No shot came.

Instead, she heard him shout in Russian, his frustration transcending through the language barrier. She opened her eyes and saw the man above clamber onto the scaffolding. Entering the arena. Climbing onto the spider's web.

She acted scared, gingerly moving away from him, allowing him to close the distance. She looked down at the other man sixty feet below and said, "Keep him away! I won't help if he tries to hurt me."

He said, "That's okay. You'll talk soon enough. You continue climbing down, or you'll end up smashed on the floor. Either way, you're coming here."

She maneuvered over the top of him, putting her body directly above, waiting, acting as if she were paralyzed in fear. She screamed hysterically when the man from the balcony got within five feet.

"Don't come closer! Don't do it."

The man below said, "Or what? You'll jump? Climb down now. We won't hurt you. We just want to know."

She said, "I . . . I can't." She began to hitch her breathing, saying, "I'm going to slip. I can't . . . I had nothing to do with this. . . . I'll tell you anything . . . just get me down."

The man below shouted in Russian again, and she waited. The killer on the scaffold reached her. She clung to the steel like it was life itself. He was surprisingly gentle, telling her she had nothing to fear. Telling her he would keep her alive.

He gave her instructions on what to do. How to get back up to the balcony ten feet away. When she looked below, he told her to never do that again, thinking he was helping her fear of heights. Not knowing she was judging the impact of his body, like a forward observer determining the strike of a mortar.

He reached out and touched her sleeve, smiling, letting her know he was no threat. She grimaced back, tears streaming down her face. She wrapped one arm into his and said, "Please don't let me fall."

He smiled, saying, "That won't happen. We won't hurt you. Follow me back." She nodded, then laced her legs around the steel beams, locking her ankles together. He saw what she did and had a spark of confusion on his face, not realizing she still held his arm. He started to encourage her again, and she let go of the scaffold with her other arm, slapping her hand into the clothing on his shoulder and ripping backward with all of her might.

Jennifer saw his eyes grow wide and felt his body begin to peel from the scaffolding. He tried to lock his feet into the steel like she had. They grunted in the exertion, her straining to remove him and him fighting to prevent it.

She started to win, his body inexorably losing its last tenuous hold on the metal latticework. He tried to hit her, but the motion caused him to lose precious inches with his legs. She heard the man below shout, but knew he couldn't shoot without hitting his friend.

Her target's feet slipped free and he slid out, held sixty feet above the ground by Jennifer's strength alone. He said, "Don't do this, don't do this, we weren't going to hurt you, don't do this."

Hanging upside down, holding his hands like a trapeze artist, she looked him in the eye and said, "Tell that to Decoy."

And let him go.

Before the body had even impacted, she raised herself up and caught the scaffolding in her hands, moving at lightning speed. Scampering like a monkey, she looked down and saw she'd missed with her dive-bomb, but not by much. The man below was lying on the ground, rolling about. He'd been struck, but it hadn't taken him out. Next to him was the body, lying on a splatter of liquid like a water balloon of red paint had exploded.

She scrambled across the latticework and reached the center of the cathedral on the far side, away from the killers. She dropped down and raced across the stone to the courtyard outside, looking behind to see what followed.

Her pursuer was still sitting on the ground holding the head of the man she had tossed, covered in his bodily fluids. He pointed his pistol and squeezed the trigger over and over, the rounds punching the air, but none of them found their mark, the one-handed grip not providing nearly enough control for him to hit her at this distance.

She ducked and sprinted out, the bullets snapping around her like bees. The weapon locked open on an empty magazine, and he screamed, "You are fucking dead! I will skin you alive!"

She hit the courtyard and kept running.

36

I stared out the window of my little hostel room, disgusted with my protectionism because the detainee was female. Upset that Jennifer had apparently corked my ability to kill without remorse. Taking another life was not an easy task, in combat or otherwise. The action required a healthy bit of emotion and a purity of deed, something Jennifer had somehow drained from me—at least as far as killing defenseless female assassins went.

I said, "You're lucky you're not a man."

Testing the rope tying her to the pipe, the detainee said her first words. "You're American."

I turned from the window, looking at her.

She sounded like an Australian, but the accent had a little tilt at the end. Something I couldn't put my finger on, but it was a tic I'd heard somewhere before. And it wasn't from any time I'd spent in Moscow.

Get her talking.

I leaned back against the wall and said, "Yeah. I'm American. Only I'm *really* from the United States. More so than you're from the land down under."

She ignored that and said, "Are you CIA?"

"Shit no. Did you see me pay someone with a suitcase of cash to jerk you off that bike?"

For some reason that brought a smile. But not enough talking. I asked, "What's your address in Australia?"

She rattled one off in a monotone, clearly having memorized it. But I knew I could crack that soon enough. I got a pen and paper, asking her for her hometown newspaper, nearest grocery store, price of gas, favorite radio station, and other mundane things that anyone would know if they really lived there.

She seemed smug, believing I couldn't prove any of her answers were wrong, knowing she was just being tested on how quickly she could think on her feet. On how much she could *seem* authentic. Right up until I said, "When we checked in there were two Australians sitting in the lobby. I'm going to take these questions and answers to them. When they don't pan out, I'm going to start inflicting pain."

Her smugness vanished. When I moved to the door she shouted, "Why do you give a damn about a Syrian?"

I stopped and said, "What Syrian?"

"You said I'd killed your friend. The Syrian. When did they become friends of the United States? When did you start to favor them over your real friends?"

Her words solved the puzzle, causing all the pieces to fall into place. I looked at her with new curiosity, kicking myself for missing the clues. She was dark haired with black eyes. She wasn't classically pretty, but attractive enough in a tomboy sort of way. In an *I served in the Israeli Army and never learned to be a girl* way.

Small waist and small breasts, she didn't look like the typical Jew I'd seen in Israel, but that's what she was. I was sure of it. The accent tic was from growing up speaking Hebrew. She'd managed to get rid of most of it, but a small amount had trickled out under stress.

The Uzi machine pistol and Australian passport were the kickers. No way would the Russians use an Uzi, a weapon invented and built in Israel. They had their own machine pistols, like the piece-of-shit

AEK-919K that the Russkis thought was the greatest thing since sliced bread.

Besides the gun, Mossad had conducted some high-profile targeted killings over the last few years, and they were known for using Australian passports for their operatives. It had become something of a signature.

I squatted in front of her until our eyes were six inches apart.

Looking for a reaction, I said, "I could give a shit about any Syrian. Why does Israel protect Boko Haram?"

She was good, I'll give her that, but there was still a tell. A small bit of shock that flitted across her face. She said nothing.

I said, "Look, I think we're working on different lines here. The man you killed was meeting the man I was following. Do you understand? We both were picking a terrorist thread, but from different directions."

When she remained silent, I slapped the ground and said, "Jesus Christ! I'm the one who could maintain an air of being a tourist. You pumped thirty rounds into a man from the back of a motorcycle in front of fifty people. Saying you're an Australian sightseer is stupid at this stage. We can help each other. There's someone protecting my target, and that someone killed my teammates. All I know is he's Russian."

I saw a flash of recognition. I'd hit a nerve somehow. She said, "I am not your enemy. I can prove it. Give me your phone. I can contact my boss."

I rolled my eyes. "What, some call center in Austria? I'm not stupid. You get my number, and your location is tracked."

"Go buy a cell phone. Let me use it, then take it out and throw it away."

I tried to poke a hole in her plan, but it was actually pretty solid. I could turn it on five seconds before, then off five seconds after. In one call, the most they'd get was which tower had registered the phone. And that would still leave about forty bazillion buildings she could be in.

I grinned and said, "That's not bad for an Australian tourist."

Before she could reply, my phone buzzed. I answered, hearing Jennifer. I smiled at her voice and said, "I was beginning to think you were in a Turkish prison like in *Midnight Express*."

She said, "Decoy's dead."

The smile faded from my face. Stupidly, I said, "What?"

She relayed what had happened after their initial call at the café. Relayed the savagery of the attack. Relayed what had become of Decoy, and her inability to stop it. Her voice broke, the pain as real as if it had come from a physical blow. Memories of Decoy floated in my mind's eye, and Jennifer's words accomplished what I couldn't on my own. She ripped the scab free.

And the blackness began to flow.

37

President Warren said, "Why does Kerry want to meet early?"

Alexander Palmer said, "I don't know. All he told me was he needed five minutes, and wanted me here. This was the only time we had available."

It was past six P.M., and they were meeting to determine a plan of attack for yet another congressional inquiry into the machinations of US intelligence. Looking to score points at home prior to election season, some congressional committee had decided to chair a hearing, purportedly because the administration had done something heinous. In reality they were probably hoping to generate enough waves for a shot at the nightly news, with committee members sternly discussing the transgressions in front of thousands of registered voters.

This time it was the budget. The so-called black budget. There was nothing they were going to find digging around that white whale, but the president still needed to ensure he understood the state of play, because he'd surely be asked at least one *When did you know . . .* question.

I'd really like to have Kurt go over there and brief them about the Taskforce budget. That would cause some heads to explode. The image brought a smile to his face.

Palmer said, "What?"

"Nothing. Kerry had better hurry, or we're going to have everyone here."

In addition to the D/CIA and the national security advisor, the meeting would include the secretary of defense, Mark Oglethorpe, and the director of national intelligence, Bruce Tupper. The SECDEF because the Department of Defense owned fully eighty percent of the operating intelligence community and the DNI because, well, he was the DNI.

Kerry Bostwick entered the Oval Office saying, "Sorry, sir. Traffic."

President Warren waved him to a chair and said, "So what crisis is there at the CIA?"

"You remember the thumb drive mission? The one the Israelis are after?"

"Yes?"

"Well, they cracked the encryption, and the good news is that there was no information other than directions to another thumb drive. Just like what happened with us."

"And the bad news?"

"No *real* bad news. Just sort of bad. I've passed the intelligence to Kurt, and he's prepping the team as we're speaking. The problem is that Bruce is intimately involved in this operation. I should have realized he would be, given the nature of the information we're trying to recover. As the DNI he's never really gotten down in the weeds before, but he is now."

"So why's that bad?"

Kerry paused, then said, "Well, he's demanding to know the particulars of the recovery operation. I can't tell him he has no need to know, because he's the damn DNI. Especially given the target. On the other hand, I don't like lying to him."

Palmer spoke for the first time. "You mean because of the Taskforce?"

"Yeah, exactly."

President Warren said, "What's the big deal? You keep the Taskforce secret from a host of official people. Do you feel bad about that as well?"

Kerry smiled. "No, of course not. But that's lying by omission. We just don't tell them what's going on. Basically the same thing I've been doing with the DNI since you appointed him. Now he's asking for specifics. What station, whether I'm deploying a team from here or using in-country assets. That sort of stuff. Even going so far as asking me the names. Besides me just not liking it, the guy is a legend in the CIA. He knows a ton of people, and no matter how secret we think we are, they'll talk."

Palmer said, "But they don't know anything."

"Precisely. Bruce is no idiot. When he isn't satisfied with my answer, and he goes to the old boys' network, he's going to get squat. Which is going to look very, very strange."

"What are you getting at?" asked President Warren. "You want to read him on?"

"Yes, sir. I do. He's the *director* of national intelligence. I understand the reason the Taskforce is so close hold, but keeping this from him is dysfunctional. It's just not right."

Palmer said, "You know why we did that, right?"

"Yeah, yeah, I get it. He's going to shit a brick. But in my mind, if you couldn't trust the director of national intelligence to be on board with your little unit, then you picked the wrong DNI. Or . . ."

Palmer said, "Or what?"

"Or maybe the unit isn't such a great idea."

President Warren started to bristle, and Kerry held up his hands. "Sir, you appointed me as D/CIA because I was candid. I'm just calling it like I see it."

Before the president could answer, the door opened again and the DNI and SECDEF entered.

Walking in front, Bruce moved right up to the Resolute desk and shook President Warren's hand, saying, "Another day in the inquisition. You never told me following the law was irrelevant when I took this job. I'm so glad I did."

President Warren thought Bruce Tupper was the correct choice when he'd nominated him, and still thought so today, but the man *was* a little bit of a kiss-ass. Something he had to tolerate as president. He smiled and said, "Well, from what I've read, it's you old-timers breaking the law that caused all the issues."

Bruce sat down, growing serious. "I completely agree. It just pisses me off that even when I *agree* with these assholes on oversight, it does no good. Because of what happened years ago, people pop up out of the woodwork, making accusations over smoke, and everyone believes it. Today it's the budget. Tomorrow it'll be something else. Hell, speaking of budgets, they ought to have a hearing on how much all these hearings are costing the taxpayer."

President Warren looked at Kerry, then Palmer. Both nodded. Bruce swiveled his head at both like he was watching a tennis match, then said, "What's going on? I feel like I'm the only one here who doesn't know what's about to be said."

Bruce turned to Oglethorpe, the SECDEF, who looked as confused as he did. President Warren said, "Palmer, get Kurt over here. Might as well get this over with."

Bruce said, "Get what over with?"

President Warren said, "We've got the location of the thumb drive."

"That's great news." Bruce looked at Kerry. "Do you have someone moving to intercept?"

"We do. The man Kerry's calling will give you a complete read-on."

"Read-on? To what? How is there a covert action occurring that I don't know about? Is there a finding?"

"Sort of. Just wait. It's not your typical covert action."

Bruce leaned back in his chair, surveying the group. He said, "This sounds like the same thing that caused the problem with the thumb drive in the first place."

"What do you mean?"

Bruce sighed, then said, "The Red Prince wasn't a paid asset. He wasn't a source. He was someone I was working on the side, off the books. He believed he was using the US, and I let him. If I'd followed procedures, he would have been given a crypt and the chief of station would have known about him. He would have been reported on. Munich might have been prevented."

"Why didn't you?"

"Why doesn't anyone? I was a young case officer full of piss and vinegar looking to make a name for myself. He was Yasser Arafat's number two. A huge coup, but if I'd have told anyone about him, he would immediately have been taken from me and given to someone with more experience. Which is what should have happened."

Kerry said, "You were paid to execute your judgment. So you pushed the boundaries. So what. You didn't cause Munich. You can't predict every twist and turn in the intelligence game."

"No, you can't, which is why we've got the left and right limits we do. Why there are procedures in the first place. I overheard him talking on the phone about the Olympics. If I'd had more experience, I would have connected the dots. At the very least, if I'd turned in a report, someone *else* could have connected the dots. After Munich, I *did* turn him over. It was agreed that I'd fucked up, but everyone just let it go. Robert Ames began to run him for real, and he got results. The PLO never attacked an American target while they were working together. The Red Prince died in '79 at the hands of the Mossad, then Bob was killed in Beirut in the '83 embassy bombing. And I learned a valuable lesson."

Nobody spoke for a moment, embarrassed at the personal nature of the disclosures. Palmer shifted his legs and President Warren broke the silence. "What was that, Bruce?"

"Never go off the reservation. Work the problem within the constraints given. It's gotten tougher over the years, with the House and Senate oversight committees, and especially the last year and a half with all the leaks, but doing otherwise breeds a culture of arrogance.

It breeds an organization that believes it is above the law, and some-times the organization begins to act that way. Begins to flout the Constitution in the name of the Constitution. Like I did in '72."

President Warren glanced at the other three men, then said, "I think you'd better get a glass of water. And maybe a paper bag to breathe into."

The other three men smiled, but Bruce narrowed his eyes. "Why?"

"Because Colonel Kurt Hale will be here soon, and he's going to tell you about an organization that flouts the Constitution in order to protect the Constitution."

38

I left the room as soon as I recognized Kurt Hale's voice, not wanting my captive to hear the conversation. He sounded like a skipping compact disc, forcing me to move to a window in the hallway for a better signal. The digital encryption of our Taskforce smartphones was unbreakable, but it also put a strain on the cell network. I said, "Sir, you broke up. Say again?"

He snapped, "Don't pull that shit on me."

He thought I was making it up, like radio operators used to do in the old days to prevent getting an order they didn't like. *"Assault that hill full of machine guns, over." "You're coming in broken and unreadable. Out."* In this case, I really couldn't understand what he was saying.

"Sir, I'm serious. I didn't hear you. Did Knuckles pass my SITREP?"

It was close to one in the morning, and the entire Taskforce was working to resolve the crisis we'd found ourselves in. First on the plate was protection of Taskforce assets, meaning we had to deal with the death of Decoy and prevent any clandestine associations from getting out. Second was to find out who'd killed him.

I'd remained in the backpacking hostel and called Knuckles, giving him a full situation report and setting in motion an invisible machine. He'd been shocked, of course, but he'd dealt with enough combat deaths that it wasn't debilitating, and as the team leader he had quite a bit to do. He began the intricate process of ensuring any investigation of the death ended as a random shooting near the bazaar. Decoy was going to become a victim of terrorism as an unlucky civilian. Acting as a vice president of Grolier Services, Knuckles had begun coordinating with the Turkish police and the US embassy for identification of the body and transport home, seeding a cover story of what Decoy was doing, both for his in-country status and his actions at the bazaar.

At the same time, the Taskforce casualty affairs group swung into motion, tying off any loose ends that might cause an unraveling of Decoy's Grolier Recovery Services employment. If there was any silver lining to the whole mess it was that Decoy was single. There would be no late-night knock on a wife's door, with a follow-on fabrication about a training accident. Something the wife would undoubtedly know was untrue, but would accept nonetheless.

While Knuckles worked the casualty extraction and cover firewall, I continued to press for information on Decoy's killers. I was one hundred percent sure that the chick I had roped to the sink was Israeli, but only about fifty percent sure she didn't have something to do with Decoy's death. I didn't think she knew who'd pulled the trigger, but I wasn't convinced it wasn't a case of mistaken identity. The killer might have believed he was also Israeli, that Decoy had been involved in the killing of the Syrian. Either way, I wanted to know what she knew.

After getting the initial report on the assault, I'd given Jennifer directions to my little safe house. While the phone call was all business, I could tell she was having difficulty dealing with the trauma, something I understood. Jennifer had known people who'd been killed, and had even killed herself, but Decoy was the first combat fatality of someone she was close to. It was the first time she'd lost a friend in the fight, and on top of that, she was probably blaming herself for the death. I'd seen the same thing plenty of times before in other operators.

Unfortunately, we didn't have the time to grieve. That would have to come later. Given the choice between grieving or killing the sorry sons of bitches who'd murdered him, I'm pretty sure Decoy would have told her to saddle up. Something I had every intention of doing.

When Jennifer had come in, she'd immediately closed on me, laying her head on my shoulder and starting to weep, unaware of the visitor I had lashed to a pipe. In dealing with Decoy's death and worrying about getting Jennifer off the streets, I had neglected to say anything to her about my prisoner. I put my arms around her and gave her a squeeze, then lifted her head, looking into her eyes.

She started to talk and I held a finger to her lips, saying, "I caught one of the killers on the motorcycle." She looked confused, and I pointed behind her.

She saw my prisoner and turned back around, whispering, "Is she Russian?"

"No, why? Because of the guy I fought in Bulgaria?"

"No, because the other men chasing me spoke Russian. I'm pretty sure I killed the asshole you fought."

I held a finger to my lips and led her outside the room into the hallway, out of earshot. She managed to give me a thorough debrief, only breaking down once when describing Decoy's demise. When she got to the part about the Hagia Sofia museum, she began to shake. But she continued to talk, because it was expected of her. In the soft glow of the single incandescent bulb, her body trembling in reaction to how close she had come to dying, she kept talking.

I could see the toll, and when I'd heard enough I stopped her and brought her close. Letting her vomit her emotions out. Letting her know it was okay to do so.

I understood she was going to beat herself up over Decoy's death, but *he* wouldn't have allowed it. She had shown a real talent, both physically and mentally. It was a miracle they *both* weren't dead. Decoy's assassination was something she'd have to work through, but in the end, it had nothing to do with her abilities. It might take awhile for her to figure that out, and I'd help as best I could.

Right after I killed the fuckers who'd done it.

I held her until the trembling stopped, then told her about the cell phone plan for the Israeli, asking if she was up for finding a drop phone. She pulled back and looked at me like I was insane, and I'd felt like an ass. Before I could retract the statement, she agreed, wiping her eyes and getting back into the mission. I gave her some cash and directed her to the shopping area of Ordu Caddesi, the four-lane boulevard only a couple of blocks away.

I spent the time she was gone coordinating with Knuckles and developing a linkup plan with the captive's boss. Coming up with a method to keep an Israeli hit team from storming my room. When Jennifer returned, I was on a final call with Knuckles. I heard someone speak behind me, and saw Jennifer talking to my captive. I hissed and got her to back away.

I hung up and said, "What was that about?"

"She told me she was sorry about Decoy. Sorry she caused the chain of events."

Huh?

Jennifer was too damn naïve to realize when she was being manipulated.

I looked at the captive, getting a blank stare back. Jennifer said, "You guys distrust everyone. She meant it. I don't think she's bad."

I said, "What, you got women's intuition? How would you know what's bad? You only see the good."

She looked at the detainee, then back at me, wanting to say something, but holding it in. Knowing I'd never believe it. I took the drop phone out of her hand and squatted down in front of the detainee.

"Time to prove you're innocent. You want to get out of here, all you have to do is show you aren't culpable for the death of my men. Get your boss here."

Sagging against the rope, she said, "You know we cannot give you what you want."

"Why? I thought we were 'friends' and all."

She shook her head and said, "Friends are people you go to parties with. We are not friends. We are allies. A totally different thing. My boss will not help you. I should never have said that before. It was a mistake."

I said, "Then what the fuck are we doing here? You said you'd help."

"I would. I really would, after what I saw. But I can't."

That did nothing but stoke the flame of my anger. I felt the darkness start to flow into the room like a fog I had no control over.

I said, "What do you mean, you can't? What the hell does that mean? You *will* call."

I looked at Jennifer, wanting her to stop what was coming. Wanting her to prevent the blackness from spreading, because if she didn't, I wasn't sure how far I would go. She did nothing, and the abyss beckoned.

I held the phone out, my voice flat-line cold, all emotion leached out of it. "Make the call."

She closed her eyes, remaining silent. My hand snapped out, seemingly of its own accord, and snatched my little captive by the throat. Her eyes popped open and began to bug out.

39

I watched her struggle with detached indifference. I said, "Make. The. Call," and Jennifer slapped my arm, snapping me out of my destructive dance. The blackness retreated like a roach caught in the light. Embarrassed at my loss of control, I sat back, afraid to look Jennifer in the eye. Not wanting to feel her disgust. When I did, instead of revulsion, I saw compassion. In that moment, I knew I wouldn't be helping her with Decoy's death. She would be helping me.

She put her hand on my biceps and said, "Don't."

I nodded, wondering if she could feel the relief flooding through my veins. I leaned forward into my captive's personal space, and in her eyes I recognized I'd lost. She knew I wasn't going to hurt her. All of my leverage had vanished.

She looked at me with something akin to pity and said, "Okay. I *am* Israeli. Not Australian. You were correct."

Amazed, I just stared at her. She said, "Give me the phone."

I said, "Wait, what happened to the Australian cover? Why would you tell me that? After Jennifer just stopped me from hurting you? After you knew I wouldn't go further?"

She looked at the wall, then came back to me. She exhaled and said, "Because I saw you with her."

Confused, I said, "What's that got to do with it?"

She said, "Everything. Give me the phone."

We stared at each other for a few seconds, and I made my decision. I leaned in and untied her left wrist, affixing the cord to the pipe above her head. I knew allowing her to have one free hand was giving her an edge, but, given the odds, I figured she was a righty.

She patiently waited for me to finish, offering no resistance. When I was done, I sat down in front of her, holding the phone. She said, "What do you want me to say?"

Off-balance, I said, "Tell him your situation. If he's an ally, as you say, he'll be willing to come talk. I'll give him the linkup plan."

I gave her the cell phone, then said, "Before you call, no Hebrew. You talk in a language I can't understand, and I'm smashing the phone."

She nodded, and dialed. In English, I heard her telling him about the killing at the bazaar, giving up any pretense of being uninvolved. She described her predicament, then what I had told her about my men being attacked by a Russian. She listened for a little bit, then passed the phone to me.

The man on the other end said, "Who am I talking with?"

His voice was deep, the English unaccented, as if he came from the Midwest.

I said, "Not an Australian tourist, that's for damn sure."

"What do you want?"

"I want who killed my men. Plain and simple."

"We had nothing to do with that."

"Honestly, I don't think you did, but I believe you know who was involved. And I want that information."

"How do I know I'm not walking into a trap? That you're not just setting me up to kill both me and Shoshana?"

Shoshana. Even sounds like a spy. "Because if I were, Shoshana here would have given you the distress signal. But she did not."

I heard only breathing for a second, then, "How do you know?"

Between the lines, he was asking if I had somehow managed to torture the distress signal out of Shoshana. Wondering if she had compromised his entire cell, laying bare much more than just Shoshana's life. Probably questioning whether Shoshana was missing fingers and eyes.

I said, "I know because Shoshana is the one who came up with this idea. I know because I'm starting to like her. I know because this isn't my first rodeo."

"What do you mean, rodeo?"

I rolled my eyes and said, "Never mind. Do you want the linkup plan, or am I going to assume Shoshana here is extraneous dead weight? I understand you're trying to track this phone, so give me an answer quickly. In another five seconds, I'm ditching it whether you're coming in or not."

I glanced at Shoshana and saw her suppressing a grin, which really pissed me off. He opted for the plan, so I gave it to him. When I was done, I hung up and said, "What's so funny?"

"He doesn't like being dictated to."

Jennifer smiled and said, "Huh, neither does Pike."

I shot her a dirty look and said, "Cut that shit out. We aren't partners, and we aren't friends. I'm not even sure we're allies." I squatted down and retied her loose left hand, saying, "She's a detainee. Period."

Now I got the look of disgust. Jennifer turned without a word and left, executing the linkup with the boss. I remained behind, sitting on the bed and feeling Shoshana's dark eyes on me. She said nothing for a while, then asked my name.

I didn't see any reason to lie, since I was here under my true name anyway. I said, "Nephilim Logan. But you can call me Pike."

She said, "Nephilim? As in Old Testament?"

"Yes, unfortunately. Which is why you can call me Pike."

We sat in silence for a moment, then she tried again. "The Nephilim were angels that came to earth as giants. Great warriors."

I said, "As far as I know, they came to my parents in a marijuana haze. The name's given me nothing but grief. Like the boy named Sue."

She looked at me quizzically, and once again, I said, "Never mind."

She said, "Can I get you to untie me, as a gesture of goodwill?"

I said, "No."

She'd started to reply when my phone rang. It was Kurt, surprising the hell out of me. I warned the captive not to try anything funny, then went out into the hallway. I wondered why he was contacting me directly instead of going through Knuckles, since he'd made such a stink about Knuckles being the team leader. The surprise ended when I was finally able to get a signal next to the hallway window. He wanted to get me under control.

"Sir, I can hear you now. Say again?"

"I said I got your SITREP. I'm sorry about Decoy, but we've got the thumb drive location. Well, not the pinpoint, but the general. The pinpoint will be coming in at any time, and we now have two priorities: protecting the Taskforce, which is what Knuckles is now engaged in, and getting that drive, which is what I want you to do."

I said, "What about Decoy? What about the Russian assassins?"

"That's not an Oversight Council priority right now. I've sent the location of the drive to your Grolier account. It's not manpower intensive, but it is time sensitive. Go ahead and recce the area so when the pinpoint comes in you can execute immediately."

I couldn't believe he was treating Decoy's death so lightly. I said, "Sir, someone's killed our men. In cold blood. This isn't like combat. It's murder. I can't let it go. I'm not going to do that. I have a person here who may know what's going on."

"Pike, no more operational acts. I understand how you feel, but it's too risky to do anything under Grolier. We need to get Decoy home and patch any holes we have, not create more."

When I didn't answer, he said, "Remember what we talked about before? About how your company fits in to the Taskforce? You told me you would follow orders."

Which is why he was speaking to me in person. He feared I'd tell

Knuckles to pack sand as the team leader, so he called to give me a direct order. One I wasn't going to obey.

I said, "Sir, we didn't talk about this. They *killed* Decoy."

I heard movement in the single stairwell, and a man reached the landing, followed by Jennifer. They entered the room, leaving the door open. He glanced at my captive tied to the sink, then put his eyes on me back in the hallway. He was dressed like a businessman, but the similarities ended with his clothes. He was furtive and predatory, like a jackal.

I heard a beep on the phone and Kurt cursed. He said, "Hold on. I got a priority call."

The man squatted down and began to whisper to the detainee, keeping me in sight while he did so. Kurt came back on the line. "That was Palmer, national security advisor. I have to go to the White House."

"The president?"

"I don't know, but I'm out of time. Are we good? You're on the thumb drive?"

"Yes, sir. I'll get your thumb drive as ordered, but I'm also going to find the men who put the hit out on us."

Exasperated, he said, "How? Pike, you've got no team. Knuckles, Brett, and Retro have stood down. They followed orders. You need to do the same. Let it go."

The man stood up from the detainee and faced me, all hard edges and unspoken threats.

I said, "Maybe I have a new team."

"New team? What the hell are you talking about?"

"Sir, I'm sorry. I'm going to find the organization that killed my friends. And I'm going to burn it down."

40

Bruce Tupper appeared so overwhelmed by what he was hearing that President Warren thought his head was going to explode. And Kurt hadn't even shown up for the official briefing yet.

Bruce said, "How long has this been going on?"

President Warren said, "Since my first term. Long before I appointed you."

He looked each man in the eye. "And all of you know about it? Why the hell wasn't I told?"

"It's not part of the official intelligence architecture. Not part of your portfolio."

"Bullshit!" Bruce exclaimed. "That's just semantics. You've got me getting skewered at one congressional oversight committee after another, proclaiming we follow the Constitution and United States code, and you have an entire organization doing exactly what the conspiracy theorists say. You've made me a fucking liar."

President Warren said, "Okay, Bruce, okay. Calm down. The conspiracy theorists talk about an unchecked intelligence apparatus doing whatever it wants without oversight. This has oversight and doesn't do anything without express approval from the very top. Meaning me, the men in this room, and about a dozen others. Now including you. You weren't lying if you didn't know."

Bruce said, "Nobody will believe that. Nobody will believe that the director of national intelligence had no knowledge of such a large, intrusive organization."

"I'm sorry, Bruce, but you understand how sensitive this is. You also understand 'need to know.' You had no need to know."

Before Bruce could answer, the door to the Oval Office opened. President Warren said, "This is Colonel Kurt Hale. Commander of Project Prometheus, the organization we call the Taskforce."

Bruce grimly shook his hand, not saying a word. Confused, reading the vibe from the DNI, Kurt clasped his hand, but said to the president, "Sir, I really need to talk to you. There are some issues that have evolved."

President Warren said, "We'll get to that, I'm sure. You brought the brief, correct?"

Kurt held up a laptop and said, "Yes, sir, but I'm not so sure now is the time—"

President Warren said, "Give him the read-on. Get done with that, and we'll talk about any issues later."

Kurt's said, "Sir, I have some information I really need to brief. Right now. It can't wait. Something that's operationally critical, but it's only for cleared personnel."

President Warren said, "Kurt, I hear you. Give Bruce the read-on, then we'll all be cleared."

Kurt looked like he was about to say something else, then went from the president to the director of the CIA. Resigned, seeing no help, he opened a laptop and set it on the president's desk.

The read-on began, as it always did, with a history of the Taskforce, discussing how the Cold War intelligence and Department of Defense architecture was causing risk to the nation after 9/11. Describing how all offensive options had been stalled because of bitter infighting between organizations or because the enormous labyrinth of laws and regulations prevented action, each new one grafted onto the skeleton of the old without thought to the repercussions.

Alexander Palmer saw Bruce roll his eyes and said, "What? You live through a different time than me?"

Bruce said, "Hey, I understand what he's saying, but everything you're talking about is exactly what I'm dealing with on a day-to-day basis. The repercussions and lack of trust. Patriot Act, NSA surveillance, secret prisons—all of it came about after 9/11, and now you're telling me that wasn't enough? We had to create something so outside the legislative process that it would be called a secret police in any country behind the Iron Curtain?"

Kurt Hale said, "Sir, I understand how you could think that just seeing the slide, but it's not true. Your statement was my greatest fear when I helped build this thing. It's not an American gestapo. It's just a tool. A tool that's selectively used when the traditional architecture fails."

Bruce said, "It's fucking secret police. I've seen enough of them in my time. I'm the one that worked through the Cold War. I'm the one who fought the assholes behind the Iron Curtain. Don't try to sugarcoat the turd just because it's American."

President Warren said, "Bruce, you can't look at the organizational structure and determine intent. All we did was basically hit a reset for the '47 National Security Act. The Taskforce operates just like the CIA did when it was first created. Before all the smothering of legal restrictions."

"You mean before our democracy found out the CIA was abusing its power and voted to rein it in. How often has the Taskforce operated in the United States?"

Kurt flipped to the next slide and said, "I was just getting there. As you can see by the charter the Taskforce operates under, it's not allowed to work on United States soil."

Bruce said, "That's not what I asked. How often has it, in contravention to the charter?"

Kurt remained silent, looking toward the president. He said, "Okay,

Bruce, you've made your point. It has conducted some limited operations on US soil, but always under close supervision of the Oversight Council."

Bruce said, "And that's how it starts. It's never an inherently evil thing. It's always for some greater good. Something that has to be done just this once. Until it becomes twice, then three times, then normal operating procedure. People in the organization end up believing they know better than the oversight."

President Warren said, "Which is exactly why I'm reading you on. You won't allow that to happen."

Bruce said nothing for a moment, then said, "Sir, I can't be a party to this. When it gets out—and it will get out—it will cause our entire intelligence apparatus to be eviscerated. And rightly so."

"What are you saying?"

"I'm saying we need to disband the Taskforce."

President Warren let that hang in the air for a moment, then said, "Right now, they're the only ones with the capability to get your thumb drive. You want to pull them from that?"

Bruce looked to Kerry. "I thought you said you had CIA assets working the problem?"

Kerry said, "No, sir. I said I had assets, but not specifically CIA. The Taskforce is tailor-made for this type of mission."

President Warren watched Bruce's face grow red. He said, "Wait, Kerry is the one who demanded you be read on. Don't go off on him."

Bruce said, "Sir, I spent my entire life fighting against organizations like this. The Stasi, KGB, you name it. At the same time, we supported other evil fucks like the Shah's Savak. I've seen what happens, and I don't want to be a party to it."

President Warren said, "Okay, let's focus on one problem at a time. Kurt, skip to the chase. You passed the thumb drive mission, correct?"

"Yes, sir. They have the mission, but there's been a problem. And it's serious. We lost a Taskforce member."

Kurt briefly described what had transpired, and Bruce became visibly agitated. He said, "It's already falling apart."

Kerry said, "Bruce, calm down. We've dealt with this in the past. Kurt, can you handle the casualties *and* get the thumb drive?"

"Yes. We're already working that."

Bruce said, "As soon as they get the thumb drive, they redeploy. They close up shop and come home."

Kurt grimaced and said, "That may be a problem."

41

Yuri ordered the cab to pull over and exited, paying the man much more than was necessary to keep him quiet. It was dark, and he'd managed to wash the blood off of his hands at a public bathing stall, but his shirt was still stained, so he gave the cabdriver every incentive to forget him.

He walked down Ordu Caddesi toward his hotel, feeling more secure when he began to pass shops with Cyrillic writing. The stores were closed, but the nightclubs were still pumping on a full tank, and all catered to Eastern Europeans with specials and sales spelled out in the Russian language. A little bit of Moscow in the heart of Istanbul.

He turned left on Laleli Caddesi, in the heart of little Russia, and finally pulled out his cell phone. He dialed Vlad, knowing that waking him up would not be pleasant. But neither would telling him the awful truth in the morning.

To his surprise, Vlad answered after the second ring, saying, "What happened? The Turks are going crazy."

"We had an incident. The Americans interceded."

"Switch your SIM card. Call me back on the second number I gave you. It goes to VOIP."

Yuri did as he asked, wishing for the encrypted phones they usually used, but knowing the signature would swiftly bring the Turkish intelligence establishment. At least the constant switching of SIM cards and the use of voice over Internet protocols would make it a matter of luck for MIT to be listening.

This time, Vlad answered on the first ring. Yuri briefly described what had occurred, relaying that he'd lost both Mishka and Dmitri.

Vlad said, "Damage?"

"Sir? They're dead."

"I understand that. I mean what is the damage to the operation."

"Mishka is covered under the consulate in Bulgaria. He was killed by gunfire, but it will be protected by the fact that the Syrian and an American were also killed. The American assassins on the motorcycle will be blamed for all three. Nobody is going to check ballistics. Dmitri was working under a private company cover, but he has no gunshot. I left him where he lay, and he'll be found in the morning. Most likely, it'll look like he broke in for some reason, climbed the scaffolding, and fell to his death."

"So no compromise with the authorities? No encounters with police?"

"None."

"Good. What is Akinbo's status? Was he harmed?"

"No, sir. I contacted him and he's okay. He's currently hiding in a mosque inside the Grand Bazaar. I have no idea how he knew to go there, but it's probably the safest place he could have found. I've told him to stay put until further orders."

"Excellent. And can you still operate?"

"Yes, but I'm down to three men."

Vlad continued as if that mattered little. "Good, because I've learned where Boris hid his thumb drive. It's in the Cistern in the old town."

The comment gave Yuri pause. As had happened with men throughout Russian history, Yuri wondered if he was being set up for a fall. He certainly wouldn't put it past Vlad, and the FSB chief showed little concern about the men he'd lost. Perhaps he was simply tidying up a few loose ends.

Because there's no way he has any information on a thumb drive or Israeli intentions to retrieve it.

He said, "You want me to go get it?"

"No. I don't know specifically where, and neither does the Israeli. That information will be coming soon, I'm sure. I want you to interdict him."

"Why not just get the drive?"

"We will, if we get that information, but I don't believe that will happen. All I may get is confirmation that the Israeli has the location. From there, our only option will be interdiction. You can recognize him, correct?"

"Yes, of course."

"Then we will not have an issue."

The entire exchange caused Yuri's survival instinct to spike. He said, "Sir, what about the men we lost? What are we doing about that?"

"What do you want me to do? I can't bring back the dead."

"Sir, we were penetrated. Someone is working the inside to Akinbo. There's no other way the Americans got here so quickly."

"No, no. That's not the information I'm getting."

Yuri thought, *Information you're getting? What does that mean?*

Vlad continued, "I believe they were tracking the Syrian as well. When they lost Akinbo, they reverted to the Syrian. He's the leak."

"Sir, that's too much coincidence. Way too much."

Vlad said, "Think about it; if they penetrated our Russian operation, why didn't they target your men first? Why did they assassinate the Syrian, then let your men simply walk up on them? Mishka killed one outright, didn't he?"

"Yes. He did."

"The assassination was tight, but the follow-up was sloppy, which tells me they didn't know about us."

"That may be true, but they do now. We should hunt them before they come back on us."

"We will. I promise we will. First, I want that thumb drive. Then, I want to get Akinbo moving again."

He said, "Sir, please, turn me loose. Let me hunt them like I did the Chechens." Then, what Vlad had said penetrated. "What do you mean, get Akinbo moving? We lost the operational objective. We don't have any chemical munitions from Syria."

"I know. But we have something else. I've come up with a different plan. One that we control. One that'll be much, much better than dealing with incompetent Arabs from Syria."

"What?"

"I want to meet in person for that. I'll send you an e-mail for linkup instructions. For the time being, get Akinbo moving to Berlin."

42

K neeling down and speaking Hebrew, Aaron Bergmann asked Shoshana if she'd been hurt. She said no, then said, "They lost a man because of our target. The leader in the hallway is on the edge. I can smell it like burning sulfur. Be careful."

"Are they CIA?"

"I don't know what they are, but it's not CIA. The man outside is hard. Very, very hard. He's a predator. The girl is skilled as well. She killed two."

Aaron took that in, reassessing what he knew. Shoshana was somewhat of an empath, with the preternatural ability to slice through subterfuge and see the true nature of people. On top of that, she was a predator in her own right. Nothing scared her, and yet this team had given her pause. He was the leader, and she would do whatever he asked, but he'd learned to listen to her. Learned the hard way, through lost blood.

He watched the man pace back and forth with the phone and saw a glimpse of what she meant. A sliver of something feral and deadly.

The girl, on the other hand, gave off no killer vibe. A tall brunette, she looked like someone who would be more at home working in an animal shelter than on some covert team.

But looks were deceiving. Along with Shoshana's statement about killing two men, the girl had just executed an elaborate linkup plan that guaranteed her protection. It wasn't the work of an amateur.

Aaron said, "What do you think?"

"I'm not sure. I don't know who they work for, and the man definitely has an edge. He's capable of anything, but the girl isn't. She
wouldn't be here if they were killing for hire. Because of that, if I were
forced to choose, I'd say they're government."

Aaron smiled. "Maybe you're just smitten."

She smiled back, saying, "She doesn't swing that way. She's with
him. They're a couple. In fact, I think she's the one keeping him in
check. He's starting to lean into the abyss because he lost his man, and
if something happens to her, it will swallow him. He'll destroy everything in his way. And I think he'll succeed."

Aaron watched the man hang up his phone and come inside, closing the door.

They sized each other up for a moment, then Aaron said, "Your
partner searched me before allowing me to follow. Can I do the same?"

The man nodded and held out his arms. Aaron conducted a brief
but thorough screen, finding no weapons. When he finished, he said,
"So what do you want from us?"

"You killed a Syrian in the bazaar. Because of it, I lost a friend. I
want to know what you know. I want to know why you targeted the
Syrian and who was helping him."

Aaron said, "Who are you?"

"Who I am is of little consequence. All you need to worry about is
what I'll do. I'm going to eradicate whoever harmed my men. You will
help, or I'll start right here, right now."

The brunette showed alarm at his words, then Aaron saw her place
a hand on his shoulder from behind. He glared at her, but didn't make
her remove it. Aaron glanced at Shoshana, and she nodded.

"Okay. Against my better judgment I'm going to dispense with the
games. I have no idea who killed your man. I had nothing to do with
it, but I spent a great deal of time preparing for my mission. Part of
that work was hijacking the various camera feeds outside of the café.

There were three, and I cut the video to hamper authorities. Forcing them to rely on eyewitnesses for their evidence."

He smiled and said, "Imagine trying to solve the Kennedy assassination without the Zapruder film. You would get nothing but conflicting reports from the people there."

The man said, "I'm not here to pat you on the back about your excellence in killing. Get to the part where this helps. Why do I care about the lack of video?"

"Because I didn't just delete the feeds. I redirected them. I have them on the laptop at my hotel, and they might help you figure out who attacked your men."

The man leaned back, skepticism on his face. The brunette said, "So you'll help?"

Aaron said, "That depends. First, what is your intention with Shoshana? Second, what assurances do I have that you won't take what I show you and attempt to use the information, either with the Turks or someone else?"

The man said, "You have no assurances other than my word. I don't give a shit about anything you've done over here. From what Shoshana's said, killing that fuck was probably a good thing, so you won't get a rise out of me. As for Shoshana, I'll release her as soon as you do what you say."

Aaron stuck out his hand, "My name is Aaron Bergmann. We have a deal."

The man shook it and said, "I'm Pike Logan. This is Jennifer." He bared his teeth in a humorless smile. "We're an archaeological firm here looking at old shit for a client. What do you do in the business world?"

Jennifer untied Shoshana, and she stood, rubbing her wrists. "His real name is Nephilim."

Aaron raised an eyebrow and said, "As in Genesis?"

Pike said, "Yes, damn it. As in Genesis by way of Woodstock. Jesus."

"Jesus? I hear he was a pretty good carpenter."

Shoshana coughed to hide a smile and Aaron saw Pike's face grow dark at the humor, believing it was at his expense. Aaron backed off. "Okay, so we've built some limited trust. How do you propose to get to my hotel without falling into my diabolical trap that I'm sure you're worried about?"

Pike said, "Call the fuckers off. Simple."

"You'd trust that?"

"No. Which is why Jennifer will stay here with Shoshana."

"Jennifer can't take out Shoshana. She has no weapon, and my girl is a killer."

"Jennifer's staying here as a backup to come get me if you try to screw us. I don't need her to fight. You pull any shit and you'll know the meaning of total destruction. I will not spare anyone. Do you understand?"

Bemused at the bravado, Aaron said, "You have no weapon either."

"Really? Look again. I *am* the weapon."

The absolute confidence from the statement caused the small grin to fade from Aaron's face. He dialed his phone.

43

Thirty minutes later Aaron pulled his rental car into the security circle of the Conrad Hilton in Beyoglu, across the Bosphorus Strait. A listless guard ran a mirror under the frame, then let him pass.

Aaron parked, then said, "There's a metal detector inside the door. In case you really do have a weapon."

Pike said, "I don't. But if I did, I'm fairly sure nobody at that security checkpoint would stop me. Unless this hotel is different from the others I've seen."

Aaron opened the door, saying, "Nope. That's about right."

They entered the lobby, passing through the metal detector. Both of their cell phones made it go off, but they were waved forward by the man watching the X-ray machine.

Aaron shook his head and said, "One day they'll regret showing nothing but a facade of security. If this were Israel I'd teach him a valuable lesson. Follow me. Elevators are this way."

He entered, placed his key-card in the slot, and punched the button for the ninth floor. They rode up in silence. Exiting out into the small lobby, Aaron said, "The man you saw on the motorcycle, Daniel, is in the room. He's not happy with you. Please do not antagonize him."

Pike said, "Tell him to keep his hands to himself and we'll be fine."

They passed ten or twelve rooms before Aaron stopped and knocked once on a door. He waited a bit, then knocked again, this one a double tap, then used his key. A wiry man with a pockmarked face, thinning black hair, and a four-day growth of beard stood on the other side, his hands behind his back.

Aaron closed the door and said, "Daniel, this is Nephilim. He's no threat."

Daniel squinted at the name. "Nephilim? As in the Old Testament?"

Exasperated, Pike shook his head and said, "Why do you people give a shit about that? Are you all Rabbis? I go by Pike."

Daniel rotated his hands to the front, exposing a Glock 17. He ignored Pike's outburst, speaking to Aaron instead. "Sir, video footage is loaded in the bedroom, ready to go."

"Thank you." Aaron pointed a hand toward the room. "Pike?"

On the bed was a fifteen-inch MacBook, the screen opened to a grainy still from a video camera. Aaron could make out a streetlight, but little else.

Daniel said, "There were three cameras on the street, none aimed lengthwise down it. All three were focused directly out from a storefront, protecting the store. Luckily for us, all were wireless, so we had little trouble interdicting the signal. It was much harder hijacking it and recording, but I felt that would be prudent."

Aaron said, "I fought him on that decision, but he insisted. I suppose you should thank him because otherwise you'd have nothing."

Pike nodded and said, "I still might have nothing."

Daniel said, "The first is from the north, the direction I came from. You'll see me go by, then I think you'll see your men."

He hit "play" and the image sputtered forward in a jerking manner, the frames skipping faster than real time in order to save hard drive space. The view was an outdoor café, people sitting around tables eating and drinking. Behind them was the street.

Daniel said, "I've chopped it to just the particulars. Watch now."

The small motorcycle came in view for a slice of time, two people on it, then nothing for five seconds. Abruptly, the people at the café all stood, some waving their arms, others looking bewildered. One male stood on a chair, and Pike said, "That's my man."

Daniel said, "I thought so." Knowing what was coming next, he said, "Do you wish to stop?"

"No."

The tape ran forward, a silent, unforgiving testament. They saw the crowd gather, then saw a bear of a man bull through them, a pistol in his hand. It spit fire, and the man on the chair's head snapped back. Aaron saw Pike begin to clench his fists, and wondered if he should turn the video off. Wondered if he should have insisted the girl, Jennifer, come as well.

Pike said, "Do you know him?"

Aaron said, "No, and I think I would remember someone of that size."

"When I met him in Bulgaria he had a card saying he worked for the Russian embassy in Sofia."

Daniel said, "It's irrelevant. He's about to die. Watch."

Aaron saw the woman known as Jennifer rise from the ground, previously hidden. She began to fight, and he was amazed she had survived. Shoshana hadn't mentioned the size of the opponent or the violence of the action.

It was hard to see on the grainy image, but somehow, she managed to disarm him, then the pistol began flashing, hitting the man over and over. Within seconds, it was done, the last image showing her stabbing the barrel into the bear's forehead, then pulling the trigger.

Aaron glanced at Pike and saw him panting with shallow breaths. Trying to dilute the adrenaline flowing through him from what he'd seen. On the screen, Jennifer took off running, disappearing from view. Pike leaned in close, then said, "Stop it. Stop right there. Back it up."

"What are you looking for?"

"She was chased. I want to see that man."

Daniel did so, going back and forth until they had the image, but the best they got was a back shot of a man running away, only on the screen for a split second.

Daniel said, "He came from the south, so maybe one of the other cameras got it."

The second feed was from the target café itself, but it showed only a narrow slice of about forty-five degrees from the front door. Zero from the tables.

The motorcycle appeared, then nothing. Three seconds after, there was a brief flurry of chaos as a jumbled mass of people ran back and forth. Finally, a man came out from the interior of the restaurant, walking underneath the camera and speaking on a cell phone. He was wearing the same clothes as the runner from the first tape, but his back was to the camera. When he turned to look down the street, giving a profile shot, Pike said, "Stop it."

The frame froze, and Aaron answered the unspoken question. "No again. He's Caucasian, but I don't know him."

"Can you print that? For future reference?"

Daniel said, "No. We don't have a printer, but I can put it on a flash drive."

"That'll work. Anything more?"

"Just the last tape, but it's farther down the street, away from the café. Around the bend, closer to the bazaar. There's not much to it."

"Run it."

They watched nothing for a moment, then caught the motorcycle flying by, the person on the back wrapped tightly against the driver. After it disappeared, a man entered the view of the camera, walking head-on to the lens.

This time it was Aaron who spoke. "Stop it."

44

The figure remained on the screen, a hand to his ear, frozen in time talking into a cell phone. Pike looked at the image, then at Aaron. "You know him? Who is he?"

Aaron leaned in close, studying the face. When he turned back, he said, "I believe that man is Yuri Gorshenko, code name Jarilo. Works for the Russian FSB."

Pike said, "How do you know?"

"It's my business to know. He's the leader of the Berlin group, a team of Russian Special Forces that target Chechen insurgents. He's killed them all over the world. Last year, he took an interest in supporting a Palestinian we had under watch. Nothing ever happened between them that we could prove, but we kept our eyes on the group because of it."

"The FSB operates externally? I thought they were like our FBI?"

Aaron said, "Seriously?"

"Yeah, seriously."

"I guess that answers the question of whether you're CIA. The FSB is the Russian security apparatus that took over from the KGB. They started out like your FBI, but they're much, much more like the old KGB now. If you were a spook, you'd know that."

"Like I told Shoshana, I'm not in that racket. I deal in substate terrorist threats. I don't follow state security organizations unless it has to do with terrorism directed at the United States, so my knowledge is limited to what you would expect. You and the Mossad, Iranian IRGC, Saudi Arabian Mukhabarat, that sort of thing."

Aaron said, "They weren't on my radar either, until they started connecting with Palestinian terrorists. The FSB has grown deadly, with no moral restraints and a lot of organized criminal connections. Their roots run deep through the government as well. It's run by Vladimir Malikov—known as Vlad the Impaler—an old KGB hand who thinks Stalin was soft."

Staring past Aaron, thinking, Pike nodded his head. "That name rings a bell, but I have no idea why. It'll come to me." He focused back on Aaron. "Okay, so this Berlin group is somehow involved with my Boko Haram guy. They're protecting him, which means they've got a plan in motion and it's not about selling counterfeit Amway products. They're going to attack someone."

Aaron said, "Perhaps."

"So you should want to help me here. Help me stop them."

"No. I should not. This isn't my fight. I have other priorities. Anyway, whatever plan they had in motion was destroyed by Daniel and Shoshana. There will be no attack."

"Maybe. Maybe not. Why do you know so much about this Vlad guy?"

"Because we do not trust him. He's linked to terrorist events."

"Precisely. So you should want to help me get rid of the Berlin group, beyond killing the Syrian. You stopped the symptom, but I'm talking about halting the disease."

"Why are you asking for my help? You're the mighty United States."

"Yeah, well, even that's not enough sometimes. You've already done the work. You could give me a lead to Yuri right now, if you wanted. Couldn't you?"

Aaron said nothing for a moment, considering. Then: "As a matter of fact, Vlad the Impaler is here, in Istanbul right now. He doesn't know we know because he thinks he's clever, but we track him fairly closely."

Pike considered that. "Your point is, it's not a coincidence he's here? He's got something to do with the meeting you broke up?"

"I'm not saying anything. Maybe he's just here for the food and the women. He's meeting someone tomorrow at a restaurant that's about a quarter of a mile from the Russian consulate. He never strays far from there when he's in town. I can give you the specifics of the meeting, but that's it."

"How do you know that?"

Aaron smiled. "Your NSA is powerful, but not the only agency in the world with collection capability. We can do a thing or two ourselves. We intercepted an e-mail about the same time you were interrogating Shoshana."

"Can you get me the selectors? Get me something to track on my own? The e-mail address? Phone number, ISP, anything?"

"No. No way. I give that to you and it'll be compromised within twenty-four hours. The United States isn't the best at keeping secrets, and we'd lose our ability to monitor him."

"Does he travel with a smartphone, or some Soviet-era brick cell phone? Do they even have smartphones in Russia? At least tell me that."

"Yes. He has a smartphone. And yes, it accesses the Internet, although it's encrypted." He pursed his lips as if to stop something from coming out, then reconsidered. "It's a Russian country code. That's all I'll tell you."

"Thanks," Pike said. "Will your people be on him tomorrow?"

"No, like I said, I have other priorities. Electronic monitoring is good enough to keep tabs on him."

Aaron heard a muted vibration. Pike removed his phone, said hello, and exited the bedroom.

Daniel said, "Why are you helping him?"

Aaron put a finger to his lips, then one to his ear, wanting to hear the conversation. It wasn't much.

"When did we get it?"

"Did you tell him you needed help? That we need three?"

"Okay. Retro's fine. Cut Shoshana free and get out of there. I'll call you in a minute with a location."

By the time he reentered, Daniel had prepared a disposable flash drive with the intelligence from the meeting and the videos.

Pike said, "Looks like you're not the only one with other commitments."

Daniel handed him the drive and Pike said, "Shoshana is free. She'll be back shortly."

Aaron said, "Good. I appreciate working with a man who keeps his word. A fight between us would have been messy."

"What would it take to get you to keep working with me? I'm not going to let this go, but my boss has other priorities."

"A vital interest to Israel. Something that would cause my people to sit up and notice. Like the Syrian did. Sorry, your man getting killed isn't vital."

"You have a way I can contact you? I mean that you don't mind me having?"

Aaron laughed. "No. I don't need the NSA up my ass."

Pike said, "Come on. Make one right here. An e-mail account. You can burn it in a week, and I'll be the only one using it."

Aaron agreed, and in seconds he'd created a Gmail account and passed it to Pike. "Now your NSA can keep tabs on both of us."

Pike smiled, held up the flash drive, and began walking to the door. "Thanks for this. Sorry I ripped Shoshana off the bike."

After he'd gone, Daniel said, "What was that all about?"

"Getting Shoshana home."

"Why'd you help him?"

"Because that fucker Yuri killed our countrymen. I can't prove it, but we ended up picking the pieces of a Palestinian suicide bomber off the streets of Tel Aviv. Yuri had contact with him. Don't worry, Nephilim will cause them some much-needed trouble, but we won't be seeing him again. He's good, but he's no match for Yuri and Vlad by himself."

"Nephilim. That's a bad omen. Bad name."

"Stop it with your damn superstitions. Did we hear anything about breaking the second encryption?"

Daniel snapped his fingers and said, "Yes! Yes, we did." He bent down to the computer and began rattling the keyboard.

"I forgot about it because of your call, but we have the pinpoint location. We can get the drive tomorrow."

45

I called Jennifer as soon as I was out of the room, telling her to come across to the Beyoglu side of the straits. I'd decided to stay right here in the Conrad, figuring getting away from all of the action in Old Town was probably a good idea. Also, the Russian consulate was on this side of the strait, just down the street from Taksim Square. Aaron had said the meeting was within a quarter mile of it, giving me another reason to remain here.

Jennifer said, "So you finally figured out that all of the pubs and bars are over on that side, huh? I wondered how long that would take."

I smiled. "You've been keeping that from me so you could stay near all the old shit. Anyway, I figured you could use a stiff drink."

Softly, barely loud enough for me to hear in my phone, she said, "I'm okay."

I said, "I saw the video. I saw what happened. I'm sorry."

She said nothing. I continued, "I have a picture of the man who I think chased you. We'll find him. I promise."

She said, "I'm not so sure I want to do that."

"You don't have to be afraid of him. I'll take care of it."

"Pike, that's not what I'm afraid of."

This wasn't something I wanted to address on the phone. I saw where she was going, and knew her heart. She would never take a life for revenge, nor would she participate in an operation that resulted in the same. But that wasn't what I was doing. Well, not completely, anyway.

The fact remained that this Berlin group was focused on facilitating known terrorist organizations that were antithetical to Western civilization. They'd failed with Chiclet, but that didn't mean they'd quit trying. Reducing their ability to operate was nothing more than reducing a clear and present danger. I knew that Jennifer wouldn't see it that way, though. All she would see was my bloodlust.

Since I'd brought her into the Taskforce, Jennifer had been forced to do some pretty unsavory things. She'd killed in self-defense, to protect her life, and killed offensively in support of Taskforce objectives when her life wasn't in danger, but it wasn't until she'd attempted to manipulate me into slaughtering a man who had raped her that she began to question herself. In the end, she'd deemed the man's death worse than the damage the killing would do to her psyche. After setting me in motion, she'd tried to prevent me from harming him because of her inherent moral compass.

She'd failed.

I changed the subject. "Where's the thumb drive?"

I hadn't even had the time to check the initial report for the operational area, and now we had a pinpoint. Things were moving quickly, and I had to make this good or Kurt would have my ass. The only thing that had prevented a thorough reconnaissance—and thus potentially missing the opportunity to get the thumb drive—was the operation that had gotten Decoy killed. The one I'd begged Kurt to let me execute, against his better judgment.

Jennifer said, "It's on the railing near the Medusa head in the Basilica Cistern."

"That means nothing to me."

"I'm sure it doesn't. Don't worry. I'll get the damn thing. The Cistern opens at nine in the morning. All we need to do is be the first in line."

"So we don't need to recce? You're confident?"

"I've already been online. There are thousands of pictures of the Cistern, and the pinpoint mechanics were done by a professional. We should probably get out by eight just to scope it, but it shouldn't be an issue."

"Sounds fine by me. Knuckles was good with giving us Retro?"

"Yeah. He wants you to call. There are some complications."

I said, "I'll bet. I'm wondering if I should call Kurt."

"Talk to Knuckles. He's on your side, although I don't think that's smart."

I said, "I'll call him now. See you soon. I only got one room, since there's no Taskforce bullshit."

She said, "Pike, I'm . . . I'm really tired."

I laughed and said, "Wow. You must think I'm a robot. I'm just saving Grolier Services some money, since this is now off the government dime."

There was a pause, then I heard, "Okay."

I said, "Tomorrow's coming early. Get in bed and get some sleep. Room's under Nephilim."

"Where are you going?"

"Talking to Knuckles. I'll get your luggage while I'm there."

She took that in, then said, "Okay. See you when you get back."

I said, "You good?"

"Yeah. I'm as good as I could be, but don't go bar hopping with Knuckles."

"I won't. I'll be back soon. Call if you want to talk."

She said good-bye, and I went to find a cab, dialing Knuckles to give him a warning that I was coming.

The drive over to our old hotel took longer than I wanted. We'd picked a spot on the European side, just west of the airport in a business district, which worked well for our cover but was hell and gone from Beyoglu—or Old Town, for that matter. It was closing in on three in the morning, and eight o'clock was going to come quickly. While Jennifer and Retro would be doing the work tomorrow, I still needed some sleep.

The only good things about the trip were I'd finally found a cabdriver who spoke English and during the drive I remembered where I'd heard the name Vlad the Impaler. Well, the cabby pretended to speak English, and I wasn't sure I remembered, but I thought I did. I'd have to check it after I retrieved my computer, but if I was right, it might be the edge I needed to get Aaron into play.

After a repeated conversation with the cabby, where he responded to every damn thing I said with, "Yes, yes," I finally got him to locate the DoubleTree Hotel. After driving in circles for an additional twenty minutes, we pulled to the front door. About to boil over, I tossed money into the front seat and left, not even waiting on him to count it.

Knuckles was in the lobby drinking a Styrofoam cup of hotel coffee. He looked sunken, like a man who'd just left the doctor with a catastrophic diagnosis. Something I expected. He'd recruited Decoy into the Taskforce after I'd left. They had both served in the same SEAL team at one point or another, and had grown close.

I shook his hand and said, "How're you holding up?"

He said, "I'm good. This bureaucratic stuff is bullshit, though. Our State Department is doing absolutely nothing to help me with the remains. You'd think he was a crack addict or something."

I sat down at his table, asking, "Taskforce?"

"They're not willing to bring any pressure. Too delicate." He sat down again and said, "Too much heat with the death of Turbo and Radcliffe because they'd already brought pressure in that incident. They're afraid something will split out of this mess, exposing them. Someone will make the connections if they press again."

"What's the status?"

He took a sip of coffee, then leaned back in his chair, looking at the ceiling, his head resting on the top spar. "Best case, I get him home in two days."

I said, "You know I'm not coming with you."

He sat back up, saying, "You need to think about that, Pike. Kurt is on the warpath. It's going to get messy. I mean it's going to get messy for *you*. You've pushed things before, but this is outright mutiny."

I said, "I know. I probably should let it go, but I'm not. Those fuckers have killed three of our men, and came damn close to killing Jennifer. I can't let it go."

"You know you're losing the rock-star bird, along with the package. I'm taking it with me."

"Yeah. I know. But I'd appreciate it if you let me raid it before you left."

"What have you learned?"

I filled him in on the Israeli connection and the probability that the whole thing was designed by a Russian kill squad out to protect Chiclet.

"So you think there's something more going on with Chiclet? That he's on his jihad?"

"I think he *was* about to run amok, but I'm pretty sure the Israelis chopped off his nuts on that. They believe the Syrian they killed was bringing in a Sarin arty round. Now that he's gone, so is Chiclet's ability to harm anyone. He's dropped out of sight. The phone we were tracking is dead, and he could be on a ferry to Libya for all I know. Anyway, he's just a linkage at this point. I'm going after the Russians. I have a meeting location tomorrow night, and I could use a Pwnie Express box. Along with the Goblin IMSI grabber."

"You got a target?"

"No, but I will tomorrow."

"You think you can exploit Bluetooth?"

"Yeah, I'm pretty sure with the Pwnie I can get in."

He put his cup down. "You can have anything you want. Whatever you want. Just put Decoy's killer down. Will you do that? For me?"

His eyes were vibrating in anger, and I saw a tic in his hand. A tremor that hadn't been there before.

He said, "Maybe I should go with you."

"No, you shouldn't. You've always been the calm one. Let me take this. I promise, I'll put him down. Just have Retro at the Conrad in Beyoglu no later than eight tomorrow morning with the kit. I'll keep him until the night, and you can tell Kurt it took longer than we thought for the thumb drive mission."

"You want me to tell Kurt you're headed off the reservation and into the badlands?"

"No. I'll do that myself, after I've gotten this incredibly important thumb drive. Might give me a little cushion."

Knuckles gave a brittle laugh and said, "Yeah, it'll be like throwing a Dixie cup of water onto an oil well fire."

The attempt at humor was swallowed by the reality of the night. We sat in silence for a moment, then Knuckles said, "You *are* going to get them, right? I've never asked anything of you before. I've taken the backseats and I've taken the lumps because I trusted you. Because I believed in you. Tell me you're going to burn them down. I want to hear it."

I could feel the pain leaking out of his being, reminding me of a dog hit by a car: lying on the pavement and keening, knowing it was hurt but not understanding why. I knew at that point it was good he was going home. Good he was escorting Decoy.

I said, "Yes. I'm going to find them, and when I do, Decoy will be the first to know, because he'll be counting the souls popping into the afterlife."

46

I got back to the Conrad just after four A.M. If I was lucky, I'd get three hours of sleep. I snuck into our room, making as little noise as possible, which was difficult considering I was dragging all of our luggage from the other hotel. I saw Jennifer's slumbering form and paused. When she didn't move, I sat down and booted up my laptop, the soft glow filling the room. I pulled up the files Kurt had sent me dealing with how important the thumb drive recovery was and saw what I had hoped I would. A connection that might get me an ally in Aaron.

I shut down the laptop, shucked everything but my underwear and T-shirt, and crawled into bed. As I was pulling the covers over me, I felt the mattress tremble, as if someone were lightly tapping it. I stopped all movement, and heard Jennifer weeping.

The sound ripped a piece of my soul out. I pulled her close and whispered soothing nothings in her ear. Telling her everything was going to be better tomorrow.

Not believing a word of what I was saying, but hoping she did.

47

Usman Akinbo awoke forty-five minutes before the *Fajr*—dawn prayer. For a moment he was disoriented, unsure of where he was. The small mosque inside the Grand Bazaar was still silent and cloaked in darkness, but the pungent smell of spice brought back his location. He sat up and looked at the time on his phone. The new "operational" phone, as it were.

He'd almost tossed it away as swiftly as he had the other cell. The one he'd used to call his spiritual advisor and read the message he'd been given. If he had any doubts about the abilities of the Great Satan's magical capacity to track him through technology, they were now banished forever. That one call had brought a world of hurt, and he was convinced that any electronic item in his possession was begging to become traitorous.

After the shooting, he'd run in a blind panic, convinced the Americans were on his heels like a djinn from hell. He'd run to the first hiding spot he could think of—the small mosque at the corner of the Grand Bazaar. He'd begged the imam to let him stay, and the man had agreed, building a pallet on the floor out of prayer rugs and blankets.

After the imam had left, Akinbo had smashed the first cell into bits, ensuring nothing was serviceable. He was about to do the same to the second when it had rung. He'd considered letting it ring out, then decided to connect. On the other end was the man he knew as Jarilo.

Refusing to answer any questions about what had occurred or how they were going to proceed, Jarilo had simply asked if Akinbo had the money he'd been given on his person. When Akinbo had said yes, he'd told him to forget about his belongings in the hotel and to purchase a train ticket to Berlin, Germany. Just like that. As if he were asking Akinbo to purchase a bottle of water in the bazaar.

The truth was that Akinbo had no idea how to even *begin* researching how to purchase a train ticket to Berlin. Yes, he'd traveled quite a bit as a child, but he'd always been handed his means of transportation. It wasn't like he'd set up his own family vacations.

On top of that, he was getting beyond annoyed at how the Russians treated him, like something subhuman. It was the very reason he despised the West to begin with, their obsession with material things and disregard for the purity of life. Because he came from a poor area, full of poverty, they assumed he was less than them. The truth was he was much, much more. It wasn't like this mission—conceived and run by them—had so far been anywhere close to smooth. He was sure he could do better. Something he would show them.

For now, he decided to continue on. To see what Berlin held. He sat in the dark and waited for the sunrise prayers. Waiting for the imam, so that he could ask for help getting a train ticket to Berlin.

Yuri's head slipped off his hand and cracked into the side of the van, snapping him brutally awake. He rubbed his crown and cursed, aggravated at the lack of sleep. He put his eye to the scope, tracking the exit down the street. It was still too early for anyone to use it, but he had nothing else to do for the moment. Unlike last night.

Problems had piled on like a school of piranhas, feeding on the flesh of his mission, and he had done what he could to mitigate the damage. He'd passed Mishka's information to the Bulgarian embassy through Vlad, letting them deal with his death as an unfortunate terrorist act, and had finally located Akinbo in the Grand Bazaar mosque, getting him moving to Berlin as Vlad had demanded. The one thing he regretted was not being able to do anything for Dmitri. The man had been with him for years, and now would be completely abandoned, as he had no diplomatic cover. He would end up in a pauper's grave somewhere on the Turkish peninsula.

The thought incensed him. Especially because the female who'd killed Dmitri had escaped. Not once, but twice. He prayed he would get a chance to even the score. He would make the death personal. And painful.

After covering his team's tracks as best he could, he'd begun a cursory Internet reconnaissance of the Basilica Cistern, preparing for the Israeli mission. He'd been at it for all of fifteen minutes when he'd decided to get some much-needed sleep. No sooner had his head hit the pillow when Vlad had called and told him the trigger was met.

True to his word, Vlad had no pinpoint location. Whoever his source was had only managed to signal that the Israelis had triggered, and would be attempting to retrieve the electronic archive on the thumb drive.

Now forced to study for real, he'd spent the remainder of the night planning his attack.

The Basilica Cistern was, at the end of the day, nothing more than an underground aquatic tank. Used in the sixth century to provide water to the ruling elites, it was lost in time for a thousand years. After it had been rediscovered, it had remained a source of Turkish pride and now stood as an ancient wonder for tourists to see. Yuri didn't give a load of crap about any of that, and skipped through webpage after webpage on its history, looking for something specific he could use to accomplish his mission. He finally found it on a tour-guide website: The Basilica had a separate entrance and exit.

To tour it—or to retrieve the thumb drive—one would enter at one location, go underground, and exit at a separate location. Which was all he would need to execute.

He'd placed one of his men, Kristov, at the entrance, giving him a photograph of the Israeli agent he'd taken in Bulgaria. The man would wait until he spotted the target, then alert Yuri. He, in turn, would wait until the Israeli appeared at the exit.

Then kill him.

That had been the hardest decision to make. Should he attack up close? Or have Kristov interdict under the ground, in the Cistern? Or should he attempt a follow once he exited, taking him at a place of his choosing?

He decided to split the difference. Trying to take down a trained Israeli agent in close quarters would be hard. Especially one who was on an active mission. Kristov would be lucky to simply remain undetected, much less able to close the distance for an interdiction inside the Cistern. Compounded with that was the lack of precise location of the thumb drive, and thus a lack of precision on when to attack.

But allowing the Israeli to leave and tracking him had its own risks. The man might never go to a good location for interdiction. They would be at his mercy. Worst case, he exited the Cistern and was picked up on the street in a vehicle, lost for good.

Yuri had decided to take him just as he exited. For one, they would know he had the drive. For another, with the weapon he had in mind, they could reach out and touch the Israeli without risk, dropping him to the ground.

Kristov, instead of following behind the Israeli to the underground, would simply move around the block and lock down the exit after the Israeli went below. When the agent was hit, he would retrieve the thumb drive.

Yuri had contacted Vlad at the crack of dawn, asking for two things. Within an hour, he had both. Now, at eight thirty in the morning, he was sitting in the back of a nondescript panel van, which was his first request.

Dinged and dented, the paint scraped, it had one back window shattered. In its place was a section of tinted plastic sheeting haphazardly taped around the gaping wound of missing glass. To anyone looking, it appeared to be a sad reminder of someone's bad luck.

To Yuri, the van had become a mobile sniper's nest. From the outside, the opaque plastic blocked the view of the interior. From Yuri's perspective, he could see out just fine, and the sheet would allow a bullet to pass through it without altering its trajectory. Something he would need to utilize for his second request.

Sitting on a makeshift bench rest was a VSS Vintorez suppressed sniper rifle. Based on the AS Val suppressed assault rifle, it fired a unique 9 x 39 subsonic round, basically a necked-up AK-47 cartridge.

With an integral suppressor, the weapon was nearly silent, and very deadly. Its only drawback was its limited range, as the heavier bullet and subsonic characteristics gave it a ballistic arch of someone throwing a bowling ball. It shouldn't matter here, though. It was only a hundred meters to the exit—a known range he had already dialed into his optics.

He'd parked the van early, before the city began to move, getting a spot down the street from the Cistern. From his scope, he could see the stairwell leading up, and there was nowhere for the people leaving to go but left or right. The street he was parked on—the same one running by the exit—had a railing preventing people from crossing at the Cistern exit, thus the target would either be moving toward him or directly away. Neither direction would hamper the shot like lateral movement would.

He looked at his watch and saw it was just past nine A.M.

Any minute now.

He was sure the Israeli would enter early, before the massive crowds of tourists began beating down the door to see the Cistern.

He put his eye to the scope again and watched as a man set up a small vending booth right outside the exit, laying out a display of what looked like bracelets. He fiddled with the rest, moving the natural point of aim a smidge until it was settled over the skull of the vendor. The man never felt the death tracking him. Would never know how fragile his life was. The thought reminded Yuri of why he was the better hunter. The stronger predator.

He leaned back, satisfied, when his earpiece chirped. "Jarilo, I'm in position, and I have no one resembling the target photo."

Irritated, Yuri said, "Then why the fuck are you calling me?"

"Because I have the girl. The one who killed Dmitri. She's in line with another man."

48

Jennifer let Retro buy the tickets and followed him down the steps into the cavern that was the Basilica Cistern. They were supposed to be a couple, but she wondered if anyone took notice of the difference in dress. He was wearing jeans, running shoes, and a long-sleeved shirt with an oversized collar, looking like he had just stepped out of a disco. It didn't match her more contemporary style, and would have looked odd in America. Here, it probably didn't matter.

Moving down the stairwell into the darkness, the air became noticeably cooler, smelling of damp stone.

Reaching the bottom, Jennifer surveyed the area to determine her ability to operate. She liked what she saw. The Basilica Cistern was basically a giant cavern, the roof held in place by dozens of columns, giving the appearance of a stone forest. Threaded throughout was a cement pathway built about a yard above the water, facilitating the tourist's ability to explore the majority of the space. The lighting was a soft glow offered from a smattering of incandescent bulbs, giving the cathedral a flickering, Halloween crypt feel. The meager reflection off the black water reminded Jennifer of Gollum's sanctuary in *The Hobbit*, making her wonder if the koi swimming in the darkness were blind.

According to the instructions, in the northeast corner were two blocks of stone carved into a likeness of the head of Medusa, both used as a base for columns supporting the ceiling. One was lying on its side, the other upside down, the Turks who had co-opted them when building the Cistern caring little for their Roman pedigree.

The path wound around them, with a small alcove behind to allow a larger group of tourists to view the heads. According to the pinpoint mechanic instructions, she was to find the head that was upside down, move around it to the alcove hidden in darkness, then run her hand along the lower railing. The thumb drive was supposedly there.

Standing on the entrance to the pathway, Retro said, "You want to execute now, or wait a little bit?"

She was surprised at the question, as she always was when one of the men deferred to her opinion, but the amazement was a little less each time it occurred. The decline saddened her, as it reminded her of an innocence she'd once held, now being chipped away a piece at a time. One day, she knew, the surprise would be gone, and she wondered what shell of a person would remain when that happened.

Last night had been a terrible reckoning. Decoy's loss and the actions she'd had to take because of it ate into her like acid. She wondered if, instead of her becoming immune, the trauma was filling up and starting to overflow. That each action stayed with her forever, only to be buried by the next, until her soul was full. Pike's comforting the night before had stopped the weeping and lulled her to sleep, but that had only allowed her dreams to haunt her from someplace rotten.

Perversely, she used this mission to tamp down her reaction to the last. Needing something else on which to focus her attention, she'd chosen to move further into the Taskforce embrace.

She considered Retro's question and said, "I think we should wait a bit. I thought there would be a bigger rush."

She'd wanted to get in early to beat whatever team or teams were also trying to get the thumb drive, but now she saw that the dearth of people was going to become a hindrance, not a help. The only thing on the pathway right now was a smattering of security guards. In order to access the alcove without looking suspicious, she needed a herd of wandering tourists to block her action.

Retro tossed his head to the right and said, "Let's do a touristy thing and read a couple of placards. That'll kill some time."

Looking where he indicated, Jennifer saw a makeshift photography studio, with a rack of costumes to the left of the camera. Next to it was a sign of some kind, describing a piece of the Cistern. She nodded, and they meandered toward the edge of the platform, fending off the photographer trying to sell them a tourist photo, the Turkish version of the ghost town Western picture.

They read the plaque for a minute or two, and the tourist floodgates opened. A steady stream of people started to filter down, and now Jennifer became antsy, worrying about losing the thumb drive to the Israeli agent. She told Retro she wanted to execute. He nodded without judgment. Letting her run the ball.

They went down the pathway at an easy pace, not rushing or drawing attention. They followed a sign for the Medusa heads and separated from the main track, going down a narrow walkway that eventually ended in a short staircase. Rounding a corner, they finally saw the two Medusa heads. Jennifer identified the one that was upside down, then glanced behind it, seeing a security guard leaning against the railing.

Damn it.

Retro saw the problem and said, "We can't stand here forever. After a couple of photos, it's going to look weird."

Before she could answer, her phone vibrated. She answered, looking at Retro, knowing if Pike was calling it wasn't good.

He said, "The Israeli team is in line. They'll be down in a matter of minutes."

She said, "How do you know? Can you send me a picture for identification?"

"You don't need one. It's Shoshana."

49

Sitting on a park bench down the street from the entrance to the Basilica, I wanted to punch myself for being so damned myopically tunnel-focused on my vendetta against the Russians. How on earth I hadn't made the connection between Aaron's team and the thumb drive mission was beyond me. I mean, how many Israeli James Bonds could there be running around Turkey?

Aaron hadn't shown up, giving the mission to Shoshana as a singleton. At least he wasn't with her. I watched her purchase a ticket, and made the call to Jennifer.

She said, "Shoshana? Really? I just assumed you'd cleared them from this."

Okay, rub it in.

"Well, I didn't, and this isn't a coincidence. She's going after the thumb drive."

"Pike, there's a security guard leaning on the pinpoint location. I mean leaning right on the thumb drive. I can't get it right now. I need a diversion."

I watched Shoshana get swallowed in the darkness of the Cistern. "She's coming down. She'll be at your location in seconds."

"What do you want me to do? She's going to recognize me, but I can't abandon this position. She'll get the drive."

"Get out. Leave Retro. Let him execute. He's an unknown."

She said, "He's supposed to be my security. My interference in case of trouble. Who'll back him up?"

"Nobody. Move. We're out of time."

"Okay, okay, I'm off. Retro has the ball."

"Put your phone in radio mode—break, break, Retro, this is Pike, radio check."

"I got you, and I got the ball. I can't stand here forever, though."

"Understood, we'll take it one piece at a time. If—"

"Jennifer's coming back down."

Huh?

"Pike, this is Koko. Shoshana must have sprinted. The path for the entire Cistern is basically a U shape, but there's a single ribbon off of it leading to the Medusa heads. I was going up the stairs and saw her. If I tried to reach the main path to leave the Cistern, she'd have seen me for sure."

I stood up and began walking to the entrance. "So now what are you going to do? She's coming right toward you."

"I'll try to hide between the columns. She'll fixate on the location of the drive, and I'll be twenty meters away, over by the head on its side."

I said, "Stand by," and paid for a ticket. I started down, saying, "I'm coming in."

"Pike, she's going to recognize you as well."

"I know. I'm thinking that's not such a bad thing."

I reached the bottom of the stairs and took a moment to get my bearings in the gloom, wondering if a dragon was going to slide out from between the columns. I followed the crowd but moved slowly, letting them pass me while keeping inside their bubble.

I scanned for Shoshana through the people flitting about and saw her leaning against the rail, peering intently at a narrow sidewalk shooting off of the primary concrete path.

Must be the path Jennifer said goes to the gorgon heads.

I said, "I got the target. She's looking hard. How's your heat state?"

Retro said, "I'm okay. There are enough people around here that I'm not standing out. Yet. But I need this fucking rent-a-cop to move."

Jennifer said, "I'm good. I'm on the far side, next to the sideways head. I can hang out here for a while."

I saw Shoshana raise a phone and start to talk. From the expression, I knew she was talking to Aaron. Knew she was aware of our presence, and was now coordinating how to skin the cat with us in play. I said, "Jennifer, you're busted. She's spotted you. I don't know how, but she has."

The Israeli hung up and began to rapidly move down the path, keeping the crowd in between her and the offshoot that led to the stone heads and the thumb drive. I followed, uneasy about what she was going to do.

We looped around, now headed on the final leg of the U toward the exit. I wondered what her plan was, running through my head what I would do in her shoes. I saw a café to the front and questioned if she was going to hide in there, although I had no idea what she could execute if she did.

She held up about fifty meters from the café and the stairwell to the exit, next to a little concrete platform jutting out from the main path. It had a lower railing and a placard announcing something. I could see people leaning over the lower railing, staring into the water.

I watched her closely, and she settled in with an eye to the path coming from the stone heads and my team. Luckily, I had already gone past her position because I was forced to stay with a crowd to remain undetected. I was now between her and the exit, and she was focused on the path to the stone heads, away from me. She pulled out her phone and began to talk. I saw her face harden at whatever was said. She hung up, and in that instant, I knew what Aaron had ordered. He was going all in, and was going to have her interdict Jennifer for the drive.

Shoshana was preparing for an ambush.

I considered my options, wondering if this damn thumb drive was worth the problem. I could call the team off and just go over to her, telling her the thumb drive was hers for the taking. I had half a mind to do that anyway. The whole scheme of stealing the drive from an ally didn't sit well to begin with.

But I knew I couldn't do that.

I keyed the radio. "What's your status?"

Jennifer said, "I'm still holding."

Retro said, "Barney Fife is still here."

I took a deep breath and said, "Okay. Get ready. I'm going to give you your diversion. When the cop leaves, get the drive and haul ass out of here."

I began moving toward Shoshana, making sure she was still focused on the path coming up. Her face was hard, thinking through the attack plan on Jennifer. Retro said, "What's that mean, Pike? What about the Israeli?"

I whispered, "Get ready. Ten seconds."

Jennifer said, "What are you going to do?"

Closing the distance to a meter, I slipped to the rear of a family, getting me directly behind Shoshana, not saying a word in response. I waited a beat for the family to clear, leaving me exposed. She sensed my presence just as I struck, hooking an arm under her leg and flipping her over the rail to the water a meter below.

She slapped her hands onto the rail, attempting to stop the rotation, but it did no good. She snarled and I saw her eyes lock onto mine, the recognition flashing through her.

She splashed into the black liquid and people began to shout. I immediately leaned over the rail in a show of helping the poor tourist who'd fallen in, shouting into my earpiece, "Execute, execute, execute."

Retro said, "Security guard is headed your way. I'm in."

Leaning over, my hand held out to the swimming "tourist," I whispered, "You got about twenty seconds."

Shoshana thrashed around in the water, then slapped an arm over the low railing. She looked up at me with pure hatred. I said, "Sorry. Come on. I'll help you out."

She grabbed my hand and I heard, "Jackpot. Moving to exfil."

I hoisted her up with other tourists now joining to help. We got her onto the deck and she stared at me with smoldering anger, still not talking.

I said, "It had to be done. You know it."

I saw her eyes flash to the crowd, fixating on something behind me. I made the mistake of turning, fearing a threat from Aaron or another partner of hers. Instead, I saw Jennifer and Retro speed-walking away. Before I could turn back, she hooked my leg and flipped me to the ground, my back hammering the concrete. I rolled right and she straddled my waist, driving a spear hand straight into my throat, hitting it hard enough to bruise my larynx but stopping short of killing me.

She said, "Next time I won't hold back. Leave well enough alone."

She sprang off of me and began to run, following Jennifer and Retro. I rolled onto my knees, hacking and holding my damaged esophagus. I coughed out, "She's coming. I say again, she's coming."

50

Yuri began to grow anxious. He could see Kristov outside of the exit, just beyond the vendor selling bracelets, and he'd watched scores of people leave the Cistern, but hadn't seen the woman. Considering she was one of the first ones in, and should have moved straight to retrieve the thumb drive, he didn't understand how she hadn't come out yet. Too many others had leisurely roamed the Cistern and were now moving on to other tourist destinations.

He said, "Are you sure she couldn't have come back out the entrance?"

Kristov said, "No. They wouldn't let her, and anyway, that's very poor tradecraft. She would have had to make an excuse to do so. Why would she do that? Why raise a signature when she could just exit like a tourist?"

"Maybe she made us. Maybe she knows I'm here."

Kristov started to respond when Yuri saw her, the head bobbing in the reticle of his scope. Ripe for the taking.

He cut off the conversation, saying, "I have the target. Preparing to engage."

Kristov said, "You have the man? Caucasian with a mustache, dressed in old clothes."

He panned the scope and found the other American. "Yes. I have him as well."

"Pick your target. One of them has it. I can't search both. You need to put the correct one down."

Yuri cursed. The plan had been based on the single Israeli coming out. Now he had two targets. Which to shoot?

He settled on the woman, his bloodlust rising to a fever pitch. He wanted to kill her. *Needed* to kill her.

"I'm taking the girl."

Kristov said, "Wait, wait. They're moving to you, and the man is digging into his pocket. Give it a moment."

Yuri watched the action from one hundred meters away, his finger subconsciously taking up the slack in the trigger. Wanting to see the plume of red over the bitch who had killed his men. The man held out something, showing the girl as they rapidly moved away from the Cistern exit.

He cursed again, the mission taking priority over his desire for revenge. He shifted focus, settling the reticle on the man, compensating for the range with the mil-dots in his scope.

He said, "I see the drive in the man's hand. Shooter ready."

Kristov said, "Send it."

He gently pulled back on the trigger and felt it break. There was a soft clap, and the weapon cycled. The recoil was negligible, and the target remained in view of the scope. In the split second between the trigger breaking the plane of no return and the subsonic round exiting the barrel, an unknown woman tackled the man from behind, grabbing his hair and jerking him off of his feet.

He saw the round strike, but instead of splitting his head it hit the man in the shoulder. The pair tumbled to the ground, falling behind a row of trash cans, the woman's upper torso the only thing in view.

He centered the weapon and squeezed again, the round's impact lost. He saw Kristov arrive, attempting to get the drive, blocking a further engagement. The woman who had tackled the man drove the palm of her hand into Kristov's nose, and Yuri saw him recoil in pain.

He cracked another round, feeling the slight recoil and seeing the plastic puff out once again.

The woman rolled, the bullet missing, and the bitch who had killed Dmitri entered the fray, jumping on Kristov, grabbing his arm, and rotating it in a direction it was not intended to go.

Yuri flipped the selector switch to automatic and squeezed the trigger, peppering the impact zone with rounds, not caring if Kristov was one of those hit.

I bounced onto the sidewalk at a dead run, racing to the tangle of people on the ground. Praying that Shoshana hadn't been so pissed that she'd force Retro to hurt her. Or worse, that she'd harmed him.

For some dumb reason, I genuinely liked her, and I didn't want to escalate this little Easter-egg hunt into harm on either side. It just wasn't worth it.

I closed on the tangled mass and saw a third man behind a garbage can, nose bloodied and Jennifer on him cranking his arm in a debilitating joint lock. I was close enough to hear it pop, and definitely close enough to hear him scream.

What the fuck?

Shoshana ducked behind the cans, holding her arms over her head, then I saw the dust kicking off of the brick wall. Retro sat up, his expression a daze, his shoulder a mass of red. The realization hit home, and time slowed, like the final step off of a high dive.

Bullets. Someone's shooting.

I heard nothing. No crack of rounds, no pop of gunfire. But it was real, and my mind began computing the means of escape at the speed of light. How to get into the kill zone and rescue all three without being hit.

I knew it was impossible. I bore down on them, waiting on the slugs to tear into my flesh, the people around the scene gaping at the tussle, unaware of the death floating in the air. Absurdly, the movie *Unforgiven* flashed in my head, as it had numerous times in combat before.

In the climactic scene, when Clint Eastwood was asked how he knew whom to kill first, because a gunfighter always knew, he'd said he was just lucky. Then he'd said, "But I've always been lucky."

That scene raced once more in my head as I slid into the vortex. Praying that I would be lucky yet again.

I rammed into Shoshana, ducking low behind the cans. She whipped around, trying to strike me. I parried the blow and said, "Get Retro on his feet."

I turned without a word and hammered the guy Jennifer held, striking him right above the nose and bouncing his skull against the stone. I felt a round impact the wall next to my head and ducked, slamming Jennifer into the pavement behind the cans, out of view from the sniper.

I screamed, "Forward! Get around the building."

The garbage cans worked fine for concealment, but offered no protection. Eventually, a lucky round was going to come through and hit one of us. It was counterintuitive, but our closest cover was running into the gunfire, and I knew by the lack of noise the killer was shooting subsonic, which meant the bullets were coming out in an arc, hell and gone from a flat, supersonic round. Any change in distance would give us an edge, as it would force him to compensate his hold for a kill.

Shoshana had Retro to his knees and I threw him over my shoulder, hearing him bellow he could run. I had no time to triage him and didn't want to find out if he was wrong. I told him to shut up, and heaved to my feet in a fireman's carry. I nudged Jennifer in the ass and I took off at a shambling trot, rounding the building with the brick chipping around me.

We got to the back side, surrounded by stone cover, and I dropped Retro unceremoniously in the dirt. He groaned from the impact, and

I began checking him out, relieved to see an in-and-out flesh wound to the shoulder. Nothing else. He'd have some serious recovery time, but he wouldn't die within the next few minutes.

I told Jennifer to put pressure on the wound and began running exfil through my mind. I turned to Shoshana, saying, "Where's your vehicle?"

She said, "I'm out of here," and began to stand. I grabbed her wrist and twisted, bringing her to her knees.

"You're going nowhere. You want to fight and we'll spend our time wrestling until the cops show up, but I promise when I go to jail you'll go to the hospital. Or the morgue. We leave *together*. I can't get my man out without your help. Understand?"

She saw the truth in my eyes. She said, "Let go of my arm."

I did so and she got on her phone. She spoke in Hebrew for a moment, then hung up.

She said, "Follow me."

51

Bruce Tupper lay on his back, replaying the conversation with Kurt Hale in his mind. He watched the ceiling fan above him spin lazily, the reflections of his bathroom nightlight dancing on the blades in the darkness.

He rolled his head on the pillow, seeing his wife of twenty years slumbering, a soft snore escaping with each breath. He wondered if they would finally split. If the firestorm coming from the latest revelation—and he was now sure there would be a firestorm—would cause the end of their marriage.

Fifteen years ago he'd been prepared for the cost, willing to take the separation about as badly as someone totaling his car in an accident. Some sense of loss, but not catastrophic. Tonight, it brought a sense of melancholy. He'd actually grown used to her. If not love, at least he *liked* her company. And the sex hadn't hurt.

Twenty years his junior, Lilith wasn't a looker by any stretch of the imagination, but she had been willing to explore, and that had always been something that brought him back. She was a little frumpy and plump, but the extra size extended to her breasts, something he had learned to enjoy. Especially when she let him tie her up.

Fond memories.

He gave up on sleep and threw off the silk duvet. He slipped out of bed, putting his arms in a bathrobe as he padded down to the second floor, to his art room. He clicked the outdoor lights and illuminated a balcony that overlooked the Potomac River. One of the very few mansions that did so.

He looked out of the French doors, but at three in the morning, it was too dark to match the sunset he'd been painting with the landscape outside the glass. He prepared a palette of paint anyway, mixing the yellows and blues until he was satisfied. At the end of the day, he had the terrain. The rest was his imagination anyway.

Working the paint mindlessly, he wondered if the thumb drive had been recovered. Given the time change, it should have been. He considered making direct contact, but decided not to. One, it was terribly risky. Two, he didn't want to give those assholes any leverage. Right now, they still considered him in the stronger position. If he kept groveling for information, that might change. One thing was for sure: He was no longer willing to sacrifice his life for the mission.

When he was starting out, he never would have dreamed that one day he'd become the head of all US intelligence. He'd acted accordingly, working as if the sword of Damocles were hanging over his head, sure that each day was to be his last. That attitude had given him freedom, and he'd operated with commensurate risk, not caring how close he was walking to the edge. Now, the world was markedly different, beginning with the fall of the Berlin wall.

The demise of the Soviet Union—the mighty USSR—was a clear demarcation in the life of Bruce Tupper. Before that time, he conducted his work out of patriotic zeal. After the wall fell, it was a confusing new world. His whole life had been dedicated to the matching of wits in the Cold War, something that no longer mattered with the crumble of the hammer and sickle. For a time, he did nothing. He simply coasted along in the bureaucracy, wondering where his career would go. Wondering, with the loss of the Soviets, if he shouldn't simply leave.

He eventually realized that he needed to refocus. Leaving wasn't the answer. Yes, the USSR was gone, but the United States still faced turbulent times, and he could actually help with those new threats. Something he would never have dreamed while the USSR was around. But his focus shifted from patriotism to personal survival. That one thing superseded everything else. Even his marriage. And now that survival was threatened by a rogue element of an illegal counterterrorist organization he had no control over. Because the FSB had killed their men, the Taskforce was going to take revenge and, in so doing, expose that Bruce Tupper was working for the FSB.

The irony was incredible.

He was the most highly placed mole the United States had ever allowed, his climb higher than the defunct KGB could have even dreamed, and he was now at risk because of the actions of his new FSB masters. An amateurish operation the KGB would *never* have conducted.

Before the fall of the wall, his case officers had assumed he would last a year. Maybe two. Just making it through the CIA training would be considered a coup. Instead, he'd not only finished, he had thrived. His one misstep had been Ali Salameh—the Red Prince—which had almost caused his discovery. Ever since then, he had toed the line, ensuring he would never be investigated for anything. Too much had been put into his infiltration, and he'd come way further than he should have.

Born in Canada to a Soviet diplomat, he'd spent his first sixteen years in North America, his father following one diplomatic post after another, all attached to the Soviet embassy in Ottawa. By the time he was seventeen, he spoke Russian with a North American accent, and spoke English like an American from the Midwest.

His father had finally been reassigned home, and he'd immediately been snapped up by the KGB. Not that he'd minded. The sense of importance was exhilarating, the praise lavished on him intoxicating. He'd gone through four months of rudimentary training on tradecraft, and then been inserted into the United States on his own. Using the name of an orphan who had died years before, he never saw his family again.

Uncommonly intelligent, and with the help of an underground Soviet machine, he'd achieved a scholarship to the University of Virginia. Graduating summa cum laude, he'd applied to the CIA, with everyone holding their breath. Waiting on him to be caught.

He had not been.

He served diligently, doing what he could, becoming the star of the Soviet crown. With the fall of the USSR, Bruce not only lost the purpose of his existence but the anchor of his life. Adrift and petrified he was now going to be discovered without anyone having his back, he began to work for the CIA for real, proving his worth and ostensibly dedicating his life to US security.

Eventually, he'd grown comfortable in his role, the duality of working to enhance the security of the very state he'd undermined previously causing no issue. He'd bumped into Lilith at a White House function, a woman twenty years his junior, but smitten with his cloak-and-dagger past, and he'd found another reason to continue. He'd asked her to marry, more a function of his perceived safety than any feelings of true love. Well, that and the sex.

Then, a KGB man had taken over the presidency of the new Russian federation. One of the handful that even knew he existed. The rest had been killed or purged in coup after countercoup, and somehow *this* one had ended up as president. Bruce had had a good ten years before the knock on the door. When it had happened, it had shocked him to his core.

At the time, he was a deputy director of the CIA, and the contact had made him feel like the ground was shifting under his feet, his reality crashing into a new one. Luckily, his placement and access were so high that he was treated with kid gloves, spending his time shaping US efforts instead of directly passing information. Like he had when he'd facilitated a high school dropout's ability to steal an entire library of NSA secrets, then successfully flee to Russia.

When the CIA had purchased the original secrets from Boris, he'd been caught off guard. Informed at an intelligence update, he'd been petrified that his true secret would be exposed. He was relieved when the greatest leak had been his efforts with Ali Salameh and the connection to the 1972 Munich Olympic massacre. He found it ironic that the head of the FSB—his counterpart in the Russian intelligence architecture—was the case officer for the Red Prince on the "opposing" side. Neither had known about the other, as often happened in the wilderness of mirrors.

When he'd learned of Boris's second potential sale of information to Mossad, he'd passed that information along to Vlad in the hopes that he would interdict it, but the Russians had already killed members of an organization he didn't even know existed. And because of it, Bruce Tupper stood to lose everything.

He could control all aspects of paramilitary activity in the guise of director of national intelligence, using his position to sway anything in the panoply of the US intelligence community, as he had with Edward Snowden, but could do nothing about an organization outside that system. Especially an organization with men like this Pike Logan. Even the damn Oversight Council he'd just been informed existed couldn't control him.

Pike was on his own agenda, and his actions against Vladimir's men would burn them both to the ground.

52

I pulled up my e-mail and was pleasantly surprised to see a message from Aaron. After the mission at the Basilica Cistern, I figured there was a fifty–fifty chance he'd blow me off.

"Jenn, he responded to the e-mail. Looks like we're a go."

She gave me an incredulous look. She said, "After what we just did to them? He must really want that thumb drive."

"Maybe it's Shoshana. She's probably smitten with me. Happens all the time."

Jennifer rolled her eyes and said, "She's a lesbian, Pike. I'm pretty sure she's not smitten with you."

Wanting to spark a little jealousy, that was the last thing I expected to come out of her mouth. I said, "Why would you say that? How do you know?"

"I just do. I knew it the minute I talked to her. I don't know how."

I closed the computer and said, "So you think she's smitten with *you*?"

She punched my shoulder and said, "No, you jerk. She's not *smitten* with anyone. They want the thumb drive."

Squinting my eyes and looking at the ceiling, I said, "Hmmm. That's too bad. We need someone from their team on our side. She needs to be smitten. Man, we could use Decoy for this. If anyone could change her stripes it would be him."

I smiled and saw Jennifer's face grow dark, the humor falling flat. She said, "Pike . . . that's not . . ."

I rubbed her shoulder, saying, "I'm sorry. That was too soon."

A grim smile floated across her face and she said, "It's okay. Decoy would agree. I'm just glad we're not making jokes about Retro."

After the shooting, we'd hobbled along behind Shoshana as fast as we could, me with Retro over my shoulder, watching her vanish into the cloistered neighborhood next to the Blue Mosque, weaving down one alley after another. While Retro was bleeding pretty freely from his shoulder wound, he finally convinced me to put him down. Well, not through his voice, but through me growing tired of running with him on my back. It turned out he could use his legs just fine.

We turned a corner to see Shoshana sitting in a van, a scowl on her face. Daniel was behind the wheel, also looking pretty grim. We piled in and Daniel goosed the engine, skipping forward and asking where we were going.

I directed them to Knuckles's hotel while Jennifer treated Retro. She cut a hole in his shirt and he complained about the damage. Shoshana said her first words at that point, snorting in disgust.

"You care more about your clothes than the operation. Typical. And that damn shirt is twenty years out of date and quite possibly the ugliest thing I've ever seen."

I smiled, glad for the conversation away from the thumb drive. I said, "Everything he wears is twenty years out of date. He shops at thrift stores."

She looked at me for a moment, then said, "What about the drive?"

Shit.

I said, "I know nothing about that. I appreciate you helping us, though."

She pursed her lips and nodded. She said nothing for the rest of the trip. Pulling into the hotel, Knuckles met us in the roundabout with a towel. He threw it over Retro's shoulder, hiding most of the blood, and escorted him past the front desk. Jennifer trailed behind.

I thanked Shoshana and Daniel one more time and told them to tell Aaron to check the Gmail account he'd given me. She'd nodded and slammed the sliding door in my face. Daniel hadn't said a word.

Inside Knuckles's room I found out that exfil plans were in full swing. Brett would take Retro and the rock-star bird to Landstuhl, Germany. They'd meet a Taskforce liaison who'd get them into the military hospital located there. He'd get treated as a military member, then continue home once he was stabilized. Knuckles would wait here and fly home with Decoy's remains via commercial air.

That left me and Jennifer to continue to track the men who had caused all of this pain. Both Knuckles and Brett asked if I wanted them to remain behind. I'd told them the same thing: "No."

Brett said, "What about weapons? This is your last chance to ransack the bird for equipment."

I said, "Yeah, I know. But I don't want to get you guys in trouble. I'll keep the kit Retro brought. I need that for the next step, and he had no sensitive items. Taking NODs, thermals, or weapons would cause you guys to pay a price. And I'm not going to do that."

Brett said nothing for a moment, waiting on Jennifer to clear out of earshot. He looked around to ensure nobody else could hear, then said, "I get all this Taskforce accountability bullshit, but I can get you some black weapons that nobody can trace. *Nobody.*"

Brett had come over to the Taskforce from the CIA's Special Activities Division, so Lord knew where the weapons he was talking about came from. I smiled, gratified by the support. "I hear you, Blood, but I don't need the help. I'm good with the electronic stuff Retro brought. It's a bare minimum, but it's enough."

"What are you going to do? Spit at them?"

I leaned back, checking to see if Knuckles could hear me. Not because I was afraid he'd turn me in, but because I wanted to protect him.

When I saw I was clear, I said, "Back when we started the Taskforce, before you joined, we put in some caches around the world. We had no idea what we were doing, just flinging shit all over the place because money was no object. Burying kit in a multitude of countries to give at least a little cell of capability around the world. We learned early on that hiding all that shit was a waste of time. There were easier ways to get operational capability in-country. We hardly ever used any of it."

Brett said, "And there's a cache here?"

"I'm not sure. There's a Taskforce guy whose sole job is servicing the caches. Pretty sweet gig if you can get it. I'll have to figure out how to contact him, but I'll have no trouble getting bullet launchers. If I need them."

Knuckles approached and I said, "You good to go with everything?"

He said, "Yeah, I'm good to go. The question is whether you are. Did you talk to Kurt?"

"Not yet."

"You need to think hard about what you're going to say."

"I know, but you've got the thumb drive. We accomplished the mission."

He shook his head. "Yeah, I'm not sure how much that'll matter. The last time you pulled something like this you were able to camouflage the op inside another one. This time, it's all up front, especially now that the thumb drive mission is complete."

A couple of years ago, while in the middle of an operation, I'd found the man who'd murdered my family. Knuckles was talking about my efforts against him while simultaneously conducting another kill/capture mission. While I'd stepped off the path for a span of time, I'd eventually come back and gained operational authority from Kurt and the Oversight Council. This time, I was going to thumb my nose at them from the get-go, which wouldn't be a comfortable conversation.

We left it at that, and Jennifer and I had returned to the hotel to wait on the Israeli response. Three hours later, looking at my e-mail, I knew that dreaded phone call had just come one step closer. I hadn't wanted to tell Knuckles about me trying to get help from the Israelis because if I did he'd be insulted and demand to stay, and so would the rest of the team. I wasn't going to put them in the crosshairs of the US government. What he'd said before still held true: Unlike me, they were subject to official government sanction. I was a civilian. I would leverage that as best I could.

I hadn't called Kurt yet precisely because I didn't know if the Israelis would help, and if they wouldn't, I was more than likely just catching a later flight home. I couldn't affect any good outcome with only Jennifer and me. But the e-mail told me that Aaron was at least willing to talk. Now it just remained to be seen whether the little ace up my sleeve would rise to the threshold of "affecting Israeli interests"

53

Aaron said, "Shoshana, I want you to come with me. Daniel, stay here. If I need something, I'll call."

Meaning, *Keep your guns handy*.

The meeting was set for one P.M. in the business center at the top of the Conrad Hotel. Aaron had tried to establish the linkup in his own hotel room, but Pike was having none of that. Not that that was surprising. Aaron wanted the thumb drive and wasn't above physical coercion to get it, something he was sure Pike understood.

The executive lounge was a good choice to thwart those efforts. It was close and neutral territory, but most of all it was staffed by members of the hotel concierge and security. There was no way Aaron would be whipping out a weapon and demanding the drive. Not that he thought Pike would be stupid enough to bring it to the meeting in the first place.

Shoshana said, "I'm not sure you want me in the room. I think I'm angrier now than I was this morning."

Aaron gave a little grin. "Come on. It can't be that bad. All you did was fail your mission by being tossed in the water by a man you should have seen coming."

Incensed at the comment, she said, "I get the chance, and I'm going to kill that man. I should have done so in the Cistern."

Daniel said, "And why didn't you? It's bad luck to allow him to continue. The cards said someone would die. You can't alter destiny. All you did was put *us* in danger. Someone *is* going to die, and it should have been him."

Aaron saw her eyes flash and knew a fight was close. Shoshana did not take criticism lightly, and she and Daniel butted heads more than they didn't—especially when Daniel's superstitions came into the discussion. He, personally, didn't care about Daniel's beliefs, but they tended to aggravate Shoshana. It was a volatile relationship that worked well under duress, but was a constant headache for Aaron when bullets weren't flying.

She took a step toward him, saying, "Keep your ridiculous superstitions to yourself."

Aaron interrupted. "Stop it, both of you. What's done is done. Why do you think he wants to meet? Did he say anything in the vehicle?"

Shoshana said, "No. He said they didn't get the drive. Nothing else."

"You believe that?"

"No way. They got it. If this is about the drive, then it's tied into what he wanted before. Vengeance for the men he lost."

"A trade?"

"Maybe."

Aaron saw the time and said, "I guess we'll find out shortly."

Shoshana slipped a small .380 automatic behind her back and followed him to the door. Once inside the elevator, away from Daniel, Aaron asked, "Why *did* you let him live?"

She glanced away and said, "I don't know. Perhaps because he didn't kill me when he had the chance. Maybe it was my 'destiny.' " She spat the last words out with sarcasm, then, much more softly, said, "Maybe I'm getting soft."

Aaron didn't think so. While he scoffed at Daniel's juvenile beliefs, he would never admit to anyone that he had his own superstitious thoughts about Shoshana. That he believed Shoshana had an ability to see through other's souls, to discern hostile intent through her mind alone. It was silly, but he'd seen her in action enough to begin to believe it to be true. Watched her go through shoot or no-shoot situations, making decisions that had confounded him given the evidence that was available, but had ultimately proven correct.

She'd been kicked off quite a few different teams because of it, ending up with him. She was the only one in his group who wasn't originally a Samson member. While the Israeli IDF had female members in combat roles, they still weren't in any of the Sayeret Special Forces units. Strangely enough, she'd been a helicopter pilot in the Israeli military, then had joined the Mossad when her conscription had ended.

He didn't know her story beyond the fact that she'd been pretty damn effective on some cross-border missions—and then had become controversial. She'd allowed herself to be used as a honeypot, sleeping with a Palestinian terrorist, then had refused to implicate him, saying they were targeting the wrong man for reasons she couldn't articulate.

She'd become a pariah after that mission, and had come to him as a Mossad-forced replacement a few years after the Samson element had transitioned from a Sayeret to the Kidon mission. When she'd landed on his team, nobody had wanted her. Word on the street was that she simply didn't have the mettle to accomplish the mission.

Initially, Aaron had assumed that the Samson team's enemies in the Mossad had dumped off some dead weight. After working with her for over a year, Aaron had learned just the opposite. She was a stone-cold killer, but only when it suited her internal code. Figuring *that* out was the issue.

He said, "What do you think I should do? If he asks for help in exchange for the drive?"

"I don't think it's our call. Headquarters will tell us what to do. Someone *did* try to kill me today, but they were after the Americans, not us. At the end of the day, that thumb drive isn't going to rise to the level of turning a Samson team loose against a Russian threat."

"But we might be able to leverage his desire for vengeance."

She said nothing for a moment, considering his words. The elevator reached the concierge level and she said, "No way. You won't be able to trick him into giving you the drive. You want it, and it's going to be paid in blood."

The elevator doors opened and they entered the Conrad executive lounge. A quick sweep of the area turned up nothing. Shoshana flicked her head to the outside deck, and Aaron saw the brunette named Jennifer, sitting at a table by herself. She didn't indicate she knew him, but her eyes tracked his movement to the door.

He went through the open glass to the deck and around the corner, at a table adjacent to Jennifer, he saw the man called Pike, along with two empty chairs.

He sat in one, and Shoshana sat at Jennifer's table, close enough to interdict her if anything happened. He saw a tiny smile flit across Jennifer's face, an effort at peacemaking. Shoshana glared at her, smoldering anger seeping out. Jennifer broke from Shoshana's gaze and scooted her chair to the left, ignoring her and watching Pike.

Aaron said, "So here I am. Against my better judgment."

"Yes. Here you are. I appreciate it."

"What do you want?"

"You know what I want. Help in interdicting a known supporter of terrorists."

Aaron said, "That isn't going to happen."

"Look," said Pike, "as Shoshana knows, my man was shot today by those same Russian assholes. I can't prove it, but that's who it was."

"So? Like we talked about earlier, I can't help you with that."

"Bullshit. After watching Shoshana in action, I'm pretty sure you could if you wanted. And I think I have something your boss might like."

"Let's quit dancing around the topic. You have the thumb drive, and you want to use it to leverage us as some mercenary force. What

I don't understand is why. I'm flattered with the request, because we really are better than your bloated special operations forces, but that doesn't explain why you're asking."

Pike's answer surprised Aaron. "I don't have the thumb drive, and I'm not using that as leverage. I'll quit dancing as well: The death of my men by the Russians is something my command is willing to forgo. I am not. What I'm doing is off the books. I'll get no help from the United States. I want help from you."

Aaron smiled, outwardly showing confidence, but inside Pike's words confused him. Without the thumb drive there was no leverage. "Why on earth would I help you kill Russians when you have nothing I want?"

Pike said, "But I do. That thumb drive you were after was offered to us first. I have some of the information from it, and I think your boss would be very, very interested."

Aaron shook his head. "There's nothing you can tell me that would get my country to take on Russia. We already know how they support terrorist groups antithetical to our nation. We know all about Assad and Iran. No matter how specific your information is, none of that will cause them to engage in hostilities against Russia."

Pike said, "You remember 1972? The Olympics?"

The words hung in the air for a moment. Aaron saw Shoshana lean forward, now extremely interested. He glanced her way, telling her to calm down with his eyes alone. He was unsure how Pike knew to push that button, but was convinced more than he had ever been that Shoshana had some ability that extended into the ethereal plane. Some ability to see into Pike even if she didn't realize how she did it.

Pike noticed the glance and said, "So you guys *are* interested?"

Aaron said, "*We* aren't interested, but Shoshana is. Do you know anything about that history?"

"Just what I've read."

He waved his hand at her, commanding her to relax. "Shoshana's grandfather was the wrestling coach. The first one to die, in the Olympic dorms." Aaron smiled. "So you've got her attention, but not my command's. Why do you mention this? It's old history."

Pike pulled out a sheaf of documents from a backpack at his feet. "These are from the file the US gleaned. A duplicate from the thumb drive you were trying to get. The man you call Vladimir the Impaler is mentioned throughout. He's in charge of Yuri, the man who killed my men here in Europe, and almost succeeded in killing me. I want your help in destroying him and his hit team."

Aaron flipped through the paper, saying, "I believe you, but I told you there's nothing that will convince my command to do such a thing."

Pike said, "He has a long history of killing. A long, long history. Read the file and I think you'll change your mind."

"Why?"

"Because Vladimir the Impaler murdered your athletes in '72. The Palestinians were the tool. He was the one wielding it. He ordered the deaths of your men. He crushed your hopes. He caused your pain. And now he's done the same to my team. You told me he's meeting tomorrow with Yuri, and I want your help to build a pattern of life."

Aaron saw Shoshana leaning forward to hear Pike's words, the bloodlust clearly evident on her face. The Olympic massacre had been the reason she'd joined the Mossad. Through melancholy stories passed down from her grandmother and mother, it was a touchstone that transcended all others, a pain she had long ago vowed to rectify. He saw her assimilate what Pike said and knew she wouldn't even need to read the words on the pages he had passed. She'd already sensed it in Pike. Already seen the truth and now understood why she'd left him alive.

Aaron read her face and knew Pike had just won. Shoshana was going on the warpath whether he followed or not.

54

Staring at the small portable monitor, Jennifer said, "Vladimir's here. Moving to the elevator."

I relayed the call to Daniel, then looked at the screen in time to see him enter the car, lost from view. A few minutes later Yuri entered, our color Wi-Fi camera giving much more definition to his features than the cheap security crap used next to the bazaar.

He had four other men with him, only one of whom I recognized. The one who had attacked Retro after he'd been shot. He wasn't hard to spot because he had a bandage on his face where Shoshana had clocked him. Or maybe it was from my punch.

Yuri poked the elevator button and I got a full view of his face. Coal-black eyes and skin as pasty as a chalk outline, he looked like a damn vampire. The sight brought enough adrenaline to make my hands tremble. I couldn't wait to get them around his neck. But, unfortunately, that wouldn't happen. I was relying on my new friends to execute, a compromise I'd worked out with Kurt.

After I'd secured the help of Aaron and his deadly little sidekick Shoshana, I'd made my fateful call to Taskforce headquarters. Naturally, it hadn't gone over too well.

Kurt had tried simply ordering me home, then had threatened me, then had finally gotten around to asking just what the hell I was doing. I'd told him the truth: I was going to hang around for a few more days and see if I could help some other players take action. The same players who had killed the Syrians. I didn't tell him who they were, but it wouldn't be too hard to figure out.

He'd said, "So let me get this straight: you're not going to kill anyone?"

"I didn't say that. My skills might come in handy."

"Damn it, Pike, you will not execute any lethal operations with Taskforce assets. Do you understand?"

I could feel the frustration vibrating through the phone, like he was screaming at a dog who refused to quit digging up the yard. Knowing his words were doing nothing, and hating it. Through the aggravation, I also sensed a little support, something I hadn't expected.

I said, "Can I execute nonlethal operations? With Taskforce assets? Truthfully, sir, I don't have any Taskforce weapons. Only tech kit. Can I use that?"

"Why?"

"To develop a pattern of life so that someone else can execute."

"No Taskforce fingerprints? No killing?"

"Absolutely not. The intel I'm working came from outside the Taskforce, and all I want to do is refine it for the other players. Let them handle the lethal aspect."

"How did you get them to play? Why are they doing your bidding?"

"Let's just say we have mutual interests, like killing the Syrian the other night. I want them gone because they killed our men, and coincidentally, they want them gone for doing the same thing."

"Are you saying the Russians have killed Israeli agents as well?"

Well, I guess my "partners" are no secret.

I went all in. "Not agents. Athletes. They found out that the Russian guy in charge of the hit team facilitated the '72 Munich massacre."

I heard nothing for a second, his mind running over our successful thumb drive mission and the fact that I had held the information. Then: "And how did they find that out?"

I said, "I don't know. They *are* the Mossad."

"Did they *find out* about the DNI? About his involvement?"

The sarcasm came through loud and clear. Along with the fear. We'd been as close as brothers over a multitude of combat actions— well, at least as him as the older brother to my younger-brother antics—and for the first time I heard him asking if I would compromise national security for a personal agenda. Like I actually had that in me. It was a little depressing, but given what I'd put him through, understandable.

"Of course not, sir. They aren't *that* good."

I heard him sigh. I wasn't sure if it was because he was relieved about the protection of the thumb drive information, or whether it was because he was wondering how on earth he'd been saddled with the likes of me.

He said, "I can get you forty-eight hours. Pattern of life only. Understand?"

"Yes, sir. Perfectly. I have a meeting tonight, and all I'm going to do is interdict the conversation."

"Keep me abreast of what's going on. At least make it *look* like you're listening to me. Give me a reason to help you."

"Roger that, sir. I'll shack up a complete SITREP when I'm done. With the time change, you should have it before you go home tonight."

After that phone conversation I felt a hell of a lot better. It was a clear indication that Kurt wanted the killers of Decoy, Radcliffe, and Turbo as much as I did, and it gave me a boost of confidence that he was willing to let me continue. All I had to do at that point was coordinate with the Israelis.

The meeting was taking place at a restaurant called 360 Istanbul. It was a hot little joint on the top floor of an old multiuse apartment building on the Beyoglu side of the straight. Located on Istiklal Street just a few blocks away from the Russian consulate, the entire area was a walking promenade that had a host of bars and restaurants running down from Taksim Square, the famous chunk of terrain that had seen all of the major protests against the Islamic influence of the government in the recent past.

While I didn't really care about the politics, the bottom line was Istiklal Street was the center of the universe for "occupy"-type young people, and thus a location where we could get some work done fairly easily. It was counterintuitive, but any focus would be directed against the Turkish population. Being a white guy would cause immediate dismissal from the local security forces, as they only had so many assets to leverage against their perceived internal threat. Something I'm sure Vladimir appreciated.

Jennifer and I had run a recce and—apart from learning I'd be coming back for a beer as soon as I could—I found the two things I needed: a Wi-Fi hotspot and a European wall outlet next to a table.

We decided that Daniel would be the man who'd penetrate the restaurant, mainly because he was the only one left who hadn't had a close encounter with one or more of the Russians. Shoshana and Aaron would remain on the street as backup, and Jennifer and I had found a little hiding place off of the kitchen one floor below.

Daniel would take up a laptop with an American electrical plug, and would use a modified Pwnie Express hacking device that looked like a European converter. Pronounced *pawny*, the company was a play on words from *pwned* in the gaming world, whereby someone cleans your clock and owns you, and *pony* from the old Pony Express. Its entire catalog of products was hardware and software exploits for "pentesting" or penetration testing of various networks. Basically, they sold hack-in-a-box devices for security professionals to test their system against a multitude of different hacking capabilities.

Or, instead of testing, you could just go ahead and hack, which is what I was going to do.

The original Pwnie Plug looked a lot like a DC power supply. We'd altered the form factor so now it looked like a US-to-European electrical plug converter, and Daniel was going to slap it into the wall, then plug in his computer, ostensibly to draw power, but the computer wouldn't be getting a charge. Instead, it was going to exploit the Bluetooth of Vlad's cell phone, turning it into a digital microphone.

Once we had the phone, the conversation stream would be directed over Wi-Fi to my location, where I would record it for future use. Before any of that could occur, though, I had to lock his phone from the cell system, which is where my last piece of kit, the Goblin IMSI grabber, came into play. Just like we'd executed with Chiclet in Bulgaria, it would act like a mini–cell tower, attracting all phones to it and rejecting every number but Vlad's. When that one triggered, it would hold it in place until we were done.

Over my earpiece I heard Daniel say, "Vlad's seated."

I said, "Roger. Locking the phone now."

Aaron hadn't wanted to give me Vlad's number, but since we were now "partners," he'd eventually relented. I punched the number into the keypad, said, "Executing," and powered up the Goblin. I saw hundreds of phones sucked in and rejected, but none were Vlad's. Thirty seconds into the cycle, I shut the Goblin down.

We either had a wrong number, Vlad's phone was turned off, or he was using a different handset. If the cell given to me by Aaron was active in the restaurant, I would have owned it.

Damn it.

I started working through the ramifications, trying to decide what I could do next, when Daniel said, "Yuri's just exited the elevator. He took a seat opposite of Vlad. Two men are checking the restaurant, and two men are going down the stairs. Security sweep."

I said, "They're coming down the stairs? To the kitchen?"

"Roger that."

55

Seeing Vlad at a corner table, Yuri ignored the hostess and moved straight to him, whispering to his men as he did so. Although the restaurant was filling up, it wasn't nearly as crowded as it would be in a few more hours, when this place became a hot spot for young, upwardly mobile Turks hell-bent on partying through the night.

The security broke off, two moving to check the outside deck, and two back toward the stairs. Before he even reached the table, Vlad stood.

Yuri said, "Did you have time to read my report?"

"Yes, I did. And I'm not very impressed. You failed again. It's becoming somewhat of a tradition."

Yuri glared at him in silence, then sat, not waiting on Vlad to give him permission. He was growing a little impatient about Vlad's superiority. And nettled by his barbs. After all, *he* was the one in the line of fire. His men were getting killed.

He said, "You never said anything about the Americans. I was supposed to interdict a single Israeli agent—not a platoon of commandos."

"So the Vympel no longer plan for contingencies?"

Yuri held back what wanted to come out, saying, "We are only as good as the intelligence we operate with. How did you know where the thumb drive was located, but not who was going after it?"

"That is none of your concern."

Yuri studied him for a moment, then said, "You have someone on the inside of the American intelligence architecture. That's how you knew about Boris in the first place. But you didn't know about the surveillance against Akinbo. We had to confirm the action for ourselves. So your source has some access, but isn't very powerful."

Vlad leaned back and smiled. "Very good. Mistaken, but good. Maybe you aren't as prone to mishaps as I thought. He—or she—is very well placed, but whatever forces interdicted the meeting with the Syrian are not part of the normal US intelligence architecture."

"You mean the team that killed my men."

Not a question. A statement.

"Yes. It's something new. A group like the Vympel. My source just learned about them."

"So he can track them now, and they have the drive. Get him to give me a thread, and I'll get it back for you."

"No reason to bother. The US already had the drive. Like you said, it's how I knew to get you on Boris in the first place. When the CIA gleaned the first copy, my source informed me about it. Why the Americans went out of their way to prevent the Israelis from getting the second copy I don't know, but they did our work for us. The damage with the US had already been done."

"But what about my men?"

"Casualties of war. Anyway, the Americans are going home with their tails between their legs, taking the drive with them. Your attack was enough. I don't need you to worry about the drive anymore. I need you to get back on Akinbo."

"I don't get that. Why? We don't have the chemical munitions. Why did you send him to Berlin?"

"You remember planning for Barbarossa II? Before the wall fell?"

"Of course. That's what the Vympel existed for. After a full-scale invasion from NATO, I would infiltrate Western Europe."

"And what would you do? Once you were there?"

"Sabotage, guerrilla warfare, that sort of thing."

"You mean with sticks and rocks? Or with an RA-115s? Thor's Hammer?"

Yuri was unsure what to say. Vlad was the head of all of the FSB, but the program he mentioned was classified at the highest order, and he'd never breathed a word of it since the USSR had disintegrated.

Vlad waited a bit, then said, "It's okay. Remember I have your file. I know you were on the team that practiced parachuting with the device, and I'm not going to ask you what your target was. All I need to know is that you can put it into operation."

Yuri nodded, unsure what to say. Afraid to open his mouth.

Vlad said, "A device such as that will still accomplish our mission. We can't lay the blame on the Syrians with the chemical weapon, so we'll lose the chance to embroil the US in that country, but we can still cause them to sink in the quagmire of Nigeria."

Yuri found his voice. "But they're all gone. Destroyed when we were afraid of them falling into enemy hands during the riots and coups of the nineties. Long gone."

"Not all. There's one that we couldn't get out. It was cached in a very delicate location, and when the Berlin Wall began collapsing we couldn't react fast enough. Actually we didn't think to act at all, since we were worrying about other things. The rest of the devices were in Soviet control. This one was simply hidden."

"You think it's still there?"

Vlad scoffed. "You think if someone would have found an RA-115s it wouldn't have made worldwide news? Yeah. It's still there."

Yuri felt his phone vibrate. He pulled it out, seeing nothing but a text advertisement from Vodafone.

Vlad said, "I'm sorry to inconvenience you. Please, by all means, play with your phone."

Yuri said, "Sir, my men are conducting a security sweep. It might have been an alert."

"And is it?"

He set the phone on the table and said, "No." Then Vlad's words sank in. "You want to give a nuclear bomb to a savage like Akinbo? Even a small one like Thor?"

Vlad said, "No. You remember your training? Remember how delicate those devices were? How they had to have constant power and all the other restrictions? The device is still there, but it's degraded by now. It'll just be a small explosion of radiological waste. What the West calls a dirty bomb. It may not be a nuclear explosion, but the radiation poison will be just as effective. It'll cause the United States to react in a frenzy. Make no mistake, they'll end up invading Nigeria because of Boko Haram."

"We'll be blamed. Nobody else had a program like Thor's Hammer."

"Not true. Any nuclear power can be blamed. Once it goes off, the only thing they'll know is that radiological material was blown apart by conventional explosives. Material they could have gleaned from a multitude of places."

Yuri considered his words, then moved on to the next problem. "You have a detailed description of the location? Berlin is a big place."

Vlad slid across a sleeve of papers, yellowed with age. "These are the original cache instructions. Of course, that was close to thirty years ago, so you'll have to improvise once you get there. The place is now a museum."

"And the arming, timing, and PAL control for the weapon? I'll need those as well."

"They're in the cache instructions."

Yuri leaned back and asked, "What's the target?"

Vlad slid across a brochure. When Yuri saw the first page, he said, "Here? Not in America?"

"No. Much easier to get the device into that country, especially with Akinbo. You'll have to get him new documents, but you have that capability in Berlin, correct? I mean, you were called the Berlin group for a reason."

"Yes, sir. I can do that. Why here, though? This is global, not American-centric."

Vlad tapped the page. "Read the specific target. You'll see why it was chosen."

Yuri studied the package, then began to smile. Vlad said, "So you see. It's poetic."

Yuri said, "Well, I don't know if it's poetic, but it'll get the US going, no doubt about that. Anytime you include their little Jewish lapdogs you'll get an exponential reaction."

56

Hearing that two men were coming down the stairs was the last thing I wanted. I knew Yuri or Vlad would be worried about security, but didn't figure they'd do some sort of *Check all the mailboxes and pull up the manhole covers* security review. Which is why I'd manipulated the lock to an old storage room next to the kitchen, right below the meeting site.

Just great. Every second I wasted hiding was a second I wouldn't have of the conversation.

Jennifer was already breaking out a cattail, a pencil-thin flexible cable with a camera on the end. It was no more high-speed than a multitude of cable cameras on the market, with the exception that it mated to our smartphones via Bluetooth, giving us a built-in monitor without having to plug a USB cable into a computer.

She slid it under the door, rotating the lens to get the view right side up while I killed the small lamp we'd found. In the glow of her phone I saw the pair turn the corner from the stairwell and hold up, staring down the darkened hallway at the row of doors presented. This would be the key, no pun intended. If they tried the lock of the first door they found and kept moving, we'd be good. If they attempted to disable the lock and enter the room, we were in for a world of hurt.

I said, "Keep watching them," and went to explore the back of the storage room. I'd cleared it earlier, but that had been just to make sure we weren't interrupting some waiter stealing a nap. Now I needed to find an alternate exit.

At the right corner was a collection of tables, one overturned on top of another. Above the stack the ceiling tiles had been moved, showing an iron rib holding up the roof. I climbed up and flashed my pen light inside, seeing we could plug ourselves there, but we'd definitely be cornered.

I heard Jennifer hiss.

I went back out front and said, "We can get into the ceiling. If they check further than that, we're screwed."

She said, "Don't worry about it. All they did was rattle that door and keep moving. We're good. They're two doors down and still coming."

Whew.

I called Daniel. "I have an idea. I'm going to suck in everyone's phone, then isolate all with a Russian country code. I'll send a text to those phones, one at a time, basically duplicating an ad for the local cell service here. You see who looks at their phone. If it's Vlad or Yuri, we're good. If it's someone else, we keep going. You copy?"

Jennifer withdrew the cattail and held a finger to her lips. I watched the doorknob go left and right, an irrational fear spiking that the lock would fail and they'd fling it open.

They did not.

She stuck the cattail back under, then gave me a thumbs-up. I said into the radio, "Daniel, you copy?"

He said, "Roger. Standing by."

I fired up the Goblin and it began to do its work. Within fifteen seconds, it held six phones with Russian country codes. I pulled up the text messaging on my smartphone, scrolled until I found the Vodafone ad I'd received earlier, then typed the exact same message into the Goblin. I targeted the first phone and hit "send," knowing the message would register with some weird number like 404-05. It would look real.

Daniel said, "Security man at the other table just looked at his phone."

"Roger." I targeted the next one on the list. Daniel said, "Nothing."

Might be the guys walking around down here.

I hit the third, and Daniel said, "Yuri just looked at his phone and set it on the table."

Bingo.

I rejected the other phones, and kept his. I said, "You're a go. That's the phone we want." I read off the number, and he went to work. A minute later I was getting Russian over Wi-Fi, all of it recorded for posterity. I was proud of myself for solving the problem, right up until the conversation ended a mere minute later.

That was quick. I said, "What's going on? I have no more voice."

Daniel said, "Vlad's stood up. He's leaving. Yuri's still in his seat."

Damn it. "Okay. We stay until Yuri clears the area. Once that's done, we can break down."

I wanted some ability to target Yuri, some clue in their conversation, but the meeting hadn't gone on very long. I wondered if I'd recorded enough information to facilitate future operations.

57

Vladimir Malikov exited the elevator, nodded at the lone security guard, and entered the mass of people on Istiklal Caddesi. The crowd split around him as they fought to reach a tram running down the middle of the street, people hopping on and off as it rolled along.

He pulled a felt hat down on his head and began weaving through the throng, walking back to the Russian consulate. He passed the Church of Saint Anthony of Padua, now locked up to prevent the revelers from invading and defacing the stone with graffiti. He paused to listen to a man and woman sing a cappella in the foyer of the front gate, a mass of people listening.

He joined them, blending into the throng. He pretended to enjoy the entertainment as if he gave a shit about their voices, but really used the pause to conduct a quick surveillance check. He saw nothing. He began walking again, reflecting on his conversation with Yuri. Before, the man had been obsequious to the point of embarrassment, but tonight he had been more forceful. More prepared to rebut what Vlad had said.

On the one hand, it was to be expected. Vlad's reputation had always preceded him, and it was larger than life, to the point that people who had not met him compared him to some boogeyman from a nightmare. When the men saw that he really *was* a human, they tended to lose their abject fear. But allowing even a hint of insubordination was unacceptable.

When this mission was done, he might have to make an example of Yuri. Rekindle the "Impaler" reputation, as it were.

What most concerned him now was Yuri's quest to leverage Vlad's source in the United States, the asset known as Angus. Clearly, he wanted vengeance for the loss of his men, and he wanted the asset to set the Americans up for him. He would push for access again, Vlad was sure, and such prodding might cause issues if it piqued the interest of the wrong men. Such knowledge was a valuable commodity, and not something to be shared.

Vlad had been coy when discussing Angus, as if he was in complete control as the primary case officer, but in truth, he knew little about the man. Vlad hadn't even known he existed until two years ago, when he'd been directly handed the communication methods by the president of Russia. At that time he'd been given strict orders not to initiate any contact whatsoever; his only job was to respond and report. Since that time, he'd learned of Angus having facilitated Snowden/Calypso's escape to Russia, the collapse of the US-planned military strikes on Syria, and a host of other national strategic intelligence priorities, but he still didn't know where the asset worked.

It had to be somewhere very high up, since the president of Russia was the one who had passed the connection, but if so, how is it he didn't know about this new US team? Yuri's question had been spot-on. How could Angus know the location of the thumb drive— meaning he had direct access to a Mossad leak, which would be very, very sensitive—and yet not know an American team was on the hunt for it?

It either meant the team was something above Angus's clearance— which, given what he'd already accomplished, just didn't seem possible—or someone suspected him and had cut him out deliberately.

The thought hit Vlad hard.

Had someone kept Angus out in the cold on purpose?

It was something to explore, but he'd have to get permission to initiate contact. The last thing they needed was Angus getting turned and facilitating their own security disasters.

He passed by the Swedish consulate and approached a crowd, all listening to a man playing a guitar. He threw some money into a pot and circled around behind him, not wanting to walk into the street with the mob of half drunks.

He skirted along the building's wall until it disappeared, an alley snaking off in the gloom, no more than four feet across. A woman with a small cart appeared, selling handmade goods. Before Vlad could protest, she draped what looked like a flower on a ribbon around his neck.

Aggravated at the sales tactic, he started to pull it off and saw it wasn't a flower. It was a plastic medal that looked like Olympic gold. He heard a minibike coming down the alley, and his fate crystallized.

The hunters had found his secret.

Holding the toy medal in one hand, eyes wide, he turned to the woman and saw the black tunnel of a barrel capped by a large suppressor aimed at his chest. The assassin bared her teeth.

He said, "Wait, wait—"

And she pulled the trigger, two short coughs drowned out by the guitar player and the clapping crowd. He hit the ground backward, the blood from his destroyed heart leaking into the cobblestones. He screamed as loud as he could, hearing a whimper escape like air from a hole in a balloon.

The woman yanked the toy medal from his neck and stuck something in his shirt, wiping his blood with it. She got on the back of the motorcycle and turned, looking back at him.

As the life drained out of his body, he thought he saw compassion. He held his hand out to her. It hung in the air for one second, then fell to the ground.

She tapped the driver of the minibike, and in the waning glow of his brain he understood it wasn't compassion. It was the opposite. She wanted to ensure he would die.

With her eyes still on him, she placed a helmet on her head and snapped down the visor. He saw his body in the reflection, a twisted, cracked thing. It reminded him of something, but he couldn't remember what.

The motorbike left, and he couldn't remember anything at all.

58

I woke up the next morning itching to get my translation of Vlad's meeting from the Taskforce, barely able to contain my anticipation. I went into the anteroom of our suite and saw my phone blinking. Kurt had called.

Huh. What's up with that?

It was seven A.M., which meant it was midnight in the states. I dialed him back, hearing the crypto software program going through its handshake. I heard a noise that sounded like Charlie Brown's teacher. It grew stronger, and I realized it was Kurt. Yelling before the encryption took hold. When it cleared, his voice came in loud and clear, and I got an immediate earful.

"Hello? Hello? Can you fucking hear me now?"

"Yes, sir. I got you."

"What the fuck are you doing over there? You killed the head of the Russian secret service?"

"What? Whoa . . . wait, sir. I don't know what you're talking about."

Jennifer came out in her robe, the front open and a little smile on her face from something that had happened before I'd seen the phone. She saw my expression and I waved her to the door, where our newspaper would be hanging on the other side.

Kurt said, "We just got word that the head of the FSB, Vladimir Malikov, was assassinated in Istanbul. Tell me that wasn't you."

What the hell?

"That wasn't me. I swear, this is the first I'm hearing about it. We did the collection mission just like I told you, and I sent the MP3 back for translation. Nothing else. No drama."

Jennifer had her robe closed and the Turkish paper opened, and sure enough, on the front page was a picture of Vlad the Impaler, although I'd seen him looking a hell of a lot better just hours earlier. The story said they'd found him clutching a bloodstained computer printout of a Chechen named Musa Atayev, apparently some type of spokesman for the Chechen insurgency. He'd been murdered in Istanbul in 2011, with almost everyone pointing the finger at the Russians. The paper's conclusion reported that Vlad's death was a revenge killing.

I didn't believe that for a damn minute, although I hedged my bets on the phone. "The news here says he was found with the picture of a Chechen murdered in Istanbul in 2011. And the Israelis told me that Yuri—the guy who killed our men—was a member of some team called the Berlin Group that ran all over the world killing Chechen insurgent leadership. He's done three in Istanbul alone."

Kurt came back, still with unbridled fury. "And you want me to believe this has nothing to do with you passing off classified information to the Israeli Mossad? You talk to them about a Russian, and he conveniently ends up dead twelve hours later?"

"Sir, I'm telling you I had nothing to do with this. *Nothing.* It's either a revenge hit, or it's something outside my control."

"Outside your control is what worries me."

I said, "Sir . . . let me get back to you."

"Okay, Pike. You send me a message as soon as you figure out what the hell is going on. For now I'm not mentioning a damn word about your plans to the Council. The news story stands until I hear otherwise."

I said, "Thank you, sir," but he'd already hung up. I turned to Jennifer and saw she'd heard enough of the conversation to understand.

My anger was reflected in the fear on her face. Fear of what I was about to do.

I said, "Those motherfuckers. They took my information and completely ignored us. They conveniently facilitated our mission to keep us occupied while they killed Vlad."

I was throwing on my clothes as I spoke, the anger building up. Jennifer began dressing as well, attempting to tamp down the flame.

"Pike, it looks bad, but you don't *know*. It *might* be them. That's all."

I sat down and put on my boots, cinching the laces as if I were trying to garrote someone's neck. "Bull*shit* I don't know. Those bastards undercut us."

She threw on her sandals, hopping on one leg and following me to the door.

"I think you should calm down. I'm sure they have their side of the story."

I flung open the door and stalked into the hall, saying, "Let's go hear it."

I knew the location of at least one Israeli room from the night I'd seen the videos, and it was only two floors above me. I ignored the elevator, banging open the door to the stairwell and taking the stairs two at a time. I heard Jennifer's sandals clacking right behind me.

I broke out into the hallway and went into a light jog, fueled forward by my sense of betrayal. I reached the door and Jennifer grabbed my arm right before I brought my fist down.

"Pike . . . stop."

I started to rip my arm out of her grasp, pissed at her interference, when her eyes caught mine. No longer wearing the brown contacts, they were gray ice and shooting sparks.

She said, "Calm. Down."

Anyone else, and that wouldn't have made a shit's worth of difference. With her, it caused a complete deflation of my anger. She slowly shook her head back and forth, and all two hundred and fifteen pounds of me turned into a bowl of Jell-O.

I fucking *hated* it.

I pulled her hand away from my arm and said, "Okay, damn it. I won't go in swinging, but I'm going to give them a piece of my mind. Can you live with that?"

She squinted her eyes, unsure if I was telling the truth. I filed the look away, surprised and happy to realize that she didn't understand the depths of her hold on me. I *could* bluff and get away with it.

Something to remember.

She said, "Go ahead. But you turn into an ass, and I'm taking over."

I banged on the door, my entire attack plan decimated by some acrobatic chick I'd had the misfortune to meet a couple of years ago.

I am pathetic.

There was a flash in the peephole, and I heard the chain being removed. When it opened, I saw Aaron.

He said, "Pike. A surprise. Why are you here so early?"

59

I pushed the door, throwing him back. I said, "Cut the shit. You fucking killed the head of the FSB because of information I gave you. You didn't coordinate with me, you didn't inform me, you didn't do a goddamn thing but ignore me."

I cleared the door, allowing it to close, and saw Daniel and Shoshana deeper in the room, Daniel's arms crossed behind his back. I knew what that meant.

Aaron said, "We had no such agreement. I facilitated your operation against Yuri, and took appropriate action against a target of the state of Israel."

"You fucking *liar*. You used me. Letting me think the operation I conducted was to facilitate a follow-on mission against Yuri. All you wanted was to get me out of the way. You had no intention of a follow-on."

I advanced into the room and Daniel brought his arms forward, showing a Glock just like last time. Truthfully, because of Jennifer, my anger had been a little forced up until that point. A little make-believe. When I saw the weapon, it spiked again for real.

I said, "You think that thing is going to protect you?"

I looked at Aaron. "Remember what I told you about trying to harm anyone on my team?"

Shoshana seemed to realize the elevation of my anger from fake to real. Understood the terrain I was now on. She put her hand on Aaron's arm and said something into his ear. He said, "Pike, calm down. We did what you wanted."

I clenched my fists and said, "Bullshit, man. You did what *you* wanted. Yuri's going to flee now. No matter what I found out from that meeting, it's irrelevant. Best case, he would have given the details for a follow-on meeting we could interdict. That'll never happen now. *Never*. And my damn command thinks I tricked them into letting me assassinate Vlad."

He said, "Yuri was never my target. After your information, all my command wanted was Vlad. Sorry, but as you Americans say, they don't call it 'show friends.' It's show *business*."

His admitting to purposely using me sparked my anger like a match touched to gasoline. I snapped toward him, drawing my arm back. I saw Daniel raising the Glock and I shifted midstride, ducking low. I wrapped my left arm over his wrist, trapping his gun hand, and swept his legs out from under him. He slammed backward into the ground and I jerked the Glock from his hand, flinging it toward the front door, my subconscious understanding that the last thing I needed was a gun in my hand.

I said, "I fucking told you who the weapon was, asshole." And punched him square in the face, once, twice, three times. His head slapped the hardwood floor and I heard someone shout. I whirled and saw Shoshana aiming her own weapon at my head, a foot away.

Her expression was stone, showing me she intended to use it. I growled and she locked eyes with me, shaking her head slowly from side to side. We both heard a slide rack, and Aaron was forced into view, Jennifer holding Daniel's weapon to his skull, her other hand in his hair.

Hands in the air, he said, "In all fairness, you never told Daniel you were the weapon. You told me. It's probably my fault for not relaying."

Shoshana looked at Jennifer and said, "Put that down. You know you won't use it."

I said, "You put *your* weapon down, or I'm going to shove it up your ass."

Jennifer said, "Jesus, Pike! Stop it." To Shoshana she said, "I'm dropping my weapon. You do what you will, but we mean no harm."

Daniel was slowly rising from the floor, rubbing his face. Before I could stop it, she released the magazine, racked the slide, and handed the weapon to him. He took it with a look of shock.

Shoshana nodded, then dropped her weapon to her side, but didn't clear it.

I glared at Jennifer and said, "You know I could have taken her."

Shoshana said, "Wouldn't help. I don't swing that way."

I turned and saw her smirk, proud of her ability to yank my chain. Not unlike Jennifer herself. But I also saw respect. She was at least halfway on my side.

I said, "So I understand from Jennifer. Apparently females can sort that out through telepathy."

Shoshana gave Jennifer a sidelong glance, and the gaze aggravated the shit out of me. As she probably wanted. Jennifer saw my expression and rolled her eyes.

Aaron said, "Actually, Shoshana *is* good at that sort of thing. I don't know how, but she found you."

"Huh. So *me* ripping *her* off the back of a motorcycle is her 'finding me.' I guess that's right in line with you not 'fucking me over.' Do me a favor and shut the hell up."

Aaron held his hands up again and said, "As you wish."

Jennifer heard the words and flashed her eyes from me to him. He saw the look and said, "What?"

I said, "Nothing, damn it." To Jennifer I said, "Stop that. It's a coincidence."

The words *As you wish* held a special meaning for Jennifer and me, but I'd be damned if she was going to take the fluke and turn this into some psychic connection. I'd had enough of that with Shoshana. The whole conversation was turning into a comedy of who's on first, and it was getting me nowhere.

I said, "Look, I ought to beat you within an inch of your life, but I'm done. You screwed me over, and you win. I got played, and you got what you wanted. We're out of here."

I started walking toward the door and Shoshana said, "Sort of like you tossing me into the filthy Cistern water, huh?"

Hand on the doorknob, I said, "That was just business. Yuri is personal."

She said, "So was Vlad. Don't stomp out of here like you lost. You screwed us over first."

I read her eyes and saw the truth of what had happened last night. I said, "You pulled the trigger, didn't you? And you know what I mean. I trusted you. The ghosts of my men trusted you. This isn't just business. Of anyone, I thought you people would understand that."

She started to utter a smart retort, but the words died on her lips after she saw the real pain on my face. She looked at Aaron. He said, "I'm sorry, Pike. I truly am. You would have done the same in my shoes."

I opened the door and let Jennifer out. Shoshana stepped forward and said, "We don't leave here for another day."

Behind her, I saw Daniel glowering with his Glock and Aaron stone-faced. Not a lot of encouragement. I said, "So?"

She glanced back at Aaron and said, "So maybe you can come up with something else that'll hit Israeli interests."

I said, "Sure. I'd love to give you a shot at screwing me over again."

She winked and said, "Maybe I just want another shot at Jennifer."

The comment left me speechless, my mouth opening and closing with nothing coming out. She closed the door in my face.

60

Yuri felt the wheels leave the earth and was embarrassed to realize he was relieved. Happy to have lived long enough to get on an airplane out of Istanbul after the death of Vlad.

He'd awoken this morning thinking of Akinbo and the various contingencies that could occur, the usual amount of mission planning that happened this close to execution. He'd turned on the news and literally fallen into the hotel chair at what he saw, shocked to his core. Yuri knew that if anyone else was on the target deck, he was a front-runner, and if they could get to Vlad, they were probably tracking him right now.

He'd ordered an immediate evacuation for his team, sending most on their way to Berlin, but he kept his communications expert with him in Istanbul.

He'd already given them a brief the night before, right after he'd returned from his meeting with Vlad, preparing them for the journey to Berlin. All he'd done this morning was speed up the process. Originally, he'd decided on travel by train because of the lax border crossing he'd witnessed coming from Bulgaria, which would facilitate the infiltration of their weapons and communications package into the European Union. The odds of discovery were virtually nil, since there was no chance of a Russian being selected for a random search at the Bulgarian border. Once across, they would be in the EU and not subject to another search for the rest of the trip.

He'd remained behind, telling them he'd come via commercial air later in the day. In truth, he was unsure if he would follow, even unsure if the mission was still a go after Vlad's death, but he had to get them out of Istanbul, and Berlin was as good as anywhere else. In fact, better.

There were a few hard rules that Yuri always followed while in Istanbul—especially since his targeted killing of the Chechens two years ago. One of those was to never enter the Russian consulate because of the risk of association and the subsequent lack of invisibility, but the assassination of Vlad overcame any fear of discovery. With his Control dead, he needed to get inside to the secure communications room, and he had no illusions about ever coming back to Istanbul. It was a risk, but worth the reward.

He was granted access without incident, and, as he expected, the consulate was vibrating from Vlad's death, with people scampering about and phones ringing. Before long, he was brought to the secure room. He closed the outer door, then entered a shielded room-within-a-room called the bubble. Using an ancient secure telephone, he dialed his old Control, but someone he didn't know answered. After a brief conversation, he hung up, and dialed another office. Once again, he connected with an unfamiliar FSB officer. He left his name and location before disconnecting.

He exited the bubble and asked a secretary for the office Vlad was using. She directed him down the hall. He found it with little effort due to the noise coming out. He entered and saw four men digging out files and folders, stuffing them into a satchel. One turned and said, "Who are you?"

"I'm Jarilo. Vlad was my Control."

The man stared at him for a second, then said, "And what do you want here?"

"I'm in the middle of a mission. I gave him my laptop last night. I need to get it back."

"We've already been to his hotel. The only laptop was an FSB one."

Yuri had no idea if a separate laptop existed, but thought it a good bet. Vlad's American asset had contacted him somehow, and he assumed it was through the massive data flow of the Internet vice, something like a phone call that the NSA could suck up and trace. He was also betting that the asset was so protected that he would be firewalled from just about anything and anyone else at the FSB. Meaning a communication method air-gapped from whatever malicious eavesdropping software would surely be installed in an issued FSB computer.

Yuri said, "Have you seen one here?"

Before the man could answer, the secretary entered, meekly saying, "Jarilo? Are you Jarilo?"

"Yes."

"You have a phone call in the bubble. Someone from the president's office."

The men in the room quit working at her words, the mention of the president bringing them up short. They watched him leave in silence. He retraced his steps, wondering who on earth would call him here. Hoping it was his old Control, he reentered the bubble, closed the door, and said, "Yes?"

"Jarilo?"

"Yes."

"I understand you have lost your Control, but we want to make sure you are still working your mission. You have your orders, correct?"

"May I ask who this is?"

"No. But I speak for the president. You will continue with your mission. Understood?"

Yuri stared at the wall, unsure what to say. Unsure that the man on the other end wasn't trying to trick him. Finally, he said, "How do I know you speak for the president? How do I know you're even privy to the mission my last Control gave me?"

"I know all about the mission. I know your file for Barbarossa II,

I know your asset is in Berlin, and I know what he's there to collect. Don't force me to prove it. That would be unwise."

Yuri swallowed and said, "Yes, sir. Understood."

"You still have your contact method with Vlad? The e-mail address?"

"Yes."

"That is how we will communicate. Send a report every day. If I require further information, or I have a change, I will respond. Otherwise, just assume we are listening."

"Yes, sir."

"Any other questions?"

"No."

"Good luck."

And Yuri heard the phone disconnect. He held the old handset for a moment, staring at it as if he would glean some further information. A relic from the cold war, it reminded him of how his life was still buried in the past. How his *country* was still buried in the past. And how he now had the means to bring it forward. Vlad's death should have left him adrift. Instead, it made him feel whole. The future of the motherland was now his responsibility.

Before, he was but a tool. One of many working for the Russian Federation. Now, he was the master. The one man remaining who could revive Russian greatness. With the death of Vlad it rested on his shoulders alone.

61

Yuri left the bubble, walked down the hall, and reentered the office Vlad had been using. The four men were wrapping up their work, the room looking more like a display in a furniture store now, with all evidence of Vlad's presence gone.

Yuri said, "Did you find a laptop?"

"Not a laptop per se, but a cheap netbook. Is that what you were looking for?"

"Yes. Where is it?"

"In the inventory satchel. We have our orders. You want it, you'll have to go through headquarters."

Feeling the power of his phone call, Yuri said, "I just did. Give it to me."

The men looked at each other, unsure what to do. Yuri played on the fear he had just experienced. Played on the paranoia that permeated his service, understanding how Vlad operated for the first time.

He said, "Give me the fucking netbook. My crypt is Jarilo. Put that on a receipt and turn it in. You will get no pushback. On the other hand, if I put that name in a situation report and tell them how you obstructed my mission, you will regret ever having come to Istanbul."

With no further argument, they'd given him the netbook.

He'd taken it back to his hotel room and passed it to his communications man, telling him to clone the drive and bypass any security.

While the team member worked on hacking the hard drive, he'd purchased plane tickets for both of them to Berlin.

By the time he'd checked out of the hotel, the clone was done, transferred to another cheap netbook. He hadn't had a chance to explore the new computer, and patiently waited for the seat belt light in his aircraft to go dark. Finally, it did.

He retrieved the netbook from the overhead bin and booted it up. In addition to bypassing the security of the original netbook, his communications operator had collated all potentially interesting files on the desktop. Dismayed, Yuri saw more than two hundred.

He spent close to an hour wading through irrelevant documents that would do him no good. Finally, he found something interesting: protocols for covert communication using the deep web and TOR.

Vlad was from the old generation of chalk markings and physical dead drops. While he could leverage technology, it had always remained somewhat foreign. Clearly, someone had provided Vlad the cheat sheet as a reference for the application.

Yuri realized that he was looking at the communication for the American asset. He put all of the instructions together and saw how serious the asset treated his own safety. Not content to use anything provided by the FSB, the man clearly understood how corrupted the Russian systems had been by the American NSA. *Before* Snowden's arrival.

Yuri considered his next steps. According to the instructions he'd found, even Vlad was restricted from initiating contact with the asset. He was allowed to receive the intelligence the asset sent, but could never attempt to task the man for anything. Clearly, the FSB was afraid the asset would vanish if pushed. The thought gave Yuri some hesitation, but he made a decision. One that would reverberate far deeper than he intended.

He connected to the in-flight wireless and began the laborious process of establishing his own NYM e-mail account. Once that was done, he accessed the TOR network, then the Blofeld SMS service, typing out a simple message. An introduction.

He took the SMS URL and placed that into an encrypted e-mail on the NYM remailer network, working through a labyrinth of layers. Finally complete, he stared at the screen, seeing nothing but a URL in an e-mail message. Innocuous to anyone looking, but as volatile as the weapon he was about to retrieve in Berlin. Well, potentially to him, anyway.

He knew if he let the message fly he might be causing his own death. He was playing in an arena at the highest level of his government. A place beyond anything he'd participated within before, and a government that had no compunction about killing. Yuri, more so than most, knew that because he himself was one of their tools of destruction.

Yuri's finger hovered over the "enter" key, knowing if he hit it the asset could very well disappear forever, or worse, contact the FSB about his disloyalty. It was a risk, but Yuri couldn't accomplish his second mission without the asset's help: exterminating the team that had killed his men. Specifically, the female.

He thought about Dmitri falling from the scaffolding, screaming all the way down. Replayed in his mind the pathetic attempt to catch the body, the force driving him into the ground as Dmitri's head exploded on contact with the stone. Remembering the promise he'd made as the female assassin ran out of the museum. The promise to skin her alive.

And he hit "send."

62

Kurt Hale wondered how Bruce Tupper would present himself in his first formal Oversight Council meeting. He was one of the first to arrive and had sat silently, not even acknowledging the other men who entered. Acting like he was still a little steamed about having been kept in the dark.

In truth, when Kurt had told them that Pike was attempting to track the team who'd killed his men—even after he'd been ordered to stand down—everyone in the Oval Office had become a little steamed, to put it mildly. He'd cushioned the report, stating that Pike was still working the Chiclet thread, trying to decipher a terrorist threat and that the men who'd killed Decoy were a part of that. On the surface, the report was true, but Kurt knew that Chiclet had taken a backseat and Pike was hunting the killers on his own.

Now, with the head of the FSB dead a mere twelve hours after Pike had accused the Russians of the murders, Kurt knew it looked like Pike was running his own assassination ring. He'd been more than a little relieved at the digital recording of Vlad's meeting, as it showed a distinct threat. Something that would help with the Oversight Council.

President Warren was the last to arrive, and, as usual, he wasted little time on pleasantries. Every Oversight Council meeting he attended had to be explained. Someone had to account for the time interval in official journals, making it appear as if he were somewhere else. As the president of the United States, his attendance alone was asking for compromise. All it would take was a single question of where he was at X time, and the crack might turn into a flood. Because of that, he tended to keep the meetings short.

Kurt got out a single "Sir," and President Warren rolled his hand, telling him to get on with it. Kurt nodded and brought up his first slide, a summary of where they stood with Decoy and an assessment of the status of the Taskforce cover.

He said, "Knuckles has control of the remains now, and a reservation on a flight tomorrow—Istanbul time—to bring him home. Brett took Retro in the Gulfstream to Ramstein, and he's been successfully entered into Landstuhl hospital as a member of the Fifth Special Forces Group from Afghanistan. Brett's got a few issues with tail numbers on the bird, but we don't see—"

Secretary of State Billings said, "Whoa, whoa, whoa. Am I the only one who watched the news this morning? Your top story isn't the death of Vladimir Malikov, the head of the Russian state security apparatus?"

Here we go.

Kurt's face remained neutral. He said, "Sir, I'm aware of the killing, but it has nothing to do with the current problem set. It isn't a Taskforce issue."

Billings gave a theatrical look of incredulity, making Kurt want to punch him. He said, "You told us yesterday that Pike believed the Russian government was protecting Akinbo, and in so doing, they had killed Taskforce members. You went so far as to say you thought Pike was attempting to track them. Now, a day later, the head of the Russian intelligence agency is dead. You're saying that's just a coincidence?"

Kurt said, "Secretary Billings, I have spoken to Pike and I can assure you that the Taskforce had nothing to do with the killing of Vladimir. Pike was working the Akinbo connection, period. He—"

Billings scoffed and said, "Convenient, don't you think?"

Kurt let out a breath and said, "Sir, I'm not the person to ask about the assassination of the FSB chief. From what I've seen, it was a retaliation hit by Chechens, but you'd have to ask Mr. Bostwick or Mr. Tupper. This is their field."

Kerry Bostwick, the director of the CIA, said, "John, that's what it's looking like. The FSB has a history of killing Chechens. This is nothing more than a retaliatory hit."

Billings said, "Bruce? What's your take?"

Kurt thought Tupper looked a little green, but given the amount of information he'd been read on to in the last few days, he understood the emotion.

Tupper said, "I believe their missions just caught up to them. Like the killing of our chief of base at Camp Chapman in Afghanistan. Sooner or later, the hunter becomes the hunted."

His words hung in the air, the slow wisp of the overhead air-conditioning vent the only noise. Kurt watched Billings. Waited on his response.

He said, "So Pike Logan gets a pass yet again." He looked at President Warren. "Sir, we're not going to continue this charade, are we? Does the fact that this asshole runs amok without any oversight scare the shit out of anyone besides me?"

The statement was the segue Kurt wanted. He said, "Secretary Billings, Pike continued working the associations with Akinbo even after Decoy's death, and he's found a distinct threat. I understand your reticence, but if he hadn't taken the initiative, we'd be in the dark."

"Bullshit! Jesus, that's what you bastards always say. Every time someone dies, it's for the greater good."

He was working himself into a full-on spastic frenzy when President Warren raised a hand, shutting him down. Warren asked, "What do you mean? What threat?"

Kurt said, "Sir, Pike penetrated a meeting with Vladimir Malikov hours before he was assassinated. He recorded the conversation, and it's worth following up."

He clicked to the next slide and said. "Vladimir Malikov and Yuri Gorshenko met last night at a restaurant in Istanbul. Pike managed to clone one of their cell phones and turn it into a remote microphone. According to what we could ascertain, they are planning an attack against American or Israeli interests."

Kerry, the CIA director, read the summary and said, "This transcript is the best you could do?"

Kurt maintained his stone face and said, "The phone was on the table in a crowded restaurant. For context, imagine if you called someone on your cell phone in a venue full of people. Instead of talking with the phone to your ear, you set the cell phone on the table, then continued the conversation. That's what we were dealing with."

The secretary of defense read the summary slide and said, "So you think this Thor's Hammer is an RDD? We've talked about that before, but it's never panned out."

RDD stood for radiological dispersion device, an acronym Kurt hated. In his opinion, it was putting lipstick on a pig, like calling a common streetwalker a "sex-care provider."

Kurt said, "Yes, sir, we do. While a lot of the recording is unintelligible, we can clearly hear Vladimir say 'dirty bomb,' and Yuri states he fears that Russia will be blamed, presumably because of how hard it is to get radiological material, which is why this scenario has never panned out before. It takes a state system to cooperate. In this case, Russia."

President Warren said, "And you feel this is tied in to Akinbo? He's the one that will release it?"

"Yes, sir. He's not mentioned by name, but they do discuss procuring documents and providing funding, and he was the linkage that led to the meeting in the first place."

The president's national security advisor, Alexander Palmer, asked, "What's the target?"

"We don't know. They specifically mention that the target is *not* in the continental United States, and also mention striking 'Jewish lapdogs.' Initially, this would indicate Israel as the target, but the reason given for ignoring the US is our security. Getting radiological material into Israel would be exponentially worse, so we don't believe it's either country. At this time, all we can do is exclude the two. We can't get any more refinement without further exploration."

"Why? What does Russia gain by facilitating Boko Haram?"

"Most of that answer is tied up in the target. We can't analyze *why* they would do it without knowing *what* they want to hit, but rest assured Russia would hurt the US any chance it can get."

Kerry nodded and said, "I agree. Russia has never become a real democracy, and it's now ruled by a bunch of KGB thugs. If they see a benefit, they'll kill innocents without issue."

Palmer said, "What about interdicting the material? Short-circuiting the whole plan?"

"Same problem as the target question. All we know is the stuff is somewhere in Berlin. They mention a museum, but that's it. Actually, we don't even know if it's in Berlin. It might simply be close enough to use the city as a base."

President Warren said, "What are you recommending?"

"Well, I would say give me Omega for an operation in Berlin, but there are significant elements to consider. One, the only thread we have is the leader of the so-called Berlin Group. We have Yuri Gorshenko's cell number and can track it, but he is a member of the Russian FSB. A state entity, and thus outside the charter of the Taskforce."

Kurt saw Bruce Tupper shaking his head, but he continued. "Two, the only team that can react in time is Pike's, and that means it's going to be just him and Jennifer. I can't pull Knuckles from the recovery mission without causing significant risk to the Taskforce cover, and Brett's tied up with Retro in the hospital."

President Warren said, "It seems issue two makes issue one a moot point. You don't have enough men to execute even if it were a sanctioned Taskforce target. Are you saying you want to wait until Brett and Knuckles are free?"

"No, sir. I can get Brett in motion in another day, two at the most, and he's already in Germany, but that's still not enough manpower. Knuckles can be free in maybe three days, but the problem won't wait that long. We need to start moving immediately. Pike thinks he could do the mission as a joint operation, using the men who helped him with the eavesdropping mission. Which means working the target with the Mossad."

Billings said, "Absolutely not! I can't believe we're even considering this. Two days ago Pike Logan flouted every bit of authority we had. I wouldn't let him be in charge of the janitorial pool at this point, much less let him freelance with another intelligence agency. This is crazy."

The secretary of defense rolled his eyes and said, "It wasn't that big of a deal. If he hadn't, we wouldn't even know about the threat. Which, by the way, is a radiological dispersion device. A fucking dirty bomb. I'd be willing to work with the devil to prevent that thing from being released."

Billings said, "You do this and you'll get your wish. Pike *is* the devil."

President Warren raised his hand and said, "Enough. Put it to a vote."

As the chief of staff for the Oversight Council, Alexander Palmer nodded and said, "All in favor of authorizing Pike to work with the Israelis, say so now."

Kurt saw everyone's hand except two.

Palmer said, "Those opposed."

Secretary of State Jonathan Billings and director of national intelligence Bruce Tupper raised their hands.

Billings said, "This is a mistake."

President Warren said, "So noted. Bruce, what is your concern?"

"You're doing exactly what I said you'd do. Exactly what happens to every secret organization, no matter how well intentioned. You're breaking your own rules."

Palmer said, "There's no rule about working with other intelligence agencies."

"But you're about to authorize the Taskforce to go after a state target. Aren't you? Otherwise why vote?"

Palmer said nothing. President Warren said, "I understand your concern, but in this case the threat *is* worth the expansion of the charter. The only reason that rule was made was to prevent a duplication of effort with the established intelligence architecture. It wasn't for some prevention of nefarious action."

Tupper turned to Kurt and said, "What about equipment? Are we expecting the Israelis to provide that as well?"

"No. When we started the Taskforce we placed equipment caches in just about every major European city. Berlin is one of them."

Tupper said, "How will he service it? What happens if he's found trying to recover the cache? There's more to this mission than simply waltzing in and interdicting the Russians."

"It's not like it's buried or built into the wall of a building. We didn't go all Cold War like you guys did. He'll be able to access it fairly easily."

"So he already knows where it is?"

Wondering why the DNI was beating through the weeds, Kurt said, "No. He knows the cities, but he'll have to linkup with an in-country asset."

"How will he do that?"

Palmer said, "Christ, Bruce, who gives a shit? He answered the question."

Tupper said, "Sorry, but it's the mundane things that get your cover blown. Just my old case officer coming out."

Kurt said, "Sir, he'll get an e-mail on his Grolier Recovery Services

VPN. It'll come from the Taskforce headquarters but look like it's coming from his server. It'll give him the bona fides and the location for the linkup. Trust me, we put some thought into this."

Tupper nodded, saying nothing more.

President Warren went from face to face, then said, "Okay, are we granting Omega to Pike?"

63

I disconnected the VPN, staring out the window at the Istanbul skyline. I heard Jennifer say something, but the words didn't penetrate.

Again, she said, "Did Kurt just say what I thought he said? Are we cleared hot to engage the Israelis?"

I closed the laptop lid. "Yes. We are. But it's Chiclet only. No freelancing. Apparently, those Russian assholes who almost killed us are actively trying to kill a hell of a lot more people using him."

"What's that mean?"

"It means Shoshana gets a chance to hit on you again."

I felt Shoshana's eyes on me through the door peephole. She cracked it and looked left and right down the hallway, presumably for a pack of American ninjas preparing to attack. She saw it was just Jennifer and me, then opened it wider, saying, "My, my. You two just can't stay away."

I pushed through the door, saying, "I couldn't stop thinking about you."

Shoshana's face shone in a genuine smile. "That must be torture. Like a Bedouin craving ice cream. A mythical thing that'll never happen."

I said, "A man can dream."

"He's in the back room. Go give it your best shot. Jennifer can stay out here with me."

"She would be honored. But fair warning: She already has her mythical wish."

Shoshana said, "That being you, I suppose?"

"Yep."

I winked at Jennifer, and she rolled her eyes up to the ceiling, clearly not amused at our witty repartee.

Daniel exited the bath just as I entered the bedroom, one eye black and the left side of his face swollen. Aaron was packing a bag on the bed.

I said, "How come every time I visit the entire team is here. Do all of you sleep together? In America we get a per diem for each person. The Mossad doesn't pay for separate rooms? Man, I thought you folks being cheap was just a stereotype."

Daniel tossed aside the hand towel he was using and advanced on me, his jaw quivering. Aaron said, "Stop."

He did so, but he wasn't happy about it. Aaron said, "To what do we owe the pleasure?"

I said, "I need your help. I got the translation from the meeting, and it's pretty bad."

He carried the suitcase into the other room, saying, "I've told you this before. I can't do anything because they killed your men. I'm sorry."

I followed, Daniel right behind me, rubbing his hands together like he was itching to get them around my neck. I said, "Yeah, yeah, I heard you. It's not 'show friends,' yada, yada, yada. I'm not here because of my men. Vlad and Yuri weren't stopped by your interdiction of the Syrian."

I now had his full attention. Aaron said, "What do you mean?"

"I mean Yuri's on the hunt regardless of you smoking Vlad. He's executing a plan, and if we don't interdict it a lot of people are going to die. Specifically Jewish people."

"How do I know you aren't just saying that? Telling me a lie to manipulate my team?"

"Because unlike you, I wouldn't do that. If I'm lying, you can keep Jennifer."

Aaron smiled at my words. Shoshana tried to maintain a stoic face, but she couldn't. Even Daniel let a small grin slip out. Only Jennifer failed to see the humor.

Aaron said, "I'll have to send a message back before I can do anything. I'll need some proof."

I said, "I'll show you what I learned from the meeting, but it's still just my word that it's the actual translation. Do what you must, but make it quick. Yuri's not going to wait on us to catch up."

64

Yuri left two men at the entrance to the warehouse and carried the case inside, the cool fog of dawn exchanged for the pungent smell of bat guano and stale oil.

At twenty-five kilograms, the case was awkward, but not impossible for one man to manage. Yuri had always scoffed at the hysterical western news reports of "suitcase nukes," with pictures of something the size of a briefcase. Yes, Thor's Hammer was man-portable, but the container was more like a footlocker than a briefcase.

He swept his feet along the ground, kicking aside years of accumulated trash, and gently set the case down. He unlocked the four twist fasteners, hearing a slight hiss of air. He raised the lid and was surprised at the pristine nature of the device, having expected it to show some signs of decay. Instead, he saw a gentle pulsing light, indicating a sufficient charge remained for initiation.

The actual explosive device looked like a cartoonish bomb without the fins, a bulbous head thirty inches long seated into a custom Styrofoam bed. An egg of plutonium surrounded by a shell of explosives, it was utilitarian and ugly. In the front of the case was the permissive action link—or PAL—that allowed the timing and arming of the device. An ancient red LED screen, it was three inches by one inch and reminded Yuri of one of the first digital watches. Something that was ultramodern in 1978, but now looked dated.

Beneath the PAL screen were two sets of numeric keypads, requiring the input of two different sequential codes at the same time. In effect, requiring two people to arm the device. Remembering his training, he initiated a self-test sequence, and forty-two seconds later the system told him that it was green, capable of detonation.

The Hammer was alive.

He'd fully expected a fault. The RA-115s was a very delicate piece of equipment that had required constant attention in order to be capable of successful employment. There were literally a hundred things that should have gone wrong over the ensuing twenty-five years it had been stored. Something in the numerous chains of fail-safes, in the PAL, the triggering mechanism, or simply the decay of the plutonium itself should have registered as a fault, telling him he held nothing more than a very, very expensive conventional bomb. An IED with a unique twist in the form of the radiological waste it would throw out.

Instead, it was telling him the Hammer was capable of critical mass. He was unsure what to do now. He'd already made contact with Akinbo, preparing him for a linkup with the device. But that was when he thought the damn thing was just an improvised radiological explosive device. Not a nuclear bomb.

Should have known when I saw the power cable.

Four hours earlier, he and two men on his team had penetrated the location where the Hammer had been hidden. The defunct headquarters for the East German Ministry of State Security, otherwise known as the STASI.

Located in the old East Berlin section of the city, on a campus between Ruschestrasse and Magdalenenstrasse, the STASI had the unenviable reputation of being the most efficient and ruthless mechanism of state control ever created. And that was *including* the KGB and the gestapo. Yuri had been to the headquarters exactly once, when on a tour using the cover of a USSR diplomatic flunky. That had been years ago, and did him little good now, since according to the pinpoint mechanics of the cache instructions, the weapon was behind a panel ostensibly in place to service the electrical system.

Along with the device, the headquarters building housed the STASI museum, with displays on the first, second, and third floors. Run by a nonprofit, it wasn't a tribute, but a warning for future generations.

Yuri had executed a quick reconnaissance, and found the rest of the campus being used for storage or rented out by other companies. Modern capitalists turning the fearful history of the STASI into a mundane office complex. Luckily for him, the least amount of security was in building one, the headquarters, as apparently the nonprofit couldn't afford much more than an old guard who looked to be about seventy, armed with nothing more than a whistle. Beyond that, all he would have to contend with were standard door locks. Maybe they figured the association of the STASI alone would keep people out.

Building one was in the center of the campus and was the tallest structure on the compound, eight stories of utilitarian Communist brick and concrete built into an unimaginative rectangle. The primary entrance in the center of the building was also the museum entrance, with the rest of the building off-limits and not used. This, of course, would be exactly what Yuri would leverage.

Given the dilapidated nature of both wings of the headquarters, it had taken little effort to defeat the locks and penetrate the building away from the museum. Following the map he'd been given by Vlad, he'd descended below ground level, using a wall-mounted ladder to gain entry to a subbasement. He'd removed an access panel to an electrical junction box and had found the weapon. In among the myriad of electrical cables running up, down, left and right, he saw the RA-115s on a custom-built shelf. Looking like it belonged there. Still attached to a power source. Still gently blinking in the darkness as if it were 1984. Waiting to be employed by another Vympel team.

He'd disconnected the power cable and retraced his steps, struggling to carry the heavy box up the subbasement ladder. He'd rested for a moment, then had exited the building. He and Kristov were picked up by the team, driving the hour and a half to the abandoned Soviet Air Force base in Magdeburg, Germany.

They'd scouted the base earlier while looking for a secure location to give Akinbo the instruction he'd need for the device. Driving among the cracked and faded Cold War buildings, Yuri had picked a warehouse set off the end of the flight line, its position providing early warning for anyone attempting to interfere.

Now, watching the self-test light smugly blinking green, telling him the box held much more explosive power than he intended, he was unsure of his next steps.

65

Bruce Tupper heard his wife in the hallway, forcing him to tap the laptop keyboard. By the time she entered, he was playing a game of computerized chess.

Wearing a worn terry-cloth bathrobe, she faked a theatrical scowl and said, "I thought you were working. When are you coming back to bed?"

"Soon, honey. I couldn't sleep."

"Problem at the office?"

She knew not to ask anything more specific. He said, "Yeah. Something that's still spinning in my head. Keeping me awake."

She opened her robe and said, "Come back to bed. You don't have to sleep. I'll take your mind off of it."

Surprisingly, given what was hidden behind the chess game, he felt a warmth flow into his groin.

"Soon, honey. I promise."

He heard her pad back up the stairs, waiting an additional three minutes before minimizing the chess game. Behind it was a message in the Blofeld SMS window ready to be encrypted into a URL, asking the source on the other end where and when he would prefer to ambush the American team.

Tupper couldn't manipulate a damn thing the Taskforce controlled, but it didn't mean he was powerless. As the director of national intelligence, it was his job to arbitrate the allocation of intelligence assets, from top secret MASINT satellites to the omnipotent SIGINT capabilities of the National Security Agency. In this case, he'd issued instructions to intercept e-mail traffic from Grolier Recovery Services, layering it deep within the bureaucracy of the NSA. The only question now was whether he would replace them with instructions of his own.

In effect, setting up an ambush.

He'd been relieved when he'd found out about Vladimir's death, not really caring about the impact to Russian intelligence. He was much more concerned about his own secret, and Vlad being gone cauterized a potential leak.

The relief had been short-lived, however. It vanished when he received contact from an unknown agent on the special system he'd devised. At first he thought it had been Vlad reaching out to him from beyond the grave. A message sent before he'd been killed. As soon as he read it, he knew that wasn't the case. It was an introduction from Yuri Gorshenko, the assassin working for Vlad whom Kurt Hale had spoken about at the Oversight Council meeting. After providing his bona fides, Yuri gave—of all things—a tasking for intelligence on the new Taskforce team.

Tupper had never been tasked before, and the precedence was unsettling, especially when given in the same e-mail providing an introduction.

He had no idea if it truly was Gorshenko, but he was inclined to believe it. Clearly the agent had talked to Vlad, as the procedures for contact were very complex. It wasn't like Yuri had just stumbled onto an e-mail address and fired off a message. All of the proscribed methods had been used, including the NYM remailer and Blofeld. Which made Tupper wonder how many other people Vlad had confided in.

A long-term problem.

The immediate decision was whether he should help the Russian agent or remain on the sidelines. Whether he would choose the United States or the Russian Federation.

If he did nothing the Taskforce would probably locate Yuri using his phone, and if that happened Pike would kill him, erasing yet another thread. But there was a risk. A chance that Pike and his new friends might actually capture the agent. After hearing about Pike's past actions, he couldn't see that happening, but if it did Tupper was under threat of significant exposure.

The other solution was to work the problem from the opposite end. Eliminate Pike himself. If Tupper set him up, walking him right into his own death, the threat of exposure would be over, at least in the short term.

As he mulled the decision he absently checked his message. He realized one thing was missing. He typed, "Destroy current phone. Being tracked." He read it one more time, ensuring his instructions were clear, then had the Blofeld application turn it into a URL. He placed the URL into a NYM e-mail message, then stared at the screen.

Stay or go. Go or stay.

At the end of the day it may be a moot point. If Kurt sent the linkup instructions before Yuri replied with his own, he wouldn't be able to switch the messages. And did he really wish to start the precedent of being tasked by Yuri? Is that what he wanted?

But he *was* an agent of the USSR. The highest mole they had ever produced. He still had some patriotism buried in his heart.

Patriotism for a government and country that no longer exists.

He grew tired of the back-and-forth. This was only a first step. If he changed his mind he could always just ignore what came back. He hit "send" and opened a drawer of the credenza, pulling out a set of handcuffs. He had more pressing matters to attend to.

Like his wife's breasts.

66

The sun crested the horizon and began to burn off the early morning mist, exposing the cracked cinder blocks and broken windows in the old Communist warehouse, the building a metaphor for what Russia had become.

Yuri's cell chirped with a text that Akinbo was ten minutes out. Ten minutes to decide what he was going to do.

He'd expected to find a fault in the system, the device unable to reach critical mass, leaving the explosive charge to simply spread the plutonium into a giant, deadly radiation cloud, but now he had a real nuclear weapon. Something he couldn't give to Akinbo, as it would point the finger back at Russia.

Velcroed to the top of the hood was a sleeve. He peeled it off and opened it. Inside were two keys and a slip of paper with Cyrillic writing, both bringing back memories of his training on the device and a potential solution.

How could I forget the failsafe?

Each key was two inches long with a square end a half-inch wide, looking like a miniature paddle. At the start of the neck the key grew very thin, with notches on both sides. Farther down, it expanded into a complex laser cut. The keys were designed to be inserted then broken off at the notches, preventing anyone from reversing the procedure.

There were two, not because the designers intended for two people to utilize them in order to arm the device. That was already taken care of by the PAL. The key slots were right next to each other and could be worked out of sequence. No, the number was to determine how the device would react once armed. Two was for nuclear detonation. One was for self-destruction.

The Vympel had trained for the deep penetration of Western Europe, with each team having a selection of targets in various cities. He had no idea where this Hammer was destined to go, but it was probably the German Chancellery in Bonn. Given the distances that had to be infiltrated, there was a great chance for discovery of a Vympel team. A chance for the RA-115s to fall into enemy hands. Because of this, there was a built-in method for destroying the device. Do everything as required, but only use one key.

An Implosion bomb—like the Hammer—was created by surrounding the plutonium pit with high explosives, which, when detonated, compressed the pit, causing a chain reaction. Simple in theory, but very, very technical in execution because the compression had to happen with mathematical precision. If any of the explosive failed to fire, or fired out of sequence, it would not produce critical mass. It would simply explode with the force of the conventional munitions.

The use of one key did the latter. It caused the explosives to fire out of sequence, which destroyed the device, preventing it from falling into enemy hands. At least that was the intended use. In this case, it also created a dirty bomb, flinging out a large cloud of poisonous radiation that contaminated everything it touched.

He bounced the keys in his hand, considering. With one key inserted, once the PAL was initiated there was nothing anyone could do to alter the device's destiny. It would be on the path to self-destruction. On the other hand, he *would* be giving a live nuclear weapon to Akinbo. A weapon that would be out of Russian control.

But the African knows none of this. He has no reason to suspect.

He heard tires crunch on the torn concrete outside and saw Kristov wave from the door. He said, "Get his passport photos first. Then send him to me."

Five minutes later Akinbo shook his hand, saying, "Jarilo? Is that right?"

"Yes. I'm here to help you with your mission. There are several critical things, so I need you to pay attention for the next few minutes."

Akinbo nodded and pointed at the box. "What's this?"

"It will replace the chemical weapon the Syrian was bringing. It's a radiological dispersion device. Basically, a hunk of plutonium material surrounded by explosives. You understand what that means?"

"Yes. I have read about it. The radiation is poisonous. They call it a dirty bomb."

Yuri smiled, thinking that maybe the savage would work out after all. He said, "Yes. Exactly."

He knelt down and opened the box, showing Akinbo the PAL and the key slots. He said, "The screen there has two windows. The bomb was designed to be initiated by two people as a safeguard. Both key codes have to be worked in under five seconds, and each code has a sequence of two keys being pressed at the same time. The numbers on the pad itself and the one in the corner, which works like a 'shift' key on a computer. You'll notice the 'shift' key is out of reach of a single hand. In other words, it prevents one man from typing on both keyboards simultaneously."

"Wait, wait," Akinbo said, "I don't have a partner. I only have myself."

Yuri smiled, "I know, which is why I'm teaching you. I trained on these for a great deal of time, and on my team we never liked the two-man rule. There may only be one man left for the mission. We learned a trick or two, and I'm going to show them to you."

Akinbo said, "What mission? I understood the weapon was created for me, but now you're talking about teams and two-man rules. What is this thing, really?"

Yuri wanted to knock him off of that line of questioning immediately. "It is what I said. I built it from other parts I used to train with. That's all."

Akinbo nodded slowly with his eyes squinted and Yuri hesitated, a tendril of concern coiling at the back of his brain. Not dread or fear. Only concern, but it was there nonetheless.

Yuri began to work through the procedures, starting with the permissive action link dual pads. He showed Akinbo the codes passed to him by Vlad, then showed him the tricks of manipulating the keyboards. He taped a tongue depressor to the heel of his palm, wrapping the tape completely around his wrist, the wood sticking out like a deformed finger. Using that, he pressed the "shift" key while inputting the code with his fingers. After Akinbo understood the concept, Yuri outfitted his hands with the tongue depressors.

He said, "Work each hand individually, then we'll start working them together. It's critical that you input the codes correctly. If you make a mistake on either hand, it will force you to start over. Three such mistakes and the pads are locked. It's a safety procedure to prevent unauthorized access. You will be unable to unlock them."

They continued for forty-five minutes, until Yuri was confident Akinbo could manipulate the keypads under pressure. He said, "Okay, you know the codes for each pad, but that's not the entire sequence. Getting the weapon to detonate is a three-step process."

He pulled a key from the vinyl sleeve in his pocket and said, "First, you input the PAL code. Once that's done correctly, you'll get three flashes on the screen. When you see the flashes, insert this key." He pushed and twisted. "Once it's rotated, you'll see this light. After that is complete, the screen will show zeros across both displays. When you see the zeros, you know you are set."

He pointed at a small cover with a single tab projecting out. "That is the detonation button."

He flipped up the cover, exposing a red button. "You get the zeros, indicating successful arming, and you press this button."

Akinbo nodded, telling him he understood. Yuri inwardly smiled at the deception. He wanted Akinbo obliterated—along with any evidence of Russian involvement—so he'd made a little omission about the arming sequence during the weapon deployment. The zeros weren't there to indicate successful arming. They were there as a timing capability. With the timer set to zero, the weapon was set for instant detonation, but there was no reason for Akinbo to know that.

Yuri said, "You see how the key is shaped?"

Another nod.

"It's designed to be reusable if the operator wants it to be, like we're doing now, but also designed to be permanent. If you rotate the key to the 'on' position, then give the paddle a sharp blow, it will break off, leaving the key imbedded. From there, nothing will stop detonation."

"What is the other key for?"

"What other key?"

"There are two keyholes. What is the second hole?"

Yuri fumbled his words, then managed to get out, "Nothing. It's a backup."

Akinbo said not a word, but his expression told Yuri he didn't believe him. Yuri said, "Walk me through the sequence in real time, but do not turn the key."

Akinbo did as he asked, using the tongue depressors, placing in the key, then flipped open the cover for the detonation button. Yuri was satisfied.

"The same man who brought you here will take you home. Tomorrow, we will take you to the overseas freight company DHL. Using the passport we will provide, you will ship the weapon to this address."

He passed a slip of paper.

"The man will then take you to the airport, where you'll board a flight to meet the weapon. From there, it will be up to you."

"What is the target?"

"You will find out tomorrow. Have you made a martyr tape?"

Akinbo said, "I have no target. How can I proclaim the target was struck in the name of the Prophet when I don't know what it is?"

Yuri pulled the key and placed it back in the sleeve. He said, "You'll get the target tomorrow. And you *will* mail the box to the address. I will want to see a receipt before I pass you the key."

Akinbo said, "What's the other key for?"

"I already answered that."

He pointed at the sleeve Yuri was putting in his pocket. "You said the second key slot was just a backup, but there are two keys in that case."

"It's a backup as well."

"That makes no sense."

Yuri slammed the lid of the Hammer closed and said, "We're done. Get the fuck out of here. We'll pick you up tomorrow. Be prepared to fly."

He watched Akinbo leave and felt the little sniggle of warning raise its head like a foul odor seeping from under the floor. Once again, nothing concrete. Nothing specific. Just a faint wisp of something decayed that was gone before he latched on to it.

He got back to the hotel and accessed his computer, checking his NYM account on TOR. He rubbed his eyes as the TOR network went through its handshake, shifting his ISP to a hundred different computers in an endless stream, protecting his anonymity.

He leaned back into the cheap hotel office chair, the weight of sleep pressing down on him. He'd been awake for close to twenty-four hours and felt every minute of it.

A small jolt went through him when he saw he had a message, and the urge for sleep melted away when he read it.

It was from the sleeper agent in the United States, handing him the American team on a platter.

67

Lamar Redinsky stepped out of his hotel in Berlin, barely able to contain his excitement. Finally, after years of mundane work, he was going to execute a mission.

Well, not *execute*, per se, but at least facilitate the mission. At least brush up against the tip of the spear. The thought alone put a spring in his step.

Fifteen years ago, he'd started out as a logistician in the CIA. A number cruncher. A guy that kept track of where the weapons were dropped. Actually, kept track of anything that was given away to the myriad of people the CIA dealt with. Medical supplies, radios, explosives, you name it, it was his job to track, because sooner or later some congressman would come looking. And he wouldn't be asking the questions because of his love of the CIA. He'd be looking because he wanted to put someone's scalp on a wall so that he could get reelected.

Lamar had knocked around the CIA for over a decade before being recruited to a new supersecret high-speed organization. A counterterrorist command that was going to *really* take the war on terror global.

After the many read-ons and signing the myriad of nondisclosure agreements, he'd been told about his job: maintaining caches around the world.

At first, he thought he was being misled. The job description was like a Hollywood movie that depicted the "truth" of the intelligence world, but failed to take into account the reality of budget limitations. In films, money was no object to the spook world, with intricate safe houses and entire wings of aircraft sitting around just waiting to be used.

Working with the CIA, he knew better. There was always someone counting the beans, and rarely was anything purchased in advance because it *might* be needed. There just wasn't that much leeway in the CIA. Far from building a Hollywood secret infrastructure, more often than not, missions were put in jeopardy by recycling something from a previous operation. That's the way it was in the CIA, but not in Project Prometheus. Here, money *was* no object.

His entire job was to travel to various caches emplaced around the European continent and maintain them. Replace batteries out of date, rotate ammunition in magazines, occasionally replace communications gear with newer versions. Basically, ensure the equipment was ready for instant use. In truth, it wasn't unlike the giant armor packages kept in Germany during the Cold War, ready to be pulled out when the Soviet Union exploded through the Fulda Gap.

The job was a dream one for him. A bachelor, he literally traveled all over Europe doing nothing more than checking on storage facilities. Like the guy who painted the Golden Gate Bridge for a living, when he reached the end it was time to start again at the beginning.

With the government paying him for travel and per diem, it was the perfect life. No stress and no danger. But it had ultimately grown old. He'd maintained the caches and felt a sense of self-worth because he knew they'd eventually be used to protect America. But they never were. Ever.

He'd become a little jaded about the job, growing bored and beginning to think the entire effort was just a waste of government money.

Maybe the CIA had a point about fiscal restraint. Then, yesterday, he'd received the request for bona fides for a team in Berlin.

He'd almost been unable to contain his excitement. Finally, a linkup for recovery. He'd sent back the instructions and made his way to Berlin via rail.

After arriving, he'd checked the cache one more time, even though he knew it was complete, then found a hotel near the linkup location, waiting in the room in anticipation. At seven P.M., he exited the hotel, walking nonchalantly to the beer garden at the end of the street in the warm summer air.

He entered and asked for a booth in the corner, afraid he wouldn't be able to get one with the gorgeous weather. He was in luck. The hostess, wearing a cartoonish alpine costume that caused her breasts to explode out of the top, led him to a spot situated deep in the foliage of the garden.

Nothing more than a picnic table, it was the perfect place for a meeting. Off the beaten path, outside of view of the street, and away from anyone else in the restaurant.

He pulled a newspaper from his bag and laid it out on the table, then placed a Houston Astros ball cap on his head. It was a signal for the man who entered that, one, he was the contact waiting to meet him and, two, that the meeting site was secure.

He ordered a beer from Miss Titsalot and waited, knowing exactly when the contact window would open. At fourteen minutes after nine P.M., a man appeared carrying an umbrella in his left hand. There were, in fact, a few clouds in the air, but that wasn't why he had it.

He advanced on the table and Lamar saw he looked like a vampire. Very pale skin and jet-black hair. The man said, "Do they serve wine here?"

Nervously, Lamar replied, "No, but they have a very good selection of local beer."

Lamar relaxed when the vampire smiled, pleased at his success on the verbal bona fides. They shook hands and Lamar said, "You're the first operator I've ever met."

A waitress approached, silencing the conversation. The man ordered a beer to match Lamar's and waited. When the barmaid was gone he said, "I don't want to screw around. Give me the instructions."

Lamar was a little disappointed, wanting to learn a little bit of the world he was only allowed to skate around. Wanting to be appreciated. He passed across a key and an envelope. "The location is a mini-storage facility. Full security and climate controlled."

Vampire said, "You keep your weapons and communications in a rental lot? Seriously?"

Insulted, Lamar said, "Yes, it's the best place. The equipment is camouflaged in crates. It's not like we have it lying on the floor, and the building has built-in security. There's no chance of compromise, and people are coming and going all the time to service the place. Of course, I suppose you'd know better."

He finished his little statement of indignation, knowing—as a support guy—he was on the edge of upsetting an operator. He no longer gave a shit. Dracula could get as pissed as he wanted. He'd been traveling all over the continent for years just to facilitate this asshole's mission. Dracula could take his indignation and stick it.

Lamar never realized the risk. Never saw the death floating in the wind. He wanted to be a part of a real-world mission, but not in the way his future would play out.

The pale man placed the envelope and key into a bag without saying a word. Then he pulled out something large. For as long as Lamar had worked for the CIA, and then the Taskforce, he had never seen a pistol with a suppressor attached for real. Like most of the world, he'd only watched them in action movies. Because of this, when Dracula leveled the weapon at him his brain refused to assimilate that it was genuine. Refused to believe that someone from Project Prometheus would ever be a risk. Didn't understand that the man in front of him wasn't a part of his trusted brotherhood.

He was still working to process the situation when his brain was split open by a subsonic hollow-point round, the bullet expanding in the tissue, creating an enormous wound channel, and failing to exit the rigid wall of his skull.

68

Akinbo flipped through the television channels one more time, mindlessly watching the screen with the sound off. Four long hours before lunch, he had nothing to look forward to but more boredom.

His operational phone split the silence, startling him. Aggravated, Akinbo let it continue to ring, debating on whether to answer. After five he snatched it up against his will.

"Yes."

"Are you ready to fly?"

"Yes. What is the target? Where am I going?"

"A car will meet you in thirty minutes. Be out front."

Before Akinbo could say anything else, the phone went dead, driving a spike into his mood. He hated being at the mercy of the white *Kafirs* for this mission. They were no different from any Western regime. Corrupt and bloated, destroying every country they touched. And they touched them all.

He packed one small bag and checked out of his budget hotel, the clerk asking if he needed the shuttle. Just outside Tegel International Airport in the northwest of the Berlin metro area, the establishment catered to the cheaper business traveler, with most customers reliant on the hotel transportation. He told the clerk no, that he had a ride, and went outside to wait.

The building butted right up to a six-lane thoroughfare with no benches or other amenities. He considered going to the coffee shop inside but decided to simply lean against the granite wall, his bag at his feet.

He checked his phone to ensure he hadn't missed a text or call, then noticed a car slow. The man he knew as Kristov pulled to the curb. Akinbo picked up his bag as Kristov leaned over and flung open the passenger door.

Kristov pulled away before Akinbo even had the door closed, not saying a word. Akinbo waited a moment, then said, "Where are we going?"

Kristov said, "Just a short distance."

Akinbo clenched his jaw at the terse answer and turned toward the window, watching the city pass by. Shortly he was lost in thought, recounting yet again what had happened yesterday, trying to puzzle out the device he'd been trained on. He was absolutely convinced that it wasn't something Yuri had cobbled together out of spare parts. He was by no means an expert, but one didn't have to be a demolition man to see the device was purpose-built, with everything fitting tightly together and lying in a custom bed of reinforced foam. There were no indications of improvisation. Nothing taped down, no wires running loose or mismatched screws.

On top of that, the security procedures were unreal. The dual key-pads were almost impossible to operate and not something he would have chosen if he were "cobbling together" a bomb out of spare parts. Especially a bomb that was to be passed to another person. Even with no experience in working with explosives, he understood that simpler was better.

Then there was the slip of the tongue about teams and missions. Jarilo was no ordinary soldier. If he was tasked with a mission, and his team had trained on the same device, it wasn't to blow up a NATO ice-cream factory. It was something strategic, and if it involved that device, it meant the weapon was a strategic asset as well.

Last night, using the laptop Vlad had given him, he'd googled Soviet dirty bombs and fixated on the rumor of a so-called suitcase nuke. Nobody could prove or disprove they existed, with some Russians claiming they'd seen upward of one hundred at one time, and that the old USSR had lost control of them. Others said it was just a myth of the Cold War, a rumor fueled by fear.

He searched further, and had found the W54 SADM, or Special Atomic Demolition Munition, a backpack nuclear device. It wasn't Soviet, though. It was a weapon created by the United States in the Cold War. So they *did* exist, and if the United States had them, he had no doubt the Soviets had followed suit. He was fairly sure he had seen one yesterday.

The final clue had been the separate initiation keys. The excuse of a backup key and a backup keyhole made little sense. The two keyholes were purpose-built. And he knew the purpose. Now all that remained was to get them.

Kristov pulled into the parking lot of a roadside café and said, "You'll find Jarilo at a table in the outside section. Leave your bag here."

Akinbo exited, went through the interior of the café, the heavy aroma of baked goods and coffee reminding him he hadn't eaten breakfast. He found Jarilo at a wooden table in the back, hands around a mug of coffee and a folder next to him.

Akinbo sat down, waiting on Jarilo to speak. He started right in without any pleasantries.

"Inside this folder is a confirmation code for a flight to Brazil. It leaves at two P.M. today going through Amsterdam. Also inside is a new passport with a visa for Brazil. You will be on that flight."

Akinbo said, "I'm getting sick of asking. Do you want me to pick my own target?"

"No. Inside here is a detailed description. You still have the address I gave you?"

"Yes."

"That is your safe house. Before you fly, you will ship the weapon to that address. They know you are coming, but don't know when."

He passed across another slip of paper. "This is their e-mail address. You'll see it's the same domain as yours. Nobody from the US will track it. When you land in Brazil, contact them."

Akinbo nodded and said, "How will I ship the weapon?"

"There is a bill of lading and a prepaid invoice in the folder. The weapon is categorized as tools. If you follow procedures, there will be no issues with customs. All you need to do is drop it off, fill out the delivery paperwork, and sign for it."

"Where do I do this?"

"You will be taken to a DHL storefront near the airport. You don't have to worry about that."

Akinbo opened the folder and studied his passport, then the target. He nodded in agreement, saying, "This is good."

Jarilo said, "I'm glad you approve. We've put a lot of research into helping you."

He slid across a prepaid credit card. "That'll get you through until the attack. Pay attention to the expiration date, martyr."

Akinbo saw that the card expired the same day as the execution of the mission. Meaning he was supposed to die in the event. He had no intention of doing so.

He said, "I see it. What is your point?"

"I don't think I need to spell it out."

Akinbo leaned forward and placed his hands over Jarilo's forearm, pulling him close. He said, "I will execute. I have not lost my focus. You people are the ones who lose the stomach for the fight at the first bit of trouble."

Jarilo jerked his arm away and said, "You have three days to create your martyr video. Can you do that?"

"Yes, but I would like a picture of the weapon to prove it was me and not just someone claiming credit. Can I do that?"

"No. No way. The photo might connect my country to your actions. We are willing to help, but only so far."

Akinbo thought, *Because someone will recognize the device for what it is. Someone will know it wasn't created in a basement garage out of spare parts.*

Yuri continued, "There will be enough evidence found with the DHL shipment and your flight itinerary. The world will believe you."

Akinbo said, "What about the keys?"

"You'll get the key when you provide proof of shipment to the address I gave you. Then you'll go to the airport."

"I'll get both keys?"

"No. You only need one."

"I thought the other was a backup."

"It is," Yuri snapped. "Now, if you have no other questions, the next time I hear about you should be because of a radioactive cloud."

It will be. A mushroom cloud.

69

The wheels touched down in Berlin, the old octagonal airport terminal in the distance. I glanced behind me and saw Jennifer leaning toward the window. Once again enjoying the history around her. Before we'd taken off, she'd explained to me that Tegel International Airport was the famed landing spot for the Berlin airlift when the Commies tried to strangle West Berlin during the Cold War.

I turned on my Taskforce phone, more pressing things on my mind than the history of the place. We were going to need equipment and weapons, and Aaron's team had left theirs in Istanbul in order to fly commercial. They'd gotten approval to help us based on my voice cuts from the meeting at the 360 restaurant, but getting their infrastructure moving was only marginally faster than ours. When I heard it would be two days before they could set up a pipeline to get their weapons and equipment out of Istanbul and into Berlin, I'd told them to forget it, and that I'd provide the equipment.

We'd pretty much given up pretending with each other about our occupations. Well, at least pretending that Grolier Recover Services was just a business for exploring old shit. They didn't know who I worked for, but understood it was some sort of US government organization. They couldn't figure out if it was military or intelligence, which was fine by me, and they were really perplexed about Jennifer.

Aaron and the Mossad had a pretty deep understanding of the

United States's secret squirrel organizations, and they knew that the CIA had no femme fatales like Jennifer. No killers like the Mossad had in Shoshana. Case officers and analysts, yes, but nobody who could have survived the ambush Jennifer had in Istanbul. It really made them curious. Especially Shoshana.

As much as we were allies, Israel was distinctly different from the United States for a multitude of reasons, not the least of which was the fact that they lived on the edge of annihilation. People in the United States had long forgotten what it was like to live in fear of losing their way of life, but Israel endured with that specter every day. It was like comparing a twenty-first-century soccer mom to a woman fighting wolves on the prairie in the 1800s.

Shoshana lived in a world that may not exist tomorrow, much like the citizens of West Berlin in the Cold War. She was a lethal killer who, while not immoral, was definitely *amoral*.

There were plenty of people in the Taskforce who leaned toward her worldview, including me, but every single one had a Y chromosome. We'd never had a female on the killing end of the spear, and because of it, Shoshana was curious. She saw a skill in Jennifer that might even exceed her own, but also a lack of will to use it.

In Shoshana's mind, the mission came first, followed by her life. Without question, both were worthy of killing to protect, the ends completely justifying whatever means was used. In Jennifer's mind, *everything* was up for question. The mission came first, but only if it was worthy, and, unlike Shoshana, she would sacrifice her life if so doing would ensure the greater good. She hadn't grown up with the wolf, and because of it her worldview was different. Shoshana saw this qualification as weak, but I knew better. Jennifer was stronger than the both of us.

I'd ended up next to Shoshana for the flight out, with her in the middle and Daniel in the aisle. Jennifer and Aaron were in the row behind us. I'd offered to switch, but Aaron had said he was fine. He didn't fool me one bit. He wanted the opportunity to explore what was next to him, which gave me a little concern. Jennifer had been trained and knew better than to give anything away, but I still didn't like her in the crosshairs.

It didn't take long for me to understand we were both in the crosshairs. Like every Israeli government individual I'd ever known, Shoshana began to interrogate me as soon as our wheels left the ground. Unlike the others, where flattery usually hid a quest of information, she started off by poking me in the eye.

"I'm surprised you convinced Aaron to come along. We don't usually follow someone with such a poor record of success."

I said, "What the hell would you know about success? You're the one who slipped in a patch of soap. *I'm* the one who ripped you off your bike."

I saw a small grin leak out. She was clearly not upset. In fact, it was almost like she was hitting on me. She said, "You aren't like her. Why is she with you?"

The change of subject threw me off. I decided for sarcasm. "I didn't think you cared. I didn't think I had a chance with you."

"You don't."

I leaned in close, brushing her thigh as I did so. "Really? You sure about that? You seem to be pretty interested for someone who doesn't swing my way."

The invasion of her personal space didn't affect her at all. With my face inches away from hers, she frowned and said, "I guess I was wrong about you. And so is Jennifer."

I pulled back and said, "What's that supposed to mean? You don't even know me. Or Jennifer."

"I know you. You're right, though. I don't know Jennifer. She's strange."

I'm talking to a female Spock.

I said, "You don't know me at all, damn it."

She said, "You just rubbed my thigh in an attempt to get me to back down. You use your sex as a weapon, and it's very clumsy. You are no different from every man I've ever met. I *do* know you. What I can't figure out is why Jennifer is with you. She seems to see something everyone else on the planet misses."

I felt anger, then embarrassment. Who the hell was she to diagnose my psyche based on a single conversation? She had no idea what had happened between Jennifer and me. I gave up on the tricks and looked her in the eye, "Jennifer saved my life, and I don't mean in a physical way. When we met I was in bad shape. I was within a couple of months of killing myself. Maybe not by my hand, but it would have been suicide all the same. She pulled me out of the pit. You asked why she's with me, but you don't understand the relationship. I'm with *her.*"

She studied me for a moment, searching behind my eyes for the lie that didn't exist. It felt like she was reading my soul, and maybe she was. She slowly nodded and said, "Perhaps Jennifer was right to do so."

I broke the gaze and said, "I'll never know why she did it. I don't know what drives her. She has her own moral code, and it's pretty set in stone."

"And you think it's better than your own."

"It *is* better than my own. Better than yours too, I'm sure."

"Can she kill on command? Will she do what's necessary?"

"She'll kill, but not like a robot. She has to know why she's doing it."

"You Americans always want to know *why*. It's a weakness we cannot afford."

I looked between the seats and saw Jennifer talking to Aaron, a smile on her face. I said, "It's not a weakness. It's a strength, and it's served us well."

She said nothing, reading my glance at Jennifer. I got a little sick of the Vulcan mind meld and said, "You don't mind, I'm going to get a little shut-eye."

She put her hand on my arm, stopping me from closing my eyes.

She said, "Your recording said they were targeting Israelis, and that's good enough for me. You think any of these other Russians had anything to do with Munich?"

"You really get a hard-on about that, huh?"

I saw the feral glint return to her eyes. The same one she'd shown when she'd found out about Vlad. She said, "More than you know. The world needs to understand how far our reach is and how long our memory runs. It is the only way to prevent future attacks."

"You don't think it just starts a cycle? Your grandfather was killed in Munich, and now you take the lives of the killers. You know Ali Salameh had a baby before he was targeted? A son? You ever wonder if the daughter of that son is now hunting you?"

She snorted. "So what you do is better? Because you kill them from the air with a Predator strike, it's more humane than what I do?"

"Don't insult me. Did you see a drone in Istanbul when I found you? And yes, I do wonder sometimes. In the end, I know there are things that can only be resolved through violence. Certain men only speak five-five-six, and I'm more than willing to talk to them in their language. There are plenty in America who don't understand this, but I do. I also understand that violence alone isn't the solution. All it does is keep the bad man away for a little bit. It creates some distance."

She said, "You don't need to worry about any of that with the Russians. They're as bad as they come. You need to know that going in. We tangled with them once before, and I learned early to shoot first, period. You don't, and you'll be dead."

I said, "I get that, trust me. I could give a shit about any second- and third-order effects with them. They picked the wrong team to hit, and now they're going to pay."

The little devil grin flitted across her face and she said, "Sort of like Munich."

I scowled at the comment; her ability to twist my words and back me into a corner grated on my limited good nature. Before I could respond, she said, "You better get Jennifer in the same mind-set. She starts questioning why she's doing something with these guys, and she'll be dead before the thought settles."

I said, "Don't worry about her. When her back's to the wall, she finds a way to win. She always has."

She traced her finger across my thigh very close to my groin, causing me to stiffen then slap her hand away. She smiled at my reaction, completely opposite of her own response to the same approach just minutes ago. She won that round, and she knew it.

She said, "I'm glad. I'd hate to lose my chance at showing her the light."

I gritted my teeth, furious at her getting the better of me. Daniel tapped her on the shoulder from the aisle seat. She pulled back, maintaining eye contact. He whispered in her ear and our conversation ended, the two now debating something I wasn't privy to.

I'd leaned against the window, spending the rest of the plane ride pretending to sleep, the discussion playing in an endless loop. Once on the ground, I focused on the mission and ignored her ability to mess with my mind.

Just as our plane arrived at the gate my phone locked on to a cell signal and began a data transfer. I had an e-mail from my "company," and was relieved to see it was the linkup plan with the asset. The good news was the person who maintained the cache was available to meet tonight.

The bad news was he wanted to execute the linkup in Magdeburg, Germany, two hours away.

70

When Akinbo exited the restaurant he saw that Kristov had been replaced with a new man. He attempted to engage the driver in conversation, but all he managed to learn was his name. Oleg. Something that sounded as foreign to Akinbo as the heavily accented English the man spoke.

Akinbo felt Oleg looked exactly like what a Cossack thug should be. A single thick bony brow and a coarse beard. The man's breath stank of boiled eggs and stale cigarettes, making Akinbo want to roll down the window.

They rode in silence to the DHL storefront, Akinbo worrying the problem in his mind. How to get both keys.

There was no question in his mind that the second key held the means of mass destruction. There was no other explanation. What he questioned was why the Russians were willing to use him to set off a dirty bomb, but not a real nuclear explosion. The only reason he could see for the self-imposed limitation was the fear that the world would understand Russian complicity in the attack. Like all the cowards in the West, they feared the wrath from using the device instead of embracing it.

The truth was he hated the Russians as much as any of the infidel regimes. They *all* stank of boiled eggs and stale cigarettes, and they all needed to be cleansed. There was no such thing as coexisting in peace. He'd watched his village live in poverty since he'd been adopted, the people scraping by trying to compete in a world that was inherently unfair. The south owned the oil, and because of it, they owned the happiness. Exactly opposite of what the Prophet preached. There was no help from anyone who believed the West. No help from the Christians. The only help was through their own exertions, and the only path was through Allah.

The dim memory of his father shamed him, as he was once one of the oppressors. It made Akinbo quiver in quiet rage, praying harder and harder for forgiveness. Praying that he would get the chance to strike back at the inequality. And now he could.

He said, "Oleg, I was told I would get the key for the weapon. Do you have it?"

"I do, but you won't get it until you mail the package. That's your ticket."

"Where is the package?"

"In the trunk."

"And the key?"

Oleg looked at him with his snake eyes, drawing on a cigarette. He said, "What fucking difference does it make?"

"The difference is I'm about to risk my life on a bill of lading you created, taking a bomb into DHL. I'd like to know I'm not being used."

Oleg stopped at a red light. He glanced at Akinbo, then reached behind the seat, pulling up a small black corduroy nylon bag. Military looking, with loops and velcro all over. Oleg unzipped a top pouch, showing the vinyl sleeve with the two keys. Deeper in, Akinbo saw a pistol and what looked like brass knuckles.

Oleg said, "There it is. Now shut the fuck up."

They drove in silence for another ten minutes, then Oleg pulled into a parking lot. He said, "The DHL store is around this corner. The device is in the trunk. I'm sure they have cameras, and I don't want to be seen driving in. When your attack is done, everything will be analyzed. You will drive from here."

Akinbo nodded slightly, then said, "You'll wait here? You won't leave me?"

Oleg laughed and said, "No, I'll be here. Don't wreck the damn car."

Akinbo said nothing. Oleg reached behind him, pulled out his go bag, and exited the vehicle. He said, "You're gone more than twenty minutes, and I'll hunt your ass down. You won't like the results. I promise."

Akinbo put the car in drive without responding. He saw the DHL storefront as soon as he turned the corner. He pulled in, parked, and opened the trunk, seeing the weapon inside. A square piece of plastic luggage that looked like a modern Pelican case, complete with butterfly closures. It was something that transported a myriad of innocuous equipment around the world on a daily basis, now secured with padlocks to prevent entry.

He went inside, initially nervous, but he gained courage by watching the actions of others. He presented his bill of lading, filled out the paperwork presented, then signed. The machine spit out a complex receipt, and he took it. He went to the car, hoisted the box out, and placed it on a dolly, wheeling the weapon inside. When the man behind the counter placed his hand on the dolly, Akinbo said, "Does this have to go to an address, or can I pick it up?"

The man said, "Yeah, you can pick it up. Save you some money, actually."

Akinbo smiled and said, "That would be better. The address I gave you isn't for sure yet. I'm worried about losing these tools, but I won't be able to pick the box up immediately. Can you hold it?"

"Yes, but not forever, and it'll have to be at a distribution facility."

"I understand." Akinbo pulled out his wallet, saying, "I'd like one in São Paulo. Can you do that?"

The agent squinted and said, "That's nowhere near this address."

"I know, but my company is located in São Paulo."

"Okay. If that's what you want. I need to redo the entire transport application, though."

Eight minutes later he was back in the car, slowly driving back to Oleg and wondering what his next move would be. In order to get the second key, he needed to separate the man from his bag. What would do that? How could he get Oleg to turn his back and leave something that was as attached to him as a pacemaker?

He pulled around the corner and saw Oleg standing next to the shell of a pay phone, the phone itself long gone. He parked next to it and waited until Oleg was inside, then said, "Here is the receipt. Please pass the keys."

"*Keys?* You only get one key."

"What about the padlocks on the outside?"

Oleg unzipped his go bag and pulled out the vinyl sleeve, saying, "Use bolt cutters. I don't have the keys for them."

Akinbo took the single key and said, "Why can't I have the backup as well?"

"Cause Jarilo said so. Let's go. Head to Tegel Airport. You got about two hours before your plane takes off."

Akinbo pulled into the street, feeling his opportunity slipping away. He drove south, weaving through the congestion toward the airport. He glanced out of the corner of his eye, and saw the bag sitting in Oleg's lap. No way to get to it.

Ten minutes of fruitless thinking later and he reached an intersection with a sign proclaiming TUNNEL FLUGHAFEN TEGEL. The Tegel Airport tunnel. Once he entered that, there would be no further chances. The next stop would be the terminal building.

He glanced again and saw nothing had changed. Oleg held the bag on his lap and was gazing out the window. Through the glass, Akinbo saw a police officer mounted on a late-model BMW motorcycle.

He returned his eyes to the front, seeing the light still red. The police officer jarred loose a single thought: *Oleg will hide the bag from him*. He made his choice, goosing the gas pedal.

Oleg shouted, "Whoa!"

Akinbo slammed on the brakes just as they skidded into the car in front of them, an old Peugeot sedan, crumpling the bumper. They had traveled no more than five feet.

Oleg leaned forward, surveying the damage to the car in front. He slapped the dash and said, "You fucking idiot. What the hell are you doing?"

Akinbo said, "Police officer to the right. He's coming this way."

Oleg stuffed the bag under the seat and said, "Stay here. Don't say a fucking word." He pulled the rental agreement from the glove box and exited, waving at the police officer.

Akinbo waited until they were talking, then reached beneath the seat. He unzipped the top pouch, slid his hand in, and took the second key. He left the vinyl sleeve as camouflage for what he'd done. He heard someone tap on his window and jerked upright, seeing the driver of the Peugeot staring at him curiously. He palmed the key, wondering what the man had seen. He rolled down the window and said, "I'm so sorry. Very sorry."

The man said something foreign and Akinbo pointed at Oleg and said, "I don't speak German."

Oleg took over, speaking German to both the driver and the police. Twenty minutes later he came around to the driver's side, watching the police officer motor away. He slapped Akinbo's head, telling him to get in the passenger seat.

He sat behind the wheel and pulled out his bag, zipping open the pouch. He saw the sleeve and closed it back up. He put the car in drive and entered the tunnel, muttering under his breath. Two miles later he pulled into the departure lane outside of terminal A.

He said, "Your flight is KLM. You do know how to get on an airplane, don't you? No chance of you causing it to crash into something, is there?"

Akinbo gritted his teeth and said, "No. I can get on an airplane."

Oleg said, "Then get the fuck out."

Akinbo did, barely having enough time to grab his small carry-on before Oleg sped away, leaving him standing on the curb by himself. Clutching two keys in his palm.

71

Yuri handed across the locker key and the envelope of instructions he'd gleaned in the beer garden the night before, saying, "Tell me the bona fides again."

Oleg said, "Simple. One: right time, right place. Two: The designated linkup enters the cul-de-sac alone, turning off his lights. From inside the headquarters office, I flash twice with a penlight. Three: He responds with two flashes from his headlights, then approaches the door. Four: He knocks four times, I reply with two, then open the door."

"Good. Get him inside and subdue him. Do not, under any circumstances, kill him. Remember that. Capture only. We'll kill them once we round up the entire team. It could be the female coming in. If it is, rest assured the male will be close. We're lucky, we'll shut this down in one night."

Oleg nodded and said, "You're not worried about them getting the locker key and real instructions?"

Yuri racked a round into his PP-19, aiming through the holosight at an imaginary target. "No. I'm more worried they'll smell a trap. I don't know if those things are a one-off, or another safety signal. They can hold them for the forty seconds it'll take before I collapse their world."

Oleg said, "Good enough for me."

After Oleg left, Kristov said, "You want me here? Or on the airfield side?"

"Airfield side. I want to block all exits. Peter stays in the vehicle in case we need a chase team, but you and I will choke off the entrance to the cul-de-sac."

Kristov nodded and said, "I'm headed out. I want to use the light while I got it."

As he left, Yuri said, "Check for bums. We don't need any witnesses."

Kristov said, "Will do," and slammed the door.

Alone in the dilapidated building, Yuri's thoughts shifted from the Americans to Akinbo. He considered sending a message to his cryptic presidential contact about the status of the mission. He decided not to. Better to do his own cleaning. There was no reason for the FSB to know that Akinbo now had the means to initiate a nuclear explosion. Not yet, anyway.

Oleg had come back with his story of the accident, cursing Akinbo and generally badmouthing his bad luck to be assigned to handle the African savage. Good-natured bitching until Yuri had asked for the receipt and the key. What he got was the receipt and the vinyl sleeve. The Cyrillic instruction for the keys' use was still inside the pocket, but the key was history.

In a panic, Oleg had ripped the car apart, to no avail. The key was gone. It could have ended up on the side of the road, but Yuri knew it had not. Akinbo—the savage they thought was so stupid—had taken it.

Reeking of fear, the sour odor wafting out as Oleg flapped his arms in the air, he'd begged Yuri to let him fly to Brazil. Let him get it back. Yuri had declined, although he did think about killing Oleg for his stupidity.

Instead, Yuri had contacted the Control of the safe house in Brazil. Thinking about what Akinbo had done, he figured the man would try to protect his theft of the key. He had to in order to penetrate the safe house and gain access to the weapon. Yuri had the DHL receipt, so he knew that's where the weapon was going, but Akinbo would be on edge, trying to determine if he'd been found out. The last thing Yuri wanted was a spike, whereupon Akinbo knew they were aware of his treachery and afraid to enter the safe house. No, he wanted Akinbo chained to a toilet until he could arrive and provide some corrective action. Then force him on his little mission with a single key.

He'd fired off an e-mail to the safe house, instructing them to send Akinbo an innocuous introductory message from their address. Ordering them to lull Akinbo into complacency. He ended the message by giving them Akinbo's itinerary, stating in no uncertain terms that if they failed to capture Akinbo when he arrived, the repercussions would be dire.

In the end, he was surprised at Akinbo's skill and cunning. He'd thought the African was an ignorant peasant, and for that Yuri was now paying the price. But not for long.

Akinbo had managed to get the key, but he'd still shipped the Hammer via DHL. Yuri had the tracking number and Akinbo's flight itinerary, which meant he could stop the weapon from ever arriving in Akinbo's hands. Yeah, he had been smart about the key, but he was woefully inadequate in modern-day logistics.

Yuri wanted to gut the African as much as he did the American team, but first things first. He glanced out of the cracked window, seeing the sun dip below the horizon and knowing that his position was about to get dark, the electricity having been long since cut off at the old air base.

He keyed his radio, getting a confirmation from Oleg in the linkup position, Kristov on the other side of the cul-de-sac, and Peter in the reaction vehicle. He said, "Keep your eyes out. This is about as easy as we've ever had, but it could still go wrong. Peter, after early warning you're still in play. I call, you'd better be able to react. Kristov, I have the west. You got the east. Nothing escapes."

They acknowledged and he had one final command. "Oleg, it's your mission now. You understand what that means?"

"Yes, sir. I do."

"Remember Dmitri. Remember what they did. I want that bitch. I want that team. I told her I would skin her alive when I caught her, and I intend to keep that promise."

72

I rolled out of the truck, hitting the ground harder than I wanted, feeling the impact in my bones. I slid to a stop, knowing that damn woman was driving *way* too fast. I saw Aaron tumble out a good fifty meters away, proving my thought. I saw the glow of the taillights disappear and hoisted my backpack in the darkness. I scuttled to his location and said, "You okay?"

"Yeah. Some bruises."

"What the fuck is Shoshana's problem? It's like she wants to punish you every time she does anything."

He grinned in the soft glow of the moonlight and said, "She's punishing *you*."

I had no time for that. Jennifer was going to be on short final for the linkup, and we needed to get in position to lock down the location.

I had no idea why the Taskforce contact had chosen to conduct a linkup on an old Soviet Union air base, but I was sure it was for a good reason. I'd learned early not to question the recce force. Nine times out of ten, as the assault force, you thought the linkup procedures or the information provided was weak, with you being a "smarter" operator trying to "fix" the problem. Then, after the assault had gone down, you found out the recce ground truth was real.

No, you can't walk right up to the breach point wearing a banana costume. No, we don't have X-ray vision of the hinges in the interior of the building. Yes, that minefield will prevent your movement from the wood line, but feel free to ignore our report.

This, though, was stretching things. The Magdeburg air base was out in the middle of nowhere, full of decaying buildings that had been abandoned shortly after the wall fell. Why on earth we were meeting here was beyond me, but I wouldn't put it past the Taskforce to cache a supply bundle at this location. Hell, I'd have done it just for the humor, but I figured whoever had created the caches was more mature.

The linkup location was at the end of a cul-de-sac on the edge of the flight line. It was a narrow strip of asphalt lined with row after row of concrete government buildings, now being reclaimed by nature. Right at the end the road took a turn to the left, running about fifty meters straight up against the runway, with a small cul-de-sac that held what must have been the best of the best for office space. I suppose it was an effort to create somewhat of a view for whichever Ivan had the pull back when the base was active, but for me it caused an issue of security.

I knew the Taskforce guy we were meeting was no threat, but I wanted to prevent anyone from interfering with the linkup. Truthfully, it was overkill, but since we had the manpower, I figured we might as well control the site. In so doing, I also hoped to get a feel for my new teammates. So far, after bouncing on the concrete, I wasn't too impressed.

In twenty minutes, Jennifer was going to drive up the middle of the pipe, execute the bona fides, then linkup with the asset. Shoshana, the little femme Nikita, and Daniel, the guy who planned his life by a Ouija board, would take the eastern exit. Aaron and I would block the western side, which happened to be across the old runway, leaving us a two-hundred-meter crawl to get in position.

I wasn't too happy about Jennifer going in alone, but the bona fides from the asset had demanded a singleton linkup, and I'd do more good on the outside, controlling the operation and the team. Plus, it gave

Jennifer some extra experience and gave me a chance to evaluate the Israelis.

Aaron took a knee and I pulled out a set of binoculars. They weren't night vision, but they were better than nothing to determine any activity across the airfield. I scanned the houses, not seeing anything unusual. Just a bunch of broken-down old Communist block buildings, looking like something from a postapocalyptic movie.

I said, "Looks clear. You ready to go?"

Aaron nodded in the dark and said, "You want point?"

Wanting to check him out, I said, "No. You take it. You see the building right where the road turns toward the runway?"

"Yeah."

"That's our target. Shoshana and Daniel should park and go dismounted to the house on the other side."

He nodded, pulled a black watch cap on his head, and proceeded to snake his way down a drainage ditch, the path taking him farther away from our objective initially, but giving him cover. He disappeared into the scrub of the ditch and I scrambled to catch up.

I fell in behind, watching him move, and knew instantly that he wasn't just an intel collector. He'd done this for real more than once in an operational role, which meant he was some version of Sayeret— Israeli Special Forces. Beyond the fact that he'd picked the exact same route I would have, you could always tell when someone was comfortable moving in the dark. No fumbling around, no hesitation or stutter-stepping, walking with the hands to the front, afraid of running into something he couldn't see. He glided along at a rapid pace, dodging limbs and stepping over rocks as if he had some Yoda skill. Something that could only be gleaned through experience.

We reached the edge of the ditch and he paused. "We have to cross fifty feet of open ground to get to the back of the building."

"And?"

"And we can belly crawl or we can run."

"What do you think?"

"Belly crawl will take forever. It's the movement that will get us compromised, so the less time out in the open the better. I say run, both at the same time."

I smiled in the dark. *My thoughts exactly.*

I said, "Sounds good. Stay away from the line of sight of that back door."

He nodded, and we cleared the open area as fast as possible, sliding up against the rough cinder block. We remained still, listening for any movement. Nothing happened.

I worked down the back side of the building and peeked around the corner. I couldn't see the street due to overgrown landscaping. I looked at my watch and saw we were close to the time window. Jennifer would be rolling in shortly.

I whispered, "Time for the belly crawl. Get down the wall until you can see the road. Stay below the windows."

He nodded and said, "What are you going to do?"

"Stay back here and control things. I don't want to get a bunch of ticks."

I couldn't see the scowl too well in the dark, but I'm sure it was there. He started moving, working his elbows into the ground and slithering forward through the brush like a snake. I sat on my haunches, running through the mission and what I would need out of the cache.

Suppressed weapons were a given, but the bigger issue is what we'd stocked technology-wise for a manhunt. For some reason, Yuri's cell phone had dropped off the grid, so we'd need another way to find and fix him. Tagging, tracking, and locating gear and whatever else I could think of. Moore's law caused the tech kit to go extinct very rapidly, and I had no idea what was stored here. If everything was no longer relevant, at least I still had the kit from Istanbul. The Goblin IMSI grabber, Pwnie Express, and other knickknacks.

The mental inventory gave me an idea. I could use the IMSI grabber right now. I set my pack on the ground and my phone vibrated with a text. It was from Aaron and said two words: "Headlights coming."

I texted back, "Roger," then switched my phone to Taskforce internal, saying, "Koko, status?"

"Coming in right now. Making the turn to the cul-de-sac."

None of the Israelis had the capability of tying into the Taskforce smartphones for group encryption, so our commo would be text-only, but at least I could talk to Jennifer.

I set the IMSI grabber on the ground and turned it on, the screen glare flaring out with a blue glow. I violently tapped keys until the display was more muted, hearing Jennifer say, "Got the flashlight signal. Exiting the vehicle."

I said, "Roger all. Tell me when linkup is complete."

She assured me she would, and I fired up the Goblin grabber.

The old air base was so far out in the middle of nowhere that anyone close who had a cell phone would register with it. It wouldn't give me a location, but it would tell me how many people were around. Which should be exactly four, outside of our Taskforce phones.

The computer began listing the cell numbers, and there were a lot more than four. I heard a noise and snapped my head around, raising my fist.

It was Aaron. He held up a finger and whispered, "There's a guy in this building. He just lost light discipline with a flashlight. He has a weapon."

Weapon?

I returned to the captured phone numbers, something about them tickling the back of my brain. Then it broke free. They were Russian numbers.

I shut down the grabber and keyed my phone. "Koko, Koko, this is Pike."

Nothing happened. *Because you just locked her phone. It's got to find a tower.*

I waited a beat, then tried again. I got nothing. I pointed to the door at the back of the house. The one we'd avoided when we ran across the open area. I pointed to the building, then ran a finger across my throat.

Aaron nodded and began sliding that way. I finally heard Jennifer. "Pike, this is Koko. Knocks complete, all bona fides met. We're secure. He's unlocking the door. You want to wait until I've met him, or come on down now?"

I hissed, "It's a fucking trap. I say again, it's a trap. Get out!"

73

Jennifer heard Pike's command in her Bluetooth earpiece, the words shooting adrenaline through her body, burning into her muscles like high voltage. The door cracked open and she saw a brutish man with a thick brow. He pulled it wider, a ghoulish smile on his face. She stepped back, raised her leg, and kicked hard, driving the door into his body and flinging him into the foyer. She leapt through the opening before he could recover.

The brute hit the floor and rolled, reaching behind his back and drawing out a pistol. She threw a low snap kick, knocking it out of his hand and sending it skittering across the floor, stopping short of a hole in the dilapidated structure. He hissed and punched her thigh, bringing her to her knees. She threw her arms up and ducked as he lashed out with a jab, rabbit-punching the back of her head. She rolled with the blow, springing back to her feet and facing him.

He made no move toward his pistol. He raised his hands and said, "Don't fight me. We won't hurt you. I have orders not to hurt you."

She heard the accent. *Russian*. She remained silent, glancing at his weapon on the floor seven feet away.

He stepped toward her. "Don't even think it. You'll only get yourself killed."

She could barely understand his English. He stepped forward again, and she slid sideways. He saw her intentions and closed the gap, both hands out in supplication. He was leaning toward her right, toward the pistol. He took one more step forward, inside her range. She snapped two quick jabs, a left followed by a right, catching him in the nose and popping his head back. She followed with a knee to his stomach, the strike missing and sliding off.

Ending slightly to his rear, she stuck a leg behind his knees and levered his body backward, causing him to slam into the floor a second time. As he went over, his flailing arms grabbed her hair, yanking her to the ground. She screamed and jerked free, scrambling for the pistol in the corner on her hands and knees.

He leapt on her back, circling his arms around her neck, clamping down on her throat and driving her face-first into the floor. She saw sparks flash in her eyes, the pain consuming her. She swept the floor blindly, desperately trying to grasp the pistol. Her hand brushed the grip and she swung it back again, slapping the pistol forward. It disappeared into the hole in the floor.

He pounded her head into the ground, paralyzing her for a moment. She quit searching for the gun and struggled to her knees. She swam a hand between his arm and her throat, using all of her strength to pry it back, but only gaining a half inch of space.

She fought to her feet, then drove her legs backward, forcing him to backpedal to stay upright. She picked up speed and slammed him into the wall near the entrance door. It did little good.

He pressed her head forward, cinching down his arms, his face next to hers. She smelled stale tobacco on his ragged breath, and knew it might be the last thing she ever sensed.

She drove her legs backward again and he used the momentum to whip her around, throwing her into the wall face-first. The impact stunned her enough to make her go limp for a split second. He bent over, holding her weight off of the floor. She saw the light of the stars through a window and feebly flung her right heel back, trying to damage him.

Window.

She put her hand on the sill and pulled herself toward it.

In between breaths, he said, "Quit fucking fighting. Stop it."

With her last bit of strength, she whirled her body, making him rotate with her and getting his back to the wall. She staggered to the right, dragging him along. He jerked her neck and she could go no farther, praying she was within range.

She went limp again, forcing him to bend over and hold her weight. She gathered her feet underneath her and exploded off of the floor, driving him backward. She barely heard the shattering of the glass and kept pushing, jamming his body through the window. His lower back embedded in the jagged glass in the sill, causing him to scream.

And breaking his hold on her neck.

She whirled around before he could recover, grabbed him by the hair and jerked his head to the right, embedding his neck in broken glass. She ripped the head down, raking his neck on the transparent razors, then fell back, gasping for air.

He pulled himself out of the window, his eyes wide-open and both hands on his neck, blood jetting out obscenely. Even as she scuttled backward like a crab, she stared in morbid fascination, amazed at the volume of fluid.

He fell face-first, one arm outstretched, the fingers clawing the dirty concrete.

74

Yuri heard the early warning call from Peter and a smile crept across his face, a sinister, savage thing devoid of humanity. It was the woman approaching. The one who had killed Dmitri and Mishka. The one he had promised to flay. A promise he very much wanted to keep.

Two weeks ago he would never have considered an operation such as this. One that was so far away from his primary tasking. To do so would be tantamount to treason. He would have simply swallowed the bitter pill he'd been given and continued on, like he had on numerous operations in the past. That had been before the death of Vlad. With it, he'd discovered a newfound freedom. It was more than a lack of oversight. It was something growing inside of him, a desire to make his own destiny instead of blindly following orders.

He'd still accomplish Vlad's original mission even if he had to set the dirty bomb himself, putting Akinbo's dead body next to it, but he would have his vengeance here first.

Headlights pierced the window of the building he was in, forcing him to duck beneath the sill. They vanished, and he watched the car coast forward with nothing but its driving lights. It reached the edge of the cul-de-sac and flashed its lights. Once, then twice. On the second flash he thought he saw movement in the shrubbery of the building next to his.

The car door opened, and he watched the female exit and begin walking to the center building at the end of the circle. He returned to the shrubbery, raising his night vision to his eyes. He could barely make out a shadow. Maybe a man, maybe not. He flipped out the folding stock of his PP-19, brought the weapon to high ready, and slid out the door.

He went around the back of the building, away from the street, sliding along the concrete cinder blocks. When he got to the edge, he peeked around the corner, using his NODs. From this distance he could clearly make out a man crouching in the dark, staring at the linkup site.

He saw no weapon, the man apparently just watching. He had to be a member of the American team. Yuri slid the PP-19 around to his back and pulled out a six-inch fixed-blade stiletto. He began to creep ever so slowly toward his prey.

He got within five feet when the man answered a cell phone. Yuri strained to hear what he said, but couldn't make it out. An instant later he understood why. The man wasn't speaking English. In fact, he wasn't speaking a language Yuri recognized.

He listened for a second more, happy for the call as, like a texting driver, it focused the man's attention on the phone and distracted him from his surroundings. A dangerous mistake on a highway, but positively lethal in combat. All Yuri needed to do was wait until the call was over, get him in the sweet spot while he was still focused on the conversation but after he'd disconnected, preventing whoever he was talking with from realizing something had gone terribly wrong.

He put the knife in a reverse grip and crouched, staring at the grainy green image through his NODs. He saw the arm drop, paused a moment to be sure, then was taken by surprise when the man snapped upright and exploded out of the bushes, running straight toward the linkup building.

Yuri remained still for exactly one second. That's all the time it took for his brain to assimilate the action, the purposes behind it, and the second-order effects of letting the man continue. He sheathed the knife, ripped off the NODs, and began sprinting, bringing up the PP-19 Bizon. He entered the street and saw the man was almost to the building.

He took a knee, flipped the lever to full auto, and squeezed off a three-round burst. The PP-19 was a submachine gun, accurate at short ranges but not designed to kill at a distance. He watched the dust spray at the man's feet. He raised his hold and let loose again. This time the man tumbled to the ground, rolling to the sidewalk just outside the building.

He was mentally congratulating himself when the window to the right of the door exploded outward.

What the fuck?

He raised his NODs and saw Oleg holding the girl, him on his back and screaming. Yuri dropped the goggles around his neck and began sprinting again, his eyes glued to the window. He reached the sidewalk and took a knee, raising his weapon and hitting the window with its mounted light. He saw the girl rip Oleg's neck on the left side of the shattered window, the blood spurting out black in the harsh illumination.

He heard a guttural scream from the right and whirled in time to deflect the charge of another man. The attacker dove at his head, attempting to tackle him. He rolled back, planting his foot on the man's stomach and using his momentum to flip him neatly over his head and into the ground. The man rolled, springing to a crouch unhurt, charging again. He saw it wasn't a man. It was another woman.

He pulled his weapon up and she lashed out with her leg, knocking the barrel off. She closed inside his range and began ripping his face with elbows and spear hands, tearing the skin above his nose and pounding his brow, all sharp edges and pain. She jabbed his left eye, blinding him, and he kicked out, pushing her back. She growled and charged again, like some demented being unconcerned about her welfare.

He popped her hard in the temple, then grabbed her hair with one hand and wrapped his arm around her waist with the other. He slammed her into the ground, then raised her head by the hair, exposing her neck.

She looked him in the eye and said, "You are fucking dead."

He said, "Not tonight."

And raised his fist.

75

I heard nothing else from Jennifer and left the whole IMSI grabber mess of computers and cell phone paraphernalia where it lay, running down the back of the building to catch up with Aaron.

I slid in behind him and said, "This place is fucking crawling with Russians. We were set up."

Working the lock to the door, he said, "One's inside here. He's got a submachine gun."

"I have to get to Jennifer. Right fucking now."

I started to move away and he grabbed my arm. "Don't. There's a killer in here with a weapon. You leave, you expose us all."

He was right, but it didn't help my mood. "Then get this thing open, or move aside and let me do it."

He went back to work on the lock, whispering, "She will be okay. Shoshana thinks Jennifer is like your Star Wars movies. Something special."

"What? A fucking Jedi?"

He said, "Yes."

I whispered, "That's fucking crazy. She's no match for a bunch of Russians."

The lock broke free and he turned the knob slowly, inching it forward from its decayed grave, wanting to prevent the rusted hinges from making noise. He said, "Shoshana's never wrong. She thinks the same of you, but I don't know why."

He pushed it open enough for us to enter and I slid in through the door, now quiet, getting far enough to allow him to follow. We both crouched, letting our eyes adjust to the starlight. The entry room had two exits. One straight ahead, and one to the right. He touched my arm and pointed to the door to our front. I nodded, moving to the opening on the right. Before either of us could take two steps, a black blob exploded out of my door, straight toward me.

The man held a long gun of some sort and was wearing night observation goggles. He saw me and skidded to a halt, bringing his weapon up. I launched straight at him, slapping the barrel high and driving my fist into his throat. He fell to his knees, gasping for air through his shattered larynx, the giant Russian goggles bobbing up and down.

I dropped a step back and lined up a roundhouse kick, whipping my entire weight behind it and catching him just behind the ear. He slammed into the ground like he'd been poleaxed. Which I suppose he had.

Aaron and I both sat still for a moment, hands out in a fighting stance, assessing whether anyone else was coming. We heard nothing. I turned to him, seeing his eyes in the dim moonlight. Looking at me with respect.

I started searching the body and he pulled out his phone, saying, "I see Shoshana was right. Remarkable reflexes." He grabbed the Russian's subgun with his free hand, and I slapped it away, jerking the PP-19 from his grasp.

I said, "In my world the Jedi gets what he earned."

His phone connected and he said something in Hebrew.

I pulled off the NODs, found a pistol, and threw it to him, saying, "We need to move. Going out the front. I'll lead."

He said, "Daniel is on the way. Don't shoot him."

I took off at a fast trot, reaching the front door and jerking it open. I surveyed the street with the Russian NODs before exiting. They worked okay, but reminded me of stuff we used in the 1990s. In the green glow I saw a man running toward the linkup building.

Daniel.

I jerked the NODs off my head and started sprinting through the grass. I hit the pavement, my legs churning as fast as I could make them go, and saw another man to my right, seventy-five meters ahead. He took a knee and raised a weapon. Even at this distance I recognized him. It was Yuri, the pale-skinned, vampire-looking son of a bitch who had killed my men. He let loose a burst and missed. I took a knee and raised my own weapon. He fired again, and Daniel tumbled to the earth. I squeezed the trigger, throwing rounds downrange in a bid to take him down. I missed. The man stood up, unaware of my attack. He began running straight toward the building.

The window next to the front door exploded in a shower of glass and I saw two bodies locked in mortal combat.

Jesus. Jennifer.

I leapt up and began running as fast as I could, desperately trying to close the distance, knowing if Jennifer wasn't dead, she would be shortly. The man had reached the edge of the lawn and had stopped sprinting. He raised his weapon, aiming it at Jennifer. I threw my own weapon up to my shoulder, still running flat-out. I screamed and squeezed off a burst.

A dark flash came from nowhere, tackling him. He grappled with the wraith, slamming it into the ground. I saw him wrap his hands into the person's hair and realized it was Shoshana. The man raised his fist in a killing blow, and I shouted again.

Yuri finally realized I existed. Still holding Shoshana's hair with one hand, he reached down with the other and grasped the PP-19. He raised it, shooting one-handed. I dropped and rolled, getting out of the line of fire, diving behind an old defunct junction box. The bullets pinged the cheap metal, sounding like rain on a tin roof. I crawled to the right and raised my weapon.

Yuri fired two more bursts at the junction box, snarling like a chained dog. The girl in his grasp rolled to the left, torquing her body around the hand in her hair and trying to kick him. He hammered her forehead with the butt of his weapon, drawing blood. She curled into a ball, hands over her skull.

Down the street he saw headlights spill into the cul-de-sac and knew it was Peter. Reinforcements on the way.

He said, "You idiots picked the wrong fight."

He placed the barrel against her head, then heard a noise behind him. The door to the building had opened. He whirled and saw the woman from the linkup coming. The killer of his men, holding a section of pipe and swinging. He raised the PP-19 and the metal slammed into his shoulder, crunching bone and drawing a scream. He rolled to the left, letting go of his captive to get away from the club. He brought the weapon up again with his weak hand, holding it out in front of him toward the satanic bitch with the pipe, but she'd already moved. He turned, desperately trying to find her.

The pipe came down on his good arm, shattering it and causing him to drop the submachine gun. He looked up at her, now helpless.

He said, "Go ahead. Do it."

She said nothing. She dropped the pipe. His face split into a rictus grin.

"You fucking weaklings. I cannot believe we lost to people like you."

He felt fingers snake through his hair, then snap his head back.

The other woman said, "Say hello to Daniel on your way to hell."

76

I leveled my weapon at Yuri, but didn't pull the trigger. He had lost my location, but I couldn't shoot with what I had. The PP-19 wasn't an accurate weapon to begin with, and this one certainly wasn't dialed in for me. If I fired, I'd stand as much of a chance of hitting Shoshana as him.

Headlights from the rear rolled over my position. I turned around to see a vehicle approaching at high speed. The car launched right at me, bouncing in the air over the curb. I leapt over the top of the junction box, losing my weapon as the vehicle smashed into it, ripping it off the foundation but stopping the forward movement.

A man spilled out of the driver's seat, raising another PP-19. I rolled over, sweeping the ground for the weapon and knowing he had beaten me to the draw. Praying his aim was off. A shot rang out and a dark mist exploded from his head, silhouetted by the glow of the headlights. He fell forward, revealing Aaron standing behind him, holding a pistol.

I nodded at him, then began moving forward, hearing Yuri scream in Russian, cracking off rounds that snapped through the air and caused Aaron to dive into the dirt. I darted around an overgrown patch of shrubs and heard Yuri shout in pain. When I regained line of sight I saw he was down, Jennifer above him holding a length of pipe.

I slowed, the night coalescing into one image burning into my brain: her standing.

Alive.

Yuri started squirming on the ground and I began running again, closing the distance. Shoshana muscled him upright, sitting behind him and holding his head. I slowed to a trot and grinned, thinking he'd just entered his worst nightmare.

And I was right.

A long blade appeared in her right hand. Her left pulled his head back. I saw the future and screamed in futility, trying to stop her. Jennifer dove toward her arm, but was too late. Shoshana slid the knife across his neck and it split open like an obscene mouth, the blood flooding down his shirt.

By the time I reached them, he was dead. Jennifer sat heavily in the grass, the murder overwhelming her.

I kicked the knife out of Shoshana's hand. "What the fuck are you doing?"

She leapt up and bared her teeth, on the verge of striking me. Aaron jerked my arm from behind and I whirled around, throwing a punch that didn't connect. He slapped my fist away, dancing out of range.

I stood fuming. I flicked my head back and forth between them and said, "We don't know where the African is. We don't know where the bomb is headed. You just killed our only lead."

Shoshana said, "That fucker killed Daniel. He was going down. No other way."

I rubbed my face with my hand and said, "You people really need to get over the vengeance thing. Munich was a long time ago."

She stood and wiped the blood off of her hands on her thigh. She looked at Daniel's body and I saw a tear tracking down her cheek.

"Don't lecture me. There is no bigger issue than my family. None. You told me you would do the same. He killed your men too."

She broke her gaze from her dead friend, glancing at Jennifer, then at me. She said nothing, but I understood completely. I *had* said that. It was a shitty deal all the way around.

I said, "I'm sorry. I really am. But there's a terrorist on the loose who's going to attack a lot more people than just your friends."

She looked at Aaron and said, "Daniel was right. I should have killed him."

Confused by the statement, I looked at Aaron. He slowly shook his head and said, "That's not true, Shoshana."

"Yes. It is. Daniel said someone was going to die, and because I spared Pike, Daniel paid the price. This is my fault."

I said, "What the fuck are you talking about? You think because you didn't kill me in the Cistern you caused Daniel's death?"

She said, "You wouldn't understand."

Jennifer cut in, surprising all of us. "Yes, he would. He understands more about the pain you feel than anyone here. There's a reason he's still standing, and you know what it is. You believe it just like I do."

Now really confused, questioning if I was the only one wondering what the hell we were talking about, I said, "Believe what?"

Shoshana gave Jennifer a slight nod and said, "Believe in the name Nephilim. Believe that you have a purpose beyond just aggravating the hell out of me."

77

As the men filed into the cramped briefing room of the old executive office building, Colonel Kurt Hale surveyed them closely, looking for signs of deception. Someone had sold the linkup information to the Russians, allowing them to set up an ambush, and Pike was convinced there was a mole buried inside the Taskforce. Given that Kurt had handpicked every member, he thought the idea far-fetched, but he had begun the laborious process of screening anyone who had access to the support and logistics of the cache infrastructure. A mole sitting on the Oversight Council itself was beyond discussion, yet he still couldn't help but study the men as they circled around the table.

The last to enter, Alexander Palmer, told him that the president would be late and to begin without him. Kurt showed no outward emotion, but internally he grimaced. He wanted the president's support, knowing this meeting was going to become contentious.

Now I know why he wanted a private briefing.

At President Warren's request, he'd given an update earlier this morning, so he knew how the president would vote when the time came.

Kurt began, "Gentlemen, this is the update briefing for Project Prometheus operations targeting Boko Haram."

That was the only statement he made where someone wasn't shouting a question or demanding a further explanation. Before he had finished relating the actions of Pike's team from the night before, Bruce Tupper became agitated, interrupting him.

"You said you did these operations all the time. That you weren't amateurs. I remember saying linkups like this caused compromise and, sure as shit, you got compromised. How?"

"Sir, we're investigating that. Right now, we believe the weak link was the man we had servicing the caches. Somewhere his operation was penetrated, and his information was used to set up an ambush for Pike's team."

"You mean a mole? Jesus. This is like the 1980s all over again."

"No, sir. Not a mole. Our men and women are personally vetted by me, then they undergo the same lifestyle and CI polygraph as anyone working in the intelligence community. Each and every one. The cache controller worked for the CIA for over a decade before he began to work for us."

The DNI slapped the table and said, "Have you ever heard of Robert Hanssen? He was a damn spy in the counterintelligence division for thirty years. Handpicked!"

Kurt held up his hands and said, "Sir, we're taking precautions. Everyone associated is going through a polygraph procedure. All information technology systems are being forensically checked."

Tupper said, "Everyone in your organization gets one. You understand? Don't cut anyone slack in your building. That's how Aldrich Ames lasted as long as he did. People simply couldn't believe he could be the mole."

Kurt said, "Yes, sir."

Tupper continued, "What's the cache asset's story? What's he saying?"

"We haven't located him yet. We're working it, but the man posing as him at the ambush had the real-world cache instructions and the keys to the drop site, which isn't a good sign."

Tupper scowled and said, "Cauterize anything he has touched. Do it now."

Kurt nodded, saying, "Already done."

Tupper fidgeted, looking for another line of attack when Palmer cut in. "Did Pike get anything from the ambush? Any intel?"

Glad for the change of topic, Kurt said, "Yes. First, there was a DHL receipt for a package getting mailed to Brasília, the capital of Brazil. We assume it's the device, but the tracking number is no longer valid. We've already been through DHL trying to piece together why it's being rejected, and apparently, it was never active. No package ever entered their system with that tracking number. Second, we have a vinyl sleeve with Cyrillic writing. Translated, it's some type of instructions for keys to be used in an explosive device. Pretty much proof positive that the Russians are involved in this up to their eyeballs."

Kurt failed to mention the biggest pieces of intelligence. Pike had also found a computer with folders on the desktop, all in Russian. He'd hooked it to the Internet, allowing the hacking cell to search the hard drive from Washington. They'd found some interesting communication methods involving the deep web, but no hard information. Kurt believed it was for talking to Chiclet, but Pike was convinced it was for communicating with a mole. He'd managed to talk Kurt into keeping the communications method secret in case it was used again.

The light above the door began flashing red, telling Kurt that someone wanted to enter the secure conference room. He waited, and Palmer let in the president.

Warren took Palmer's seat at the head of the table and said, "Where are we?"

"Just getting to the intel indicators from the ambush."

"Did you brief the Cyrillic stuff?"

"Yes, sir."

President Warren turned to the secretary of state, Jonathan Billings, and said, "I want quiet pressure brought to bear on Russia. We don't know if it's sanctioned or not, but someone in their government is helping Boko Haram, and I want them to know we know."

Billings nodded and said, "A sleeve with Cyrillic writing isn't much to take to them. Do we have any other proof?"

President Warren scoffed and said, "Seriously? Yeah, we have more proof. The head of their intel agency was heard talking about a dirty bomb to a guy who ambushed Pike. And who also conveniently had the sleeve."

Billings curled deep into his chair at the outburst and President Warren softened his tone. "Look, I don't want this to be a Cuban Missile Crisis moment, with pictures thrown down at the UN. We don't know what their involvement is at the end of the day. Do it quietly."

Billings nodded and President Warren leaned back, saying, "Go ahead, Kurt."

"Sir. I'm about done. We assess that Chiclet and the device are headed to Brazil, and I'd like permission to continue with Pike's team. I believe we're under the gun on this."

Lindsey Bamf, one of two civilians on the Council, said, "Assuming it is Brazil, why there? Why not here in the States?"

Billings said, "First off, the vice president is down there right now. Along with a contingent of the Senate. They're due to return in four days."

"Would anyone know that?"

"Well, yeah. It's all over the press."

Kurt said, "The original voice cut also said they thought it would be too hard to get inside the United States. As for Brazil, the World Cup is starting. The tournament is played in twelve different stadiums in twelve different cities throughout Brazil, but we don't think that's the target. It's a catalyst for the target."

He clicked a slide, showing the teams of the World Cup. "This year is the first time since 1970 that Israel has qualified. Because of it, the prime minister of Israel is visiting the team, showing his support. Remember that the voice cut indicated Israeli interests?"

President Warren nodded and said, "I see where you're going."

Kurt clicked to the next slide. "The prime minister of Israel is meeting the Brazilian president along with our vice president two days from now. With the address on the DHL ticket being the capital, Brasília, we believe that's the target."

Bruce Tupper let out a bitter chuckle. "Snowden just keeps on giving."

The secretary of defense said, "What's he have to do with this?"

Billings said, "The president of Brazil went spastic six or eight months ago when our surveillance operations inside the country were leaked. We're trying to rebuild relations, but the vice president isn't the man to discuss this issue. It's way, way over his head. He had to pay a courtesy visit, but we didn't want it to be alone, one-on-one. In order to keep the discussion on the weather or something else innocuous, we invited the Israeli prime minister to attend."

Palmer said, "Can we call it off?"

Kurt said, "Sure, but calling off the meeting isn't going to call off the attack. Chiclet will just look for a new target."

President Warren said, "Okay, okay, get Chiclet's information out there. Let the Brazilians know there's a threat on the loose and it may be directed at a World Cup venue but more likely at the seat of government. Get them on the ball."

Bruce Tupper said, "And how do we know this?"

President Warren smiled, "Tell them it was an NSA intercept."

Everyone politely chuckled and Alexander Palmer said, "Sir, I'd recommend sending in NEST as well."

"Yeah, right. Of course. Palmer, you got the ball with the department of energy."

Palmer nodded and said, "Kerry, I need you to talk to the CIA liaison in Brazil. Let 'em know our nuclear emergency support team is coming to the capital, and they're going to have sensitive equipment that needs to get through customs discreetly."

Kerry said, "Easy day. Kurt, what's your recommendation for the Taskforce?"

"Have them investigate this address. See what they can find."

Tupper said, "They're in Germany. Isn't this time sensitive? Can't we use something on the address besides this illegal Taskforce operation?"

Kurt said, "Retro's stabilized in Landstuhl, so I broke Brett free. He met the team in Berlin with the Gulfstream IV. They're halfway across the Atlantic now."

Tupper blew up. "Are you fucking kidding? What happened to oversight? Who gave you permission?"

Kurt said, "Sir, I had to get them out of Germany anyway. My recommendation is to get them into Brazil, but if you guys say no, then they'll simply fly home."

Tupper looked at President Warren and said, "I emphatically vote no." He raised a hand and theatrically began ticking off fingers. "One, they have no cover for action in Brazil. No way to explain what a supposed archaeological firm is doing with a bunch of Israelis who have nothing to do with them. Two, they've shown a willingness to disobey our instructions, and giving them permission to continue is tantamount to condoning their past actions. And three, they've had a hostile penetration of their organization and we don't even know how. For all we know, everything they do will be exposed by the Russians. They're a walking time bomb of compromise."

President Warren said, "Kurt, what about that?"

Kurt said, "Pike's team has all the information on Chiclet. There are a bunch of intangibles that he can connect intuitively. Sending someone new to start now isn't the same. You can't manhunt by committee. Something will get missed. As far as compromise goes, the Israelis will help rather than hurt. If it blows up, we can always throw them to the wolves. Finally, I'm running this one personally. Everyone else is firewalled. No support teams, no logistics, no other involvement besides the men in this room."

The secretary of defense said, "You guys are stomping on the ants and missing the elephant."

Tupper said, "You call exposing an intelligence organization operating outside the laws of the United States an ant?"

"Yeah. When you compare it to the death and panic of a dirty bomb going off. *That's* the fucking elephant."

78

Akinbo saw the DHL sign and attempted to pull over, only to jerk back into his lane after a bleating of horns behind him. Sweating profusely from fear, he circled the block, the task of driving in this place sending a rancid flow of nausea in his stomach.

Unlike Berlin, São Paulo was a free-for-all of vehicle operation, with everyone vying for position as if the most reckless behind the wheel created the driving rules. It scared the hell out of him. All he wanted to do was get the package and find a place to stay. Get some rest before tomorrow.

Everything had gone perfectly fine leaving Germany. He'd destroyed the Russian's operational phone, buying his own inside the Berlin airport with the credit card he'd been given. He'd accessed his e-mail account—the one supposedly protected from the United States—and seen an e-mail from the safe house, waiting on his response as if they were completely unaware of his theft of the keys. Which was more than he had hoped. He'd responded to the e-mail, saying he was on the way and looking forward to meeting, then e-mailed his contacts in Boko Haram, asking them to create the propaganda tape. They'd replied, telling him it would be done, then had asked him to create a Twitter account for spreading the video. He'd done so, using the handle @Bokoharambrazil. Finally, he'd paid a change fee and changed his ticket. Instead of landing in Brasília, he'd opted for São Paulo. The Russians had an agenda for him, but he'd chosen his own target.

Everything looked to be tracking, including slipping from the noose of the Russians. They expected him to arrive today and attack in two days. Instead, he would attack his target tomorrow—provided he could get the device.

Circling the chaotic streets of São Paulo, he wondered if he was going to fail simply because he didn't have the nerve to drive among the lunatics in this city. Approaching the DHL location for the second time, he put on his blinker and changed lanes, ignoring the bleating horns and the driver behind him slamming on his brakes.

Sandwiched on the ground floor of a ten-story structure, surrounded on all sides by glass and steel office buildings; there was nowhere to park near the DHL store. Not willing to pass by a third time, he took a cue from a van ahead of him and hopped the curb, parking on the sidewalk.

He exited, eyes downcast to avoid the angry stares of the pedestrians on the street, wondering how on earth he was going to drive the five hours to his destination. It had looked so easy on Google Maps.

He went to the counter and presented his receipt. The clerk asked for identification and he slid across his passport. The man studied it intently. Sweating profusely, Akinbo patted his forehead with a cloth. The clerk disappeared into the back. After five minutes, Akinbo began to suspect that Jarilo had set him up, and that the clerk wasn't searching for a box, but waiting for a team of policemen. Every minute that passed increased his unease. He called to the back but received no answer. At the eight-minute mark his survival instinct trumped his desire for the weapon. He pocketed his passport and trotted to the glass doors, seeing his car outside. He pushed them open and heard someone shout behind him.

He turned, preparing to flee, and saw the clerk waving his receipt in the air with one hand. The other was pulling a dolly.

He said, "Where are you going? Don't you want your tools?"

79

I took another look at the reconnaissance video, the glow from the computer getting brighter in the back of the van as the sun dropped in the sky. I was searching for an additional breach point, but didn't find one. It looked like the only way in was either the front door or the two windows in the back. Both had bars on them, complicating the issue.

The house itself was connected to the buildings left and right, with no space in between, the area in a decidedly seedy part of the capital. Called Ceilândia, it was a borough created in the '70s to relieve the *favelas* or shanty towns being built downtown. Of course, you couldn't expect a government neighborhood created specifically to house people living in homemade shacks to be a place to brag about. Our target was on a road that wasn't even paved. I'd read about the *favelas* in Rio, most run by drug gangs and crime lords. I hoped Ceilândia wasn't a duplicate of that city, because I didn't want to have to fight my way out if we raised a ruckus. I was beginning to have second thoughts about our little detour to Brazil.

While waiting to linkup with Brett and the rock-star bird, I had briefed Kurt Hale on what we had, letting Aaron and Shoshana deal with Daniel's body. I don't know what they did—something with their own Mossad connections—but I felt badly about the loss. Shoshana had taken it hard, and technically she was right: It *was* because of me. He was killed in an ambush targeting Americans, not Israelis.

I was convinced some sorry bastard inside Taskforce headquarters had intentionally leaked our information, but Kurt didn't feel the same way. He was sure the asset in Europe had simply been sloppy and had been penetrated by the Russians, maybe years ago. I thought he was using blinders because he'd personally approved all the operational members of the Taskforce. Admitting there was a mole instead of shitty tradecraft was admitting he'd screwed up. Tough pill, but he might have to swallow it.

I'd told him everything we'd found, from the DHL address to the computer, and made him promise he wouldn't divulge to anyone the deep web messaging protocols I'd discovered. I was sure it went to the traitor, and I'd used it to send an innocuous message hoping someone would reply. From there, I was going to set up a trap. *If* we had a mole, that is. The communication method could have been used by Yuri to buy anything from black-market firearms to kiddy porn.

After the Israelis had returned we'd taken off from Berlin with a flight plan to Charleston, South Carolina, where my company was located. Aaron had questioned that decision, and I'd told him I didn't have authority to execute anything yet. That caused Shoshana to demand they fly commercial—in effect, cutting ties with us and continuing on their own. Daniel's death had bitten deeply, and she wanted Chiclet as much for his scalp as for stopping the attack. She didn't trust us to continue. After some discussion, I'd managed to convince her that the flight plan was just a formality, but I wasn't so sure about her judgment. She was on the edge, looking for vengeance.

After my initial outburst at Magdeburg, I'd let what she'd done to Yuri drop. It was clearly wrong, but I wasn't sure I had room to cast judgment. If I had seen Decoy killed in front of me, then had his murderer in my arms—helpless or not—I was fairly sure on what I would have done.

Jennifer didn't see it the same way. She *knew* it was heinous. As soon as we were alone she had stated her unease about what had occurred. In return, I had asked her about the man who died from the fall off of the scaffolding, the implication clear: She had killed him out of necessity, but it was necessity wrapped in vengeance.

Her eyes had watered, and she'd said, "Don't say that. Don't tell me I'm a murderer. I can't bear that coming from you."

I said, "Whoa, that's not what I meant. Don't ever think that. It's just very complicated. Yuri was a bad man. *He* was the murderer, and he got what was coming to him."

"That's not our call. Not like that. It makes us like him. By tolerating it, *I'm* becoming like him."

I shook my head, saying, "No, you're not. The fact that you question makes you more than Yuri. Make no mistake, he would have killed you without remorse and slept like a baby later."

She'd nodded as if she believed me, but whispered under her breath, "I wonder if Shoshana used to be like me. If it's only a function of time."

I'd kept my eye on Shoshana on the flight, looking for symptoms of a ticking bomb, but she seemed to have returned to the smart ass she was when we'd first met, needling me at every opportunity. Jennifer had sat with her, which was alarming because I knew she was still questioning her actions. I didn't need Shoshana trying to twist up Jennifer's moral compass. I let it go, and I eventually saw them laughing together. From across the cabin I'd caught Jennifer's eye, and she'd smiled.

Whew. One less issue.

The flight was a little over twelve hours, and at the nine-hour mark the copilot had awakened me from some much-needed rest to say that we'd gotten the mission to explore the DHL address. I spread the wealth by waking up the Israelis. The news made everyone happy. I wanted to say, "See, I told you we were going to execute," but in truth, I'd had my doubts that the Oversight Council was going to allow us to continue. As much as I loved Charleston, I had dreaded going there with two pissed-off Israeli commandos.

We'd landed at the capital and I'd had Jennifer rig up a rental sedan with covert cameras, then launched her and Shoshana on a recce mission while the rest of the men loaded up a panel van with equipment we might need. After they'd returned with the video, I had started deliberating assault options.

The video running one more time, I said, "Man, I would love to breach from the back alley, but I'm not assaulting by climbing through a window. The only way in is through the front door, and a breach out there is asking for trouble from neighbors."

Brett, sitting next to me in the van, said, "We could go mechanical and get in fairly quickly."

"It won't be quick enough to surprise them, and I don't want to give them time to get ready for a fight."

"Explosive breach?"

I slowly nodded. "Yeah. It's looking that way. We're going to wake the neighborhood, though."

From the front passenger seat Aaron said, "What about the roof?"

I rewound the video, judging the height of the building. It looked like a story and a half, with some sort of storage on top that wasn't a full floor. We could get up on the roof with little trouble. Especially with Jennifer. To Brett I said, "You bring a Wasp from the plane?"

He was already breaking out the case. The Wasp was a very small unmanned aerial vehicle with day/night optics. It had only a little over two feet of wingspan and an electric motor, making it damn near invisible. With the sky rapidly going dark, Brett would have no trouble doing a flyover without compromise.

I kicked him out and waited, going over a potential assault plan in my head. We had a team of five, with three assaulters I could count on and two I wasn't sure about. I said, "Aaron, don't take this the wrong way, but have you done a building assault like this before?"

He smiled and said, "In my real job, this is what I do. The intelligence work is a sideshow."

"And Shoshana?"

"Not the same skills as Daniel and me. She was a helicopter pilot." He patted her knee to let her know it wasn't meant as an insult. "She has other skills, though."

I nodded. "I have no doubt."

Shoshana said, "What about Jennifer?"

"The same. She's got some unique skills, but building assault isn't one of them."

"What unique skills? That sounds like something I'd like to see."

My face began to shade crimson, causing her to smile. I blurted, "She's a great climber. If the roof works out, she'll get a ladder up there for us."

I glanced at Jennifer, and I'll be damned if she wasn't grinning like Shoshana. She was enjoying my discomfort. *What the hell did they talk about on the bird?*

I said, "What is your problem, Shoshana? You drop me out of a car going ten miles per hour too fast, one minute you want to kill me, the next you don't, and you're constantly trying to get a rise out of me."

Aaron laughed and said, "It means she likes you. Trust me, if she didn't, you'd really feel the pain."

Looking at Aaron, but talking to me, Shoshana said, "Aren't you going to pat Jennifer on the knee? Show her she's still a valued team member while you talk about her shortcomings?"

I said nothing, wanting no part of that fight. Aaron scowled and she turned to me. "If you're not, can I do it?"

I felt my face flush again and said, "I need to stretch my legs."

I slid open the door, and Brett pulled up. He climbed in the van with the Wasp case, the UAV now neatly stowed. I said, "And?"

"And Aaron's idea was spot-on. It looks like Koko's getting in some climbing."

80

Six hours later I was watching Jennifer free-climb up her little ninja grapple, a caving ladder made of wire rolled and strapped to her back. The alley was littered with black trash bags, and it stank of spoiled vegetables and rotting meat left to sit too long in the sun. Two houses over I heard a dog losing his mind barking. I hoped he did that every night and it didn't cause the owner to come out and investigate.

We'd opted for a dismounted infiltration, walking about a half mile through the twisting alleys, holding up at the corners while Brett checked the next block with thermal imaging. It was slow and tedious, but the last thing I wanted was early warning on the target. We needed surprise, which was why we weren't driving right up to the front door.

I'd outfitted Aaron and Shoshana with our standard gear from the package in the rock-star bird, giving them each a suppressed H&K UMP .45, a Glock 30, and a set of night observation goggles. Since we didn't have enough Taskforce smartphones to pass out, we'd all reverted to old-fashioned FM radios with earbuds. I'd put Brett on point, me running slack, and staggered Jennifer in between Shoshana and Aaron. I'd given him tail gunner.

We'd made it to the rear of the target without issue, then the damn dog had started barking. Jennifer had tossed up her grapple, taken a couple of tugs, and begun scampering up like the Dread Pirate Roberts on the Cliffs of Insanity. Moving as if someone were hoisting her from above and walking straight up the quarter-inch rope with hand strength alone.

I have to admit, I'd seen Jennifer climb her way up all manner of things, but this was in a whole other class. I was impressed. And a little proud. I looked at Shoshana with a smug grin.

Gun aimed out into her sector of the corner, she leaned in and bumped my knee. I ducked my head toward her and heard, "Wow. I should have patted her knee. She *does* have some skills I'd like to see alone."

I wanted to punch her in the mouth, the comment and humor completely lost in the middle of a mission. She was no operator. No Jennifer. She was flighty, emotional, and unable to maintain a serious role. It was late to realize that, but it was true.

I rotated around without a word, making sure we had 360-degree security and were all ready to go. I heard the dog go crazy again and turned that way, focusing on the gate to the house. I felt another tap on my thigh. I expected to see Brett or Aaron leaning in, but it was Shoshana again.

She pulled my sleeve, drawing our heads together. She said, "I'm sorry. That wasn't funny. I'm not really flighty. We're about to get in a gunfight and you don't know me well enough. I won't let you down."

The fact that she used the same words that had flitted through my head freaked the hell out of me. Aaron had said she was an empath, but it was clearly more. She was fucking Carrie.

I nodded, unsure what to say. I was saved by the caving ladder rolling down with a soft clatter on the ground. I looked up and heard in my earpiece, "Pike, this is Koko. Roof secure."

Shoshana whispered, "Koko? That's what you call her on the radio? Sexy."

My mouth fell open at her words. *She is insane.*

I grabbed the ladder and hissed, "Koko's a fucking talking gorilla."

I saw the whites of her teeth in the grin. "Touché, Nephilim."

I said, "You ever crawled up one of these things?"

"No, but how hard could it be? Anyway, I thought I was on the ground. 'Squirter control' or something."

I said, "You are. Squirter control, that is," then keyed my mike. "Jennifer, Shoshana's going to need you to stabilize the ladder. Come on down."

She said not a word. I saw the ladder whip a little and knew she was on the way. I pulled the cable taut, letting her scramble down without the end flailing all over the place, something she would have to do for Shoshana. Getting up such a ladder wasn't easy on the best of days, but it was made infinitely harder if someone wasn't pulling down on the end, turning it into a facsimile of a real ladder instead of a whipping beast that had to be conquered into submission. Jennifer could handle it, but the task was definitely not something I wanted Shoshana to attempt for the first time, in the dark, on an assault.

Jennifer dropped between us, giving me a look, questioning why I'd made her leave her security position on the roof. I said, "You and Shoshana have squirter control. You've seen the terrain. We're coming in hard. Hopefully, we trap them all before they can react, but you know how that can go. Anyone escapes, they'll be coming out the front."

Jennifer understood the situation immediately and said, "Can Shoshana do that?"

With a little bit of venom I said, "Probably not, so be prepared to do a singleton takedown."

I got an up from my three-man team and started climbing, Jennifer pulling hard on the bottom of the ladder. I heard Shoshana below me say, "What is he talking about?"

Jennifer answered, sounding embarrassed. "The buildings are connected all the way to the end of the block. There's nowhere to hide.

We can't circle around and sit in the street, waiting for someone to run out. We'll be spotted. We're going to do it from the roof. If someone comes out, we'll have to drop to the street below. I understand if you can't do it. I'll handle it."

I reached the top, pulling myself over the parapet, and heard, "Fuck that guy. . . ."

I smiled.

Two minutes later my three-man assault element was on the roof, the squirter control still climbing. I said, "Okay, Brett, where's breach?"

He led us behind an old AC unit, now defunct. Through my NODs I saw a plywood hatch. I leaned down and stuck a knife in the seam, then levered it up. It fought me for a moment, then sprang free with a pop like a party favor. We all stopped movement, waiting. I heard a scrape behind me and said over the net, "Koko, Koko, freeze."

The faded scuffling from the ladder went silent.

We waited for an additional minute, then I hoisted the thick piece of plywood out of the way, saying, "Koko, good to go. Continue."

Laying the plywood on the roof, we all stared down into the pit, the IR lights from our NODs providing an eerie *Blair Witch* movie view. I saw a shelf below full of discarded insulation and pieces of machinery. No movement. I signaled Brett, and he lowered himself down, taking a knee. I pointed at myself, making sure Aaron saw me, then followed. Thirty seconds later, we were all inside, the attic space barely five feet tall, forcing us to kneel. Brett pointed to the closest side and I saw a glow of light penetrating from below, illuminating a wooden ladder affixed to the wall fifteen meters away.

I nodded, and he began moving toward it slowly, one step at a time. I felt the floor crinkle with his steps, making a popping noise. He stopped, glancing back at me. I raised a hand, giving an unspoken question.

What's up?

He slowly shook his head. I broke noise discipline over our ear-pieces. "You see something?"

He whispered, "I can't move."

"Why?"

"The ceiling is dry-rotted. I'm on a sheet of thin ice."

I said, "What?" then heard multiple pops, like bubble wrap being twisted. And watched him disappear through the ceiling.

81

A cloud of dust popped into the attic space like a Wile E. Coyote cartoon. I darted forward, hearing the plywood snapping. I leaned over and saw Brett getting to his knees on the floor below, three men sitting up and yelling, coming out of a deep slumber. The only way down was the ladder, which was across the hole he'd created. Clearly the roof wouldn't support that.

Uh-oh.

I looked back at Aaron and said, "Time to get in the fight."

He said, "How?"

I clenched my teeth and jumped up in the air. When I hit the tinderbox of wood, it splintered like it was made of glass. I smashed straight through to the floor below.

I hit the ground and rolled to the right, bringing my weapon up.

The three men were fully awake and starting to react. One grabbed a pistol on his night table and Brett drilled him. Another began sprinting out of the room. He'd almost reached the door when Aaron came crashing down, knocking him in the head with his full weight. The final man managed to get out through a side door leading to a hallway. I took off after him, but was hampered by the chaos in the room.

I reached the corridor and saw it was empty, two other doorways open just before it took a bend to the right. I keyed my radio. "Koko, Koko, got a squirter."

My target knew where he was going and could run flat-out, while I was forced to clear each room in case he'd opted to hide. I did so, finding nothing but a closet and a bathroom. I heard the front door open just as I rounded the corner of the hallway. I raced to the entryway, now open from the man's flight, and saw him come crashing back inside. Shoshana straddled his waist while Jennifer closed the door.

I called Brett. "Status?"

"Target secure."

We lumped all of them together in the back room. One was an indigenous-looking tough. The other was a pasty-faced Caucasian. I was sure he was Russian, but when he shouted at us, he did so in English, and had no accent. Brett and Aaron cinched flex-ties on them, hands behind the back, feet shackled with a two-foot shuffle room.

I said, "Search this place. Documents and electronics are the priority."

Brett and Jennifer left, but Aaron and Shoshana stayed. I said, "You guys are wasting time. We need to get out of here."

Shoshana said, "I'm better at interrogating. I know how to do this."

I looked at Aaron, and he said, "She's right. Let her take a crack at it. She's scary good. She's school trained and has done many, many of these before."

I thought about it, then nodded my head. Given where she'd come from, she probably had more skill than I did at this. I'd conducted a number of interrogations over my career, but I always defaulted to the trained interviewer when I had one.

I said, "You know what to ask?"

She said, "Yes. Trust me, if he knows the location of Chiclet, so will we."

The Caucasian said, "Fuck all of you people."

Shoshana kicked the detritus on the floor, searching. She stood up holding a thin finishing nail. She said, "Fuck me indeed. I wonder what I could do with this? It looks like a catheter, doesn't it?"

I flinched at her words, as I'm sure every man on earth would. She brought her eyes to bear on the Caucasian, and they were floating in evil. Sinister. The detainee took one look and made a break for the door, a pathetic shuffle in the flex cuffs like he'd been drinking and didn't trust his steps. Shoshana stuck her right leg out and he splayed forward, unable to protect his fall because his arms were behind his back. He landed face-first, his head hitting the wall as his body slammed into the ground.

She leaned over him and said, "I'm not going to ask any questions just yet. This is called the warm-up."

I looked at Aaron, wanting some confirmation I was doing the right thing by leaving him alone with Carrie the Empath. He nodded and winked. I went to help with the search. I was digging through a cabinet when I heard a scream. A thin wail that cut through to the soul, like someone was being skinned.

I took off running back to the small room, bumping into Jennifer moving the same way. She shouted, "What was that?"

I said, "I don't know. Shoshana, I think."

We reached the room and I saw the man on the floor, hands free but legs still cuffed, Aaron over the top of him. Shoshana was standing in the corner and panting. I saw the wild eyes and knew I'd made a bad choice. I had understood she was on the edge, but hadn't thought Aaron would allow her to outright harm the detainee.

Jennifer ran to the man on the floor and I stalked to Shoshana, saying, "What the fuck is going on?"

She said, "He stabbed himself."

Now furious, understanding the state of play, I said, "*Stabbed himself?* With his fucking hands behind his back? Really?"

Brett entered the room. He took one look at the tension floating in the air and said, "Got a laptop. Outside when you want to see it."

He left.

Shohsana said, "I freed him. For the interrogation."

Aaron rolled him over, and I saw a knife sticking out of his chest, the front of his shirt liquid red. Jennifer checked his pulse, looked at me and shook her head.

I got within an inch of Aaron's face and said, "What the fuck is wrong with you people?"

Aaron said, "Wait, Pike, it's not like that. Shoshana really *was* conducting an interrogation. She untied his hands to give him water. It was all part of the plan. Shoshana threatens, then becomes nice. We don't coerce unless we have to."

I stabbed my finger at the corpse. "Then how the fuck did that happen?"

Shoshana began talking in short, choppy sentences. She seemed genuinely shaken. "He began answering questions freely. He seemed to be relieved that we had him, and that I wasn't resorting to violence. He's a reporter from the Associated Press. The Russians pay him for access to their servers."

She took a deep breath and rubbed her face with both hands. "Everything was going fine until I asked about Yuri. The name sent him over the edge. He started crying, talking about how they were going to torture him to death, and begging me to kill him. Before I knew it, he dove across the table, grabbed a knife, and stabbed himself."

I went from her to Aaron. He nodded. "That's what happened."

I said, "Where'd he get a knife? He was clean when we cuffed him."

"Yes, he was. It's his room, though." Aaron pointed to a nightstand on the floor, a drawer ripped out. "He knew one was in there."

Jennifer had studied Shoshana for the entire exchange. She said, "She's telling the truth."

I started to give a sharp retort, then caught Jennifer's eye. She slowly nodded her head. Jennifer had sensed something I couldn't.

Aaron said, "Pike, we can argue about what happened later. The information we did get is critical. The assets here were directed to capture Chiclet because he was disobeying orders. He doesn't have a dirty bomb. He has a real one."

"What do you mean? Real one?"

"He has a live atomic bomb. A suitcase nuke, and he's going to set it off day after tomorrow at the meeting with your vice president and my prime minister."

82

Kurt Hale watched the people leaving the Oval Office, all of them confused as to why they were being forced out. None were read on to the Taskforce, but they knew if the president's schedule was interrupted to this degree, it had to be something awful. Even President Bush continued reading at the children's school after the first plane had hit the World Trade Center.

He waited a beat, allowing them to clear the West Wing, then entered, surprised to see Bruce Tupper standing next to the president's desk. Kurt closed the door and said, "Sir, I didn't expect you here, but it's a good thing. We have an issue that you can solve immediately."

President Warren, already in a foul mood after having his meeting broken up by Kurt's emergency phone call, said, "He's supposed to be at an NSC debate on Nigeria in ten minutes. What was so God-awful important?"

Kurt cut straight to the chase. "Pike sorted through the DHL address. It *is* tied to Chiclet, but he doesn't have a dirty bomb. He's got a Russian suitcase nuke."

The president's mouth dropped open and Tupper said, "Wait, wait. What? That's an old wives' tale. There's no proof that those things exist. Congress had a huge investigation on them in the nineties and couldn't come up with any credible evidence besides some testimony from Russian environmental scientists."

Kurt said, "You want to trust some congressional committee or what Pike's found? We had nuclear munitions like that, why shouldn't they?"

President Warren said, "Why would they give Chiclet a nuclear weapon? What the hell is Russia thinking? That would start a war."

"According to the interrogation, they didn't expect it to be nuclear. It was supposed to be a dirty bomb and cleaned of Russian fingerprints, but that's really irrelevant, sir. The immediate target is the bomb. The Russians come later."

Tupper said, "What do you know about the weapon? What's its power?"

"We know jack shit about the Russian systems, but we can look at our own. In the seventies and eighties we had Special Atomic Demolition Munitions for Special Forces to use on deep penetration raids behind the Iron Curtain. Those weapons were implosion devices that weighed about seventy pounds and could be dialed from point-one to one kiloton. Given that every bit of Soviet technology was stolen through espionage from our nuclear program, theirs are probably similar."

Warren said, "What's that mean to me?"

"Some good news. The Hiroshima bomb was fifteen kilotons. This is probably a max of one kiloton. A kiloton is a thousand tons of TNT, so, in perspective, this will be much less than the fifteen thousand dropped on Japan."

"Well, that's great for a *Jeopardy!* question, but it still doesn't give me a feel for the damage."

"Remember Timothy McVeigh and the Murrah Federal Building? What his bomb did?"

"Yes."

"This will be like eight hundred of those bombs going off at the same time. Unlike Hiroshima, instead of the entire city being wiped off the planet, it'll be the city center. Or something like that. The nuclear fallout will still be severe."

"That's good news?"

"Well, better than the alternative. The other thing we learned was that we assessed the target correctly. He's planning on hitting the vice president's meeting. For all we know, the bomb is already placed, but it gives us two solid days to find it."

Tupper said, "What leads do you have? How are you going to find and fix Chiclet?"

"That's the problem you can solve. Right now, we're sitting on the house, basically waiting on Chiclet to show up. That's not what I would call a solid plan for success. The guys in Brazil also thought the weapon was going to be delivered by DHL, but we know that's not happening. The DHL receipt went nowhere, so it's likely the same will happen with Chiclet. He knows the Russians didn't want a true nuclear blast, and he's not going to show up at the house and let them stop it."

"How can I help?"

"We have four Associated Press e-mail accounts, all tied to American journalists. We need to see the content."

President Warren said, "What? You think the Associated Press is involved here? That's crazy."

"No, no. Not at all. We think these are mirror accounts the Russians developed through the asset in Brazil. The Russians control Snowden, and they know we won't touch something as sensitive as Associated Press reporters. They're using the mirrors to communicate. At least that's my theory. On the surface, they're legitimate, so it's a tough call."

Tupper said, "Not that tough. All I have to do is get a warrant through FISA."

President Warren leaned back and rubbed his eyes. He exhaled and said, "No, you can't. Without extensive background proving the viability of the warrant, the court will deny it. And we can't give that background. The days of the rubber stamp are over."

Tupper said, "What about using Taskforce assets? Why do I have to do anything in the first place? Two days ago Kurt was briefing me on their computer network operations."

Kurt said, "We could do it, but it'll take time. Time we don't have. We're totally focused on foreign systems. Getting into the AP without compromise will be hard. Yeah, we could smash and grab, but we'll be exposed. The NSA has already established the back doors."

Tupper frowned and said, "You're asking me to order someone to commit a felony. Basically, do the very thing everyone is afraid we'll do. Crush the Fourth Amendment."

Kurt said, "I don't see a choice. It's the only lead we have. Chiclet's phone is no longer operational."

Tupper said, "And that's how it starts. Every single time."

President Warren said, "Enough of the damn semantics. Get it done."

Tupper said, "Sir, I hate to look like a weasel, but I'll be the one standing up in front of the intelligence committee. I'll have committed a felony."

Kurt said, "Goddamn it, there's a nuclear bomb loose in the hands of an Islamic psychopath who thinks the world would look better without electricity! Who gives a shit about who's going to get blamed?"

President Warren raised his hand, silencing Kurt. He said, "Par for the course inside the beltway. Bruce, do what Kurt's asking. If it goes bad, I'll take responsibility. I'll step forward."

Tupper said, "Sir, I didn't mean I wouldn't do it. Just that there's risk. Of course I'll do it."

President Warren said, "Yes, you will. If that bomb goes off because you didn't do everything you could, I'm throwing *your* ass to the wolves."

83

I saw a vehicle park opposite of our target house and perked up, the little spike of adrenaline helping to relieve the growing lethargy from lack of sleep. Two men exited, neither of African descent. They ignored the house in question and went inside two doors down.

I was positive that there was no earthly way Chiclet would be stupid enough to show up at this target carrying a Commie SADM, but we had little else we could do until the Taskforce could provide us another thread from the e-mail addresses we had found, which was taking longer than expected. It turned out they were encrypted with an open-source protocol called Pretty Good Privacy—or PGP—and each e-mail had to be cracked separately.

The NEST team had arrived with some FBI escorts and I'd convinced Kurt to break one of the eggheads free to help out my efforts. Composed of scientists from places like the Sandia and Alamo national labs, they were the front line of locating and rendering safe a nuclear device. The only problem was they needed the search area necked down a little smaller than a city.

I'd sent Jennifer and Shoshana to linkup with our NEST professor, then piddled around on my computer, but eventually had run out of things to do. Brett and Aaron were taking catnaps in the front seat, but someone had to stay awake to watch the one remaining detainee we had. He was shackled five feet away, and snoring. We'd left the dead guys in the house to rot. If/when the Brazilian police found them, the trail—if it led anywhere—would point back to Russia.

I rubbed my eyes, wanting to close them for a good five hours. The orbs felt like they had sand grating on them. I opened them back up, about to tap Brett on the head and get him back on guard duty when I saw I had a new e-mail from the Taskforce.

I double-clicked it and found a plethora of information. The e-mails had been cracked, showing Chiclet had been in contact with Boko Haram as well as the Russians. Initially elated, I went through the data, growing more and more frustrated. It was a lot of smoke about the attack, but nothing concrete to help us find him. We had the ISP and could track that, but it was located in São Paulo, which meant he'd sent it when he'd landed. Not something we could use for catching him.

Why did he land in São Paulo instead of Brasília?

The only thing I could think was to throw off the Russians since they had his itinerary, but he hadn't used it.

The rest of the information dealt with the making of a video claiming responsibility and the creation of social media accounts, to include a damn Twitter handle of @Bokoharambrazil. It aggravated the shit out of me. The guy was going to destroy a city, then tweet about it like he was on MTV's *The Real World.*

I stared at the screen, then had an idea. I called the hacking cell: "Hey, thanks for the work."

"Don't thank us. Big NSA did this job. We'd still be trying to get into the system, much less cracking the encryption."

"Oh . . . well, can you get into Twitter?"

"An individual account, or corporate databases?"

"Individual account."

"Yeah. We can do that."

"Get into Chiclet's account. He had to send real verification information in order for the Twitter account to go live. I want that information."

I hung up and saw Brett roll in his chair and rub his face. "What's up?"

"We got a lead on Chiclet. Well, we might have one."

We waited in silence for twenty minutes, then my phone rang.

"Hey, it's Chucky. I got in. I'm on his account right now. The e-mail registered is the same AP one."

Shit. No help.

"So there's nothing else?"

"No, not really. Hang on. I'm still scrolling through privacy settings."

I waited impatiently for all of two seconds when he said, "Whoa, no way!"

"What? What is it?"

"He's enabled a mobile phone for Twitter. And I have the number."

"What's the country code?"

"Four nine. Germany."

"Geolocate that fucker, right now! Send me the map location."

The commotion awakened Aaron. He sat up in the driver's seat and said, "What's going on?"

I said, "We might have a location for Chiclet, but I'm not holding my breath."

Brett said, "Why on earth would he use his real phone?"

"I don't know, but he didn't need to put a phone in at all, so putting in a fake one would be a waste of time. Maybe it's part of his propaganda plan for mobile use. Maybe he needs the connectivity."

My phone vibrated. Chucky said, "You got it? It's on the mapping app."

I changed windows on my laptop and saw a blinking blue marble in some town called Curitiba, south of São Paulo. A wrong location.

Brett said, "What's he doing down there? That's hell and gone from Brasília."

Aaron was staring intently at the map. He said, "I've lost track of time. What's today's date?"

I told him and he said, "Mother of God. I know what his target is. Today's the opening of the FIFA World Cup."

Brett said, "Soccer?"

"Football, yes. The matches are played in twelve cities. Curitiba is hosting a match today. Between the United States and Israel."

84

Akinbo finished his prayers, took a shower, and packed his minimal amount of clothing into his carry-on. He didn't bother to check out of the hotel, as he'd rented the room for two days. He didn't want to raise any unnecessary signature by interacting with the staff, so he'd paid for an extra day. It was really irrelevant, as this building would be vaporized before his checkout time came.

He went down the back stairwell, exiting the hotel from the side and crossing the street to the parking garage. He traveled up to the third floor, popped the trunk, and saw the device. Next to it was a set of two-foot bolt cutters.

He glanced left and right, but nobody was about. He'd picked this corner spot precisely because it was out of view of the two cameras on the floor, allowing him to arm the weapon before taking it to the final destination.

He slid his hands into his jacket pocket and withdrew the keys. He laid them in the trunk, one beside the other.

He snipped the padlocks and released the four butterfly clips holding the device closed, a slight tremor forming in his hands. Lifting the lid, he glanced around once more, seeing nothing alarming.

He removed the two tongue depressors that had been left inside the device. He taped one, then the other to the heel of his hands, shifting the one to the left a smidgen.

He placed his hands on the two keyboards, levered the piece of wood on top of the shift key, and typed in the code. Midway through, his left hand slipped, causing a failure. He felt sweat bead on his forehead. He only had two more chances before the device locked out. He willed his hands still, positioned them over the keys, and proceeded, deliberately moving slower.

The screen flashed three times, telling him he was successful. He inserted the first key and twisted. A small light illuminated next to the keyhole. He inserted the second key and turned, getting a second light. A row of zeroes appeared on the screen, flashing three times. The weapon was armed. Yuri had told him to press the button at this stage, getting instant initiation, but he knew that there was no way the Soviets would have made a suicide device. No way Yuri had trained to kill himself. He wasn't the *shahid* type, especially when it would be so easy to build in a timer.

From now on he would be working in a vacuum. If he was wrong, he'd end up as a *shahid*, and though he wasn't afraid of that outcome, he saw no reason to hasten his death if it wasn't necessary. Not when he could simply set a remote detonation.

The game started at three, and he wanted to make sure the stadium was full. With a forty-five-minute half, he would set it to go off at four P.M. He looked at his watch and computed the math. *Five hours and thirty minutes.*

He placed an index finger over the five and tapped. Nothing happened. The zeros remained unchanged. He switched keypads, using the five on the second one. A red block five appeared as the last digit. He exhaled and typed in the remaining digits.

The timing complete, he placed the edge of his hand next to the keys, wondering how hard he should strike. He gave a small karate chop, sweeping his hand forward and snapping the keys off at the heads, the shafts breaking much easier than he expected. He leaned over and saw the key shafts inside the keyholes.

No *turning back now.*

He flipped open the metal plate protecting the arming button. According to Yuri, pushing this with the zeroes in the window caused immediate detonation. Akinbo would now learn if there was any correlation between the numbers and the button. It had crossed his mind that there might be a separate method for initiating a countdown, and that this button's sole existence was for detonation. A fail-safe, emergency way to initiate the bomb regardless of where the countdown stood.

He closed his eyes, whispered, "Allahu Akbar," and pressed the red button. Nothing happened. No explosion, no whirring or clacking of the machine, no sound at all. He opened his eyes and saw the seconds counting down. A relentless march to victory.

He wiped the sweat from his brow and closed the trunk, his hands trembling. He exited the garage to Buenos Aires Street. He was still three blocks away, but he could see the giant Arena da Baixada ahead. Constructed in the late nineties, it was one of twelve stadiums used for the World Cup, and one of the few that wasn't built from the ground up to meet the requirements dictated by the World Cup governing body.

Two blocks from the stadium Akinbo noticed a large spike in police presence. They were everywhere, and the game was still five hours away. He reached within one block, the stadium straight ahead, and saw a checkpoint, the police searching every vehicle before allowing them to continue. He took a left, then a right, avoiding the checkpoint and driving aimlessly, thinking.

He had hoped to park next to the stadium and walk away. He wanted to put the weapon at ground zero and leave no doubt about the target, but that was no longer possible. He thought about it and realized that *ground zero* was a relative term. From what he had read online during his research, this device should eradicate a huge swath of the city in a giant ball of fire. All he needed to do was park close.

He found himself on Presidente Affonso Camargo Avenue, driving past a rail switchyard he had reconnoitered earlier. He saw his escape platform still parked in the switchyard, a freight train destined for São Paulo. He would be leaving his car here, and wanted a clean break out, so he had decided to hop a freightliner back to São Paulo. No tickets purchased, no rental agreements in a computer system, no identification shown, nothing to connect him to Curitiba.

He'd hopped freight trains plenty of times in Nigeria, as it was one of the few ways available to travel long distances, and in truth he felt more comfortable stowing away than he did trying to decipher the mass transit system or brave the five-hour drive back to São Paulo with the lunatics on the streets around here.

He would watch the detonation in real time from São Paulo, access Twitter, post the video, and then fly back to Nigeria using his original passport.

But where to park the car? The stadium was out since he couldn't get past the police. Parking on the street was out. Too much chance of getting towed or broken into. He considered. Why not just return to the parking garage? It was three blocks away, but that distance was negligible, and he'd paid for the spot. He could park in the same location, free from interference.

He turned the car around, heading back the way he'd come, humming a mindless tune.

85

We were on short approach to the São José dos Pinhais International Airport in downtown Curitiba when the little blue marble began to move. Unfortunately it was going outside of town, which left the unsettling thought that he'd hidden the nuclear needle in the haystack of the city and was now fleeing.

Choices, choices. Focus on finding the bomb, or focus on capturing Chiclet?

I said, "Doc, given the soccer stadium, how quickly can you locate the radioactive material?" I pointed at his boxes in the plane. "I mean, will this stuff start pinging a mile away, or do you need to walk right up on the bomb?"

Shortly before taking off, Jennifer and Shoshana had come back with our NEST expert, a thin bespeckled man with a thatch of red hair. He'd brought all sorts of detection equipment with him, so I was hoping we could solve the problem fairly quickly.

He said, "That all depends. Is the material highly enriched uranium or plutonium? Is it shielded? If so, with what? How much material is there? Is it—"

I cut him off. "Jesus Christ, give me an answer. It's a nuclear bomb. Can you fucking find it?"

"I don't know."

Looks like it's Chiclet.

I turned to Brett. "What's he doing?"

"He's on a highway headed north toward São Paulo, but not moving too fast. About fifty miles an hour."

"Can we catch him, or should we go to São Paulo and interdict him coming south?"

"We don't have time to do that. It's a five-hour drive from São Paulo to Curitiba alone. The game's in four and a half hours."

I turned to Jennifer. "Tell the pilot to get us down, now. Declare an emergency and cut in line." To Aaron: "Figure out the rental companies on the ground. Get us two vehicles."

I started to ask Brett a question when he said, "He's not on the highway anymore."

"So he's not headed to São Paulo?"

"Uh . . . I don't know. He's still headed north, but according to this map, he's running right through the woods."

"On a dirt road? An unmarked road?"

"Not at that speed."

Shoshana leaned in and said, "He's on a train."

She's right. I said, "Get on that other laptop. Figure out the trains to São Paulo. See where that thing is going to stop."

The plane started a steep descent and Aaron said, "Got two vehicles lined up. One SUV and one sedan."

"Perfect."

Much too quickly Shoshana came back. "There are no passenger trains to São Paulo. In fact, there aren't very many passenger trains in the country of Brazil. Lots of metro inner-city, but no long-haul between cities."

"So it's not a train?"

Brett said, "No, it's a train all right. It's on the map now. The other imagery must be from before they completed the tracks."

"So he's acting like a hobo? Hopping a freight train?"

"I guess."

The wheels touched down and I said, "Figure out where the next switchyard is."

Twenty minutes later Aaron, Brett, and I were hauling ass out of Curitiba headed toward a town called Campina Grande, about forty-five minutes away. We weren't sure the train would stop, but satellite imagery showed that the tracks led to a switchyard there. Given that Akinbo had at least a half-hour head start, all we could do was pray the train spent some time doing whatever it is that trains do at switchyards.

I'd tasked Jennifer and Shoshana with running the doc to the soccer stadium to see if they could find anything. If they did, it would be up to them to render the bomb safe. I wasn't holding my breath that it would do any good, but it was better than all of us chasing after Chiclet like the gang from *Scooby-Doo*. Although I wouldn't mind it if Chiclet ended up saying, *And I would have gotten away with it too, if it weren't for those meddling commandos.*

Luckily, the airport was in the southeastern section of the city, so we didn't have to fight our way through a bunch of inner-city gridlock and could hit a ring highway right off the bat. We'd reached the north edge of the city and joined another highway, with me driving and Brett watching the ball. He said, "Target stationary in Campina."

"Good deal."

We drove on, getting into some hill country, and I saw the tracks off to my left, running parallel to the highway. I passed a few houses, then more and more structures as we entered the town. Brett said, "Switchyard is a half mile ahead."

"Vector me in."

He did, getting me off the highway and giving me left and rights through the poor village. Eventually, we were on a dirt road paralleling a chain-link fence littered with paper and plastic bags. On the other side was a two-track switchyard and a lone freight train.

I drove forward until the chain link went to the right and our road entered a wood line. I threw the car in park and said, "Status?"

"He's still there. From the overhead it looks like the fourth or fifth car from the end."

I studied the train, seeing most of the cars were open bay coal containers. He wouldn't be hiding there. The last seven cars were enclosed and appeared to be for cattle, and from this distance, they looked empty.

"Okay. Let's go. We'll enter where the tracks exit the switchyard. Move straight to the rear of the train. I'll take the first cattle car on the train. Brett, you take the last. We'll work our way toward each other. Aaron, you stay outside in the grass for squirter control. You see him break free, give us a call."

Aaron, looking over my shoulder, said, "Pike, the train is starting to move."

I whipped around and saw the wheels slowly turning, the train jerking forward.

Shit.

"Change of plan. Aaron, you got the SUV. Parallel the train. Brett, let's go."

I tossed Aaron the keys before he could protest and Brett and I sprinted toward the gap in the chain link, the train picking up speed with each passing step. Brett, being something of a freak when it came to running, pulled away from me like I was wearing cement shoes.

He reached the train and began looking for something to mount. Behind him, at the end of the first cattle car, was a ladder rising to the roof. He slowed down, letting it catch him, then jumped up. By that time I'd made it to the tracks and was huffing to catch up, the train inexorably going faster and faster. Brett leaned out and I put on a burst of speed, leaping up and grabbing his arm. He jerked me higher and I grabbed the ladder, slamming into the wood slats of the car.

I peeked between the gaps of the second carriage, seeing an empty space, the floor filled with manure from its previous occupants. Brett tapped my arm. The train was now moving close to thirty miles an hour, and picking up speed with each passing foot, the wind and the clanking of the wheels making it impossible to talk without shouting.

He pointed into the first car in line, his hand in the shape of a gun, index finger out and thumb extended, only it was inverted, with the thumb aimed at the ground. The hand and arm signal for enemy.

I leaned forward and saw a lump balled up at the far end, a small carry-on bag next to it. I studied the car for egress points. Apparently, the sides flipped down, turning into ramps for loading the cattle, but once on the move they were locked in place as walls. On either end were ladders leading to the roof, which looked like the only way in or out.

I pulled back and pointed up. Brett nodded, and we climbed to the roof, with me in the lead. I broke the shelter between the cars and the wind punched me in the chest, threatening to throw me off. I collapsed to my hands and knees and scuttled forward, giving Brett room. I don't know what I was expecting, but in the movies guys run back and forth over trains as if they were on a rubber track. *Another myth blown.*

Brett reached the top and went through the same realization, getting down low to avoid the wind. I pointed at him, then to the near ladder hole. He nodded, and I pointed to myself and the far ladder hole at the end of the car. He nodded again and held out a fist. I bumped it and started crawling. I glanced back once, seeing him disappear down the ladder.

Moving forward on my hands and knees, advancing toward the ladder at the end of the car, I saw the locomotive at the front travel under some sort of light pole or switch control, a metal rod that crossed over the top of the train at about knee level from the roof. I needed to get to the ladder before it reached me, or end up trying to jump over while the train continued on.

The pole came inexorably toward me, but the train was long and I had plenty of time to evade. I thought I heard a shout, torn away by the wind. I crawled toward the ladder hole, and Chiclet appeared at the top. He saw me and leapt out, standing on the roof of the train. I did the same, risking the stability for the extra speed.

For a moment I thought he was going to fight me, but he turned and jumped over the gap to the next car in the chain, landing on his knees. He stood and saw the pole for the first time, too late to avoid it. He screamed and it caught him right above the knees going sixty miles an hour. He was flipped halfway over the top, then dragged backward. The pole reached the gap between the cars and I saw him fall.

Worrying about my own life, I judged my timing, then jumped in the air, playing a deadly game of Wipeout. The pole passed underneath me and I slammed back into the roof. I scuttled forward just as Brett appeared.

I shouted, "He went down between the cars."

We both leaned over, but saw nothing but the clacking wheels of the train. Akinbo was gone.

86

As we lurched forward, the wheels clapping in rhythm like a metronome, an idiotic hope flashed in my head that maybe he was clinging to the underside of the car, but I knew he had fallen, chewed up under the steel of the train. Just as I knew we had probably lost our ability to find the weapon.

Brett looked at me, his expression conveying the same thought, but we didn't have any time to mourn Chiclet's passing. I clambered down the ladder, the fresh air replaced by the foul odor of manure and cattle sweat. I ran to his carry-on and ripped it open, flinging out the few small possessions that were inside. Socks, two shirts, an extra pair of pants, toothbrush and toothpaste. Nothing else.

I unzipped the outside pouch and found a key-card to a hotel called the Sienna. The rest of the bag was empty.

I said, "Call Aaron. Tell him we're coming out. Have him check the computer and figure out how we get off this train, the sooner the better."

Brett nodded and began dialing. I called Jennifer. She answered on the first ring.

"You have him?"

"No. He's dead. Long story. What do you have? Anything?"

"Nothing at all. We've made a grid search of the stadium area, but we can't get very close because we don't have tickets to the World Cup. So far, Doctor Dolittle here has come up with squat."

"What about his equipment? I mean, he's the guy that's supposed to be able to find nuclear shit."

"Pike, I don't know. He's tried all manner of scientific stuff. Geiger counters, multispectral analyzers, something called a sodium iodide detector, and a bunch of other things that look like they came from *Ghostbusters*. He thinks the weapon is shielded. He's now saying he might have to be within five feet."

Brett hung up his phone and pulled my sleeve. I asked Jenn to hold on and gave him my attention.

He said, "Pike, we've got about two minutes to get back outside. Aaron says the train's about to cross a large lake. It should slow down when it does because of the bridge. We don't get off there and we're riding this thing for an hour until the next switchyard."

"Get off? You mean jump? Into the lake?"

"Afraid so."

"Fucking great."

I went back to the phone. Jennifer said, "What was that about jumping?"

"Nothing. We're apparently going to get wet on our way back. When's kickoff?"

I heard Jennifer bark a small laugh. "I don't think they call it a 'kickoff,' but it's in two hours." She paused, then said, "Pike, I'm wondering if we should be keeping this secret. Shouldn't we call an evacuation?"

"It'll do no good. We'll only succeed in creating massive panic. It would probably take over an hour just to get someone important enough to be able to disrupt the game, then another hour before anyone started moving. Very few would make it out of the blast radius in time, and the chaos will hamper our ability to operate. We're all in on this one."

She said, "What's the cutoff? How much time do we have?"

I knew what she was asking. Jennifer wanted to know what *all in* really meant. Were we going to search until it went off, or was I going to order our evacuation via the rock-star bird while we still had time to get out of the blast radius?

Given I didn't know what time it was set to blow, the cutoff was all a guess anyway. I said, "I haven't gotten that far yet. Let's exhaust all options."

"What options? I'm driving around in circles with a guy waving a wand in the air."

"I found a key-card to a place called the Sienna Hotel in Chiclet's bag. That's the only anchor we have."

Brett got on the ladder and pointed at his watch. I nodded.

"Look, I gotta go. Brett's saying they're announcing my flight. Exploit that room. Maybe the device is in there."

"Pike, that's not much of a lead."

"It's all we've got. We'll make the call on evac when I get back."

I disconnected and followed him up the ladder to the roof, retracing our steps to the outside rungs at the back of the car. We crawled down until we were standing in the same spot we'd found to get on this magnificent ride. I felt the train slow and leaned out into the wind like a jumpmaster spotting a release point. I saw the lake ahead, stretching out to the horizon on both sides, an old-fashioned wooden trestle bridge spanning across it. To the right I could see the highway about a hundred meters away, and a vehicle that might or might not be Aaron's.

I studied the bridge and saw that the damn thing was about thirty feet above the water. And while we'd slowed, we were still moving at a good clip.

I shouted to be heard above the wind. "That's a pretty steep drop. Aaron's sure this thing is more than five feet deep?"

Brett leaned out, then came back in and shouted, "Thirty seconds." Ignoring my question.

The earth fell away from us and we were racing across the trestle, the water shimmering in the sunlight. Brett looked at me and pointed to himself, then turned without a word. He swung out, still holding on to the rung. I could almost hear him counting in his head. *One . . . two . . . three.*

And off he went, hand over his face like he was helocasting for an infiltration off the coast of Panama. I saw him hit the water, a plume of white, then it was my turn.

I hope that lake is deep enough.

I pushed off from the train, then put my feet together and hands over my face, feeling the drop. Just before I hit, I realized it didn't matter how deep the water was. The odds of finding that nuclear bomb were so minuscule that if the lake was shallow, all I'd be doing is shaving an hour off of my life.

87

Jennifer hung up and immediately began tasking her little team. "Shoshana, get online and find a hotel in Curitiba called the Sienna. Get me some directions and vector me in. Doc, we think the weapon is inside a hotel room. I need you to start thinking about rendering it safe. Forget about detection."

Doctor Nicholas Sharp said nothing, holding the back of the passenger seat Shoshana was sitting in and looking literally like he was going to throw up, his eyes unfocused.

Jennifer said, "Doc, doc, hey! Are you listening?"

He snapped out of his trance and said, "We should get inside the stadium. He probably put it in there. I can't detect from inside a car. We need to get some tickets."

Jennifer waved her arm at the crowds flowing to the stadium, the dull roar inside heard even though they were a block a way. She said, "It's the damn World Cup. It's like the Super Bowl. Tickets sold out months ago. Did you hear what I said about rendering it safe?"

Shoshana cut in. "I got the hotel. It's only a few blocks away."

"Which way?"

"Straight north on Buenos Aires."

Jennifer began driving, fighting through the people now spilling from the sidewalks to the street, the crowd growing like a thousand tailgate parties at an NFL game, handheld horns blowing and goofy hats worn. All happy to have paid enormous money to travel to the World Cup, a once-every-four-year event, but a lifetime trip to anyone attending. A special occasion that was about to turn horrific.

Getting no response from Doctor Sharp, Jennifer's lips drew into a grim line and she snapped her fingers in front of the NEST scientist, saying, "Doc, did you hear me?"

He said, "Yes. I don't know if I can do that. I don't know enough about the device."

Jennifer shook her head. "And you're the best we've got? The front line of defense?"

"I'm not a magician!"

Shoshana said, "If it is to be, it is up to me."

"What?"

"Nothing. It's just a thing we used to say. It's up to us. Period."

Under her breath, Jennifer muttered, "I knew I should have run when Pike asked to start a business."

Shoshana laughed and said, "Too late now. Take your next left."

Jennifer turned the wheel and Shoshana said, "There it is."

"There's no parking here. It doesn't have a lot."

"Park in the street. Let's check it out." Jennifer honked the horn, clearing the crowds away from the curb, the stream of people breaking around them like a rock in a river. Shoshana turned around in the seat. "Doc, stay here. Anyone tries to move the car, tell them you're only parking for a minute. If you're going to vomit, open the door."

He nodded, holding a wand attached by a tube to a briefcase, meekly waving it out the open window.

Shoshana exited, saying, "Let me do the talking."

Jennifer said, "Okay by me." They went straight to the reception desk, fighting through a rowdy crowd hell-bent on having World Cup fun. One of the men interdicted their path, said something, and slapped Shoshana on her butt. She glared, causing him to fall back and his buddies to start whistling and catcalling. Jennifer followed in the wake, the actions appearing as if from another world. Some other place where happiness still existed.

They made a lewd comment to her as she passed and she gave a sickly smile, knowing they were doomed. Knowing they were all going to die. The man who'd groped Shoshana saw the look and his revelry faltered. He took in the pain, understanding something bad was in the room, but not understanding what it was. He let her pass.

Shoshana reached the reception desk and pulled out two one-hundred Brazilian *real* notes, setting them on the desk. The woman behind the counter eyed the money, then said, "Yes?"

"We're here for a friend of ours. He's an African. He checked out today, but he left something in his room. We came to get it back."

"What's his name?"

"His name is on the money in front of you."

She looked from Jennifer to Shoshana, considering. Then she said, "His name wasn't on either one of those bills. Perhaps it's on a different one."

Shoshana placed another one-hundred *real* note on the desk and said, "His fucking name is on that one. Understand?"

The receptionist tapped on the keys and said, "Yes, here he is. Room three thirteen, but he's not checking out until tomorrow."

Jennifer saw Shoshana's expression and knew she believed the same thing. *Jackpot.*

Shoshana said, "Give me a key, please."

Jennifer pulled out her phone as they went to the elevator. "Doc, get in here. We might be in luck. Room three thirteen."

Not waiting on him, they raced up the stairs, knocking World Cup tourists out of the way and clanging open the door on the third floor. Shoshana used the key and Jennifer went inside. It was sparse, with a small bathroom and a wooden wardrobe instead of a closet. By the time the Doc had entered, they'd searched it. And come up empty. The room was clean.

Doctor Sharp said, "I think it's time we evacuated. The game is in thirty minutes. If it *is* something besides a dirty bomb—if it's a live nuclear weapon with a one kiloton yield—we'll need all that time to get through the traffic. To get far enough away."

Jennifer dumped the trash on the bed, sorting through receipts and used Kleenex. He said, "Did anyone hear me? I think at least *I* should go back to my team in the capital. They might need me."

Jennifer picked up one receipt and studied it, ignoring him. Shoshana said, "What do you have?"

"A rental car contract. Why does Chiclet need to hop a train if he's got a rental car?"

Shoshana started moving toward the door, saying, "Because it's being used to hide a bomb."

88

They reached the lobby, the drunk guys still there, Shoshana moving back to the reception desk.

A different man approached, saying, "You speak English? You two going to the match?"

Shoshana ignored him, saying to the receptionist, "You don't have a parking lot here. Where do people park their cars?"

"We don't get a lot of people with cars."

"You got one the other day. The man from room three thirteen. Where would you tell him to park?"

She said, "Maybe it's written down on another bill."

Shoshana leaned over the counter, grabbed her by the hair, and slammed her ear into the wood. The woman squealed and said, "Across the street! There's a parking garage across the street. We have an agreement with them."

The drunk staggered back, his eyes like shiny plates, dropping his bottle of beer. Shoshana released the clerk, who fell against the counter, rubbing her head. The doctor put his hands on his knees and threw up, gushes of bile splattering onto the tile floor.

The World Cup patrons parted like the Red Sea at the bile streaming out, fleeing out the door onto the sidewalk or into the adjacent coffee shop. Jennifer and Shoshana followed them, running by the doctor to the front door. He wiped his mouth and said, "We need to go!"

They ignored him again. Shoshana saw the parking garage and swore. "That thing will have a million cars. We don't have time to find a needle in a haystack like that."

The building was five stories tall and appeared to be serviced by the entire city, with everyone at the World Cup event two blocks away using it. Jennifer knew it would house at least five hundred vehicles, maybe more if the roof was used to store cars as well. For the first time, she thought about fleeing.

We aren't going to succeed.

She said, "Shoshana, I think we've reached the point of no return. I think it's time to go."

Shoshana turned from the garage and said, "I didn't expect that from you."

"Shoshana, we need to look at this realistically. We'd need to find *and* disarm the weapon in less than thirty minutes, and all we have is a license plate."

Doctor Sharp said, "Yes, yes. Listen to her."

Shoshana bored into him with her eyes and he wilted back, hiding behind Jennifer, pretending to adjust his equipment. She said, "Jennifer, I know you don't understand, but this is just like Munich. The bomb is here to wipe out our national football team, all because we're Jewish. We haven't made the World Cup since 1970. Our entire country is watching this match, and they're going to kill them on live television. Just like the Munich Olympics."

She turned away and said, "I can't let that happen. If they go, I go with them."

Jennifer heard the dull roar of the stadium. A crowd of thirty thousand civilians from Israel and the United States, all traveling across continents to see their teams play. A man and woman passed to her front wearing the colors of Israel, laughing and joking. On the man's shoulders was a small child of five or six, blond hair flowing behind her, matching the color of her mother's. Giggling and bouncing up and down, she knew nothing of war or death. Jennifer saw the mother take the father's hand and grin. A blindly joyous expression that was about to be forever obliterated.

She said, "Go start on the bottom floor. I'll be in shortly."

Shoshana broke into a wolf smile, her teeth bared but showing no joy. She jogged across the street. Doctor Sharp's face went pale.

Jennifer started walking toward their car, pulling out her phone. Brett answered on the fourth ring, saying, "You found it?"

"No, I need to know if you packed a MLPR in the go case." She pronounced it *milper*.

He said, "As a matter of fact, I did. Why?"

"Not enough time to explain. We're in the parking garage across the street from Sienna. What's your ETA?"

"I'm not with Pike. I'm at the rock-star bird. We're prepping to get out of here. He's on his way to you. He didn't call?"

She said, "No," and her phone beeped with call-waiting. "He's ringing now. Gotta go."

She jumbled through the buttons, then Pike's voice came on. "Jennifer, I'm initiating an abort. Time's up. Move to the airport. Brett's getting ready for exfil."

Opening the trunk of her vehicle, she said, "I can't. Shoshana's staying. I'm staying."

"What do you mean, you can't? Damn it, as your team leader, I'm *ordering* you to leave. Fuck Shoshana. If she wants to stay, so be it."

Jennifer hung up without another word, then began rooting through the Pelican case that Brett had packed. She said, "Come here, Doc."

When he did, she said, "Mount this camera to the front windshield on the right side. Aim it toward the right at license-plate level, then run the cable through the window."

"We don't have time for this."

"*Do it.*"

Her tone took him aback. Her expression scared him. He picked up the small wide-angle lens and used the suction cup to affix it to the windshield, saying, "What is this?"

Now in the front seat messing with a small laptop, Jennifer said, "Mobile license-plate reader. It's used by the police to find criminals, but we use it to track terrorists. It'll scan every plate just driving by. When his registers, we stop."

He muttered, "You mean *if* it registers."

She ignored that and said, "Get in."

She goosed the gas pedal and bolted across the road, causing the flow of people to jump out of the way, two men from the crowd slapping her hood as she went by. She ignored them. She pulled up to an automated machine with a drop bar and purchased a ticket. She saw Shoshana and whistled. When the Israeli entered the car, Jennifer said, "That laptop is going to recognize every license plate we drive by. I've programmed in Chiclet's. If it's here, we'll know shortly."

She goosed the pedal and they went up the garage, much faster than was safe, causing spectators for the Cup to dodge out of the way. In back, Doc started moaning. They reached the fourth level and he said, "It's not here. It's not here. Please, for the love of God, we need to leave."

Grim-faced, Jennifer continued on, breaking out onto the upper deck of the roof, the sunlight blinding them. Shoshana said, "Nothing. No signature."

Jennifer whipped around in a U-turn, the camera now aimed on the opposite row of cars, then began going back the way they'd come.

The MLPR blared an alarm on the third floor.

89

We got caught in the traffic next to the Arena da Baixada, at least a thousand people in the street, feeding into a stadium that held over thirty thousand. The death toll made me nauseous, but the crowd had no sense of urgency. Like lambs being led to the slaughter, they continued on with their unwitting lives. I began cursing. "Fucking soccer pussies. Get out of the way!"

Driving, Aaron said, "It's football, if you're going to scream like that. And it's your team playing, so I'd think you'd show a little more decorum."

"That *is* my decorum." I would have gone on a diatribe about Jennifer to relieve the angst I was feeling, but knew it would be wasted breath on Aaron. He couldn't get in touch with Shoshana either, and I could tell it was grating on him.

We needed to get the hell out of this city, but both of them refused to answer their damn phones, forcing us to drive from the airport to their last known location. I didn't know what they were up to, but they were about to kill us all. I started to give another colorful description of the fairer sex when my phone rang. It was Jennifer.

"Pike, we've got it. I'm looking at it right now."

I swallowed my aggravation. "And?"

"And that damn NEST doc finally came in handy. He says it's an atomic demolition munition. Made to blow up dams or bridges or the seat of government-type stuff. It's a tactical weapon, not a giant nuke."

"Does that help us at all?"

We broke through the crowds around the stadium and started screaming up Buenos Aires Street.

"Only a little. It's probably one kiloton, so it's not like a TV show atomic bomb that destroys everything for miles. On the downside, he says the thing will have a multitude of dead-man switches all designed to detonate if anything is tampered with. It isn't a ballistic missile flying through space. Since it had to sit somewhere until it went off, it had built-in fail-safes. In other words, once it's set to go off, it's going off."

Aaron hit the parking garage and ignored the drop bar, our SUV shattering it in four pieces, people diving out of the way like they were in a Mountain Dew commercial. I said, "What floor?"

"Third."

"Ten seconds."

Aaron saw them before I did. Three people huddled over an open trunk in the corner of the garage like they were looking at a dead body. Which, if there was a mirror in the trunk, I suppose they were.

I leapt out before we'd even stopped, running to them. Jennifer saw me and smiled, relief on her face. The expression made me feel sick to my stomach.

Way too much faith. We should have left twenty minutes ago, when we stood a chance.

I projected a confidence I didn't feel, saying, "Okay, so what's the countdown? What are we dealing with?"

Shoshana said, "It looks like he wanted it to go off at halftime for the game, so we caught a break. We have thirty-two minutes until detonation."

Some break. An additional thirty minutes to live. I looked at the device, an innocuous egg laid in a bed of Styrofoam, two ancient LED displays counting down in synchronicity. I leaned in close and saw the broken keys in their holes. Saw the permanence built into the system.

"Doc, I know you said tampering with the system would cause detonation, like cutting a wire here or smashing the display, but what about killing the whole thing?"

Jennifer picked up on where I was going immediately, running to the Pelican box in the trunk of her sedan, shouting, "Yeah! The Stiletto."

Shoshana said, "What's that?"

"It's an experimental EMP device. It'll fry every bit of circuitry in that weapon. Kill it all at the same time. Doc? Would that do it?"

He was staring at the weapon like he was hypnotized, his left leg trembling. I put my hand on his shoulder and said, "Doc? Did you hear what I asked?"

Jennifer handed me the Stiletto and he said, "NO! No. You can't. Look, I've checked it out, and it *is* a nuclear device. It's plutonium, and it's armed. It was purpose-built. If the Russians designed it, they built in safeguards. The initiator for this device is a flow of current that's already been created, like a wall of water behind a dam. Killing the device with your EMP will do nothing but destroy the dam. Whether the timer kicks off in thirty minutes or you disable it, the current is flowing."

"So we can't shut it down? At all?"

"Not with those keys broken off." He broke down and put his head in his hands, crying like a little girl. "We're all going to die."

I smacked him in the back of the head, saying, "I don't have time for that shit. Solve the problem. We have twenty-eight minutes. Now twenty-seven."

He stopped sniveling and actually looked at me with a little steel, analyzing the problem scientifically without his life in the balance. He said, "Distance. Get this thing as far away from population as possible. The farther you get, the less people will die."

I said, "Fuck. That's it? No magic NEST shit?"

He said, "It's not an Iraqi IED. It's a booby-trapped bomb built by a state. The only difference is that there's a nuclear core. There *is* no magic. Distance is it."

Jennifer said, "We can drive it. If we hauled ass right now, we'd get it out of the center of the city. The blast radius will be half as bad, maybe a third depending on traffic."

The unspoken command was that someone would die with the device.

I said, "That's bullshit. No way is driving this thing out of here the answer." I watched the countdown continue, my stomach churning, then said, "We have the rock-star bird."

Nobody spoke for a moment. Aaron said, "I agree the aircraft would be a solution. It could get the weapon clear easily, but who will fly it? Are you a pilot?"

I knew the hitch even before I'd finished my sentence. Before he'd opened his mouth. "No, I'm not, damn it. But that thing could get it out of here."

We all looked at each other, waiting for some miracle to pop up. It did, but not in the manner I expected.

Shoshana said, "I'll do it. I'll fly the plane."

Aaron snapped his head to her and said, "You're a helicopter pilot. You can't fly that aircraft."

"Oh yes, I can. In the air, it's all the same. The hardest part is landing, and I won't be doing that. I can, and I will."

Nobody said anything for a moment. Jennifer looked at me, and I realized she was waiting for me to do something. Pull a miracle out of the mess we were in and prevent the deaths of tens of thousands of people, without it costing the death of one in particular. She trusted me so much that it hurt. I caught her eyes and shook my head. It wasn't coming. I had never let her down before, and now I would. People were going to die. The only question was how many.

Aaron said, "Where will you go?"

"Over the ocean. The Gulfstream flies at over five hundred miles an hour. I can get out of range within minutes."

"And then what?"

She gave a bitter smile. "And then I fulfill Daniel's prophecy. I prevent Munich. Remember? He talked about this very thing before you ever left to Europe. He was right in the end."

"Damn it, Shoshana, no. No, no, no."

"What else is there? You want to run now, in a car? Even if we could get outside of the blast radius, what would it get? Our national team will be slaughtered. Thousands of Israelis will die. Daniel is already dead. All for what? My life? Your life?"

Aaron looked at me for help. One more person thinking I could prevent the inevitable. I said, "If I could fly the plane, I would."

Shoshana said, "Will they charge you for the loss of the aircraft?"

I gave a rueful grin and said, "Yeah, they probably will."

"Then it will be worth it. Let's go."

I saw Jennifer's eyes water. She looked at me one more time for a miracle. I said, "Get in."

We loaded the car with the weapon, then drove to the airport, once again fighting through the traffic, the partying and happiness of the people on the street a stark contrast to what we were carrying in our trunk. Jennifer called Brett along the way, giving him the warning order that the pilot was going to have to give a crash course to someone on the aircraft. She ended by telling him that if the pilot had an issue with it, he could fly the plane himself.

We passed through the general aviation cantonment area and showed our passes. They waved us forward, and we were on an airfield with a nuclear device. I would have been pissed except they were now saving lives with their lackadaisical attitude. I saw Brett on the tarmac, then the pilot going through preflight.

We got to the plane and all four doors of the SUV opened, like we were going to a wake. Which I suppose we were. Shoshana glanced at me and I smiled, attempting to show courage. She tried to return it, but what came out was a broken thing. I felt my gut drop again.

What am I doing? Letting her die for me?

I started to help with the weapon when Brett pulled me aside.

"There's no other option here? She's got to go?"

"Unless you can talk that pussy cover pilot into flying. I'm not sure we have enough per diem to get him through eternity."

"Yeah, I know, but what about jumping? Can't we get the bird out over the ocean then parachute out?"

I said, "You can't jump a Gulfstream. You can't open the door in flight. You know that."

Brett scrunched his brow, looking at me like I was an idiot. I said, "What?"

"What? *What?* That damn bird is built for jumping."

"What do you mean? I've flown that thing forever. It's built to hide shit. It's got no operational capability."

He rolled his eyes. "I don't know where the fuck you've been, but since I've been with the Taskforce, it's had an infiltration capability. There's a hatch at the back of the tail. A clamshell comes out, like a seven twenty-seven. Instead of walking down stairs, you just inch your ass into space."

I said, "Are you serious?"

He squinted his eyes and said, "You really didn't know?"

Right then, in the heart of the mission I learned another downside to being a "commercial" Taskforce entity. Nobody bothered to tell you about operational capability because you had no need to know. If you were just an infiltration platform, it was irrelevant, only in this case, it was fucking critical.

I said, "Are there chutes on the bird?"

"Yeah. Civilian Javelins. Rigger packed, with Cypres AAD."

I saw Shoshana in the cockpit with the pilot and shouted, "Aaron! Get over here."

He jogged up, his face expecting me to tell him that I'd managed to turn off the device with my charm. I disabused him of that notion.

"We have parachutes on the plane. Shoshana can get it out over the ocean, then jump out."

He took that in, then nodded absently. "Yeah, yeah, that'll work. She might make it."

I said, "What does that mean? She's a damn commando. All we have to do is show her the exit procedures."

"She's not jump qualified."

I heard the words and felt a final kick to the gut. I had just assumed she was a paratrooper. In movies like *Point Break*, any idiot can strap on a parachute and free fall like a master, floating through the air as if it was second nature. The truth of the matter was that jumping out of an aircraft, free-falling, opening, and then landing a parachute successfully was incredibly difficult. There were plenty of military members in HALO operations—after being trained—who ended up pounding the unforgiving earth with their bodies. Without any training, I gave Shoshana about a fifty percent chance of survival, and that was even with the Cypres automatic opening device. It would fire at a predetermined altitude, but if she was upside down or tumbling the parachute would do nothing more than snarl into a ball of nylon, wrapping around her body.

Jennifer had heard the conversation and said, "We have nineteen minutes."

I said, "Brett, get me a rig. Lay it on the ground." To Jennifer: "Get her out here. I'll show her what to do, then Brett can show her how to open the door."

She said, "Shoshana won't live through this, will she?"

I said, "Yeah, she will, because I'm going out with her."

90

The rock-star bird hopped down the runway as if we were testing its shock absorbers. Buckled into the copilot seat, I shouted, "I thought landing was the hard part?"

Shoshana said nothing, working the flaps and the yoke. We bounced one more time, then lifted off for good. I thanked my lucky stars that there were no obstacles after the runway, because Shoshana flew about eighty feet off the deck forever, the aircraft slowly—oh so slowly—rising in the air. Eventually, we got high enough that I would actually call it "flying."

I said, "Way to go. Christ. If that's how you fly in Israel, remind me to stay away from El Al."

She turned the aircraft to the coast, putting the bird at full throttle. She continued to climb to fourteen thousand feet, then leveled off. She engaged the autopilot and said, "Fourteen thousand feet, as you asked."

I unbuckled, saying, "Let's get our chutes on."

The bird broke the coastline with twelve minutes left. I wondered if we were going to get out in time. The NEST doc had said three miles distance for an atmospheric blast would be safe, but I wasn't putting my life on that. At five hundred miles an hour, the bomb would be about twenty miles away after three minutes. That was my cut line. Exit with three minutes left. I hoisted the parachute on her back, then helped her with the leg straps. She stepped through, saying, "I understand your relationship now."

What. The. Fuck.

"I'd love to hear your bipolar Spock assessment of my life, but we have more pressing concerns."

I started putting on my own chute as she crouched in the back, breaking the seal on the paneling that hid the clamshell. She smiled, and I saw a genuine spark of happiness. Odd as it was, a ray of something that had been hidden was now revealed under the stress.

She said, "We have less than ten minutes. And I'm about to die. I told you earlier that you were like every other male, but you're not. You didn't have to do this. Why did you?"

I peeled back an innocuous covering near a coffee machine in the galley and grabbed the winch handle for the clamshell. I began to crank, a sliver of light that turned into the whole sky. Huge and close.

I said, "Jesus, Shoshana, you're not about to die. Believe me, if I were going to get killed doing this, I wouldn't be here."

She said, "Yes, you would. Same as me."

I shook my head, working the clamshell open. When I looked up, she was staring at me intently, reading my mind again. Unconcerned about her fate.

For me, I was petrified. I was sure *I* would live, but not sure at all that I could save her life. If she exited and flipped out, it would be like a lifeguard trying to reach a drowning man in a storm. I'd work it as long as I could, then cut the drowning man free, leaving her fate to the emergency Cypres automatic opening device. Maybe it would save her, or maybe it would wrap her in a burial shroud.

I said, "You ready to go?"

"Ready as I'll ever be."

I pointed to the floor inside the kitchen galley, the gaping maw of the open sky feet away. "Have a seat."

She did so and I got in behind her, pulling her into my groin, my legs outside of hers. I looked forward at the small opening and thought that Brett saying this plane was "built for jumping" was a little bit of an exaggeration. The clamshell was nothing more than an add-on. In order to exit, we had to scoot forward on our butts, then basically fall face-first out of the aircraft through a minuscule hatch.

I said, "Remember, all you have to do is fall flat and stable. I'll reach you. I'll pull the ball. I'll do everything. You just arch your damn back as hard as you can. It'll keep you from flipping. When you hit the water, don't let the chute get on top of you. Start working out of the harness immediately. If—"

She put a finger to my lips and said, "We're running out of time. I'm not worried."

I thought she was lying, but when she turned around, she showed no fear. I said, "You should be, because I've never done this before."

She said, "Your name is Nephilim."

I ignored that bit of uselessness. "Time to go."

She leaned back and kissed me on the lips, shocking the hell out of me. She pulled away and said, "Don't get an erection. I just wanted to show you what you were missing. In case we got in the air, and you decided that saving my life was too big of a challenge."

I gave a fake smile, now believing that she really *could* read my mind. "Don't worry. I've got Jennifer waiting, and for some reason she likes you. Coming on to me isn't going to help your chances of survival."

She started scooting forward, the hatch growing bigger, me right behind, my adrenaline ramping up now that all that remained was to exit. Setting my body on fire. She reached the end, her legs dangling into space. She stretched forward with her hands and grasped the edge of the aircraft.

She leaned back, as if to get away from the hole, and I prepared to shove her out, knowing the average human would never exit an aircraft while in flight on their own. It was just wired into our brains not to commit suicide. She screamed something, and launched into space, taking me off guard.

Crazy woman.

I scooted forward as fast as I could, seeing her tumble away end over end, which would guarantee her parachute would wrap around her in a death shroud when the Cypres fired. I fell out, tumbled once, then went stable. I executed a 360 and saw her below me, still doing somersaults. I tucked my arms into my sides and began screaming head down at over two hundred miles an hour, gaining on her.

I shot under her and flared, getting back to her level. I grabbed her harness at chest level and her pant leg at the thigh, fighting against the wind buffeting her body. She went rigid and stopped tumbling. All I needed was her flat and facedown for the parachute to successfully open, and I had that. I let go of her leg and grabbed the leather ball attached to the pilot chute at the bottom of her container. I threw it into the wind and she was ripped out of my hands by the opening shock.

I fell two more seconds, getting clear of her, then pulled out my own pilot chute. I gained control of my canopy and circled around, spotting her above me, a beautiful square of nylon over her.

I tried to find the rock-star bird, but it was already out of sight. I began turning to get behind Shoshana to follow her in when a brilliant flash split the air. I closed my eyes and felt a thermal rush. Two minutes later, the thunderclap of the explosion reached me, whipping my canopy and making me swing like a pendulum.

I stabilized just as the water approached. I flared, sank into the surf, and shucked my harness. I started swimming toward Shoshana while she was still in the air, watching her skimming above the waves. She didn't know how to flare and hit the water running with the wind, going about thirty miles an hour and smacking down like a water-skier out of control. I got to her as she started to get dragged facedown by the chute. I jerked her cutaway pillow and the canopy floated free, racing across the ocean like a giant bird.

I pulled her upright, getting her head above the surface. She coughed out water and said, "You didn't tell me I'd hit that hard."

I initiated the beacon in my pocket, saying, "You didn't listen to my class on controlling the canopy."

She wrapped her arms around my neck and started laughing, kicking her legs to tread water, her entire body trembling with the fallout of adrenaline. Glad to be alive.

She said, "You know, if I swung that way you'd be in serious trouble."

I said, "I know. Trust me, I know."

91

The Charleston humidity was cloying but I still insisted on sitting outside, as Jennifer knew I would the minute I said where we were going. Fuel was a bar and grill with a Caribbean flair built on an old gas station, and one of my go-to places for visitors. She wanted to take Shoshana and Aaron to someplace more upscale and so-called Charleston, but I was having none of it. Complete with two-dollar PBRs and an outdoor garden with a bocce ball pit, Fuel was way better than someplace with white tablecloths.

A summer breeze kicked up, wiping the heat away, and it felt good even with the humidity, reminding me I was alive. While it had been three days since our near-suicidal plane flight, I was still waking up each morning mildly surprised to feel my heart beating.

We'd floated in the water for close to three hours before Aaron and Jennifer found us in a rented speedboat. I had begun to wonder if maybe we were going to have to swim back home. Once we'd returned to the airport I'd immediately ordered everyone to buy tickets, and we settled on Charleston as a destination. Well, most of us did. The pilot of the rock-star bird was a little aggravated that I'd destroyed his aircraft, and he'd opted to fly straight back to DC, where I'm sure he went straight to Kurt Hale, crying like a four-year-old. Sure enough, I'd heard about it as soon as I talked to Kurt, but it was mostly in jest, and not something I gave a shit about on a summer day like today.

Jennifer slid her hand over mine and squeezed. She seemed to be doing much better about the whole *Am I a murderer?* thing, but I suppose saving the world from a nuclear strike will do that to your moral code.

Watching Shoshana laugh at Aaron's pitch, she said, "I never told you how much Aaron appreciated what you did for Shoshana. He cares a great deal about her."

I said, "Maybe he should be giving *us* an award."

Once we'd arrived back in the United States, I'd called Kurt. I'd sent a SITREP before we'd left, and by the time we'd landed, we had a message from the president of the United States saying he wanted to convey his thanks to the Israeli team in person. It would be private and off the record, but it was still pretty prestigious.

Shoshana caught us looking at them and winked. Jennifer said, "I think she's smitten with you."

I smiled and said, "She doesn't swing that way."

"I don't know about that. She's making all the wrong moves for someone who isn't interested in the opposite sex."

I opened the laptop and fired it up. "Maybe it's you." I squeezed her hand. "I'm fairly sure I could understand why that would happen, if last night was any indication. You know she's an empath, right? She's seen through your prim-and-proper facade."

She blushed, actually looking worried. She said, "I hope that's not true. Either way, whether it's me or you, it'd kill Aaron. I *know* he's smitten with her."

I started tapping keys, going through the laborious process of working through the TOR network and getting into the NYM and Blofeld applications.

Watching me type, she said, "So Knuckles is flying down here just to take that computer back to DC?"

"Yeah. That's his story. In reality, I think he's going stir-crazy up there. And he likes it here in the Holy City. Plenty of hot single women running around for a Navy SEAL to stalk."

"How did he sound on the phone?"

"Better . . . Here he comes."

I saw him through the old roll-up garage door next to the bar and waved. He came outside smiling, his hippie hair trailing in the breeze. Two women at the bar, wearing scrubs from the medical university, followed him with their eyes all the way to our table.

I gave him a man-hug and said, "Long flight just to get a computer."

"Yeah, I know. I might have to spend the night here. Maybe two nights."

I laughed and sat down while Jennifer gave him a peck on the cheek. "How was Decoy's memorial?"

It had happened while we were down in Brazil. For once, I hated how quickly the Taskforce did them.

"It was good, Jenn. Good."

I said, "I wish I could have been there."

He slapped my shoulder, "I know, but you were saving the world. Usual shit."

"How's that going inside the beltway? I haven't seen anything at all on the news. How are they keeping a lid on it?"

He grinned and said, "Believe it or not, your idea of flying the weapon out into the ocean has solved more problems than just saving lives. The Oversight Council is pretending it didn't happen. There are a bunch of questions being asked down in South America about a 'large explosion' over the ocean, but since every bit of evidence has been destroyed, DC is looking in the sky and whistling."

"You've got to be kidding me."

"Nope. They're just going to ignore the whole thing. Turn it into a meteor strike or something. Pretend it never happened. Keeps them from having to try to tightrope around the Taskforce."

"What about the radiation? The fallout?"

"Apparently it won't be that big of a deal. They figure it was a one-kiloton bomb, and we used to test two-kiloton airbursts in Nevada all the time without any ill effects, so it'll just disperse out in the ocean. I didn't ask them if we needed to worry about Godzilla being created, but apparently it's no threat to humanity."

He looked at Jennifer and said, "By the way, I heard you were the one who found the bomb. Saved the day. That's going a long way to spare Grolier Recovery Services from Pike's bullshit, but it's not a done deal yet."

She gave an embarrassed smile at the first part of his statement, then showed confusion at the second. I said, "I put you in the SITREP to Kurt, because you did, in fact, save the world from nuclear devastation."

She grinned and said, "What's that about GRS?"

"Kurt told me the Oversight Council was considering cutting our contract because I don't know whether I'm a government employee or a civilian. Basically, that I'm uncontrollable. We might get fired."

She looked at Knuckles and said, "Really? After what he just did?"

Knuckles said, "Don't worry about it. Kurt's on your side. So is President Warren. Just don't do anything stupid in the next few days."

I said, "Oh, we're going to do some foolish things over the next few days, trust me." Jennifer turned beet red and punched my arm, mouthing, *Pike!*

I tapped the final keys on the computer as Knuckles rolled his eyes. He said, "I really don't want to hear about the fraternization."

I no longer heard him, my brain focused on the computer screen. I had a message on my fake account. An e-mail from the mole sent four days ago. I translated the Blofeld URL. It was short and to the point.

Americans getting content on Associated Press e-mail accounts. Sanitize them ASAP.

Jennifer saw my expression and said, "What is it?" Knuckles started to lean over to see the screen and I rapidly exited the Blofeld account, destroying the message forever.

I said, "Nothing." I closed the lid and handed him the computer. "Here you go. This is what you came for. Hopefully they can find something about that mole on this."

I stood up and pulled out my Taskforce phone. Jennifer said, "Where are you going?"

"Calling Kurt. Only be a minute."

After getting shuffled around by minions, I finally got him on the phone. He said, "Hey, superhero, what's up?"

"I hear I'm getting fired."

"I already told you that. Is Knuckles spreading RUMINT? Ignore the hearsay. Nothing's changed since our last conversation. No decisions made."

"Okay, but that's not why I'm calling. The Taskforce didn't crack the Associated Press e-mails. Who did that?"

"The NSA, and I'm telling you, it was a close run thing. Tupper, the DNI, didn't want to do it. The president had to order him."

"Who knew the NSA was doing it? Who outside of you and the president?"

"Just Bruce Tupper. President Warren kept it very, very close hold because it was basically a felony. Why?"

"No reason. Hey, Jennifer's calling me. I gotta go."

"Don't let those Israelis show up late. Get them on the plane. I know how you are in Charleston."

I said, "Don't worry about that. The sooner I get them to DC the better."

I hung up, thinking. Debating. The first compromise had been internal to the Taskforce, when the cache location had been penetrated. The second one—the one I'd just seen—was outside the Taskforce completely. The mole had knowledge of both and the ability to manipulate our surveillance systems.

I thought about what I knew and my possible actions. I considered Jennifer, now content in the knowledge that she was no murderer and that the Taskforce was a force of good. That *I* was a force of good.

Then I thought of Decoy dying. Of Daniel dying. Of how close Jennifer had come to dying. How close thousands of people had danced near slaughter. I thought of the name Nephilim, of the Old Testament punishment of an eye for an eye. Of the information I had about a Middle Eastern CIA case officer's connection to the Munich massacre, and how the Americans were petrified it would fall into Israeli hands. And made my decision.

I said, "Shoshana, can I see you for a second?"

She came jogging over and I went deeper into the garden, away from the group.

Puzzled, but grinning, she said, "What, are you going to try to change my stripes?"

Her smile faded when she saw my expression. "Pike, what is it?"

"I have some information that affects Israeli interests."

92

Bruce Tupper put the finishing touches on his landscape painting, then signed the bottom with a flourish. His wife came in as he set his brush down. She hugged him, saying, "It looks wonderful. I take it by your burst of artistic energy that things are better at work?"

He smiled and kissed her. "Yes. Things are decidedly better now. It'll probably get worse again, but right now, it's pretty good."

She said, "Can we go for a walk finally? Forget about work? I haven't seen you in a week, and it's a gorgeous summer day."

"Can I smoke a cigar?"

"Yes. But just one."

He said, "I'll meet you downstairs." She left the room with a little skip in her step, and he put his paint away feeling the same. The awards ceremony today had been the capstone event for a difficult few weeks. The Israelis were courteous to a fault, and he had heard nothing from his new contact in over a week. He wondered if his secret had been completely welded shut on the far side. He dared to believe that he would never hear from the Russians again.

In this, he was correct.

He went downstairs and found his wife talking to their driver/personal security man. She saw him and smiled. He felt a warm glow. He showed their Rhodesian ridgeback the leash and the dog went wild, bouncing up and down. The entire scene was idyllic.

Something he never would have had in the Soviet Union. He had been blessed.

They exited the mansion and began walking. He let her lead the way, the ridgeback sniffing every bush. They worked around the winding neighborhood streets, the mansions glaringly massive in the dusk, the security man behind them at a respectful distance. They said nothing for the first thirty minutes, Bruce thinking of how close he'd come to being exposed and his wife simply enjoying the walk. The sun began to set and the summer evening reached that tipping point between night and day, the air still.

Bruce heard the motorcycle before he saw it, a smaller bike with two people on it, both wearing full-face helmets. He thought nothing of it, even when it pulled abreast of them and stopped. The person on the back tossed him something and he caught it in confusion. It was a plastic medal. A replica of Olympic gold. He knew instantly what it represented.

He heard his security shout, the man drawing a weapon and running toward them, but not nearly as fast as the assassin. He returned to the passenger and was staring down the bulbous maw of a suppressed pistol. It spit twice and he scarcely felt the pain. His wife screamed and he sat down heavily, his legs losing their ability to hold him up.

He barely registered the motorcycle leaving, even with his security man firing blindly in the growing darkness. His vision tunneled until he was looking at his lap as if through a straw. A string of viscous red drool fell from his mouth, dripping down from his lip. His breathing became labored as his punctured lung strove for oxygen. He coughed, spraying his lap with blood. In the center was the plastic medal, the fake gold now tarnished with red. Sitting there proudly still, as if he'd earned it.

As his brain shut down, he supposed he had.

ACKNOWLEDGMENTS

Yes, yes, I know, the Israeli national football team did not qualify for the World Cup in 2014, extending their absence to forty-four years. But at one point they were looking strong! When they failed, I had a choice of either redirecting the target or just using literary license. Since the Munich Olympics factored in heavily on the motivations of the Mossad team, I decided to use literary license to juxtapose the repercussions of the threat.

While Israel didn't make the World Cup, they did attend the Munich Olympics in '72, and their athletes were murdered in a horrific terrorist act, much like I depicted. The mastermind of that event, Ali Hassan Salameh—aka the Red Prince—was a real person, and we really used him as a source for information about Lebanon and the greater Middle East, so much so that his Force 17 commandos once protected Henry Kissinger on a state visit to Beirut. We did not, however, start that relationship until after Munich. Robert Ames, the CIA case officer mentioned in the book, was Salameh's actual case officer in life, and Robert really was killed in the Beirut embassy bombings, but Bruce Tupper and his machinations are false. It is fiction that we knew about Munich before it happened but fact that while Israel hunted Salameh, we courted him. Eventually, Israel's Wrath of God teams won. Well, conventional wisdom is that he was killed by Israel. They've never admitted to it, but the second chapter in the book is pretty much what happened.

As for the WMD, the W54 SADM is a real man-portable nuclear weapon designed for use during the Cold War by Special Forces teams—known as Greenlight teams—on planned missions that were seriously suicidal in nature. In the words of one member of a Greenlight team, "There were real issues with the operational wisdom of the program, and those who were to conduct the mission were sure that whomever thought this up was using bad hemp." Little is known about the existence of USSR "suitcase nukes" (at least on the US side of things). Congress did conduct several hearings on the subject in the 1990s, and the verdict is still out on whether the USSR had them and, if so, whether they still maintain control of them. Historically, whatever weapons system we invented, the Soviets stole and duplicated, so I don't see why this would be any different. For research, I used the W54 platform and not the wild mock-ups shown in the Congressional hearings, which were pretty much panned as unfeasible by nuclear scientists. Since the SADM was real, and had been successfully tested, it provided concrete data on size, weight, implementation methods, destructive radius, fallout risk, et cetera.

While my Director of National Intelligence, Bruce Tupper, had nothing to do with the Red Prince in the real world, he actually *is* a real person. I donated the chance to name my DNI (who up until that point was called Angus Smackmaster) at an auction to raise funds for the Georgia chapter of the Make-a-Wish Foundation, which grants the wishes of children with life-threatening medical conditions. Bruce himself was at the auction but didn't bid. Someone else did, and then, after some thought and consultation, provided the name. I will always wonder if Bruce is flattered to be in a novel or a little chagrined he ended up being a murdering traitor.

As always happens when researching my novels, I owe a debt of gratitude to an unnamed, unregistered "tour guide," this time in Istanbul. For fifty bucks he showed me everything I needed, including where the illegal African immigrants hang out, the Russian sector of shopping, and the Russian consulate, in addition to all of the usual tour stops. All it cost me was a detour into his uncle's carpet store, where I was subjected to a hard sell for an hour and a half. I had no such luck in Plovdiv, Bulgaria, but I did just fine on my own.

There's a lot more to writing books than just, well, writing books. I have to thank my agent, John Talbot, who manages all the behind-the-scenes business for me. I truly appreciate our friendship and all of your work on my behalf.

It's an understatement to say that I've been truly blessed by my association with Dutton. To have lucked into this team as a new author was nothing short of a miracle. The tireless efforts of the Dutton team are apparent in the success of my books. To my editors, Ben Sevier and Jessica Reinheim, thanks so much for giving me the leeway to follow my gut, along with astute guidance to prevent me from running off the rails. To my amazing publicists, Liza Cassity and Emily Brock, you rock! To the marketing team, especially Carrie Swetonic, thanks for putting the best foot forward for Pike and his team and always turning our requests around quickly. Finally, these acknowledgments are always about the hardcover books, leaving out Danielle Perez and the hard-working team at Signet who ensure the paperback release is perfect. Thank you!

ABOUT THE AUTHOR

Brad Taylor, Lieutenant Colonel (ret.), is a twenty-one-year veteran of the U.S. Army Infantry and Special Forces, including eight years with the 1st Special Forces Operational Detachment—Delta, popularly known as the Delta Force. Taylor retired in 2010 after serving more than two decades and participating in Operation Enduring Freedom and Operation Iraqi Freedom, as well as classified operations around the globe. His final military post was as Assistant Professor of Military Science at the Citadel. His first five Pike Logan thrillers were *New York Times* bestsellers. He lives in Charleston, South Carolina.